Boarding School

by
Clint Adams

PublishAmerica
Baltimore

First printing

ISBN: 1-4241-9696-5
PUBLISHED BY PUBLISHAMERICA, LLLP
www.publishamerica.com
Baltimore

Printed in the United States of America

Dedication

To my little buddy Eddie…

Do you remember that day at school when you were thirteen and you came to my dorm room to ask me a question that was of extreme importance to you? And do you remember also how you sat down in one of my chairs and then began to plead with me to let you move in with me? Well, I have never forgotten that afternoon. In my mind now, I can still hear you promise me that you would be a good roommate and you would always keep your things neat, and you would always be quiet whenever I needed to study. "Just say yes," you kept repeating. "Come on, please just say yes. That's all you've got to do and I'll take care of everything else. I'll even do all the moving myself. You won't have to do a thing to help. Please, just say yes. That's all you've got to do. Just say yes, please!"

Of course I didn't say yes that day. I was moved by your pleas, but I had my own selfish reasons at that time in my life which I believed were more important than any thirteen-year-old disagreements you might have been having with your roommate. And it was decades later before I learned the real reason why you were so desperate to find sanctuary with me.

A few years ago when I was talking with an old friend of ours from those days, I learned, finally, what it was that your older and larger roommate was forcing you to do with him every night after lights out. Eddie, I had no idea. I wish you hadn't been too frightened or too embarrassed to tell me why it was that you had to get yourself away from that monster. I wish I had been a little more on the ball that day so I could have figured out for myself why it was that you were so distraught over your need to find a safe place to live. You did give me a few hints about how unhappy you were with your roommate, but nearly everybody in that place was unhappy with their roommate at one time or another. So I simply chalked your complaints up to typical roommate squabbles.

You were a great kid, Eddie, one of the nicest ones there, and it haunts me now to think of the sex acts you were being forced into performing every night with that creep. If I had known, if I had possessed any idea at all, I would have moved heaven and earth to get you out of that situation that day. But I didn't know, and so I simply said "no" to your impassioned pleas.

Today I can also recall the look of utter dejection and despair on your face as you left my room once our conversation had ended. I don't remember you speaking very much to me after that. You had placed all of your hope and faith with me, and I had let you down. In the years that have followed since my learning of the truth, I have tried to find you so I could apologize for not making the right choice that day. But all of my efforts to locate you have failed. So I am dedicating this book to you, Eddie, in the hopes that one day you will pick up a copy and read this and discover how truly sorry I am for not understanding you, and that I know now that if I had simply stated a different one-syllable word—the word "yes"—I could have saved you from the nightmarish existence that must have been your world at that time. I guess when we're kids, we don't realize how profoundly our decisions can affect the lives of others. In any case, all my best to you now, Eddie, wherever you are.

Table of Contents

Chapter One
Traveling to Ulster Academy

The Callahan Tunnel. As I pass by this familiar structure so I can steer the rental car I just picked up back at Logan through the Summer Tunnel instead, I realize that it has been over thirty years now since I've called this area my home. Thirty years since I've thought seriously about the miserable way I was forced to live when I was an Academy kid, and it has taken thirty years for me to build up the courage I need to step foot in Boston again.

For those who are in my life today, my entire existence in this part of the country is now compressed down into an old school catalog, a few odd photos I took, and the words "Ulster Academy" which I will occasionally mention when the days of my youth become the topic of discussion. It was better, I always believed, if the people around me didn't know anything about the anguish I suffered. It was better for all concerned, I thought, if I didn't try to explain what it is like when a boy's innocence is suddenly stripped away from him by the base interests of others who live around him, or how easy it is at an impressionable age to be sucked up into a life which I would never on my own have selected for myself. And it was better, I decided, if I didn't embarrass myself by revealing all of the unspeakable things they made me do here.

But all of that is behind me now. Not too long ago, I decided to confront Boston...and the town of Ulster and especially the Academy itself. So I've set aside some time in my schedule today to give me the chance I need to end my years of concealment of the truth—not only for my own health and peace of mind, but for others who may be facing similar experiences and aren't sure how to cope with them. Today, after all of these years, I am taking charge of my past by going back to my old boarding school for a visit. Yes, as incredible as it must seem, I am now driving toward the town of Ulster, Massachusetts. And out of an abundance of caution, I am issuing this warning before I go on any further, because the secrets I'm about to tell are not suitable for the prudish or the faint of heart. And I am being very serious by what I'm saying here. Sometimes I handled things well, and other times I did not. But good, bad or otherwise, I intend within this text to describe in brutal detail the events which came to define my existence while I lived here. And of course, to keep me out of hot water, I have changed the names or eliminated the names entirely of everyone I lived with in those days. Also, I have given voice to these people by using the vernacular of the time. So be advised that a reader who is not up to the task of learning the truth about what I went through as a boy in boarding school would probably be better served by putting these pages down now and searching instead for something light to read, like a romance novel.

I'm driving south now on the highway which leads out of Boston. Already I can see the town of Framingham through my side window. Before I landed today, I considered the idea of stopping here first before continuing on down to Ulster. After all, my memories from this town are just as intense, if not more so, as all the others I have from this area. But I concluded that I'm not yet ready to see this place also. In fact, I may never be ready to visit Framingham again. Just the thought of taking the exit right now and getting off the turnpike sends shivers up my spine and gives me aching pains all across my stomach. And then, after a few more moments pass, the sight of Framingham in my rearview mirror seems to validate my feelings for me and I'm able again to relax. *Not this trip,* I keep saying to myself. *I'm not stopping here today.*

Another ten minutes or so and the traffic is finally beginning to thin out. Thirty years ago I thought Boston was crowded. Today it seems absolutely clogged with people. Soon though, I'm able to set the cruise control and settle in for the rest of my journey. If I don't spend much time looking around in the town of Ulster or gazing at the lake, I figure I can be on the Academy grounds in a little over one hour from now. And as I listen to the engine and the tires do their jobs for me, I remember back to that summer afternoon when the letter came. Back when all I knew of Massachusetts, besides the boating trips my dad and I occasionally took to Cape Cod, was what was displayed and described in the Ulster Academy catalog which had spent the better part of the spring and summer that year lying on the coffee table in my parents' living room in our house in Denver.

"Clint? There's a letter for you!" my mother called to me from the patio as I played around that afternoon in the swimming pool we had in our back yard. She had caught me right as I had begun to wrestle with a floating chair I had received for my thirteenth birthday a few weeks earlier.

"What, Mom?" I hadn't been able to hear everything she had just said to me because at the moment she had begun to speak, the chair was winning the upper hand and I had found myself under water during the first half of her announcement.

"I said you've got a letter. Come on in now so we can see what it says." And then my mother turned around and walked back into our house.

"Ok, Mom!" I yelled back. "I'll be right there!" Quickly then, I swam over to the side and climbed out of the water. As soon as I was on dry land again, I started for the house. I knew what letter my mother was talking about and I was just as excited as she was to find out what it had to say. So without wasting precious seconds to fuss with my towel, I raced straight into our kitchen to join my mother.

"Oh, Clint!" my mother sounded appalled when I arrived inside.

"What?" I asked innocently as I took up a position next to her at the kitchen counter.

"You're soaking wet! You're dripping water all over the floor!"

"That's all right, Maria can clean it up. Is the letter from Ulster?"

"I jus' cleaned up the floor in here, little man." Maria suddenly appeared from the other room and was not amused by my apparent disregard for the work she had just done.

Now I felt bad. "Oh, Maria. I didn't mean anything. It's just water."

"Jes', well jou can get the mop and wipe it up jourself."

"Ok, in a minute." I didn't want to get on Maria's bad side. After all, later on she might make something like liver for dinner to get back at me. "Go on and open the letter, Mom." My attention was now returned to the reason for all of this commotion.

"Hold your horses, my soggy son. Hold your horses." With a steak knife, my mom then slit open the top of the envelope from the all-boys prep school and pulled out the letter from inside. As soon as she had the paper unfolded, she began to read to herself.

"What's it say? What's it say?" I couldn't believe that she was making me wait while she found out first what was in the letter. After all, it was my letter.

Maria suddenly interrupted. "It says jou need to go and get the mop now to clean up the floor."

"Oh, Maria," I tried to make light of her comment. "I promise, I'll get the mop out in a minute."

"Ok, here we go," my mom finally began to speak again. "To 'Master Clinton Adams,'" my mother tried to make her voice sound formal as she read my letter to me. "'Dear Clint, After careful consideration of your application and academic record by our admissions committee and by our board of trustees, we are pleased to inform you that you have been accepted as a new first-year student at Ulster Academy and as such, will be expected to attend our school during the upcoming fall term…'"

"Yippie!" That was all I needed to hear. I was so elated over the news, I began to jump up and down as I shouted out my joy right there in the kitchen. "Yippie! Yippie!"

"Oh, Clint!" Mom was now upset with me again. "Now you're shaking off water all over the place. Go back outside if you're going to do that."

"Yippie! Yippie!" I didn't stop to engage my parent in further conversation. I just kept yelling as I hopped through the kitchen and back out onto the patio. "Yippie! Yippie! Yippie!…" I then kept up my hopping and yelling until I had hopped all the way back into the swimming pool. "Yippie! Yipppie! Yippie! Yippie!" SPLASH!

For the rest of that summer, my mother and I spent our time buying things I needed and getting me ready for my year away. Besides the list of suggested personal items provided by the Academy, I had a few friends at that time who had gone off to boarding schools the year before and who had already given me plenty of pointers on what I should take. So I felt confident that I knew how to prepare myself to live on my own.

The very first thing my mom and I did was to go out and buy me a bigger foot locker. The one I had been using for summer camp for the past three years was fine for month-long stays in the Rockies, but was woefully inadequate to hold everything a boy my age would need for an entire year in the east. I was also fitted for a navy-colored sport coat—the school colors were navy and red. In the rule book, which the Academy had also sent to us, it was stated that coats and ties were to be worn by all students and faculty at dinner every night, except Sundays, and for all sporting events when the Academy teams traveled to compete at other schools. Also, school-sponsored outings to Boston or Providence to hear the symphony or to see plays, were other occasions when formal attire was required. Of course the term "formal" was inaccurately used in this instance but as I learned later on, it was the common way that this type of dress was referred to by Academy students and staff. Anyway, once my mom had my measurements, she sent this information off to the Academy along with an order for a school tie, some T-shirts and a sweat shirt all bearing the Academy crest. According to the rule book, these articles would then be waiting for me in my dormitory room when I arrived on campus in late August.

On the weekends, when my dad had time to help us, we worked to pack up our house. The whole reason for me getting to go away to school had to do with the transfer my dad was taking from his company which was requiring him to go to Europe for two years. He was going to be setting up new facilities for his employer in France and Switzerland, and my mom was going along to handle the entertaining duties which went with my dad's new position. During the two years they were to be away, my parents had arranged to rent our house to another family. They had wanted to take me with them and have me attend American schools in each country, but I didn't want to leave the United States. At that time, during the early 1970s, there were too many things going on in the country that I was just becoming aware of. I was worried that if I went off to Europe for two years, I'd end up missing everything, and then I'd be forever out of step with my friends. So the plan became for me to attend school in the east during the school year, and then I would visit my folks in Europe on Christmas and summer breaks. And as far as I was concerned, this was a great plan.

The idea of going off on my own to a boarding school which was nestled in the countryside of picturesque New England appealed to me. I was always independently minded and I saw my time to come at the Academy as a great adventure. Also the photos in the Academy catalog were amazing. Besides a swimming pool and tennis courts on the grounds, the Academy was located on the shores of the largest lake in Massachusetts, and it had its own dock and sandy beach. And in the water there was swimming, canoeing, water skiing, fishing, crew and endless possibilities when girls schools came to visit. Plus in the winter when the lake froze, there was ice skating and hockey. The place looked like a paradise of athletic activity. I truly couldn't wait to get there.

"Now are you sure that going to Ulster Academy is what you want to do, Clint?" my dad asked me this question one day when he was at his desk and preparing the deposit check to hold my spot in the fall term.

"Yeah, Dad. I'm sure."

"You know you can't take everything you own when you go. You'll have to keep some of your belongings in storage with our stuff."

"I know, Dad." The box I had been carrying at this moment was heavy, so I set it down for a moment on the couch which was nearby.

Because I tended to be a packrat with my possessions, my dad wasn't sure yet if I had fully digested the point he was trying to make with me. "So? Have you given any thought to what you're taking and what you're leaving behind?" My dad always wanted me to consider issues from every possible angle. "Like your guitars. Have you figured out which one of your guitars you're going to take with you? I don't imagine a dormitory room can hold all four of them, you know."

"I know," I assured him. "I'm taking my twelve-string and leaving the others here with your stuff."

"Oh, I see. Well, that sounds like a smart decision. A folk guitar won't need an amplifier." Then my dad thought for a moment longer. "Say, isn't your twelve-string the one you use to lead the singing around the nightly campfires up at camp every summer?"

"Well, others do that too, but yeah it is," I confirmed. "In fact, did you know that another kid who plays guitar up there once liked my twelve-string so much, he offered to buy it from me?"

"No I didn't. But it's a wonderful piece of workmanship, so I'm not surprised."

"Yeah." Then a question popped into my mind about something I hadn't considered earlier. "Dad?"

"Yes, Clint." As he answered me, my dad licked the stamp he had just torn off from his roll and placed it on the envelope he had just addressed.

"Do you think I'll be able to keep up with my karate lessons at the Academy?" I had been studying the martial art now for about two years and had just won my red belt. My goal was to make black belt before I was out of high school.

My dad then turned in his chair and looked directly at me. "Actually, I checked into that already. The Academy doesn't offer karate. But I spoke with the headmaster and…"

"You called the headmaster?" For some reason I was alarmed by this news.

"Yes." My dad waited a moment for me to calm down.

"Well, how did he sound… what did he say?" I suppose I believed at that moment that I should have been the first one from our family to have spoken to the man.

My dad smiled at me. "He sounded fine, and if you'll give me a chance, I'll *tell* you what he said."

Now I felt silly. "Sorry." I decided that I must have been starting to feel nervous about the upcoming life change I was about to embark upon.

My dad's smile then broadened. "He told me that if it is possible, they will make an effort to find you lessons in town somewhere."

"Oh. Well that sounds ok." Even if it couldn't be worked out, I figured that *some* sacrifices were going to have to be made. I decided that, worst case, I could practice my techniques on my own during the school year and then resume my lessons in Europe during my summer breaks.

Finally, a few weeks later, the day came for us to leave Denver. Maria had been given a generous severance and had been released from her responsibilities with our family. I remember standing in our empty living room and taking one last look at the home I had grown up in. Our house had always seemed so warm and inviting to me but on this morning, as the harsh light from the early sun made the empty room look like a photograph which had been overexposed, the house now seemed sterile and no longer a place where we belonged. Since my parents had put their cars into storage, my dad's company sent around a car and driver to take us to the airport. So as we were chauffeured past the stately old homes and the beautiful old trees which made up our neighborhood, I couldn't help but think as we pulled out onto Colorado Boulevard and headed toward Stapleton Field, that I would not be the same person the next time I saw this city.

***

I don't remember anything of the flight we took that day. I imagine we changed planes at O'Hare, and by the afternoon we had arrived in Boston. Once we had our luggage, my dad rented a car and we then set out to find the town of Ulster which our map showed as being located just beyond the town of Worcester and near the Connecticut state line.

"Dad?" I was so excited, I would have gotten out of the car and tried to run to the Academy if I had thought that my feet could have gotten me there sooner.

"What is it, Clint?"

"Maybe you ought to let Mom drive. She doesn't get lost as much as you do in new places."

It was an old family joke. My dad was always getting himself lost when he was in unfamiliar territory. "Don't worry, Son. The instructions I got from your headmaster seem pretty simple. We'll be there in no time."

An hour and a quarter later, I was finding it agonizing to wait for my dad as he took four extra minutes out of our schedule to drive from one end of main street in Ulster to the other. I was unimpressed when he read a sign to us which said that this quaint little New England village had been founded in the year

1737. And I must have seemed borderline suicidal when my father offered next to drive us around the seventeen miles of shoreline which encircled Ulster Lake before going on to find the Academy.

It was nice of him to show me the lay of the land, as it were, but I figured there would be plenty of time later on for me to explore the area. The priority in my mind at this moment was for us to reach the Academy as quickly as we could so I could become acquainted with and settled into the place which was going to be my home now for perhaps the next five years.

According to the Academy catalog, which I had brought along with me, the school was located within a pine forest on an elevated area which looked out over the southern section of the lake and which, at one time, had been the home of the Nipmuck Indian tribe. "Come on, Dad. The town is at the north end of the lake. I really wanna get there." I couldn't stand it any longer. I felt as if I had to get to the campus as quickly as I could.

"All right, Son, we won't spend any more time in town. We'll go straight on to the Academy now." Finally my dad was convinced to end the sightseeing and conclude our trip.

"It says that the Connecticut state line lies fifteen feet outside the Academy's front gate," I was still reading from the catalog.

"Ok, Clint, we get the idea. We're going there now," my dad actually seemed a bit disappointed that we weren't going to spend any more time investigating the quiet village. "Oh, look over at the lake," he pointed with his finger as he began to head us along the highway which led south out of town. "That looks like a nice place to stay the next time we come through here. 'The Friendly Inn.' And look, guys, it even has a dock with boats you can rent. I'll bet there's a pool there too, Clint."

"Maybe," I answered with little enthusiasm. The only amenities I was interested in seeing at that moment were the wonderful ones I was expecting to discover at the Academy.

After that, it didn't take too long before it seemed to me as if a feeling of anticipation had also come over my parents. At a spot seven miles south of town, we turned off of Highway 193 and continued our journey along a winding back country road toward a huge gathering of lodgepole pine trees.

"Here it is!" my dad called out a few minutes later after we had wound our way through the woods. "Ulster Academy!" he announced with pride. After all, he had gotten us to our destination without getting us lost.

On either side of the school's entrance stood square white cement pillars—five feet high with old-style gas lanterns mounted on their tops. On the outside of the pillar on the right there hung a colonial-looking sign which plainly proclaimed the name "Ulster Academy" and warned that we were entering a private drive.

"There're the tennis courts," my mother called out.

Immediately to our right once we had gone through the entrance, perhaps fifty feet away across the lawn, was a tall chain-link fence which surrounded one lonely tennis court. It looked to me as if it hadn't been used in years. Leaves were piled up all around the base of the fence, weeds were growing through cracks in the surface, and there was no sign of a net. "Looks sort of grim," I offered.

As we continued along the main drive of the school, we all noticed that the grounds in general looked unkempt. The outsides of the drive itself were badly in need of edging and the small soccer field to our right showed no signs of ever having been limed. Except for a small gymnasium which had been to our immediate left once we had gone through the entrance, that entire north side of the drive was dense with pine trees. To the south beyond the soccer field were two small buildings. The first was a two-story house with an odd-looking one-story add-on sticking out to its west (toward the tennis court) and having three sliding glass doors which faced us. The other building was a smaller one-story structure which I suspected was a dormitory. Everywhere there was lawn, it looked to us as if a good mowing was long overdue.

"Oh," was all my mother would allow herself to say. She didn't want to let on that she was suddenly worried that we had made a terrible mistake in choosing this place.

At the eastern end of the drive, perhaps one hundred and twenty yards from the front entrance, the cement looped around to form a circle. Within the circle grew grass and four or five tall spruce trees which stood alongside a flag pole which looked sort of denuded to me since there was no flag flying from it. Also placed within this circle was a large tacky-looking rectangular sign which faced back toward the entrance and also read "Ulster Academy" in case the smaller more tasteful sign hanging beyond the gate would happen to go unnoticed.

"I don't know, Clint," my mother couldn't hold herself back any longer as my dad pulled our rented car around to the other side of the circle and then parked in front of the largest building on the campus—Ulster Hall.

The catalog said that Ulster Hall was the school's main building and was "situated on a prominence which offered a scenic and commanding view of Ulster Lake." The frame structure measured one hundred and sixty feet across and sixty feet deep and boasted a total of fifty rooms within its two stories. And as my dad turned off the engine, we tried not to notice the paint which was peeling everywhere from the siding.

The imperfections which were now so clearly causing my parents concern, didn't bother me in the slightest. To me, it was exciting to finally be on the grounds of the school where I was about to begin a life of my own. In my mind, Ulster Hall looked to have been built originally as a lakeside inn. I remember imagining as I got out of the car and followed my parents under the front foyer—located dead center on the building—and up the cement steps which led to the double doors of wood, glass and brass, an earlier, more rarified time when perhaps horse-drawn coaches pulled beneath this same foyer to disgorge their well-heeled patrons who would have come to the inn to indulge themselves in a fine dinner or maybe to dance next to a scenic and commanding view of the lake. And as I entered this majestic old inn behind my folks, I had to throw my hands out quickly to prevent the front door from snapping back and striking me in my face.

"Sorry, Clint," my dad said as he looked back at me to make sure I was all right. "That door's got quite a kick."

Once we were inside and standing in the small lobby area, I supposed my dad had expected someone to appear suddenly to greet us. Instead, nothing happened. After thirty seconds or so of waiting, we began to look in the library straight ahead, and to walk down the south and north halls, which extended through the middle of the building, to search for someone we could report to.

"Here's someone," my dad called out when he spotted a small round-faced man with mutton chops wearing glasses, a tie and a nondescript sport coat while he sat behind his desk in one of the offices along the south hallway.

But the man didn't jump up and rush over to shake our hands and offer us a hearty greeting upon our arrival. In fact, he barely looked up at us at all when he spoke. "Yes ah, just go over and wait in the library. Someone will be along in a few minutes to assist you."

Deflated, and a little annoyed at having come all this way to be told to go sit down and wait, especially when we could detect no other signs of life anywhere at the Academy, the three of us then turned around and walked back to find ourselves seats in the library. As soon as we had entered the larger room with its many windows which looked out the rear of the building toward the lake, we were able right away to find some black captain's chairs with the Academy crest painted on their backs for us to sit down in.

"Are we here on the wrong day?" my mother asked.

"No, this is the day when all students are supposed to arrive with their parents," my dad assured us.

Blue carpeting was everywhere as we then spent a moment surveying our new surroundings. From the sitting area along the library's south wall, where we now were, we looked north into the rest of the room. After an open area, there was a row of tables, each one surrounded by chairs, which ran from left to right (or west to east) the entire depth of the room. Beyond these tables were stacks of books which filled the rest of the room to its north wall. The catalog had referred to this as a "fine library," but I didn't know that a collection of books this small could even be called a library.

My mother then spotted something that convinced her that we had indeed arrived on the correct day. "Look at what they've left out as refreshments for the visiting parents," my mother said as she pointed to a white dinner plate on a nearby table with three pathetic-looking Hydrox cookies on it.

A few moments later, we began to hear what sounded like some older kids horsing around down at the end of the north hallway. Soon after that, we noticed the small man, who had no time for us still, pass by the entrance to the library and head toward these sounds. A minute or so later, the sounds had ended and the small man had returned and had entered the library so he could speak to us again.

"I'm sorry you've had to wait. I guess nobody's around anymore, so why don't you all come into my office now and we'll get you enrolled."

"Ok," my mother answered in a tone which conveyed her disapproval of the obvious inefficiencies in this place which were causing us to be inconvenienced.

The man caught my mother's meaning and spoke again to defend himself as he guided us back into the south hallway. "Everyone else has already arrived today. You're the last ones. I guess that's why my staff has already left for the day."

We followed the man back into his office and once we had all been seated, we then watched as he slurped his coffee without offering any to my parents. "I'm Donald Stuart," the man offered. "I'm the headmaster here at Ulster Academy."

Even at thirteen, I could tell that this man was overly impressed with himself. And so I sat there and listened to the conversation which ensued between my parents and this odd little man into whose care I was about to be placed. After a couple of minutes, I realized that this was one of those conversations where the child was discussed, but never engaged. And so I picked up the Academy's yearbook for the previous year which had been lying on a table next to me and began to look through its pages. Right away I was able to find a picture of this man, so I read through his credentials. Given what I had seen so far, I was shocked when I read that my new headmaster had earned degrees from Yale and Brown and had also been a Fulbright Scholar at the University of Paris. As far as I could tell, he was the only member of the faculty who was Ivy League. With an academic pedigree like his, it was no wonder that he seemed to treat we lesser people with a sort of aloof disinterest. *I wonder what this guy's doing in a dump like this*, I thought to myself.

"Say, that's a fine head of blond hair you have, Cliff," the little man behind the desk finally attempted to communicate with his latest charge.

"Yes, sir, and my name is Clint, sir." I tried to sound polite. Impressive education or not, this first acknowledgment of my existence struck me as being kind of lame. But then I noticed that he was going bald, so I presumed he was simply recalling better days.

Fortunately our meeting with Mr. Stuart didn't last very long and a few minutes later we were standing up again and about to leave the man's office. I now knew that instead of being assigned a room upstairs in the main dormitory, I would be living in room number two on the lower level (basement) of a building they called East Hall which turned out to be the small one-story structure we had noticed when we drove in. And I had a roommate.

"Oh, there's one more thing," Mr. Stuart offered as he stood up again and guided us back out into the hallway. "The kitchen is closed tonight. In fact, our food service doesn't actually begin until tomorrow morning at breakfast."

This was an astounding bit of news. How in the world, I wondered, could they have required the entire student body to show up today and then not have a meal prepared for them tonight? After all, it wasn't as if there were any alternatives available to us. The Academy was out in the middle of nowhere. There were no shops nearby. No mini malls or pizza delivery. The nearest McDonald's was twenty minutes away in Worcester. The only place where a person could find something to eat other than the school dining room was back in town, which was too for away to make walking feasible and I wasn't sure yet if I could find my way back there anyway.

"So what is everybody supposed to do for dinner tonight?" my mother challenged.

"Oh, well," my headmaster seemed to stammer for a moment. I guessed that he wasn't used to being put on the spot by a parent who was more than willing to place him there. "Most everyone has already gone up to Boston tonight to attend a James Taylor concert." Then Mr. Stuart looked at me. "I imagine we could make arrangements to get you up there, and we could tell you what section all of our people are sitting in so you could make connections with them and get a ride back afterwards."

This idea sounded insane to me. I liked James Taylor's music and I even knew how to play some of his songs, but suggesting that I go to a city I didn't know to find people I had never met and who would not know to be looking for me—remember, this was happening long before cell phones had ever come onto the scene—so I could hopefully gain a ride back, struck me as the height of irresponsibility with my welfare. "No thanks," I answered. "I'll just stay here."

"Are you sure?" Remarkably, Mr. Stuart felt called upon to press his nutty idea.

"Yeah, all I want to do is get to my room and get unpacked." Then I looked at my parents. "I'll be all right without dinner tonight. I'm really not that hungry anyway."

As soon as my parents and I had returned outside and could speak freely again, my mother was quick to voice her disdain for Mr. Stuart to my father. "Did you see the bags under his eyes and how red his nose is? He has got to be a heavy drinker."

It turned out that East Hall was right off the south end of Ulster Hall across a small parking lot which doubled as an outdoor basketball court. It seemed to me as if many people had been parked in this lot earlier in the day, but when my dad backed our car up to the front of my dorm, we had the place to ourselves.

"We'll help you get your things inside before we go," my dad offered once he had the car parked and the trunk open. Mr. Stuart had told us that in order to get into the lower hall where my room was, we would have to go through a door on either side of the building (left, east or right, west) which were each located at the bottom of a set of cement steps. He had suggested that we take the steps on the left as we faced the dorm because the door on that side was closer to my room. Also, he had cautioned that we could not get to my room by entering the door in front of us on the main level because apparently the main floor was completely cut off from the downstairs, which struck me as a strange way to build a dormitory.

Once my dad had my suitcases pulled out of the trunk, we all took a moment to acquaint ourselves with this area of the campus next to the lake. Right off we could see that we were standing at the top of a hill and that my dorm was sitting on a small plateau which had been dug into the side of this hill. The steps on the right terminated at the door downstairs, but the steps on the left stopped briefly at a landing next to the door on that side, and then made a ninety-degree-angle turn to the left and continued on down steeply past another dormitory until they ended at a parking lot in a lower area of the campus. This other dormitory, I later learned, was known as "the Annex," and we could see that it was possible to enter the west end of this building by continuing on down a few steps past the landing and then jumping off to the left and following a short path in the dirt over flagstones to a door. When the three of us reached the landing, we could see further that the other end of the Annex was attached to the second floor of a small two-story building which had been built in a spot where the lower campus parking lot lay in front of it and the lake lay behind it.

The three of us then focused our attention on the large black wooden door which was all now that separated us from the knowledge of what my room was going to look like. And like everything else around this place, this door too had gone too long since its last painting.

"Well, shall we go in?" My dad then pulled open the door which immediately caused it to let out a sort of spring-loaded, mid-range groan.

"Charming," my mother responded as she led the way inside.

We found that there was adequate lighting when we entered the stark and narrow hallway. Immediately to our right, once we were inside, was a bathroom. For an instant, I peered in through the door and found one sink, one toilet, one urinal, one shower and a window with translucent glass along the east wall. The entire room seemed barely bigger than my parents' walk-in closet back home. The four bedrooms on this floor were all off to our left and in four or five steps we were standing in front of the second door on this side of the hall.

"You've got the key don't you, Clint?" my dad puffed as he set one of my heavy suitcases down.

"Yeah, I do," I answered as I pulled it out from my pocket and slid it into the lock. And when I turned the lock and pushed open the door, I encountered a boy my age with a thick head of straight black hair who looked back at me with an expression of surprise. "Oh sorry," I reacted quickly. "I didn't know anyone was in here. I think we're supposed to be roommates."

The boy then smiled and put out his hand. "Oh, I didn't want to go to the concert tonight. Hi, I'm Matt Ramsey."

Immediately, I put down my suitcase and shook the kid's hand. "I'm Clint Adams. Nice to meet ya." I then introduced Matt to my parents and we all spent a few minutes after that in conversation.

Matt turned out to be a fairly chatty fellow. "I hope you don't mind, but I went ahead and took the bed next to the window."

"No, that's fine," I replied.

As the four of us talked, my parents and I learned, among other things, that this boy was from Grosse Pointe, Michigan, and had been brought to the Academy by his aunt whom he now lived with after his parents had been killed in a traffic accident some seven or eight months earlier. He seemed capable of talking freely about the incident, but we could tell that he was still bothered by his loss. And happily, we discovered that Matt had picked up a large deer salami and bag of potato chips in town before his aunt had brought him to the campus that day, plus my new roommate knew where the TV lounge was in Ulster Hall where we could get pop and candy bars from the vending machines which were there. So dinner, I resolved, was no longer a problem.

"I thought of stopping in town for some provisions," my dad admitted. "But someone in the back seat was in too big of a hurry to get out here."

"Ok, Dad." I knew he was joking so I pretended to feel insulted.

"Did you aunt stay here in the area tonight?" my mother asked my new roommate.

"No." Matt smiled. "She's meeting her new stock broker for dinner down in New York tonight. I think they're dating."

"Oh," my mother continued. "Your aunt isn't married?"

"No, but she'd like to be," Matt answered.

My mother then smiled. She had spent as much time on campus now as she considered bearable. "Well, perhaps we should be going now so you two boys can become better acquainted."

"Yes," my dad joined in. "We've still got a good three-hour drive to New York ourselves, and I've made dinner reservations for us tonight at 21. So we need to be leaving here pretty soon, I'm afraid."

The time had come for my folks to be on their way, and for me to finally be on my own. My parents said good-bye to Matt, and then I followed them back out to their car. It had been cloudy all afternoon and by the time we had gotten outside again, the clouds overhead had grown dark and were looking now as if they were about to open up on us.

"I've arranged for you to have an allowance of five dollars a week. You can pick up your money every Monday from the bursar's office in Ulster Hall," my dad told me as he took his place behind the steering wheel again. Later I found I was able to stretch my allowance out so that I could pay for one three-dollar small pepperoni pizza from one of the three pizzerias in town, and one can of pop per day for six days every week. "But here's fifty dollars so you can run into town this weekend and get a desk lamp and whatever else you may need for your room." My dad then smiled as he handed me the cash.

"Thanks." I appreciated the thought.

"Try to get something that will cheer up your room too, dear," my mother suggested as she took her seat in the car next to my father. "All of that pine-colored paneling against that light gray linoleum looks so dreary."

"Ok, Mom, I'll try," I answered.

There was still a little more information my dad wanted me to know as thick drops of rain began to fall on me. "Tomorrow I'm going to be spending some time in our New York office while your mother goes out and does some shopping. So we'll be spending tonight and tomorrow night at the Pierre. Then the day after tomorrow, our flight for Paris leaves first thing in the morning. So if you need us before we leave, you can reach us at the Pierre. After that, you can go to Mr. Stuart if you have any problems. He does seem a bit odd I suppose, but I think he's got everything under control around here."

"Ok, Dad. I'll be fine," I said as the rain began to come down harder now.

We then said our good-byes and as I stood there by myself in the downpour in front of my dorm and felt the cool drops of rainwater begin to soak down through my hair and come to rest against my scalp, only my mother had a sense, as she and my father drove away toward the front entrance, of the peril in which I had just been placed. Because later that night, after they had both gone to sleep in their hotel room in New York, my mother awakened suddenly in a panic and quickly awoke my father to tell him that they needed to return to the Academy immediately to get me out of the awful place. My parents never came for me though, because my father pointed out in their ensuing conversation that by this late date in the year, it was impossible for them to place me anywhere else. He also assured my mother that everything for me would be fine because, after all, I was a strong and capable boy who would be able to handle any challenge which might come my way. And so instead of returning to Massachusetts to rescue me, my parents simply turned over in their bed and went back to sleep.

To this day, I don't fault my folks for sticking to our original plans. Because frankly, how could any of us have known that as I returned to my room that afternoon and unpacked my belongings so I could get myself settled, I was now living in a place which was gripped by a sickness that was easily hidden from the view of the casual observer. In fact, it was years later before I learned that this infirmity is so common, it actually has a name. And so as I became acquainted during the rest of that day with the layout of my new world, I often found myself reflecting on those several minutes I had spent standing in the rain and watching as my parents' rental car disappeared amid the pine trees in the distance. Every time I recalled this image and relived in my mind the feeling of becoming drenched in my first New England rain, I also would remember how lonely seeing them leave made me feel. Later that night, as I lay between the sheets of my freshly made new bed and closed my eyes so I could drift off to sleep, I was utterly unaware that on this day my parents had left me at an institution which was plagued by what was likely the worst case ever of English Boarding School Disease.

Chapter Two
Settling In

The next morning at seven o'clock we were awakened by the first clanging school bell of the year. During the night before, Matt and I had hit it off as friends right away. It was odd but even though we were from different areas of the country, we actually had a lot in common. Like me he was pretty resourceful. Besides the salami and chips, he had actually been able to pick up a *Playboy* without his aunt noticing while they had been at Logan Field the day before. In those days it was considered extremely taboo for boys our age to be in possession of such material. And physically we were similar. At that time, we both stood at five feet two inches and Matt weighed perhaps ten pounds less than I did then at one hundred and eight pounds. Also, it would be another year or more before either of our voices would begin to drop.

The rest of the students had returned to the Academy from the James Taylor concert at a little after ten o'clock the night before. When that happened, we learned that another pair of first-year students had been assigned to live in room three next door to us. We hadn't been able to spend much time with them, though, because by then they were tired and wanted to go to sleep. But we were able to find out at least that both boys, Juan and Carlos, were from Venezuela. Also we discovered that apparently one person per room had been assigned to rooms one and four, and in each case they were older kids. When they entered our hall, Matt and I made a point to be friendly and say hello, but each guy just grunted at us and then went straight into his room and slammed his door shut behind him.

As we slowly climbed out of our beds during the half-hour period we were given between the wake-up bell and breakfast, we realized that we were both a little weary from the traveling we had done the day before. So it took us a few minutes to get moving that Friday morning. Nevertheless, within the allotted time, we were dressed and standing in front of a seating chart which was hanging on a bulletin board just outside the entrance to the dining room in Ulster Hall.

"We're at table one, Mr. Stuart's table," Matt read out this information once he had found our names. "Who's he?"

"He's the headmaster around here. Didn't you meet him yesterday?" I was a little surprised that I knew who Mr. Stuart was, but Matt didn't.

"No, some woman from the office checked me in when I got here."

"Oh," I replied blankly.

The kitchen and dining room were both located at the end of the north hallway in Ulster Hall. As we passed by the opened door to the kitchen and made a right turn to enter the dining room, we found that this unremarkable-looking room with a wood floor, was roughly the same size as the library, and just like the library, had large windows which looked out the rear of the building toward the lake.

Table one was the first table we came to once we were standing in this room. And as other kids began to file in for breakfast, we moved quickly to find empty seats and sit down together. Each table in this place was round, made from wood and seated six guys comfortably or seven uncomfortably. We had arrived a couple of minutes early, so my roommate and I watched as the rest of the student body and the faculty sleepily walked in and filled the tables in only the front half of the room. When we were all finally assembled and sitting down, I counted sixty-two students and ten faculty in a dining room which was built to hold one hundred and thirty people.

Next, like an emperor entering his court, Mr. Stuart walked into the room quickly and then stood behind the chair we had left empty for him at our table. Once he was still, the rest of the room stood up, apparently knowing that this was their cue to do so. Instantly Matt and I stood up as well. A moment later, once the room was quiet again, Mr. Stuart spoke.

"For what we are about to receive, may the Lord make us truly thankful. Amen!"

"AMEN!" came the refrain from everyone else in the room, and then we were all seated again.

The tables had been set for us in advance, and in the center of each one stood a tower of bowls and a meager assortment of individual boxes of cold cereal. I didn't know it then, but this was to be our meal for nearly every breakfast we were to have for the rest of my days at the Academy. And though I liked cold cereal at the time, to this day I have refused to touch the stuff ever again because of how often we were given it then.

While I ate, I was eager to get a good look at the other kids with whom I would be living for the next three seasons. Right off, I noticed something that I thought looked odd. At every table there seemed to be a random assortment of ages among the students seated, but at our table nearly every kid was first year. At this stage in my life, I was still pretty much blind to the shortcomings—real or presumed—of the adults I encountered, so I shrugged my observation off as an attempt on the part of a sympathetic headmaster to make young boys, who had probably never been away from home, feel more secure by seating them with the Academy's father figure. Then about halfway through the meal, Mr. Stuart stood up and tapped his empty glass with his spoon to get the attention of everyone else in the room. As soon as he had the room quiet, he spoke again.

"Good morning and welcome to another fine year at Ulster Academy. By now you should all be settled in your rooms and have your schedules. Classes begin at eight-thirty this morning, so make sure you're on time and where you belong when the bell rings. If any of you don't know where you're supposed to be, come by the office right after breakfast and see Mrs. Wellesley, my secretary." He then paused for a moment to let what he had just said be absorbed by our brains. "Also, let me remind you that attendance at breakfast, and for that matter for all meals except the ones you have on Sundays, is mandatory every day just as it is for all of your classes. The only way you can be excused from breakfast is with a note from the school nurse, whom you will find in the school infirmary every weekday morning for half a day." Again our headmaster paused for a moment. "I'll save the rest of my announcements for lunchtime. So for now, enjoy your breakfast and become acquainted or reacquainted, whichever the case may be, with each other and then go ahead and head off to your classes as soon as you're done eating." And with that, the man sat down to finish his breakfast.

Throughout breakfast and as we began to go through our first full day at the Academy, Matt and I tried to become acquainted with the other students. Most of them had come from the corridor which begins at Boston and then extends down through Providence and onto New York to end up in Philadelphia. There were also some foreign students attending. We had at least half a dozen kids from Venezuela, one from Iran, one from Turkey, and one from Colombia. And no matter how hard we tried to be friendly, practically everyone ignored us whenever we said hello. And we weren't just being shunned whenever this happened to us. It actually seemed as if we were being held in contempt for daring to socialize with easterners.

Our daily schedule was as follows:

7:00 AM—Rising Bell
7:30 AM—Breakfast
8:30 AM—1st Period
9:20 AM—2nd Period
10:15 AM—Morning Break
10:30 AM—3rd Period
11:20 AM—4th Period
12:15 PM—4th Period Ends
12:20 PM—Lunch
1:05 PM— 5th Period
1:50 PM—6th Period
2:45 PM—7th Period
3:35 PM—End of Classes
3:50 PM—Recreation, Athletics
6:00 PM—Dinner
7:00 PM—Night Study Period
9:15 PM—Study Period Ends
10:00 PM—Lights Out

For some reason which I never fully understood, we never had any classes on Wednesday afternoons. Apparently the reason for this quirk in our schedule was based on some ancient New England tradition which called for no work to be performed on Wednesday afternoons. In fact, I don't know if this midweek vacation is still observed today, but shops in town actually closed their doors and refused to do business on Wednesday afternoons. And so, to make up for our lost class time, the Academy scheduled classes for us to attend every Saturday morning. But come Saturday afternoon, our time was our own until breakfast the following Monday.

In the afternoon, that first day, Matt and I decided to go out for the school's soccer team. I had wanted to play soccer for some time by then, and I had been frustrated by the fact that at that time, there were virtually no teams set up yet in the west. Only in the eastern part of the U.S. had the sport begun to catch on. But after practice we learned that there were no locker room facilities where we could shower and change out of our gym clothes, so all of us on the team simply returned to our respective dormitories and took our showers there.

The next day, after we had finished with our first round of Saturday morning classes, we found hamburgers waiting for us in the dining hall.

"Oh, man. My favorite," I announced to the others at our table as I took a bun and a patty from the serving platters when they were passed around the table.

"Pass the ketchup please," Matt asked of a kid who was sitting across the table from us. "And the mustard too."

"I'll take those squeeze bottles when you're done, Matt," I remarked cheerfully. "A good hamburger has got to have ketchup and mustard on it."

While the rest of us were preparing our plates, Mr. Stuart got up again and tapped his glass with his spoon so he could make some more announcements.

This time he started off by introducing the school proctors to us. In other schools they were usually known as prefects or resident assistants, but at Ulster, the students who were paid a few dollars to have authority over the rest of us were called proctors. Of course all five of the students now standing before us were seniors. In order of rank, we were introduced first to the head proctor, who was essentially the leader of our entire student body. Next came the head waiter, whose job it was to assign students to be waiters in the dining room on a rotating basis and who also assigned kids to KP duty in the kitchen. Then the remaining three were introduced to us as being in charge of the three dormitories. It was true that some of the teachers lived in the dormitories also, but the proctors were the ones who were in charge of us outside the classrooms. As a result, each day after classes were over, the teachers would simply disappear and, with the exception of dinnertime later in the evening, not be seen again usually until the next morning. So once these introductions were completed, the proctors were then told to sit down again so that Mr. Stuart could go on to inform us on other matters.

"This afternoon, as it will be for every Saturday afternoon, the school van will be available to take anyone into town who needs to go. It will leave from right outside in front of Ulster Hall by the circle at one o'clock, two-thirty, and four o'clock. And then in town the van will leave to come back here at two o'clock, three o'clock and four-thirty. And if you're still in town after the four-thirty van leaves, then you're on your own for getting back here. All drop-offs and pickups in town will be made at the Duncan Donuts. From there you can walk to wherever else in town you need to go.

"At all times of the day or evening, there will always be one teacher who will be carrying the book you need to sign in or out of if you leave the campus. Around here we call this teacher the AOD, which means the authority on duty."

Suddenly the kid sitting next to me leaned over and whispered, "I bet it really means the asshole on duty."

"He needs to be," Mr. Stuart continued, "the last person you see before you leave the campus and the first person you see when you return. And if you don't know where he is when you need him, then you have to go and hunt for him. Because we never want to have a situation occur where your parents call wanting to talk to you and we have to tell them that we have no idea where you are. If ever you can't find the AOD, look on the bulletin board out in the lobby. If he's not around, he'll usually leave a note hanging there that'll tell you where he is."

I didn't know at this moment, but within a few weeks I came to understand what the older students already knew. It seemed that soon after the school year was underway, a majority of the teachers—out of laziness mostly—would hand the book over to students so that they could go off and do personal things which interested them more. Heck, I was even made the AOD one Sunday afternoon so the teacher who was supposed to be carrying the book could take a nap without being disturbed.

Another duty of the AOD was to go around to all of the dorms at lights out every night to make sure that all students were accounted for and that all lights were indeed turned off. But within a week we knew that only two of our teachers actually took this part of their job seriously. The rest of the faculty couldn't seem to care less about us. In fact, most nights Matt and I could have taken off at practically any time we wanted and gone someplace, if there had actually been someplace for us to go and a way for us to get there.

"And also," Mr. Stuart had one more issue he wanted to raise before he was ready to sit down again. "Does anyone need to go and see the baba?"

At this point I had no idea what this man had just said. Was he making some sort of a reference about sheep? I looked around the room quickly for clues but all I could see was hair rippling across heads which were shaking to indicate a general disinterest in whatever it was our headmaster had just offered. And then I realized what it was that Mr. Stuart was talking about. During this era—the early 1970s—it was the style for guys to grow their hair out. A few students, like the head waiter, had hair past their shoulders and nearly all of us had our hair covering our ears. So the negative reactions around the room were in response to the offer to be given a haircut. *Oh, that's it,* I thought to myself. I was still getting used to the accents and many odd habits of speech I was hearing for the first time in my life such as the New England tendency to drop the letter "R" from the end of words where it really belonged. So when I heard the word "baba," I had no idea that Mr. Stuart believed that he had just said the word "barber"—which of course he hadn't.

Finally, Mr. Stuart called for the cook to come out of the kitchen to be introduced. The man who made what I considered some of the worst institution food I had ever tasted was a large overweight African American with an extremely disagreeable personality. His name was Thomas Jefferson, and the only thing he said to us of note was that he never wanted anyone to come back to his kitchen to ask him for seconds. According to the man whom the Academy catalog referred to as a famous chef, we were always given plenty of food the first time around, so there was never any need for us to return for more. As the man spoke, I got the impression that he really didn't care at all for kids. Later, I learned that the theory among the students was that Thomas was skimming money off of the food budget so he could pay for the shiny new blue Camaro he always kept parked just outside the kitchen's back door.

When the announcements were finally over, it was nearly time for all of us to leave the dining room. By now, Matt and I were acting the way that new roommates typically do when they first become acquainted. That is to say, we were doing everything together. So with the opportunity now before us to go into town, as soon as lunch was over we took advantage of it together.

The one o'clock van was packed with kids wanting to taste freedom again, and because we had arrived early, we were able to count ourselves among the chosen few. The van was driven by one of the teachers. Students were expressly forbidden from driving the school van for insurance and other more obvious reasons. And when we finally disembarked at the Duncan Donuts, Matt and I were joined by a new friend we had made earlier that day.

Frank DeVierno was a year older than we were and was from New York City. Actually, Brooklyn was the borough where he lived with his mom, his sister, and his grandparents. This was his second year at the Academy and with his streetwise persona, he came across as a kind of tough kid who knew everything about everything. Matt and I weren't sure if he was tagging along with us to be helpful, or because he had nothing better to do and wanted to see how two boys from other planets would be spending their afternoon. Because by now, it seemed to be known all over school that we westerners were different.

"So, Frank," I asked a little later on as we were coming out of a drug store on Main Street. Matt and I had both needed to pick up some things like toothpaste and shampoo and I had also bought a bottle of baby oil. At that time, kids were using baby oil instead of sun tanning lotion because it was believed that the oil gave a person a richer, more natural-looking tan. Anyway, I wanted to have some for the upcoming occasions when we would be lying out on the

Academy's beach after an afternoon of swimming in the lake. "I've been all over the campus by now and I haven't been able to figure out where the pool is."

Frank then stared at me with a sort of amused look on his face. To me at that moment he resembled a person who had just eaten something he hadn't intended. "What pool?" he asked.

"The pool on the campus. You know, there's a picture of it in the catalog?" I was beginning to raise my voice. *How could a guy who had already spent a year at the Academy not know where the pool is?* I wondered to myself.

Frank then smiled at me. "There's no pool at Ulster, Clint."

I couldn't believe my ears. "Are you kidding?" I must have sounded as if I was blaming Frank for the bad news. "There's a picture of three or four Academy kids swimming in an indoor pool right smack dab in the middle of the Academy catalog!"

"Smack dab, huh? I didn't know people really said things like that. If you ever said anything like 'smack dab' in Brooklyn, they'd beat you up."

This was awful news. I couldn't figure out how in the world the Academy could advertise a swimming pool and then turn out to not have one. "Oh well," I said a moment later when I realized that there was no point in getting upset over the issue. "At least we've got the lake we can swim in. That'll probably be more fun anyway."

"No, you can't do that either." Frank now looked as if he was enjoying his new role as dream smasher.

"Well why the hell not?" My voice now rose in pitch. Rapidly I was becoming exasperated with the whole subject.

"Because the guy that owns the Academy doesn't let us use the lake anymo..."

"Wait a minute!" I interrupted Frank. "You said 'owns'? There's a guy who owns the Academy?" Now I was ready for Frank to clarify what he had just said to me.

"Yeah," Frank confirmed. "Some guy named Zanapolis or something like that."

"He owns it?" I still couldn't get this idea to make sense to me. "As in he makes his living off of us?"

"I guess," Frank confirmed again.

"What's the big deal?" Matt asked me.

"I don't know, I just thought private schools were never operated for a profit and were run by boards."

"Well, we've got a board," Frank volunteered.

"We do?" Matt now seemed a little more interested in our discussion.

"Yeah, Zanapolis and Stuart and I think maybe the dean of students are our board."

"Well, why don't we talk to this Zana... whoever he is and ask him if we can go swimming in the lake?" Matt always seemed to believe that there was a simple answer to everything.

"Because he's never around," Frank continued. "Sometimes he comes to the Academy in the morning when everyone's in class to check on the bookkeeping in the bursar's office, and stuff. But most of the time he just stays away. Anyway, he told Stuart and Stuart told us that he can't afford to pay for a guy with the right training to watch us all the time when we're in the lake. So the insurance company made him tell us to stop using the lake. Which is too bad really, because last year we got to go in it all the time. It was a lot of fun. In fact, we even had our own ski boat last year."

I was nearly sickened by my bad luck. I had missed all of that fun by one year. "That stinks," I protested.

"Yeah, really," Frank concurred.

"I can't believe it." And I couldn't believe it. "So there's no way that we can use the lake ever, is there?"

"What if we go swimming anyway?" Matt asked.

"Then you get detention or suspended," Frank advised.

In those days there were actually unpleasant consequences which went along with being placed on detention or suspension. So that, unfortunately, was that on the subject of swimming at Ulster Academy.

***

For the next couple of weeks I put my efforts into establishing a routine for myself. The classes I had been assigned were like classes in any school, except we always had fewer students in them. For example, my smallest class consisted of only five of us. This fact, of course, was considered to be one of the benefits provided by the Academy. A smaller student-teacher ratio was supposed to mean a greater degree of personal attention for each boy.

The one universal feature which was true for practically all of the teachers at the Academy that year was that, with only one exception I can recall, every teacher there wore a mustache. I have no idea how such a phenomenon came to be. Perhaps they had all gotten together before the school year and had colluded to grow facial hair. In any event, it was a rather strange thing to see.

The other characteristic which all of our teachers seemed to have in common was a well-developed skill for giving homework assignments. I suppose the theory was that if we were always busy with our studies, we would never have time to get into trouble. Matt and I and the Venezuelan boys next door were all good kids. We always followed the rules of the school which included our nightly observance of study hall. Every so often during this period, at least at the beginning of the year, a teacher would come through our hallway to make sure that we were actually doing our homework and not horsing around, instead. Since we were required to study with our doors open, he would come in and then stand in our doorway for a moment to say hello to us. After our response, he would then move on to the room next door and do the same until he had worked his way past all four rooms on our floor. And when he was satisfied that we were all being diligent in our work, he would then leave us by going through the large wooden door at the other end of our hallway. After that, things for us would become quiet again.

In our little hall, we were isolated from the goings-on of the rest of the school, but in time we began to hear about shenanigans which some of the students in the larger dorms would sometimes pull. This was true for both Ulster Hall and especially the Annex where the kids were all older and seemed to me to be more wild than the average Academy student.

On Saturday nights there were almost never any structured activities for us to get involved in. Occasionally a movie might be run on a portable projection screen that a teacher would set up for us in the library, and this diversion from an otherwise dull evening would help to pass the time for a little while, at least. But in general we were always left to our own devices once dinner had been finished. Also, lights out was later on Saturday nights. Instead of ten o'clock, we were allowed on this one night of the week to stay up until midnight, thus prolonging our boredom on these occasions. It was on one of my first Saturday evenings when I got to see for myself what my mother had meant when she had expressed her belief that our headmaster was overly partial to alcohol.

On the second floor of Ulster Hall, was a door that led out onto the top side of the foyer which stuck out over the front entrance to the building. The foyer had apparently been deemed unsafe to walk on because it was falling apart, so students were not permitted out onto its deck—ever. Of course on this particular night, some of our more illustrious students had chosen to ignore the "DANGER" signs which were posted on and around this door, to venture out onto the roof of the foyer anyway. And then to further draw attention to themselves, these boys elected to heave giant water balloons at anyone who might happen to blunder by on the drive below. At this same moment, I had just happened to be looking for something to do downstairs in Ulster Hall and was utterly unaware of the events which were taking place upstairs and on the drive outside. So when all hell finally broke loose and the kids on the foyer began to scatter, I was surprised to notice Mr. Stuart suddenly charging into the building from outdoors so he could confront the hooligans and dispense some discipline. An instant later, before I was able to put together that something was going on, the man had me cornered at the base of the main stairway—where I had been standing—and then he began to speak to me.

"Hey, there! Do you bizzawojabizja?" he asked angrily.

"What was that, sir?" At first I thought I was just having trouble hearing my headmaster because the open doorway to the TV lounge was nearby and the sound from the program that the half dozen or so other students in there were watching was blaring out into the north hall.

Right away Mr. Stuart understood from my reaction that he had failed to communicate with me. But incredibly, instead of hoping that I hadn't caught on about his condition and passing me by so he could run up the stairs and perhaps still capture the young assassins before they could get away, he decided to remain in front of me and give speaking another try. "Buziawoziavizia! Vizia! Vizia!" He was still quite intent on getting an answer out of me.

By this time, I'm sure my mouth was gaping open. "Huh?" All I could do was stare at the man in wonder. I had never in my life seen an adult authority figure behave so strangely. Alcohol had always been present in my family during social gatherings and holidays, but none of the male role models within my parents' sphere had ever permitted themselves to drink to the point of becoming so out of control in front of others. So I really had no idea how I was supposed to respond in a situation like this.

Apparently then, Mr. Stuart realized that I was neither involved in the conspiracy in question, nor was I deserving of his wrath. So he then tried to make up for his bluster by saying something kind to me. "Aw, vuja meeja vuz." At least the man's tone was now softened even if his meaning was still anyone's guess.

Earlier that day I had taken a nap and had apparently slept on my hair funny. So throughout this particular evening, I had a small lock which was curled out and up on one side of my head which made it noticeably independent from the rest of my hair which always hung straight down. As I stood there dumbstruck, I watched as Mr. Stuart then raised his index finger to my head and touched my little flip of hair. As strange as this gesture seemed, I supposed that this touch from him was intended to show me that he no longer considered me a suspect in the just ended balloon/foyer caper. And then, as if he needed to point out to me that he was thoroughly soused, he spoke to me one last time.

"Aw, you… cute little vujaujamoo." Then he passed me by and continued on up the staircase so he could see for himself if there were still any activities going on in the dormitory which required his supervision.

For a moment after he had left, I just stood where I was. I was still unclear over what it was exactly that had just happened to me. But before I had time to sort it all out, I could see the dean of students, apparently motivated also by the events which had just transpired outside, suddenly roar into the building through the front doors and walk straight to where I was still standing by the stairs. When he reached me, he also stopped and spoke to me.

"Did you see Mr. Stuart come through here?" he asked out of breath. The man was something like seventy pounds overweight.

"Yes, sir," I answered quickly. I was worried that I was about to be in trouble again.

"Well, what did he say?"

***

At last, my first letter from my parents arrived from Europe a few days later. After I had found the air mail envelope resting against the side wall in my mail slot, I decided that I wanted a quiet place where I could read what my parents had to say to me in peace. So after lunch I walked down to the lower campus in search of a private spot.

When I reached the bottom of the long set of cement steps which led down the hill from the landing next to my dorm, I turned to my left and walked into the small two-story frame building which the Annex dormitory was attached to on this building's upper level. Originally built as a lakeside tavern, this old structure later had become the Academy's canteen. Today, the soda fountain was gone and the place was set up as a coffee house which meant that it was still being used every so often for school parties. As I entered what was now referred to simply as the Annex, I found more blue carpeting plus dark wooden high-backed booths placed all around the perimeter of the main room next to the windows. An adjoining room hidden behind two double doors along this main room's west wall revealed a smaller bare enclosure which was adorned only with nine twin-sized mattresses spread around in succession on a dusty wooden floor. In addition, this smaller room had a recently added separate circuit of lighting which had ultimately given this little hideaway its name—the black light room. Obviously a great many hopes and aspirations had gone into the decorating of this would-be love nest, and I have to confess that as a still young and innocent teenager, I was intrigued by the idea that young couples in this part of the country were so willing to put their most intimate moments together on display in this manner. But at the moment, I was searching for a quiet place to read my letter and the black light room seemed too creepy to me to be appropriate for such an endeavor, and there were a couple of other guys talking in one of the booths in the main room. So I walked back outside and decided to try my luck around on the rear side of this building.

Lakeside behind the Annex was free of any people, but it was also free of anyplace to sit down. There were no beach chairs or wooden benches, and I didn't want to risk getting sand in my pants by sitting down on the ground. *The dock,* I decided, seemed to be my only option. So I walked quickly along the bank back toward the base of the hill that held the upper campus on its summit until I could step with my right foot out onto the dock. I didn't have a lot of time before my next class, but now that I was here I wanted to place myself at the most picturesque spot I could find, so as the wooden planks creaked under my one-hundred-and-seventeen-pound frame, I kept walking until I had made my way clear out over the water to the end of the dock. And then I sat down.

For the next few minutes, then, I read all about the items my mother had purchased in New York and about the apartment they were settling into in Paris. There was clearly a great deal of activity now swirling around them both. I also learned about the room they had prepared for my future visits, and I found myself wishing for a chance to travel to them now so I could talk with them in person and tell them about all the interesting and disappointing things I had encountered so far at the Academy. But above all I wanted to insist that the next time we were wanting to select a school for me, it was going to be imperative that we check it out by visiting the place first. Because by now I was inclined to agree with my mother. This place was a great deal less than we had expected. And the more I read, the more aggravated I became over the fact that I couldn't even talk to my parents anymore.

Long-distance phone calls in those days were expensive for a school that was so obviously hard up for money. And an overseas phone call would have practically thrown the Academy into bankruptcy, according to the way Mr. Stuart often talked about things. In fact, the owner of the school, according to what we had been told, was so worried about being charged back for collect long-distance phone calls made by the students, he had arranged for the few pay phones we had in our dormitories to be set so that nobody could ever call out on any of them. Only incoming calls were permitted, but the labels showing the phone number on each phone had been removed, so there were rarely any occasions when students would be able to talk with people from the outside world. These arrangements only added to the feeling of isolation I was already suffering from, and caused the mail to become far more important to me than it might otherwise have seemed.

Gee, if I had to get a message to my folks in a hurry, how could I do it? I wondered as I folded my letter and stuffed it into a pocket. I didn't have any other relatives. Both of my parents were only children as I was, and all of my grandparents had passed away by this time in my life. And Matt was in the same boat as I was. The only family he had left was his aunt. And from the way he talked about her, his aunt was always too busy off chasing men and trying to get married to be reliable in any way to him. *So where would I turn?* I wondered.

"Hah," I sighed as I gazed at the two boats which were tied to the dock next to me. The Academy had only two day students and each one of them lived way over on the other side of the lake near town. They both brought themselves to school every day in their own boats. When I had first learned of this, I thought it sounded like a really cool way for a kid to get himself to school in the mornings. So, as I began to inspect the crafts beside me more closely, I saw that the one in front was an in-board out-board of some sort with a wooden hull, and the one tied up behind was a nicely maintained Boston Whaler. *Could I count on one of these guys to get a message out for me if I needed it done?* I decided that the chances of success for such an endeavor were probably pretty slim since I wasn't even sure who these kids were yet. *I don't know if this school is really going to work out for me.* I knew I had no other choice, but with all the disappointments I had experienced already, this was how I had been feeling lately.

I then thought about the back country road which ran along the south side of the Academy and past the Annex parking lot. I could look down on this road from the window in my dorm room. It continued on past the Academy and went curving back up into a hilly and wooded neighborhood with perhaps fifteen houses in it. I had made friends with a boy named Jamie who was about my age and who was from this neighborhood behind the Academy. He lived with his mom and his step-dad in a green house with its own dock which we could see across the cove from the Academy stretching out from a point of land. *He might help me,* I thought. *He's got some guts.* Jamie and a friend of his named Charlie who also lived behind the Academy, and another boy named Danny who was always followed around by his German shepherd named Bandit, were the only people who lived near the Academy who had enough courage to step foot on the school grounds. The rest of the people who lived in Jamie's neighborhood, as well as those who lived in the twenty or so houses which stood along a few roads which fanned out from the main one which led to the Academy's front entrance from Highway 193, behaved as if our school were some sort of home for dangerous and misguided youth. On the rare occasions when we would see one of these neighbors driving past the campus, it would always seem as if they did so quickly and with their doors locked and their windows rolled up so they could avoid a chance encounter with any of us. And frankly, it wasn't hard for me to sympathize with these folks.

An awful lot of the kids at the Academy looked as if they were refugees from a detention facility. It didn't surprise me that the handful of people who lived around our school were afraid of us. After all, at that time the remnants of the hippie movement were still in existence. And I suppose it didn't help matters much when students would blast songs like "Mississippi Queen" by Grand Funk and "Iron Man" by Black Sabbath from their open dormitory windows as many were inclined to do all day. So as a result, we almost never saw any of these people who lived nearby. *I guess,* I decided, *I'd have a hard time relying on any of them either.*

Realizing suddenly that it was getting late, I looked at my watch and then I stood up so I could begin to walk back toward land. It was time for me to get going if I didn't want to be late for my fifth period class in the lean-to. That was the name for the odd-looking add-on to the two-story house I had seen the day my parents and I had arrived at the Academy. The two-story house turned out to be where Mr. Stuart lived, and the three sliding glass doors were classrooms where I was now supposed to be.

"Where ya been, Clint?" Matt asked me when we caught up with each other on the landing a minute or so later. We were both on our way to the same class.

"Just down by the lake. It's pretty nice down there."

"Yeah, but it'd be a lot nicer if we could go swimming."

***

One fine and warm fall day, perhaps a week later, an incident occurred which confirmed to me that I had indeed come to a strange place filled with odd and perhaps even warped people. In the middle of the afternoon on this particular day I had skipped soccer practice so I could have some extra time to finish a paper which was due on the next day for my English class. I was returning to East Hall from Ulster Hall after buying a few supplies I needed from the school's bookstore when, at the same moment I entered my hallway through the door on the east side of the building, I spotted another student entering my hallway from the other end through the door on the west side. Because he was a short kid for his age with a stocky build, he had acquired the nick name of "the Block" because apparently his appearance reminded everyone of a block of wood.

As I allowed the large wooden door to slam shut behind me, I started toward my room and pulled my key out from my pocket. Other people in this part of the country—I discovered shortly after my arrival—seemed perfectly comfortable in looking straight at someone and then not saying anything to acknowledge that person's presence. But I had been raised to be polite, so I said "Hello" to the Block while he continued to stand on the threshold and hold the west door open. In an instant I realized that he was keeping that door open because he was waiting for someone to catch up with him. This seemed curious to me because the Block didn't have a roommate.

"Hey, Clint," he replied with confidence. "You're not goin' to practice today?"

"No, I've got a paper I've gotta finish," I admitted as I slid my key into my lock and pushed open my door.

My first thought was that the Block had figured that our dorm would be empty for the afternoon and was holding the door open for a girl. After all, he lived in room four down at the end of our hallway, and it would be a quick task for him to sneak a girl into his room. And as it turned out, I wasn't too far off with my guess, even though I couldn't figure out where at an all-boys school a kid could come up with a girl to take to his room.

"Come on," the Block called to whoever it was who was now clearly coming down the cement steps toward him. "Hurry up. Come on."

That's a funny way to talk to a girl, I thought to myself. By this time I had delayed my entry into my room because I wanted to see who it was that the Block had enticed to come down to our floor for a visit. But what I saw next caught me completely off guard.

Suddenly a golden retriever appeared at the bottom of the steps and with some further urging from the Block, came into the building and began to walk around on the linoleum. I recognized this animal right away. Her name was Lollie and she belonged to a teacher at the Academy named Mr. Kelley and his family. For an instant Lollie panted and nosed around in the frenetic sort of way that dogs do.

"In here, Lollie," the Block ordered as soon as he had the west door to the hallway closed and his own bedroom door opened.

Obligingly, the dog then trotted into the boy's room. The Block then looked directly at me. "See ya, Clint," he stated with a continued sense of confidence. And then my neighbor at the end of the hall followed Lollie into his room and closed and locked his door behind him.

Man was that weird, I thought as I entered my room. I decided to leave my door open to create a cross breeze. *We all like the dogs here,* I continued to think as I opened my window to gain some relief from the heat. *But this is the first time I've ever seen anyone actually take one of them into his room.*

There were three dogs which hung around our campus regularly. Lollie and her brother, who was owned by another teacher at the Academy, and Bandit, the German shepherd that was owned by the neighbor kid Danny, were all friendly toward the students and were usually willing to retrieve a ball or two or just sit and be petted. These dogs were a constant presence in our lives at the Academy. In fact, one morning, while I was on my way back to my room after breakfast, I stopped with a couple of other guys on the basketball court in front of my dorm to watch Bandit as he roughhoused with Lollie. At first I thought that Bandit was trying to pick a fight with the young lady. But in no time he had her down and then to my astonishment, he nailed her right there in front of all of us. At the age of thirteen, seeing a sex act performed practically at my feet, even if it was between two animals, had a powerful effect on my hormone-filled body. I'll skip the details about what followed, other than to admit that my reaction to this incident, once I was inside and alone, wound up making me a few minutes late for my first class that day.

In any event, once I was seated at my desk and working on my paper, I began to hear some odd sounds coming from the room at the end of the hall. Lollie barked a couple of times, and I could hear the Block trying to quiet the animal down. I could tell also that this kid in room four had opened his window as well, because I was hearing these and other sounds come to me through both my door and my window.

After a bit, things seemed to quiet down once more, so I tried yet again to shift my mind to the homework assignment at hand. But as soon as I began to write, I could hear consistent, almost rhythmic banging and squeaking sounds begin. Quickly I put down my pen and sat back in my chair to see if I could sort out what the heck was going on now. As I focused my attention to this new interruption to my afternoon of study, I concluded that I was hearing a metal bed frame being pushed consistently against an inside wall. *The Block has his bed slid up into a corner against an inside wall and his window,* I recalled.

In no time, curiosity had the better of me and I decided that I had to find out what was happening. So I got up out of my wooden captain's chair and I walked quietly down the hall until I was standing right outside the door to room four. As soon as I was still, and while the banging and squeaking continued, I was able now to discern that the squeaking sounds I was hearing were being made by bed springs. And on top of that, I now could hear Lollie uttering a sort of doggie groan with every exhale. "Rr, rr, rr, rr!"

I can't believe this! My senses were defying my ideals of decency and proper behavior. By this time in my life I had heard jokes about Shepherds and their sheep, but what I believed was now occurring on the other side of that door, went well beyond any concept of sexuality that I had ever before encountered.

"Rr, rr, rr, rr!" Lollie continued her groans.

The more I heard these sounds, the more my curiosity grew until I reached the point where I decided that I had to know for sure what was going on in that room. *He can't be doing that...* The whole idea seemed too impossible to be true. And so I walked back down the hallway to the east door and I left the building.

I had it in my mind to walk along the wide earthen ledge out behind our floor in a casual way, so I would appear to be just out for a break from my studies to get a bit of fresh air. And as I began to pass slowly by the windows, I was just as eager to disprove what I thought was taking place as I was to prove it. As I advanced along the back side of my dorm, leaves on the ground crunched under my feet which no doubt announced my approach because once I was along side the opened window to room four, and before I could make myself turn my head to the right to look into the Block's bedroom, the kid spoke to me.

"Hi, Clint!" His voice sounded clear and quite friendly.

Right away I figured that a strong greeting like this meant that there was another more sensible explanation for the sounds I had been hearing. So with a great sense of relief, I turned my head and saw in horror as my neighbor lay on his stomach on top of Lollie—their encounter now apparently ended—while the dog lay quietly on her back underneath the boy.

"Oh… ah, hi there… Block." What do you say at a moment like this? Hey, that's a nice dog you've got there?

Lollie then twisted her head a couple of times to get a better look at me, but other than that, she seemed quite content for the moment to stay where she was.

Jeeze, I wonder if he's gonna give her a cigarette, now? I thought.

"It sure is a nice day outside today isn't it?" Although he still sounded confident, it was obvious that the Block was now trying to make conversation to break through this moment of awkwardness.

"Ah… yeah it really is." Again, I couldn't think of anything else to say. But I was aware that if I stayed there any longer, there would only be one way for this conversation to go, and I didn't want any part of that. So I excused myself. "Well, I guess I ought to be getting back to my homework. I'll see ya later, then." I was already walking away before I had finished speaking.

"Yeah ok, Clint. I'll see ya later." And that was the last we ever said to each other on the matter.

***

Her name was Ellen, and she was the first girl I ever French kissed. She had come to the Academy with the rest of the students from an all-girls school up in Boston, to spend an evening with all of us at the Academy. Everything about that night, I remember as being magical. It probably sounds strange to say now in light of the sort of world we live in today, but at the time, I didn't know that there even was such a thing as French kissing. I had merely thought that kissing was kissing. But by the time my arranged date with Ellen was over later that night, I had become a devoted practitioner of the art.

"So is everything ok here?"

I felt a hand placed on my back and a voice speak to me from above. "Yeah, great!" I answered as I looked up and saw that it was the head proctor who was expressing an interest in my well-being.

"Good. We thought you two would get along well together because you both play the guitar," he revealed.

"Oh yeah?" I then took my eyes off of the head proctor and looked again at Ellen with approval as she sat there on the small couch next to me. She was gorgeous with long brown hair and a cheery face. Our eyes met again and she smiled back at me.

The head proctor then continued with what he wanted to say to us. "Yeah, and we thought when we matched you two up that maybe you guys could play a few songs for us after dinner tonight. You know… to help us kick off the evening and everything."

"Really?" I was amazed that I had been part of the strategic planning for this occasion. "Well that's fine with me. What do you think?" I asked my date. We had only just been paired up by the head proctor and his counterpart from the girls' school a mere three minutes or so earlier, so we were still on our initial attempt to get to know one another.

"Well," she began, "I just got here, and I don't have a guitar, and we've never tried playing together." At first Ellen was less than enthusiastic with the idea. She looked around the room as she spoke and saw that people were beginning to get their plates and fill them with food. Plus it had been a long ride down from Boston on the bus, and frankly, I think she also lacked a bit of confidence in her music skills and was afraid of sounding foolish in front of everyone.

But I was used to getting up and doing impromptu performances. I thought the idea sounded fun. After all, life for me at the Academy was still relatively new and a quick couple of songs would gain me a little notoriety which, in turn, would make it easier for me to make friends, I figured. "Oh it'll be easy," I accepted the invitation for both of us. "If somebody else around here has a guitar we can borrow, we can probably have a few songs worked up in about fifteen minutes." I then saw Ellen look at me with an expression of surprise on her face. What—she must have wondered—was I getting her into?

"Great!" The head of our student body seemed pleased that we were willing to make the effort. "I know where I can get my hands on another guitar. I'll be right back." And then he vanished into the crowd of students who by now had filled in the library around us.

"It'll be fine," I tried to reassure Ellen. "If you can play, I'm sure we can put together a couple of numbers at least. Do you sing too?" I asked.

"Yes, I guess," she answered tentatively.

"Well then, we'll be fine. I sing also."

A moment later the head proctor had returned with a six-string folk guitar which apparently belonged to the head waiter. "We'll hold some dinner for you guys while you go get ready."

After that I remember taking Ellen over to my dorm room and pulling out my twelve-string. (Now, in case I was just expected to say something else here, let me assure the reader that I was raised to always be a gentleman around women. Also, at this stage of my life, I was still pretty naive about matters of sex.) About ten minutes later, after some quick rehearsing, we were as ready as we were ever going to be. So we returned to the library and took our places on a raised section of the room by the windows because it seemed to make the perfect stage for us. I have no idea now what we actually played that night, but I imagine—to be safe—we did standards like "Greens Leafs" because a lot of the time, the audience sang along with us. Our performance went fine except for the fact that the head waiter kept calling up for us to play "Wooden Ships" by Crosby Stills & Nash. At the time, that song was part of a brand-new album which I hadn't yet been able to listen to. Looking back on it now, I have decided that he was simply jealous that such a young kid like me was up there getting all of the attention instead of him. And indeed, I didn't know it at the time, but eventually I would feel the brunt of his ill feelings toward me. And, not to blow my own horn or anything, but I was a much better performer than he was. In fact, with the exception of one fellow who was a very fine pianist, I don't remember anyone at the Academy ever being able to match me in this area.

So we did the two or three songs we had prepared to solid applause, but the audience wanted more from us. So, after that, Ellen and I alternated solo numbers for a while until we decided we had been up there long enough.

"Here you go." The head proctor handed Ellen and me our dinners after we had put down our guitars and rejoined the crowd. "We put these plates together for you guys. Thanks a lot for doing this for us. I think it went over really well." And then, as an older brother might do to a younger one, the head proctor reached over and rubbed the top of my head with his hand which, of course, messed up my hair.

"No problem," I answered with a smile. "Any time." And then I lifted one of my hands and used my fingers as a comb to put my hair back into place.

"You're welcome." Ellen also sounded grateful for the praise, but I think she was just as glad to finally have the whole experience behind her.

After dinner we joined some friends and made our way down to the coffee house in the Annex. There, amid the dim lights, the posters of rock bands and the loud music of Steppenwolf, the Doors and Jimmy Hendrix, we talked and danced through a good portion of the evening. One of the funnier things I remember about Ellen was that she had recently developed an odd affinity for baby bottles. As she explained it to me, the small ones were a convenient way to carry liquids when she traveled because they never leaked. She had many insights like this and I found it fascinating just to listen to her. But eventually,

Ellen and I decided that we were restless and the time had come for us to go out and find something else to do.

We did peer into the black light room and saw that all nine mattresses were in use, but that wasn't Ellen's style. So we left the coffee house and walked around behind the Annex so we could stand on the beach and watch the moonlight as it reflected against the lake. Shortly after that, though, Ellen felt chilled, so we decided to climb the steps and return to the upper campus to check out what was going on up there. But we never made it all the way. When we reached the landing, instead of turning right to go up the remainder of the steps, we chose instead to continue straight ahead which took us directly into my dorm.

After I had hung a neck tie around the door knob on the outside of my door to signal to Matt, in case he came around, that our room was in use, Ellen and I then spent the next few minutes engaged in nervous conversation. Soon, though, we were sitting together on my bed. Ellen was a little more than a year older than I was, and as I look back on our evening together now, I realize that she was the one who was really in charge. And when we finally began to kiss, and I felt her tongue penetrate through my perimeter of teeth and then plunge itself deep into the private region beyond my gums so she could rub and play around in there freely and with impunity, my first thought was *What is she doing to me?* An instant later, though, I realized that her oral gymnastics were causing me to feel exhilarated. So I immediately reciprocated with an equal amount of enthusiasm.

This was how Ellen and I then spent the rest of our evening together until the time came for her to rejoin her friends and leave the Academy to return to Boston. I never saw her again, but a few weeks later I received a small package in the mail from her. In it I found a small baby bottle, an elastic bracelet she had made for me from blue beads, and a picture she had drawn for me which she called a dot drawing. The artwork was done in ink and was comprised of a series of dots which together depicted the image of a short man wearing a large hat. My friends at the time told me that the man looked like Arlo Guthrie. I never knew one way or the other. I was just grateful to have received her gifts.

Years later, I gave the bracelet to my daughter when she was still a little girl, because it was something of mine which she admired. My wife one day threw out the baby bottle because she couldn't imagine why a grown man would have such a thing sitting on his closet shelf, and the picture I had mounted. It is with me still today and has become one of the items from my youth which I truly treasure.

Chapter Three
The Day My World Changed

On the following Monday, a few days later, classes resumed as normal. Throughout the day I felt as if I was on top of my game. I remember receiving an "A" on my English composition that day, and at lunch I actually enjoyed what we had been given to eat. In the afternoon during soccer practice, I felt as if I was finally getting the hang of things. I had figured out the way to adjust my foot and angle my body so I could loft the ball accurately whenever I wanted. I don't know if my successes on this day had anything to do with the great lift in my spirits I was still feeling after my date with Ellen, but regardless of what the reason was, I had a tremendous day.

At dinner that night, Matt and I found ourselves assigned to a different table. Frank was now sitting with us and the rest there were upperclassmen whom, as of yet, I really didn't know all that well. The teacher who was supposed to sit at the head of our table lived off campus with his young family, and therefore was AWOL during most of our meals. This particular meal was just such an occasion, so the head proctor took charge of us instead.

Once the blessing had been said and we had all taken our seats, a couple of things happened which struck me at the time as being sort of strange. For starters, instead of one of us at the table being assigned to be our waiter, and then that boy being saddled with the task of bringing out a tray filled with serving platters and bowls filled with food, and instead of having our dinner portioned onto plates by the head of our table and then passed around family style to the rest of us as usual, the head waiter appeared instead with a tray loaded down with plates which had already been prepared for us in the kitchen. He then made a special effort to give everyone at our table the precise plate which he believed each person was supposed to have.

The whole business struck me as odd and at one point I asked one of the bigger kids sitting next to me why our table was doing things so differently. The guy responded simply that because the head proctor was in charge of our table, we were sometimes accorded special treatment. Honestly, I thought his answer sounded goofy. But I couldn't come up with a better one, so I accepted my plate and began to eat my dinner once everyone else at the table had been served.

Another thing that I remember about that meal was that instead of being served the usual fried or boiled potatoes, on this night we were given mashed potatoes. Normally, our cook never wanted to go to this much trouble for us. I loved mashed potatoes, especially when they were served with fried chicken as they were on this night, and I found them a real treat. But Matt told me afterwards that he had thought that his had tasted a little funny.

During study hall that night, I noticed that Matt couldn't keep himself from yawning. For some reason he seemed overly tired all evening and by the time the bell had gone off for lights out, he was already in his bed and nearly asleep. Within, perhaps, two minutes after I had turned out our lights and gotten under my own covers, I could hear Matt breathing deeply. It amazed me to see how quickly that kid could fall asleep.

In bed, I remember being keyed up over my day, plus I was still reliving my date with Ellen. So it took me some time that night to fall asleep. In a while, though, I did manage to drift off. Another day was finished, and another week had begun, and I was beginning to believe that things for me at the Academy were going to work out all right after all.

I didn't hear them enter our room a few hours later. I don't know if they first spent some time going through our things or if they just watched us sleep for a while. But the next thing I knew, I was feeling impressed to wake myself and open my eyes. When I did, I saw two tall figures standing over me in the moonlight with Halloween masks covering their faces. I must have been startled to see them because immediately one of them placed his hand over my mouth to silence me. Then, I saw him raise his index finger to his mouth hole.

"Shshsh!" he said. "Don't worry. It's all right, we're just upperclassmen," the first one whispered to me.

I then calmed down and the guy removed his hand from my mouth. "What's going on?" I asked nervously. "How did you get in here?" These guys were full grown and it made no sense to me to have them there in our room.

"It's all right," the second one then whispered as well. "We used a pass key. Sit up for a minute and we'll explain it to ya."

I did as they asked. Once I was upright, things didn't seem so overwhelming to me. "All right. I'm up," I acknowledged. "Now what?"

The first one then continued. "We've come to get you for a little... initiation we give to a few special first-year guys every year. It's like...a special honor."

"Oh?" I replied. "Well can't you honor me later? Like after breakfast or something when I'm awake?" I asked. I wasn't sure what to make of all of this.

The second one then answered me. "No, the tradition is to do this now. At this time of the night."

"What about Matt?" I asked. I then looked over at my roommate and saw that he hadn't noticed any of what was going on next to him. He was just lying there with his eyes closed—sawing logs.

"No, this has all been arranged just for you. Come on, stand up. A bunch of us are waiting."

"A bunch?" I was surprised to hear that I was such an object of interest for so many. I don't know why, but this was apparently enough to persuade me to get out of bed and go along with these guys. Perhaps I'm just more prone to powers of persuasion when I'm only half awake.

When my bare feet first hit that cold linoleum floor, I began to look around the room for something to put on.

"No!" the first one stopped me as I reached for a pair of pants. "That T-shirt you're wearing, and your briefs are all ya'll need. Just put on your sandals and let's go."

"Really?" I asked. "You want me to go someplace in just my underpants?" As strange as this sounded, it really didn't raise that many red flags in my mind. After all, this was an all-boys school and there were no women around anywhere at this hour of the night.

"Naw, you don't need nothin' else. At this time of night most of us are in what we normally wear to bed anyway." The first one made it all sound so friendly. As if the three of us were headed for some big pajama party and staying in my underwear would help me to fit in better. Then I noticed that both of these guys were wearing blue jeans. "Yeah, but you two guys have pants on," I observed.

"That's because I normally sleep in the nude," the first one replied.

"Yeah, and so do I," the second one now joined in again. "Hey, we're runnin' out of time. Come on, let's get going."

"Fine." I said nothing more on the subject after that. I decided that it really didn't make any difference to me at this time of night how I was dressed—or not dressed. And besides, it was normal at the Academy to see boys running around in the dorm hallways wearing nothing but their underpants, especially in the mornings before breakfast and at night before lights out. In fact it was even commonplace for guys to walk into the rooms of other students and sit down for a chat while their friends were dressing. I had figured that this general lack of personal modesty at Ulster had been brought about by the large community shower rooms that the other dorms had. With no partitions or curtains set up between the shower heads, there was little reason for a kid to hide himself after he had showered a bunch of times with practically everyone else in the school. So in silence, I walked over to our closet and slid my feet into my flip-flops. "All right, now what?" I asked once I had them on.

The first one then pulled a pair of eye shades out from his pocket. "Now we have to blindfold ya."

This idea didn't thrill me. "How come?" I asked.

The second one was ready with an answer for me. "This group is sort of like a secret society. We want you to become one of us, but you don't have to if you don't want to. So if you decide not to join us, we don't want you to know who any of us are. Otherwise our society wouldn't be secret anymore. Ya see?"

The explanation seemed to make sense. After all, they *were* wearing masks. "I guess." So I gestured for them to go ahead and put the things on me. The first one placed the elastic string around the back of my head, and then he pulled the shades down over my eyes until the plastic was resting on my nose. I then could feel both sets of their hands pulling my hair out all around from under the string and then smoothing it down straight again. I guess they did this to make sure the eye shades fit snugly around my head.

"Good!" the second one said when they had finished with my hair.

"Ok, let's go." Next I could hear the first one walk over to the door and open it. He then stepped back over to where I was standing and grabbed my arm. "We'll guide you to where the others are waiting."

"Ok," I acknowledged. I then could feel the first one pulling on my arm, so I began to walk along with him. Once we had walked out into the hallway, I could hear the second one close my door and then catch up with us. "Hey, hold up. We forgot something."

"Oh right!" the first one answered. And then we stopped walking. "Here, put your hands out in front of you," he then let go of my arm.

Without thinking, I did as he asked. "Why?" I then could feel my wrists being tied together with some rope.

"Because we're supposed to tie your hands together," he replied.

"It's all right," the second one then spoke up before I could offer any sort of a protest. "I don't know why they feel it's necessary. It's not like there's anyplace you can run away to. But it's part of the tradition, so we have to do it."

I said nothing more. In another moment my hands were tied together in front of me and the three of us were out the door, up the stairs, and on our way across the upper campus in the middle of the night.

They guided me across the basketball court in front of my dorm and then over to the circle in front of Ulster Hall. Once we had passed the flag pole, we then turned left and began to walk along the main drive toward the front gate to the school. It was still early enough in the fall for the temperature that night to be comfortable. At least I don't remember feeling cold.

As my journey progressed, I suppose my mind was working mostly on the task of trying to figure out just what all of this could possibly be about, and where in the world these guys were taking me. So when we turned off the drive just before we reached the gate, and began to follow the cement path which led to the gym, I breathed a small sigh of relief. I had been starting to worry that these guys were going to be taking me off campus somewhere. If that had happened, I figured it would be anyone's guess where I might end up. But now that it seemed clear that we were remaining on campus, I knew, at least, that I would be safe.

When we pulled open one of the doors on the front of the building and walked into the gym, it sounded to me at first as if the place was closed down. But in a few moments, as I became accustomed to the sound of our footsteps crossing that vast wooden floor, I began to notice other sounds. People were talking. I realized then that apparently some guys had gathered in one of the back rooms of the place. So I knew finally, that I was about to learn what this secrecy was all about.

"Well, here they are," I heard a voice say as we entered the coach's locker room through a door off a little side hallway in the rear of the gym. I was then escorted over to what I judged to be the center of the room where the two guys who had brought me then let my arms go so the three of us could stand side by side as if we were about to take part in a ceremony of some kind.

"Welcome, Clint!" An enthusiastic voice by the wall in front of me sounded pleased that I had come. Apparently except for the two guys standing on either side of me, everyone else in the room was lined up along this same wall. I remembered that this room measured about twenty feet square—a little large for a locker room in a building this small—and there was a door from here which led into a private bathroom with a single stall shower. I also knew that these two rooms were about as far away from everyone else on the campus as one could get. There were no windows, and outside the only things nearby were trees—and lots of them. In these rooms and at this time of night, we were truly isolated from the rest of the world.

"Hi," I answered back. The eye shades didn't fit me just right, so I could make out that the lights had been turned on in this room. Then the voice against the wall spoke again.

"You can call me 'leader,' Clint. The rest of us here have appropriate names also that you'll learn in time." The leader was making himself sound cordial. "It's so nice of you to join us here tonight. Do you know why you're here?"

"They said something about an initiation," I answered. As soon as I had spoken, I thought I could hear suppressed snickering going on around the room.

"Yes, well…an initiation is a good way to put it." The leader's cordial tone now seemed to be giving way to one of condescension.

I suddenly sensed that this situation I was now in wasn't as friendly as I had been led to believe. "But I was also told that if I didn't want to join, I didn't have to." I figured I'd better get the qualifier stated right up front.

Outright laughter then broke out around the room. I had apparently said something that had struck everyone there as funny. I now had a sick feeling in the pit of my stomach that told me I had made a huge mistake in agreeing to come here tonight. I began to think about what it would take for me to get out of this place in a hurry if I had to.

"Yeah, well… I'm sorry, Clint, but they lied to you about that. You have no choices here. All you need to know is that we've chosen you to be part of our little group and that's the end of it. From now on, you're gonna have to do what we say whenever we say it. Ya got that?"

The concept that the leader was explaining to me went dead against my fierce sense of independence. But being the smallest one there—all of their voices were deep and mine was still high—I was inclined to be cautious. "I don't understand."

"That's ok," the leader responded. "You will in a minute." Then the leader addressed the two who were still standing on either side of me. "Ok guys, strip him."

Before I had a chance to say anything else, I could feel hands begin to pull at my clothing. Instantly I threw my tied hands hard at where I judged the location to be of the stomach belonging to the guy on my left.

"Ohoof!" I scored a direct hit. His hands, then, were off of me and I could hear his body crash to the floor. I then kicked off my flip flops, took one step backward to my southwest, set myself into a side stance, and then threw a side kick with my right foot to where I guessed the other guy's head was positioned.

"Auhauh!" The guy on my right then fell away also. I apparently had nailed him where I had wanted as well.

This blind karate works pretty well, I thought. Now that I had given myself the opportunity, I figured I needed to get out of this place as fast as I could. But before I could turn to make a run for the door, I felt an impact to my head, and then I saw stars. The next thing I knew I was on the floor feeling disoriented with a fair amount of pain in my skull. Right after that a loud and angry voice began to echo in my head.

"Don't you ever try any shit like that again on any of us, Clint. I'm a black belt, you asshole. How does it feel to take a roundhouse to the head? If you ever try anything like that again, I'll tear you apart!" The leader now sounded more like a marine than he did a student of the martial arts. After that, he spoke again to the two who were sprawled on the floor with me. "Go on, finish your job!"

Hands were then placed around my waist and I felt my underpants yanked off of my body. More hands then grabbed me on both of my upper arms and an instant later I was lifted back to my feet. Then hands pulled my T-shirt up over my head and down my arms to hang over the rope which was still keeping my wrists tied together. I was now standing naked in the middle of this brightly lit room in front of them all.

"That's more like it," the leader now sounded pleased. "Yes, you look fine. You've got some hair but it's blond too, so I don't think that'll matter much."

I had no idea what the leader was talking about, but it seemed pretty certain that it wasn't going to be anything that I was going to like. "What are you talking about?" I complained peevishly.

"You'll know in a minute. Now are you gonna be a good boy, or am I gonna have to hit you again?"

"Yeah!" I answered defiantly.

"Yeah what?" the leader sounded irritated with the tone of my answer.

"Yeah, man!" Roundhouse or no... naked as a jaybird or no... I still didn't like the idea of being controlled this way. The hands gripping my arms then began to squeeze me tighter and I could sense movement in the room once again. "Ohoof!" I took a fist to the stomach. The pain from the impact doubled me over.

"What do you say!" The leader was now standing over me and practically screaming.

"Ah... yes!" I gasped.

"Yes what?" the leader demanded.

Giving into this guy wasn't enough for him, apparently. Now the son of a bitch was wanting my respect as well. Unfortunately I no longer felt in any condition to argue. "Yes... ah... sir." I forced the words out from my constricted diaphragm. No longer did I feel that defying these guys was in my best interest. The leader had made it very clear to me that going along with whatever it was that he had planned would be a lot better for my health than doing otherwise.

"Ok." Then to the two on either side of me again, "You guys take him now and put him in the shower."

My escorts then pulled on my arms for me to go with them. I straightened myself up, as best as I could, and began to walk with them. The light I had detected from the corners of my eye shades then vanished as we moved from the larger room into the confines of the smaller one. All the other guys, apparently, were remaining out in the locker room because when I was finally in the bathroom, it felt to me as if it was just the three of us again.

When it seemed certain that the leader was not around us any longer, I debated with myself over whether or not I should express a little anger at these guys for lying to me. But when one of them let go of my arm and turned on the water in the shower suddenly, I decided instead to focus my energies on what they were about to do with me.

"Now listen up!" the one on my left began to speak to me. As the water hit the cement floor, I found it a little bit harder to hear him. "From now on, you do exactly what you're told as soon as you're told to do it, and you'll be back in your bed in no time."

"After I've dried off," I added.

"That's right," the guy answered.

I could now feel the cool spray from the shower hit me on my shins. As the one on my right worked to adjust the temperature for me, the one on my left finished with my instructions.

"And if you give us any more trouble at all... then God help you."

"How long am I gonna have to be here?" I decided that another question from me now couldn't be a problem for them.

"For a while," my keeper answered. "And don't talk either unless you're asked to. Ya got that?"

"Yes, sir," I acknowledged. There was nothing else I could do at the moment. By this time the one on my right had gotten the water temperature adjusted correctly. He then turned back toward me and untied my wrists to remove the rope and T-shirt from me. A moment later I could feel his hands return to their positions on my right arm, and then the two of them led me into the shower.

As my body became wet, a hand detached itself from my right arm again and then made its way into my hair on the back of my head. A palm with its fingers outstretched was then placed against the back of my skull. A moment later, with gentle but definite pressure, my head was shoved into the running water. The shower head was one which put out a large thick volume of water over a pretty broad area. So in no time my hair became completely soaked through. The palm then tilted my head from one side to the other to make sure that every bit of the hair on my head had become drenched.

Once they were sure I was all soaked down, the guys then pulled me back from the water so I could stand dripping a few paces away. I then could hear one of them place a chair in the shower and then they spun me around and backed me into the stream again until I was made to sit down in this chair. They had done a pretty good job of estimating my position, because after I was seated, they only had to make a slight adjustment in the angle of the shower head to cause the water to pour down directly onto the top of my head.

"Now stay here and don't move! And don't take off those eye shades either!" I heard one of them order.

After that they apparently pulled the shower curtain around me as they left because I could hear the sound of metal rings being scraped along a rusty metal rod. But due to the noise created by the water as it pelted me on the top of my skull, it was harder for me to discern the sound of the bathroom door when they closed it behind them.

So now, it seemed I was being given some time to reflect on my new circumstance. The first thing I noticed was that the chair I was sitting in was small, as if it had come from a kindergarten. I had never seen a chair like this anywhere on the Academy grounds, so I figured my hosts had gone to some trouble to find it. Of course once I had made this observation, the next obvious question in my mind was to wonder why they would want me to sit in such a low chair.

I also thought about all that had just happened to me and I couldn't figure out what kind of an initiation would require a smaller kid to be beaten up, stripped and thrown blindfolded into a shower. None of these things made any sense to me, and I wondered further how long the upperclassmen out in the locker room were going to make me stay in here and what sort of things were they going to be doing to me next. And as it worked out, I didn't have long to wait for my answers.

I wasn't sure if I had heard the door open and close, but my mind snapped to attention when the metal rings were scraped along the metal rod twice again. Immediately after that, I could sense the presence of another person in the shower with me. At that moment, I quickly flashed back to times at summer camp when the counselors had made us double up in the showers whenever we were running out of hot water and there was still a long line of unclad boys waiting to get in. I didn't know why someone else was now there in the shower with me, but I was certain, at least, that it wasn't because we were running out of hot water and he wanted to get clean.

"Stand up!" a voice then ordered.

I did as I was told and rose to my feet. There was, thankfully, enough room for me to move around in here with this other person. Once after I had just arrived at the Academy, I had peered into this bathroom and concluded that the shower was kind of odd looking in the way it had been designed. It seemed too big to me for just one shower head, yet not big enough for two.

"Now turn around and face the wall."

Ignoring the running water, I turned myself around and stood with part of my face now in the stream. As I did this I decided that the voice I was hearing belonged to the leader. So I knew at least, that whatever it was that I was about to be involved in, it was important enough for the top man himself to be in there with me.

"Now bend over and grab onto the chair with both hands. Then let the top of your head rest against the wall."

I wanted to ask the leader what the point was to all of these instructions, but I didn't want to take the risk that more of his black belt training would be put to use against me. So as I bent over and gripped the seat of the chair with my hands, I could feel the water begin to hit me all up and down my back.

The leader then adjusted the angle of the shower head. As soon as he had the water pouring down mostly onto the back of my neck and head, he began to put his hands all over me. I first felt him place them on my hips as he steadied my stance. He then began to rub his hands all over my back and down my legs. After that, he played a bit with my hair and then he smoothed his hands along my face, chest and stomach and even gave my penis a couple of yanks—which didn't please me. Eventually, though, his hands wound up on my butt and a moment later I could tell that he was feeling around inside my crack for my hole. In no time he had found it and for an instant, I thought he was going to stick one of his fingers into me. But instead, the leader inserted something small, long and hard, and then I could feel a cold substance growing in volume inside my anal cavity.

"What are you doing?" I asked in a panic.

"Don't worry," the leader answered. "It's just olive oil. I've got it in one of the squeeze bottles from the kitchen.

I couldn't imagine why someone would want to squeeze olive oil into my ass. A few moments later, though, the leader pulled out the end of the squeeze bottle and then I could feel him insert an oil coated finger into me.

"Auh!" I strained. What he was doing to me now was not comfortable. Immediately I felt a huge buildup of pressure in my rectum which seemed on the verge of becoming painful.

"Relax!" the leader called to me. "This'll be a lot easier on you if you relax your butt."

I tried to do as the leader said. At the same time, I couldn't figure out what kind of perverse pleasure could be derived from sticking a finger up my ass and spreading around olive oil. So as the water continued to flow down all over my head and neck, I could feel the leader probing the inside of my anus. And when he finally did pull his finger out of me, I let out a long sigh for the relief I then felt from the pressure he had been causing.

"There, you see. Now you're relaxed. That's how you want to be when I'm in your ass."

Gee, I wondered silently. *Is he going to do this to me again?* It was only another moment before I had my answer.

"Ok, get ready," the older boy placed his hands on my hips one more time.

I next felt what I first thought was his big toe at the entrance to my hole. It was oily as well, and then in horror I realized that it wasn't his toe… it was his penis! "NO!" I shrieked. I now understood that the leader was naked in here with me and he was getting ready to… "Auhauhauh!" The pain was enormous. I couldn't believe this was happening to me. "MY GOD I'M BEING RAPED!" I yelled as loudly as I could manage.

The leader ignored my outbursts and continued to push himself gradually into my anal cavity and only stopped once he had slid himself in about halfway. "Calm down!" he ordered. "Relax like I told you and this won't hurt as bad."

"Take it out!" I screamed. "My God it hurts! Take it out, please! Please don't do this to me! Please stop it! My God, don't put me through this, please!"

My pleadings accomplished nothing. I felt as if I had just been impaled by an object that was large and blunt, like a zucchini or something. The idea of being raped was as upsetting to me as the actual pain from the act which was now beginning to sap my strength. My body then began to tremble from the strain being placed upon it.

"I said calm down. You better do as I say, because I'm not stopping." And with that he resumed his steady push until he had shoved his penis all the way inside of me.

For a few moments after that, he just stood there with his penis up my ass to allow me some time to get used to having him inside of me. Soon, he began to wiggle himself from side to side every so often to stretch me out. I struggled to get myself under control and did my best to relax my body as he had said. And after a while, I can't say that I got used to it, but I did seem to be able to tolerate him a bit better. Just the same, I still felt as if he had shoved a watermelon up my ass. And then things got worse.

"Ok now." It was time for some more instructions. "I want you to keep the top of your head pressed up against that wall. You hear me?"

"Yeah." I called back.

"What was that you said?"

"I mean yes, sir!" It seemed like an awful lot at a time like this to expect me to remember to be respectful.

"All right, fine then. Here we go."

The leader then began to slowly pull himself back out of me. As he did he pulled my body backwards slightly along with him, and the pressure in my rectum began to subside a bit. But an instant later he thrust his penis back into me and the force of his loins hitting against my butt, slammed the top of my head hard into the wall.

"Auhauhauh!" I cried out in pain. The impact had again caused me to see stars.

"I told you to keep your head up against that wall didn't I?" he thundered.

"Yes, sir," I answered almost in tears from the pain.

"Well then this time, do as I say," the leader barked.

"Yes, sir," I answered weakly.

The leader then began to pull his penis out of me again, but as before, he stopped once he had drawn himself out about halfway. "Is your head against the wall now?"

"Yes, sir," I replied. We were having to yell at each other because the sound of the shower plus the intense echo from the cement floor and tiled walls was making it hard for us to hear each other.

"Ok, I'm not gonna give you any more warnings now. So hold on." The leader then thrust himself into me again, but this time he just kept pulling himself back and then ramming his penis on in again without stopping.

"Auhauh! Auhauh! Auhauh! Auhauh! Auhauh!" With every thrust of his cock, pain shot all throughout my frame. I didn't know how much of this I was going to be able to take, and I felt as if my ass was being ripped apart while I held onto the chair for dear life.

"You're doin' fine!" the leader hollered.

"Auhauh! Auhauh! Auhauh! Auhauh! Auhauh!" I really couldn't have cared how much he was enjoying me. For a while then this became my life. He continued to ram himself into me, and I continued to scream after every thrust from the pain. In time, he increased the pace of his ramming, and the pain no longer seemed to bother me as badly. I don't know why this was, other than I suppose that if a person tries hard enough, he can get used to pretty much anything.

Finally, after an exhausting session, the leader stopped his ramming suddenly and, without removing his penis from my ass, and using his right hand, he grabbed a large hunk of my soaked hair from the back of my head, and then he pulled the upper half of my body through the stream and up until I was standing straight up again. Immediately I found it awkward to stand this way. With his penis still lodged in my ass, it seemed impossible for me to gain my balance. The leader apparently knew this because he continued to pull my body backwards beyond vertical until he had me resting against his bare chest. He then placed his left arm around my own chest to hold us together, and then he released his grip on my hair and allowed his right arm to drop to his side. As soon as he was satisfied with the way he now had our bodies configured, he resumed his thrusting, only this time he pushed my body upward.

"Auh, Auh, Auh, Auh, Auh!" The leader was taller than I was. So every time he jammed his penis into me, he lifted me completely off of my feet. Then every time we came back down, I could only touch the floor with the balls of my feet before he would have me airborne again. I hated the feeling. It seemed to me as if I had completely lost control over my body. At one point I flailed my arms in an attempt to find something I could hold onto to brace myself, but there was nothing out there for me to grasp. So faced with no choice again, I gave up and simply allowed the leader to take me over completely as he bounced me up and down endlessly.

I don't know if I can adequately explain how it is to feel someone ejaculate into you, especially if you're not inclined that way, as I was not. Because there are physical and emotional components to the experience which shook me equally. So as one might expect, before too long the time had finally come for me to suffer through the leader's climax.

Suddenly I noticed the leader widening his stance. He then hugged me tightly with both arms, and jammed himself into me extra hard three more times.

"Auhauh! Auhauh! Auhauh!" He then tightened his bear-like embrace, took some wet hair from the back of my head into his teeth, and shook us both for a few moments while he ejaculated into me. An instant later I felt him shiver… and then his thrusting was ended altogether.

For what must have only been a few seconds, but what seemed to me at the time as taking minutes, I just hung there in his arms, my feet still not able to touch the floor and my ass still filled with him. We were both out of breath, and our bodies, still pressed together, were heaving against one another as we tried to recover our wind. And I guess it was at this moment when I became aware of this emotional component I just spoke of. Because I realized, just for an instant, that I felt as if I now had a more intimate understanding of who the leader really was on the inside. It was as if he had just put his brand on me and I now belonged to him. And to this day, it is still hard for me to put into words, but it seemed to me then as if the leader and I had connected on a level that went deeper than mere friendship, and far more personal. It was almost as if we were now linked in some way.

This special feeling of a connection to the leader was an emotion which I neither sought nor cared for once I felt it. So I quickly discarded it and have tried throughout the years to not consider it any further until the time came for me to write about it here. Anyway, after that, he bent his knees so I could stand flat on my feet again, and then he pulled himself out of me and removed his arms from around my body. "Sit down!" he commanded.

When he had finally pulled his penis out of my anus, that entire region of my body suddenly felt like a beach ball that had just had all of the air let out of it. Even so, the pain I was still feeling throughout my buttocks was enormous and I couldn't believe what he was now telling me to do. "Are you kidding?" I shrieked back at my first ever sex partner. "You actually expect me to sit down now after what you just did to me? Are you in sane?" I was almost hysterical by this point. "Auhauh!" I then felt the leader's hand slap me hard across my face. His blow carried with it enough force to nearly knock me off of my feet and onto the shower floor. It was clear to me then, that the leader was not burdened by the same feelings of closeness that I was now fighting.

"I said sit down, damn you!"

He was yelling in my face now. Once again it was obvious that I was being given no choice in the matter. So, in the stream of water, I bent over and reached out to feel with my hands for the chair. When I found it, I turned around again and gently placed my bottom on the seat and moved myself around gingerly until I could find a position on one cheek which I could tolerate.

"Now stay there and don't move." The leader then re-angled the shower head so the water would again pour down directly onto the top of my head.

Any empathy I might have felt for the guy was gone after that. "Yes, sir," I called up through the water.

"There are four more guys comin' in here next, one at a time. And you're gonna have to service each of them before we'll let ya go. Ya got that?"

The news crushed what little spirit I had left. I had hoped that they would let me leave now. I couldn't imagine how I was going to make it through four more encounters like the one I had just been through, without needing to go to a hospital afterwards. "No!" I shrieked again. "Please, no more. I can't take any more. Please, I've done everything you've asked me to. I can't do any more. Please let me go… Auhauh!" The leader slapped me again, and I stopped my pleading after that.

"Shut up and don't move," was the only response he would give me.

There was not even a hint of compassion in the leader's demeanor. Apparently he had taken from me what he had wanted, and now the time had come for him to move on. It was almost as if our session together had never happened. But I knew it had happened because I was still having a great deal of trouble just trying to sit properly. A moment later, I could hear the metal rings scrape against the metal rod once, and once again. And then I knew I was alone.

Despite the coarse way the leader had just behaved toward me, he and the others did apparently recognize that I needed a few minutes to recover from my ordeal because it took at least that long before the second guy opened the door and came into the bathroom.

"Hi, Clint." This second person was someone I hadn't dealt with so far. He sounded a lot more cheery and at first I found the contrast between him and the leader bewildering. I then heard the metal rings scrape, then something was plopped down at my feet before I heard the rings scrape again.

"All right now, Clint, I've just dropped a cushion down in front of you. I want you to find it and then get off your chair and sit on it."

"Yes, sir," I answered. I then bent over and felt the boat cushion this second guy had brought for me. It felt like one from the stack of them I had seen in the little boat house which stood behind the Annex down by the lake. So, a moment later I was seated on it. As soon as I was settled on the floor, I could hear the second guy then remove the chair and drop two more cushions down on either side of me.

"Ok, now I want you to rotate your body ninety degrees to your right and then lie down flat on your back on all three cushions. And make it so the water is hitting you mainly on your body."

This guy seemed to know exactly what he wanted from me and, after all I had been through all ready this night, I wasn't willing to see what else could happen to me if I offered him any argument. So silently I complied with his instructions. But as I reclined and felt the water begin to pound me all up and down the front of my body, I remember wishing for an inkling at least of what this guy was intending to do with me.

"Now relax. Take it easy."

As I listened to his words, I could sense him sitting down on the shower floor next to me.

"There's not gonna be any pain involved with this. Now I want you to relax. So just give yourself two or three long and slow exhales so you can release all the tension from your body."

I did as he said. I took three long slow breaths and then exhaled each one fully as I tried to relax my muscles as completely as I could. The water helped too. The perpetual kneading of my skin by the dozens of thick sprays from the shower head above made me feel as if I was receiving a massage. A few of the sprays were hitting me on my face, but I found a couple of positions for my head where I could breathe with no trouble, and the shades I was still wearing were protecting my eyes. So after a short bit, I did begin to feel better.

"Ok, now just lie still and enjoy this." The second guy now seemed ready to begin something. I still had no idea what it was that he was intending to do with me, but he was making it sound as if whatever it was would be something wondrous.

When I felt his fingers begin to handle and twirl my penis, I reacted automatically. "Hey! What are you doing?" His actions were shocking to me and I didn't like it at all.

"Shshsh!" the second guy responded. "Don't say another word. Just lie still, relax and enjoy this," he answered firmly yet a bit mysteriously also.

I didn't know how to react after that. I certainly didn't want anyone to be touching me there, but I didn't know if this guy would hit me too if I tried to stop him. And even if he wasn't inclined to throw his fists at me, I had no doubt that the leader was still close by and would be more than happy to come in and knock me around some more if called upon to do so. So I made the only choice, under the circumstances, that I could. I kept still, as I was told, and allowed him to play with me.

Within just a few moments, he had made my penis supple and able to flop around easily. He then placed his thumb on the top of my shaft, and his first two fingers along the underside near the crown, and then with some pressure, he moved my loose skin downward until his second finger wound up resting at the base of my penis.

"Haah!" My body reacted instantly by forcing me to inhale sharply. He didn't move his fingers once he had found my spot. He just maintained friction on me.

"That's it. Now you're feelin' it." The guy sounded pleased by what he was causing to happen to me. "Just stay relaxed. My name is Artist, and I give the best head at the Academy," he said to me softly.

"Haah! Haah!" I had no idea what he was talking about, but at the moment I didn't care. A steady surge of stimulation was now affecting me all throughout my loins and it was beginning to shoot out into the rest of my body. At the same time, I could feel my penis beginning to swell. I then rolled my head over to the right and opened my mouth slightly as a sort of dull reaction to what was being done to me. "Uuh!" I groaned.

Every so often, Artist would move my loose skin up my shaft, then fondle my crown, and stroke the skin back down and hold it again. These movements only caused my responses to become stronger, and I could tell now that he was making me hard. Soon after that, he began to stroke me continuously. "Uuh!" I groaned again. This time my head rolled by itself over to my left.

As Artist's efforts to stimulate me sexually continued, my toes separated and my body began to tense. I could feel it now all over. The sensations now consumed me and I decided at that moment that I was no longer opposed to lying there on the shower floor and having this guy work me. In no time he had gotten me fully erect—and he had done a good job of it too. My penis was now thick, hard and strong, and staying that way.

"Ok, hold on," he advised. "Now the good stuff really begins."

And with that the guy lightly caressed my penis downward a few times with his fingertips, and then he bent down to where his head was in the stream just over me, and he took my penis into his mouth.

"Uuh?" I had no idea now what he was doing. Was he going to bite me? I had never heard of someone doing something like this. But before I could think up all of my questions, I had my answer. He wrapped his lips around my crown, and then he corkscrewed his way down my shaft with them.

"Ohhhh!" I dropped my jaw and cocked my head backwards as if I had just been conquered. I couldn't believe the way he was now making me feel. My body felt utterly paralyzed with pleasure. I was now completely under his charge and very willing to just lie there and benefit from the obvious skills this second guy possessed.

Do you know the sound that a shower makes when the water hits a person's hair? Well, the water hitting the Artist's hair became the constant sound that I heard as he began to stroke my hard-on aggressively with his lips. But I also heard a smacking sound. Sort of the way a wet wash cloth sounds when it's slapped against the side of a porcelain sink. He had created a suction in his mouth while he was stroking me and the feeling that it, plus some incredible things he occasionally did with his tongue around my crown, sent me over the edge. I was now his to command.

So we continued this way for a while. With my body now as rigid as a piece of plywood, I remained on the boat cushions in a state of ecstasy while Artist's head kept jerking up and down on me at an ever increasing pace. And far too soon, he had brought me to the point where I could no longer hold myself back—and I ejaculated.

I came hard and I came strong, and I felt as if I had emptied out all of my semen and then some. And once the spasms had ended, and I felt as if every ounce of my insides had been pumped to my outsides, my body collapsed. Every muscle I had after that went limp and I felt as if I wanted to stay on those cushions forever. "Ohhhhh!" I exhaled. I was in awe of what this guy had just done to me.

Artist then sat up and spoke to me again. "How was that?"

"Ohh… man!" was all I could say at that moment. It hadn't been that long ago in my life that I had discovered masturbation. So an experience like this was completely new to me.

"Ok, now stand up," he began to give me instructions again.

Reluctantly I did as he said. When I was vertical again, I could sense Artist returning to his feet as well. Quickly then, I could hear him remove the cushions and reposition the chair for me under the stream. "Ok, sit down in the chair again," he ordered.

As before, I felt with my hands through the running water for the chair. When I found it, I turned around and planted my bottom down on the seat again.

"So did you like that?" he asked me again as I noticed him adjusting the angle of the shower head so that the water would again pour down directly onto the top of my head.

"What?" As before, the sound of the water through my skull and over my ears was making it a little harder for me to hear him. And then it dawned on me. These guys were restricting my vision and limiting my hearing deliberately. The only sense I was being permitted to use unfettered was my sense of touch—and they were working that one overtime tonight. *So why,* I wondered, *was allowing me only my sense of touch so important to them?*

"I said did you like that?" The sound of Artist's voice then compelled me to return my focus to him.

"Oh, yeah!" I exclaimed again.

"What was that?" he asked more sternly this time.

I knew he could hear me just fine. So I realized, then, that the time had come for me to be submissive once again. "I mean yes, sir."

"Good. Well, now that you know how it's done, you're gonna give me a blow job next."

"What!" I couldn't believe my ears. I had heard the term "blow job" a couple of times the year before in school, but I had never known what it meant. Now my education was moving too fast.

"That's right, and I expect a good job too. I don't want to feel your teeth at all."

"No!" I yelled in disgust. I was horrified by the idea. I couldn't possibly allow someone to put his penis into my mouth. The very thought was too repulsive for me to even consider. "Auhauh!" Artist then slapped me hard across my face and forced me to fly off the side of my chair and onto the shower floor.

"You're going to give me a blow job now, or I'm gonna give it to you in your ass like the leader just did. And if you give me any more shit about it, I'll bring the leader back in here and let him take care of ya his way. So which way is it gonna be? Do you take it in the mouth? Or do you take it in the ass? Are you really ready to have another bone up your butt tonight? Huh?"

There was no longer any evidence that this guy had been kind to me just a few moments earlier. This was a miserable situation I was now in. "No, sir," I didn't think my ass could handle another rape job. I then felt a hand grab my arm and pull me back onto the chair.

"So are you gonna give me the blow job you owe me?"

It was hopeless. There was no good choice for me to make. There was only one way I could go that would save me from any more physical pain. "Yes, sir," I answered meekly.

"What was that? I'm not sure I heard you."

"Yes, sir," I answered a little louder this time.

"Yes, sir, what?"

"Yes, sir, I'll be happy to give you the blow job I owe you, sir." I felt ill.

As I continued to sit under the stream, I wanted desperately now to find a way out of all of this. I could then feel the insides of Artist's bare yet hairy legs rubbing up against the outsides of my thighs. He was straddling my legs now so he could bring his groin area closer to my face. But before he moved in on me all the way, he stopped and grabbed my cheeks with his hand and squeezed them together.

"What you do is... you purse your lips together like you're playing a trumpet... like this." He continued to demonstrate with my face. "And then while you're running your lips up and down on my dick, you want to sort of clamp down tightly so you can suck out all the air while you're doing me. And listen, if you have a problem with all of this at first, just think of your mouth as being detached from the rest of you and not a part of your body anymore. That'll make it easier to do."

I began to wonder what would happen if I were to throw up right now.

"But the most important thing for you to remember is to keep your teeth away from my dick. To start with, until you get the hang of it, you can cover your teeth with your lips when you start out. Any questions?"

"What if I throw up?" I asked. I was just curious.

He then released his hold on my face. "Oh, well... I'm not planning to go down your throat or anything. I think that's too advanced for you right now. For now I'm just gonna try to keep it in your mouth. But I'm not gonna know how far in I can go until I've gone in there. Anything else?" he asked.

"No." I was now depressed.

Apparently my inadvertent insubordination angered him. "What was that?" he demanded.

"I mean no, sir," I replied in a monotone voice. I now just wanted to get it over with so I could go back to my room and try to forget that this night had ever happened.

I guess Artist already had an erection going because a moment later I felt his legs slide up closer along my thighs, and then I could feel the tip of his penis poking at my lips. Automatically, I recoiled in disgust and wrenched my head away from him. Artist then grabbed my face with his hand again, squared me up, and then plunged his penis into my mouth.

"Agk!" It was awful. His penis filled my mouth and immediately caused me to gag when I felt it begin to slide down my throat. Fortunately, he noted my distress and pulled himself back out a bit as he had promised.

"Sorry. Like I said, I don't know how far into you I can go until I go in. Are you ok now?"

"Um hmm," I answered in the affirmative. There was no way at this moment that I could form any real words.

"Good. Now just sit there while I do the work." And so, the next phase of my "initiation" was begun. Immediately then, Artist began to thrust himself repeatedly into my mouth while I just sat there under the water and took it. I was now giving my first blow job.

"Purse your lips more, like I showed you," he hollered.

I tried to do as he ordered.

"Good. Ahhhhh! Yeah, that's it! Ok, now make a suction, Clint."

Again I obeyed him and began to suck on his penis as if it were a fat stick of candy or something. Soon I was hearing my own mouth making the same sort of smacking sounds I had heard the Artist make when he had sucked on me.

"Aw, yeah! Outstanding! Clint, you're really good at this. You've got great lips."

Terrific, I thought. *I can put that on my resume. "Special mentions in English, Music, and he's got great lips."* The situation was impossible. This was now without question, the worst night of my life. I hated what I was being forced to do and I kept wondering to myself what it was I had done in my life to deserve such a fate. And the more my mind fixated on these thoughts, the harder it became for me to keep control over my emotions until eventually I couldn't take it any longer and I simply began to cry. So as the Artist thrust, I sobbed and we continued on this way for the next several minutes.

Sometimes, when you are truly in a crisis, your mind begins to go to other places. As the Artist's penis seemed to now feel like a permanent fixture in my mouth, I tried to take his advice and mentally detach the lower half of my head from the rest of me so I could think of my mouth as being no longer a part of my body. I also thought about how different my life could have been had I accepted my parents' invitation to go with them to Europe. Of course, I knew I had missed my chance. It was too late for me now. After all, I had made my choice. But the idea of being someplace else at this moment did seem to comfort me—if only for a brief moment.

Then, without any warning he stopped his thrusting. “Ok, I’m just gonna stand here now and I want you to start going down on me.”

Again my new sex partner used an expression I was unfamiliar with, but I figured he had meant for me now to do all the work. And so I began to move my head forward and back so my lips could stroke down along his shaft and then stroke it back out again. In no time, I began to tire from my efforts. This, as it turned out, was a lot of hard work.

“Faster!” he ordered after I had been going for a while.

So obligingly, I picked up my pace. *Oh that’s why,* I thought to myself. It had suddenly occurred to me. The reason why they had gone to so much trouble to put me in a little kid’s chair was so that my mouth would be at the optimal height for what I was being forced to do right now.

“Come on, Clint. Faster, man.”

It was no longer possible for me to do this job halfheartedly. There was too much I had to keep track of. Besides having to keep a constant tension in my lips, I had to keep sucking all the time while making sure also that as I kept going *down* on him at an ever increasing pace, I didn’t accidentally graze him with my teeth. Before long, I realized that I was now honestly trying to bring this turkey to a climax. So to balance myself better and to give me something I could push off against, I reached out with my hands and wrapped them firmly around the back of his thighs just below his buttocks.

“Oh yeah! Go for it, Clint! You’re really workin’ me now!”

And I was. Every time I felt him tremble inside, I tried to do everything harder and faster so this entire ugly mess could be over sooner.

“Ah!” Artist gasped. “Ah… Uuh!” For a time then we continued this way. Every so often he would make sounds like these which would cause me to believe for an instant that we were reaching his end. But then just as quickly his groans and grunts would cease and out of frustration I would bear down on him even harder. Finally though, he began to moan between his gasps, which told me that we were getting close. Because I was so busy, I didn’t notice at first what this upperclassman did with me next. In silence, Artist reached out with his arms and gripped my wet hair within his fingers, and then he rested his hands on the top of my head so they could ride along as I kept my cranium in constant motion.

Now I was going all out. No more holding back. My head was moving in and out like a woodpecker’s and my lips were clamping down on his penis like a vise while I sucked away like a vacuum cleaner. It was becoming painful for me to keep going like this, but I did my best to ignore the pain. I wanted this to be over, so my entire being was now committed to bringing this guy to his climax.

And then, after a couple of false alarms, it happened. I could feel his penis throbbing between my lips as the realization of what was finally starting then hit me. He was ejaculating into my mouth!

"Ahhhhhh!" In my hands, his thighs felt as if his entire body was being electrocuted. It was awful—and just as disgusting as one would think it would be. Instantly his semen filled my mouth and tasted like a huge volume of warm snot. It was all I could do to keep myself from throwing up in revulsion right then.

"Ah! Oh yeah! Haaaaa!" The guy exhaled loudly as he squeezed out his last few bullets of semen into my mouth. To keep from getting slapped again, I kept going down on him until I could feel him stop my head movements by pulling on my hair. He then released my hair and pulled his penis out of my mouth. *Finally!* I thought to myself. I was about to spit out his semen and rinse my mouth out in the stream when Artist grabbed my cheeks to hold my mouth shut.

"Swallow it!" he demanded.

"Umm?" I was again horrified at what I was being commanded to do. "Um ummm!" I protested. I couldn't see any reason why swallowing his semen could make any difference to him at this point. After all, I'd already given him the damn blow job. That should have been plenty.

"Either you swallow it now, Clint, or I'll bring the leader in here to work you over again," he threatened. "This is something you're gonna have to do every time. Around here the rule is, you have to swallow…or else. So come on, Clint. Swallow it, man!"

He shook my face as he spoke. By now I had been through too much to want to oppose these guys anymore—so I did as I was told again, and I swallowed it.

"All right. Good for you, Clint. You did fine."

Artist then let go of my face. I did nothing after that. I just sat there, still under the running water with my head now hung down. I was beat, and I was beaten. These bigger kids had taken everything I had—physically and emotionally. They had gotten me to participate in every foul act they had wanted, and I was now feeling ashamed.

I guess it was at about this time when I decided that I didn't care anymore. Nothing seemed to matter to me any longer. They had stripped me of my clothing and then they had stripped me of my dignity. I had been handled and penetrated in every way imaginable. They had turned this little bathroom into their own private whorehouse with me as their chief whore, and I just couldn't find it in me to give a shit about anything any longer. They could turn me into a blow job machine now, and I wouldn't care. And as it turned out, that was exactly what they did to me next.

Artist turned the handle on the wall to make the water temperature hotter. In my despondent state, I hadn't noticed that the hot water had begun to run out.

"Ok, Clint. See ya." And with that I could feel Artist's legs slide down my thighs and then leave me to sit by myself again. An instant later I could hear the metal rings scrape as my second sex partner ever left me to remain behind in the shower. And then the rings scraped again. So now, apparently, I was alone once more and expected again to sit quietly under the running water.

"The asshole didn't even say thank you," I muttered to myself as I sat there, under the stream. So after that, I began to brood until I heard the metal rings scrape yet again.

I don't remember much about the third or the fourth guys who took their turns with me that night, other than I believed at the time that they had been the two guys who had brought me to the gym in the first place. Neither of them actually said very much to me once they were in the shower with me. I do recall, at least, that each of them got rough with me at the beginning of their sessions. Because when the time came for things to begin, they each slapped me first and then grabbed my head or my hair harshly before they plunged their rock-hard erections into my mouth. It was as if all in the world that mattered to them was their chance to ejaculate in my mouth—which they both eventually did. And just as it had been with Artist, each of these guys forced me to swallow afterwards.

Despite my best efforts to please these guys, I was not able to be as aggressive with the third or the fourth guy because my body and my spirit had simply become worn out. In fact, toward the end of my job on the fourth guy, I felt as if the viselike hold my lips had on his penis was the only thing that was holding me up. It seemed to me that if I were to let go of him suddenly, my body would then collapse in a heap on the shower floor and I would be unable after that to get back up. But finally I had finished with them both and then the time arrived for the fourth one to leave me.

"Ok, now don't move and the next guy will be in here in a minute," he said gruffly as he turned the hot water handle up the rest of the way for me.

By this time I had slumped my body against the back of the chair while my legs were stuck out and spread wide apart in front of me to hold me in this position. My head was flopped back from exhaustion and much of the shower was now hitting me directly on my face. I had found a spot between the sprays where I was trying to catch my breath, and I felt utterly incapable of going on. "Please..." I pleaded with the fourth guy before he scraped the metal rings, "...please let me go now. I can't do any more of these tonight. The leader said there's one more of you coming in here, but you guys have used me up. I can't do any more. Please, can't I go back to my room now?"

But the fourth guy said nothing more to me. All I heard after that was the sound of the metal rings scraping once and then they scraped again, and then I was by myself once more. *The asshole didn't even answer me,* I thought. *And after all I did for him.*

And so I waited for the next guy to come in. As I felt the water pelt my face, neck and chest, I could tell that things for me were just as dire as I had described to the fourth guy. My strength was simply not returning fast enough to make another session possible. If the next guy were to walk in on me suddenly, the best I'd be able to do would be to just lie here against the back of the chair and allow him to abuse me in whatever way he would want. Because by now, my energy was depleted.

A few minutes later, I was still by myself and the water was beginning to turn cold. I reached up behind my head to turn up the hot water handle and found that it was already up as far as it would go. "Hello?" I decided to try to find out what was going on. "Is anybody coming in still?" By now it had been a lot longer of an interval between perpetrators than any I had experienced so far. "Hello...o?"

I was still too afraid a minute later to take any initiative to find out what was going on. But when the last of the hot water finally ran out, I knew I would not be able to stay under an icy shower for very long, so I turned off the water and listened for signs of life on the other side of the bathroom door.

After yet a few more minutes, I stood up. *This is silly,* I thought. *They can't expect me to stay in here all night.* And so I lifted my eye shades and peered around the shower curtain. I was surprised but pleased when I saw that the bathroom door had been left open and the lights in the coach's locker room were now turned off. "Well what do ya know? They left," I said out loud in case someone was still around.

While I continued to drip, I walked timidly across the bathroom floor and out into the locker room. Once I had reached the spot where I figured I had taken the leader's roundhouse, I realized that there was nothing anywhere for me to put on. "My clothes are gone," I announced to no one. "I can't believe it. The bastards didn't even leave me a towel." It was maddening. My T-shirt, my underpants, and even my flip-flops were gone. In disgust, I pulled the eye shades off of my forehead and looked at them. *Could I use these to cover myself?* I wondered. I then threw them aside. The very idea seemed too absurd to even consider. And since there was nothing else I could do—"Oh, what the hell"—I went ahead and walked out into the gym and opened up the side door to the building.

By this time, I figured it was nearly three in the morning. As I stuck my wet head out the door and into the cooler night air, I could see that everything outside was still. By now the upperclassmen who had initiated me into their version of Academy life were gone and probably back in their rooms getting ready for bed. Since there were no signs of anyone around—there were still no lights on in any of the windows in the other buildings—and since I figured I had no choice anyway, I stepped outside all the way and began to walk across the upper campus toward my dorm… completely in the nude.

My feet have always been a bit tender on the bottoms, so it was fortunate for me that I was able to walk mostly on grass all the way back. Only twice did I have to cross small stretches of cement, and suffer through the pain of stepping on small pieces of gravel. And even though I made it all the way back into my hall without being seen by anyone, I had no doubt that some of the upperclassmen I had been with that night lived in Ulster Hall and had watched me make my way back home through their darkened windows on the second floor.

When I opened the door to my room, finally, and walked in, I found my clothes lying on my bed. Apparently the bigger kids had dropped my things off after they had left me. Except for this, everything else in my room was as it had been when I had left it. Though it had shifted some by this time, moonlight was still coming in through the window and Matt was still sound asleep. Apparently while all of the events of this night had taken place, my roommate had never awakened once. *Incredible,* I thought to myself. *I've heard of sound sleepers, but this kid takes the cake.*

Now that I had been running around naked and wet for a while, I was beginning to feel chilled. So I pulled my towel down off of the hook where I kept it and finished drying myself off. I then closed our door and put my underpants and T-shirt back on and quickly got myself back under my covers. Once I was settled, I found it comforting to be back in my own bed in my own room. Yet, as relieved as I felt to be among my own things once again, there was no escaping the fact that I and my things were still surrounded by the Academy and those upperclassmen who tonight had taken me into a world I had never known could exist.

There was a lot now that I was going to have to sort out. For instance, was tonight just a one-time thing, or was it the beginning of many more such occasions for me. And how was it that these guys could be so well organized and operate with such impunity at the Academy. There were many questions like this which I needed to find the answers to in a hurry if I was going to be able to figure out a way to keep these perverts from taking over my life—if that indeed was whet they had in mind. *But I'm too wiped out now,* I thought. *In the morning after I've had some sleep. Yes, in the morning I'll be able to think more clearly.* And then a moment later, I was asleep.

***

Even though it was four hours later before the piercing sound of the wake-up bell snapped my eyes open again, it seemed to me as if only four minutes or so had actually passed since I had fallen asleep. And as I became aware of the ache in the muscles in my jaw, and the profound weariness which seemed to adhere my body to my mattress, I decided that more than ever at this moment, I wanted to skip breakfast and my morning classes, so I could stay in bed until lunchtime.

"Hey?" At last, Matt was awake.

"Mornin', Matt," I replied.

"Do you wanna use the bathroom first, or should I go now?" he asked.

"You go first." I was content to stay where I was. Besides, I had peed in the shower on the fourth guy's legs right while he was ejaculating so he wouldn't notice.

"Oh. I was hopin' maybe you'd wanna go first." Matt then yawned and pulled his covers away and sat up. "I don't know why, but for some reason I'm feelin' really tired this morning," he admitted.

"You're tired?" I was incredulous. "You slept like a brick all night."

"Yeah, I know, it's weird. I shouldn't be tired at all now, but I'm just dragging." Matt then planted his feet on the cold linoleum and stood up. Then, as if he suddenly understood that there might be a deeper meaning to what I had just said, he looked at me and spoke again. "Why...were you awake last night or something?"

"Yeah, for a while." I wasn't ready to tell Matt about what had happened to me just yet because, well… I was embarrassed at the idea of explaining how I had wound up having sex with four guys in a shower. Also, until I knew more, I didn't see the need to scare him.

Matt then began to cross the room so he could head for the bathroom. "Really? Well, I was out completely," he said with sweet ignorance. Matt then opened the door and walked out into the hall.

I know, I thought to myself as I watched my roommate disappear into the bathroom across the hall. I then closed my eyes again and began to think about the events of only a few hours ago. The bright light of the daytime and our morning routine made it all seem so impossible to me now. As if what had happened was just too fantastic to have ever taken place. But it had taken place. My achy jaw and my tender behind were constant reminders to me that it had really happened.

I suppose some might wonder at this point why I wasn't rolling on the floor in abject despair over the perverse liberties the bigger kids had taken with my body. In the eyes of many, I suspect, I should have been inconsolable by now. And upon reflection, I'm not sure I can offer an adequate explanation for how I was managing to keep myself together, other than to point out that I have always tried to take adversity in stride whenever it has come my way. To be sure, I was upset. How could I not have been? And to risk the use of a cliché', I did feel violated. But I knew that a wild release of emotions would never get me out of the mess I was now in. Instead I understood instinctively, I suppose, that I had to think my way through this.

Also, I have never been the emotional type to run and blurt out information about things that are bothering me to the first sympathetic ear I can find. Besides, the events of the night before were serious and despite the normalcy of my morning, they had utterly changed the ground rules for my life at the Academy. So when Matt and I walked over to the dining hall a short while later, and took our seats at our assigned table, I quietly inspected every person we encountered along the way to see how they responded to me, and to judge whether any of them were harboring lurid thoughts toward me behind their eyes. Unfortunately, all I managed to observe that morning were a lot of bloodshot eyes. And I guess no matter how normally I tried to behave by treating everything around me as if it was just another day at the Academy, my silence was soon noticed, at least, by one. So as we concluded the blessing and then began yet another breakfast of cold cereal, Frank spoke to me.

"So what's with you?" he asked.

"What do you mean?" I asked back.

"Well, usually you're so chipper in the mornin's. In fact, sometimes it's really annoyin' how awake you are around here. But today, you're lookin' like a gloomy Gus or somethin'. So I figure somethin's gotta be eatin' at ya. That's all."

"Yeah," Matt then chimed in. "You have been sort of quiet so far today," he now observed.

I knew that the things that had happened to me had to be exposed, but a discussion at breakfast about how I had just been taught the finer points on giving blow jobs, would accomplish nothing and likely make things worse for me than they already were. So I dodged the question. "Oh, I just didn't sleep very well last night, I guess."

"Really?" Frank seemed surprised at my answer. "Yeah there're a lot of people around here who have trouble sleepin' sometimes. I know, becuz sometimes I wake up at night too and I can't go back to sleep for a while."

I turned my head and looked directly at Frank in astonishment. Did he know what had happened to me? I didn't think he was involved because I hadn't heard his voice in the gym, but had he seen me walking back to my dorm in the nude, perhaps? His comment only served to heighten my already growing sense of paranoia, and caused me to consider right then the idea of getting up from the table and fleeing from the dining hall. But at the same time, these were questions which I wanted very much to know the answers to. And so my breakfast became a maddening stretch of time wherein I kept hoping for Frank, if he really had seen anything, to tell me what he knew, yet at the same time I was terrified that a candid discussion would ensue, and I certainly didn't want to get involved in anything like that.

For his part, Frank seemed unaware of my stare. He just continued to sit there and eat his cereal while he allowed his eyes to roam around the room and look at everyone else but me. In a while I decided that the others at my table were obliviously unaware of the significance of what Frank had said. And fortunately, this included Matt.

After that, nobody seemed interested any longer in how I was doing. Matt went on to tell Frank, and anyone else at the table who would listen, about how soundly he had slept during the night, and how this compared to his usual sleeping habits. As this went on, I found I was free, then, to resume my quiet observations of the other students around the room. I figured if I could recognize a voice, I could begin to put this puzzle together. Unfortunately, though, because by this time I had only lived at the Academy for a few weeks, and because I had spent most of my time so far with the twenty or so other boys who were underclassmen—thirteen- and fourteen-year-olds like me—I just didn't know most of the older kids well enough yet to be able to notice anything familiar about any of them.

In the end, breakfast did give me the time I needed to arrive at a few conclusions. For example, although at this point in my life I was still learning about sex—the night before had increased my knowledge exponentially—I did know enough by now to realize that once a person has experienced it, he's likely to want to have it again, and again. Even I felt conflicted. As angry as I was over what those upperclassmen had done to me, I confess that I was also thinking about when I might be able to receive my next blow job. The idea in my head that morning for achieving this goal involved hitchhiking to Boston on the weekend, getting together again with Ellen, and then somehow talking her into the idea. But my own emerging needs for sex aside, it seemed pretty certain to me that, unless I made up my mind to take some sort of action now to head them off, my assailants would be back again soon to enslave me once more.

I also realized that if they could grab me in the middle of the night, they could grab anyone. Perhaps even Matt. By now I had developed protective feelings toward my roommate. He was a sweet kid, and I couldn't imagine Matt ever being able to go through what I had just endured. An experience like mine would destroy him emotionally and he would never be the same kind, innocent boy he was right now if these monsters were ever able to get their hands on him. As I thought about these things, I came to believe that it was my responsibility now to act. And so I resolved to do whatever I could—short of putting myself in greater peril—to stop those upperclassmen assholes, and to put an end to their late-night escapades.

The only person at the Academy I trusted implicitly besides Matt was Mr. Stuart. Although he had made a less than remarkable impression on me at first, over time I had gotten to know the man better. These days he seemed attentive and very accommodating to my needs. In fact, I now thought of him as just the kind of grown-up a kid could go to when he needed to talk, which I had already done on a couple of occasions. After all, at this period in my life, he was the closest thing I had to a father figure. So when breakfast was over, I told Matt I had to go take care of something, and then I left the dining room and began to walk down the long center hallway of Ulster Hall. When I came to the third door past the lobby, I turned to my right and walked in.

"Excuse me, Mr. Stuart?"

My headmaster was already in his chair and staring down at some work on his desk. He usually had his breakfast by himself over in his house instead of joining the student body in the dining hall. At lunchtime his habit was to take his meal with all of us, but unlike my dad, by dinner he was usually gone again because by then he had sunk too far into his bottle to be of any use to any of us. He looked up at me and smiled when he heard my voice.

"Well, good morning, Clint. Come on in. How can I help you?" Mr. Stuart then stood up and gestured for me to take a seat in front of his desk.

I hesitated for a moment in the doorway. "Ah… I have something pretty important I need to talk to you about. Is it ok if I close your door?" For the next half hour until classes were started, the hallway was going to be filled with teachers and other students and I didn't want anyone passing by to accidentally hear what I was about to say, or even to see me in here.

For a moment, Mr. Stuart seemed surprised at my request, but then he quickly gave me my answer. "Sure, go ahead," he said warmly. "Close it and then come sit down."

"Yes, sir." I then closed his office door and walked in and sat down in one of the office chairs in front of his desk. Once I was seated, Mr. Stuart then sat down again behind his desk. "So, what's on your mind this morning, Clint?" he asked as he took a sip of his coffee.

I then proceeded to tell my headmaster everything about what these unknown upperclassmen had done to me the night before. I laid it all out for him. I gave him every disgusting and painful detail. He listened quietly as I got it all off of my chest. At one point, I found myself nearly in tears again, but I choked them back because I didn't want there to be any interruption in what I was telling him. It was almost as if I was having to live through it all again, but once I was done I sat back and waited for his reaction.

"That's an amazing story," he observed.

"Yes, sir," I had been hoping for a bigger display of emotion than this.

"Are you ok?" he asked matter-of-factly.

"Yes, sir. I'm a little sore in a few places, but I guess I'm all right." I was beginning to wonder if I was the only one at the Academy who considered the actions of these upperclassmen to be outrageous.

"Have you discussed this with anyone else?" he went on.

"No, sir."

"Not even your roommate?" he queried further.

"No, sir."

My headmaster then sat back in his chair and thought for a moment. "I guess it was pretty hard for you to come here and tell me all of this wasn't it?"

"Well yes, sir, it was."

"And they really forced you to do all those things with them, eh?"

"Yes, sir. Everything I said."

"I guess your skin must have been pretty pruney after you got out of that shower, then?"

This struck me as a rather frivolous question for him to be asking me. But out of respect, I gave him my answer, anyway. "I don't know… I suppose it was, sir."

Then I had a question of my own. "Mr. Stuart, what about calling the police? Isn't what they did to me last night against the law?" I thought for an instant longer. "I mean, isn't it a whole bunch of crimes?"

My headmaster seemed ready with his response. "No, I'm not convinced we want to get the police involved just yet. You have to understand, cases like this are almost impossible to prove in a court of law."

"What do you mean?" At first I found this response a little tough to believe.

"Well, did anyone who wasn't part of the group last night actually see you get forced into performing oral sex on these boys?"

"No, sir. Not as far as I know. Remember, I was blindfolded the whole time."

"Right. Well, did your roommate witness you being taken from your room? And were you forced to go with them, or did you go willingly?" The man seemed to know a lot about legal matters.

"No, sir. Matt was asleep the whole time and, I'm sorry to say, I went willingly with them to the gym. It's true they never told me really why they wanted me, but I had no idea it was going to turn out the way it did."

"Well there you see," Mr. Stuart concluded. "The police would simply surmise that since there were no witnesses to say otherwise, you had sex with those four boys last night because you wanted to."

"But that's not true!" This answer really upset me. That wasn't at all the way it had happened.

"I know… I know. I have no doubt that what you're telling me is true. And because I believe you, I'm willing to do something about all of this. You know, I can inflict penalties on these boys without having to go prove my case first in a court of law. And I want you to think also about the publicity something like this can bring if the police became involved."

"Publicity?" I hadn't thought about this.

"Oh yes," Mr. Stuart continued. "If the police become involved, the whole incident will become public knowledge and then everyone will know about what you did last night."

"Oh." I didn't like the sound of this.

"No, I can keep everything quiet so you're protected and so nobody else has to find out about how you came to be involved sexually with these four boys last night."

Shit! I thought to myself. *Now he's making it sound like everyone'll think I'm a homosexual.* My headmaster was truly giving me a lot to consider that I hadn't thought of so far.

"So you did the right thing by coming to see me first, Clint."

Suddenly I felt better about my immediate prospects for the future. "Yes, sir. Thank you."

Mr. Stuart then stood up and walked around to the front of his desk. "All right. I'll begin looking into this immediately. We certainly can't have older students here at the Academy using younger ones as sex objects now can we?"

"No, sir." I then stood up because it seemed to me that he was wanting our meeting to be ending now.

"You just leave things to me now and don't worry." Mr. Stuart then put his hand on my shoulder and began to guide me toward his door. "I'll begin an investigation right away to find out who these students are so we can put a stop to this. But, you need to understand that it's probably going to take me a little time to get to the bottom of all of this. Perhaps even a few weeks..."

"A few weeks?" I interrupted. I wanted action now.

Mr. Stuart wasn't put off by my protest and continued to speak. "Now I said don't worry. My methods in matters of this type always work. And once I've started looking into this, they'll know what I'm doing and they'll probably lie low in the meantime in hopes that I won't find out who they are. But in the end I will. Frankly, I'll be surprised if they'll bother you any further now, but until we know who these boys are for sure, I think it might be best if you don't say anything to anyone about all of this. And I think this should include your roommate." Mr. Stuart then opened his office door for me to leave through. "Ok?"

"Yes, sir. That won't be a problem. I'm finding it all pretty embarrassing anyway."

"Well, I'm sure you are. So you just leave everything to me. All right?"

"All right, sir. I will. Thank you."

Mr. Stuart then smiled. "You're welcome, Clint." And then he changed the subject, sort of. "Say, I noticed you haven't been to the baba since you've gotten here. With your hair all wet last night, it should have been down in your eyes, eh?"

I smiled. I appreciated his attempt to put me at ease by making conversation. "Well it wasn't in my way last night because of the eye shades, but normally when it's wet these days it hangs down over my eyes, pretty much."

"Kind of like a sheep dog, eh?"

"Yes, sir, I guess."

"And are you planning to go to see the baba any time soon?"

"Well, not really. I like growing it out like everyone else is doing these days."

"Yes, well, I think it looks just fine. So you let it grow for as long as you like. In fact, I'm thinking of ending our relationship with the baba altogether because nobody from here ever wants to go to him anymore."

I smiled again. "Yes, sir." Then it was time for both of us to get on to other things.

"Well, you go now and run along to class and I'll let you know as soon as I've learned anything."

"Yes, sir." And then I left my headmaster's office and started back for my dorm so I could pick up the books I was going to need for my classes that morning. As I walked through the lobby and out the front doors into the dewy New England morning, I reflected on the conversation I had just concluded and decided that even though I had not gotten the huge emotional reaction I had expected from the man, I was still pleased that I had gone to Mr. Stuart with all of this. I felt relieved now that I had done the right thing and reassured that I would no longer have to worry about being molested again.

***

For the rest of that day and the one that followed, I tried to take Mr. Stuart's advice by throwing myself back into my studies. Classes and meals went off as normal, as did our soccer practices. I didn't sleep well the first night, though. I kept worrying, I guess, that I was going to have another visit and subsequent trip to the gym shower. So by dinnertime the next day, I was beginning to feel pretty tired.

"For what we are about to receive, may the Lord make us truly thankful. Amen." One of the teachers offered the blessing in the headmaster's absence.

"AMEN!" The collective response from all of us rose up in the room. And then the sound of sixty wooden chairs being scraped at the same instant along the wooden floor of the dining hall, plus the rush of nearly that many voices talking all at once, filled the room like an explosion. After that, we were in our seats and ready to eat. I was hoping for a good meal, and praying that the cook had succeeded this time in making us one that would taste good. The head proctor was again sitting at the head of our table and as we waited for our food, he turned and spoke to the kid who was sitting in the chair to his right—the waiter's chair.

"Just stay where you are because the head waiter's bringing out our plates to us again tonight."

A moment later the head waiter emerged from the kitchen holding onto a tray which was filled with plates which had already been prepared for us.

"Twice in one week?" I remarked.

"Don't knock it," the head proctor had heard my comment. "It saves me a lot of work servin' you guys."

"Well that's fine," I replied. "Just so long as it's good." And it was good. Once again Thomas had made mashed potatoes for us, this time with Yankee pot roast, and I dug into my dinner just as soon as everyone else at the table had been served.

Since most of the guys assigned to my table were older kids, Matt, Frank and I tended to say very little during meals. But on this occasion, once we had all begun to eat, the head proctor tried to engage us in conversation. "So how is soccer coming along for you little guys?"

"Fine," Matt answered.

"Yeah, fine," I answered as well just before I shoved another fork full of food into my mouth. This was the kind of dinner I liked.

Frank didn't play soccer so he didn't say anything. Since athletics weren't mandatory at the Academy, Frank chose instead to spend his afternoons sitting in his room or walking around the campus or hanging out in the TV lounge.

"Well, I think the soccer team has another game coming up next week," the head proctor continued.

"Oh yeah, with who?" Matt asked.

The head proctor named some school in a nearby town, but since Matt and I were still new to the area, it wasn't a name that either of us recognized.

As I ate my dinner, I recalled Matt's comment the last time we had been served mashed potatoes about how he had believed them to have a funny taste to them. So this time I paid closer attention to the way mine tasted. And oddly enough, by the time I had eaten about half of the portion on my plate, I decided that I wasn't going to eat any more. I didn't know if it was merely the power of Matt's suggestion, or if there really was something different about them this time, but I wasn't comfortable with the way they were tasting any longer. At first when I was hungry, I had figured I could just put up with this change in their taste, but after I had been eating for a while, a nagging feeling inside told me that I shouldn't be eating them at all. And so I left perhaps half of them on my plate.

"Would someone please pass me the bread?" Frank loved his bread. He once told me he liked bread so much because of the Italian in him. I never really understood what he had meant by that. Thomas' idea of giving us garlic bread or dinner rolls was to pull a quarter to a third of a loaf of white bread out of its wrapper, and then pile the slices onto a plate and serve it to us. It wasn't that this was a necessarily bad way to serve bread to a student body of sixty-two, it was just that, to be served bread in this manner for practically every dinner seemed to me to be far less than what we should have been getting for the high tuitions our parents were paying.

The plate was closest to me so I reached out and passed the bread to Frank. As I did I happened to notice that this time Matt had eaten all of his mashed potatoes. After dinner I asked him if he still thought they had tasted funny.

"No, they were fine tonight," he replied.

"Really?" Because of my experience this time, I found his answer surprising.

"Yeah, I don't know what it was about 'em last time, but tonight they tasted just fine to me."

To be honest, most of what Thomas cooked for us tasted odd in one way or another anyway, so I decided that today perhaps he had simply dropped his wristwatch in the pot again or something. So I didn't consider the matter any further.

During study hall that night, I remember finding it hard to concentrate on my homework. I figured at the time that I was feeling extra tired because I hadn't gotten much sleep for the previous two nights. So when it came time for lights out, I was ready for bed. And soon after we were under our covers, I was asleep.

It's a strange sensation to describe. When it occurs, there is an awareness on some level in your mind that something has taken place. Perhaps a sound of some sort registers somewhere deep in your brain. And then, after a stretch of time which is usually indeterminate in length, the impression somehow manages to work its way to the conscious part of your mind causing you finally to react.

Suddenly I awoke in the darkness and sat up in bed as if my head had just been shot away from my pillow. "Matt?" I called out without thinking. I then turned my head and looked at Matt's bed. He was gone! The covers had been pulled back and his bed was now empty. Quickly I pulled away my own covers and bolted out of my bed so I could make a closer inspection of the scene. I placed the palm of my hand on Matt's sheets and could feel that they were still warm from his body heat. "Shit, it just happened!" I exclaimed to no one. I decided the sound I had just heard had been the door closing when they all had left the room.

There was no time to lose. As fast as I could, I stuffed my feet into my tennis shoes. It took me an extra few seconds, but I knew my flip-flops would make too much noise at this time of night. An instant later I was out in our hallway, but before going any farther I made a quick check of the bathroom to make sure I wasn't overreacting. Unfortunately, I wasn't—the bathroom was empty too. So an instant later, I was down the hall, through the large wooden door and out into the balmy night air.

All of my senses were now keenly tuned to the environment around me. As soon as I had reached the top of the cement steps, I stopped moving and searched the upper campus with my eyes and my ears for signs of any sort of nocturnal life. And as I had figured, it took me only a second or so to hear voices off in the distance and then a slam as one of the doors on the front of the gym was closed. After that, everything was silent.

I was frantic to stop them before they could get at my roommate, and I was about to take off running diagonally across the campus toward the gym, when I heard another sound and noticed a dark figure emerging from the far side of Ulster Hall. I then watched as the figure began to head directly toward the gym. The guy was far enough away and in the darkness most of the time so I couldn't make out who he was. In response, I froze and squatted down to reduce the size of my frame and make me a smaller target. There was nothing nearby for me to hide behind, but I was in darkness as well, so I waited and hoped that the guy over on the other side of the campus would miss seeing me.

"Hey, hurry up. They're already in there." After he had walked about a quarter of the way to the gym, the guy I was watching stopped and turned around to call back to a second guy who then appeared also from the far side of Ulster Hall. I decided then that both of these guys had come outside through the back door to the kitchen.

"I'm comin', keep your shirt on," the second guy hollered back.

I continued to keep myself down and still as my eyes followed this second guy as he walked quickly to catch up with his buddy. I also observed that he was carrying a small item in one of his hands, and after a few moments I determined that the object was one of the squeeze bottles from the kitchen.

Looking back on it now, I often wonder what would have happened if I had just stood up and yelled at them. And then I realize that if I had done that, they probably would have run over and pounded me. I was, after all, only thirteen. At the time, though, I knew I needed to do something to try to help my friend, but I continued to be afraid for my own safety. So for the moment, I remained crouched in the darkness near my dorm and I continued to watch the two upperclassmen until they had walked all the way over to the gym, and had gone into the building through its side door.

Now that I was free to move again, I felt compelled to run to Matt's aid *and,* at the same time, stay out of sight just in case any more of them happened to show up outside. So instead of taking off directly for the gym, which would have kept me mostly out in the open, I decided to take a longer route along the perimeter of the grounds so I could keep myself behind cover more often.

And so, I took off toward the headmaster's house. A moment later, as I was passing by his front door, I gave some thought to the idea of waking him up so he could come along and end all of this. But this was a two-story house and I knew by now the man would be upstairs and passed out. So any attempt I might make to wake him would probably be useless and only succeed in drawing attention to me—which at the moment was something I was trying to avoid. So I continued my journey. Once I had passed the three classrooms in the lean-to, and I was out onto the grass again, I kept myself close to the chain-link fence which ran along this south boundary of the upper campus.

As I passed the back side of the house belonging to Danny the neighbor kid, I could see that his family were all asleep at this hour. Even Bandit failed to notice me as I passed by their back yard. A moment later, I had reached the tennis court. I remember wanting to go around to the outside of the court so I could use it for cover, but it backed up against the west fence, so instead I had to cut across in front of it as I made my right turn to head north along the front border of the grounds and toward the gym.

A moment later, I crossed the main drive next to the front gate, and then made my way along the cement path toward the front of the gym. Both of the front doors, which stood on separate ends of the building's south side, had windows with safety glass set into their upper halves. And so as I approached, I was able to see that the lights inside were turned off.

Once I had arrived at one of the doors, I took a quick look around, and then I slowly pulled the door open to avoid causing any squeaks. A few moments later I was inside the gym with the door closed behind me and wondering what in the world I was going to do next.

"I think this kid's gonna work out pretty good," a voice then said from beyond the lighted doorway at the other end of the gym. "In fact, he submits pretty easily. He may wind up being the best one yet."

Immediately I focused all of my attention onto that doorway. It sounded to me as if the person speaking was about to appear and then enter the gym, so I looked around quickly for a place where I could hide.

"Yeah, he's not nearly as feisty as the last one, and he seems pretty scared right now," a second voice, also approaching, then replied.

All I could find near me were some gym mats which had been rolled up and shoved over against the south wall. So I took a few quick steps to my right and then dove behind them just as the two figures appeared in the gym and looked my way.

"Yeah, but after a while he should get over most of that. Besides, a little fear in these kids is a good thing. Right?"

The second guy then laughed. "Yeah, you're right."

I had to come up with something fast. I knew that time for Matt was running out. I could hear the shower so I knew by now they had gotten his clothes off. So I began to wonder how I might be able to create some sort of a distraction which could clear the building long enough to give me a chance to rescue my friend. But before I could come up with any kind of a plan, I heard that awful sound.

"Auhauhauhauh! Auhauhauhauh! Auhauhauhauh! Auhauhauhauh!"

I couldn't stand it. Not only did Matt sound as if he was in excruciating pain, but his cries sounded as if they were being made by a boy who believed that his situation was utterly hopeless and that his life was about to end.

"No! Auhauhauhauh! Auhauhauhauh! Stop it, ple... Auhauhauhauh! Auhauhauhauh!"

This was too much for me to listen to. I had failed Matt and I felt terrible about it. In a moment the two figures in the doorway went back into the coach's locker room, so I decided the time had come for me to leave too. There was nothing I could do and I didn't want to stay and listen to my friend be raped by these bastards any longer. They had Matt now and they were going to do to him everything they had done to me. So I stood up and sneaked back out the same door I had come in through. And once I was outside again, and as I began to walk away from the building, I could still faintly hear Matt's voice behind me as he continued to cry out for help which could never come.

"Auhauhauhauh! Auhauhauhauh! Auhauhauhauh! Auhauhauhauh!"

***

I guess I must have drifted off after I had returned to our room, because the next thing I remember was being abruptly awakened out of a deep sleep by the sound of our door being slammed open against the east wall of our room. I then opened my eyes in time to see Matt—his body naked and wet against the light coming in from the hallway—as he crossed our room and then threw his abused body down onto his bed with enough force to cause its metal legs to scrape a short distance along the linoleum.

I froze for a moment, not sure what I should do. Matt sobbed uncontrollably into his pillow, and I wanted to do something to comfort him, but I was still feeling guilty for all of the atrocities which had just been visited on him and as such, decided that anything I'd try at this moment would be of little use to him, anyway. Besides, I knew Matt well enough to know that it would help him to go on with his crying so he could get it all out of his system. It might be said now that my inaction at this moment was a bit cowardly I suppose, but as I had already proven, I don't always make the best decisions when I'm only half awake. And so, for the next few minutes, I did nothing but listen to my friend cry.

I did, however, make sure that I stayed awake just in case Matt decided to need me for some reason. But soon, the sobbing ended and he fell silent. Worn out and distraught, a few moments later when I could hear him breathing deeply, I realized that Matt had cried himself to sleep. So with the coast now clear, in a manner of speaking, I got up to close our door and then I walked over to take a look at my roommate and see if there was anything now that I could do for him.

Since the boy hadn't dried himself off before he had lain down on his bed, his hair was still soaked and in clumps all over his head. I could see his right ear clearly where the clumps had parted, which looked a little odd to me because when his hair was dry it always covered his ears pretty much. Water was also beaded up everywhere on his skin. And I admit that I took a moment to inspect his bare bottom. Not because I was interested in it, but because when I had been raped, it felt to me as if something had torn and I was surprised not to find any blood afterwards. So I figured that Matt had probably had the same experience and I wanted to see if I could spot any blood emanating from the area around his hole. And as it turned out, I couldn't.

Finally, I decided that for now, the only way I could help him would be to cover him up so he wouldn't get chilled. And so I took one of his blankets and covered him with it. He was clearly exhausted from his ordeal, because he never noticed me. This, then, was all I figured I could do for Matt until morning. So with everything in our room now quiet again, I went back to my own bed and was asleep again a few minutes later.

The next morning was difficult for both of us. Once we were awake I couldn't get Matt to say anything. He wouldn't even look at me. He still didn't know that I already knew about everything he had been forced to go through, and when I tried to talk to him, he just rolled himself over and stared at the wall next to him.

"Matt, we need to talk." Though I was feeling extremely groggy this morning for some reason, I tried to get a conversation going. I knew that until he began to speak about it, he would be unable to come to terms with the events of last night.

There was no response from my friend. He continued to stare at the wall with his back turned toward me.

"Matt… really man, we need to talk about last night. I know all about it."

Again Matt gave no indication that he was even listening to me.

I knew he could hear me just fine, so I began the conversation without him. "Matt, I know that they tricked you into going with them. I know that they got your clothes off. I know that they put you in the coach's shower. And I know the leader raped you and the rest of them made you give them each blow jobs. I know all about it."

Matt then rolled back to face me as abruptly as he had turned away. I could see tears on his cheeks as he spoke to me. "How could you know all that? Did you have something to do with it?"

I knew that the time had come for me to tell him everything. He was in it now as deeply as I was and the two of us were going to have to stick together. Before last night we had just been roommates and friends. Now we were both in a struggle that neither of us fully understood, yet I knew that we would both be better off if we resolved to work together. And so, I confessed to Matt everything that had happened to me for the past three days. I told him every detail from the moment on Monday night when I was first awakened, to the comments I had overheard the night before about how submissive and afraid they thought he was. My friend lay there transfixed. His expressions kept shifting from disbelief to horror and eventually to anger. And when I was finished, I had never seen him as livid as he was with me then.

"Why the hell did you let them do this to me? Why didn't you warn me ahead of time that this might happen? I'm sorry they got you, but you didn't have to sit back and do nothing and let them come and take me too! I thought you were my friend, Clint." And then Matt rolled over in his bed and refused to look at me again.

And so I explained again about my conversation with Mr. Stuart. I told Matt how our headmaster had felt certain that nothing like this would happen again and how he had told me specifically not to tell my roommate anything right now. And I admitted to Matt that I was also ashamed and embarrassed over how easily they had overpowered me and forced me to do every vile thing they demanded of me. I was nearly in tears myself when I summed it all up by assuring my good friend, that if I had known for sure that he was in danger, I would have told him everything sooner. And then I stopped talking and waited to hear my roommate's response.

At first, Matt still refused to look in my direction. He was still, apparently, mulling over in his mind everything I had just said. Then, after a few more moments had passed, he turned his head around and looked at me again. "I want to say one thing."

"Ok. What?" I had no idea what was coming next.

"From now on, if you find out anything when I'm not around, I want you to tell me about it immediately so we can both be prepared together. No more making decisions for me on your own. And I don't care how embarrassed you feel or what Stuart says about it. You tell me everything. Is that agreed?"

I was relieved. I knew whatever it was that we were facing, we would be better off facing it together as friends. "Yes," I accepted his conditions. "I agree." And then I had one more thought. "And the same goes for you, ok? If you find out anything, you be sure to let me know too. Agreed?"

"Agreed," Matt said. And then he smiled for the first time today and stuck out his hand for me to shake. I took his hand and we shook on it, and then he continued to speak. "So now what do we do?" he asked.

"I don't know," I admitted. "I suppose we go to breakfast and act like nothing's happened."

"Yeah well, we're gonna have to do a better job of acting than you did on Monday."

"What do you mean?" This news surprised me.

"Frank was right. You were a gloomy Gus."

"Well, I don't know what else to do. We can't sit in here all day." Then I got an idea. "I know what… I'll talk to Stuart again after breakfast."

"No!" Matt was profoundly against this idea. "They told me last night that if I go to any teacher or the headmaster about this, they'll start breaking my bones and keep going until they get bored." A look of fear had now returned to Matt's face. It was clear that involving Mr. Stuart was no longer an option for us.

"Well, I don't know what else we can do then except wait for Stuart to get to the bottom of all of this for us," I admitted.

Matt then got an idea and perked up again. "I think we ought'a call the police. These bastards need to be arrested and put in jail."

"No, we can't do that either," I protested. I then recounted in greater detail the things that our headmaster had said about police involvement and how calling in the authorities could only make matters worse for us. "Just think what would happen if the upperclassmen were arrested and then let loose because the police couldn't make a case stick against them. Besides," I reminded my roommate, "...we can't call out on any of the phones around here except for the ones in the office."

"Oh, yeah." Matt understood. "So if we can't go to Stuart, and we can't call the police, then what do we do?"

I thought about my answer for a moment longer, but our course of action seemed clear. "I guess we simply wait for Stuart to finish his investigation and we hope that it doesn't take him too long to solve this for us."

Matt didn't look very comfortable with the idea of putting our fates entirely in the hands of a man whom we barely knew. "Are you sure he'll do it?"

"I think so," I answered. "I get along with him pretty well. I really think he believed me the other day, and I think he wants to do what he can for me." And so our game plan was set. We would wait and hope for the best. "We're just gonna have to stick together all the time from now on and let 'em know that we know what they're up to now and we're not gonna let 'em get us anymore."

Matt smiled at my challenge to be defiant against the perverts who had turned our lives inside out. "Ok," he agreed. "I guess that's what we'll do."

We continued to talk for a few minutes longer. Indeed, I had been wrong to keep what I had known from Matt. He had been right when he had said that it had been as if I was trying to inject myself into his life and make decisions for him. But I had been right about something also. The innocence in him was now faded, and he was no longer the same boy he had been yesterday. But his kindness still remained, and out of the rubble that the night before had created of his life, a stronger, wiser young man had emerged. And I guess I felt pretty much the same way about how I had come through the experience. So we went to breakfast that morning and we didn't go as two timid little boys. We went instead as defiant young men. Ready to challenge anyone who would try to dominate us.

***

Except for a big change in the weather, the rest of that day and the next one were unremarkable. Matt and I figured that in a school as small as the Academy, it would be no time at all before we'd be able to identify who these upperclassmen really were. And so we both began to pay close attention to every post-pubescent voice we encountered. Our thinking was that if we knew who these guys were, they'd lose their advantage over us and we'd be able to then go to the headmaster to have them all expelled, or something. But our opportunities to discover the true identities of our adversaries were limited. Since all of our classes were with the other first-year students, the only times we were really around the older kids was at meals or soccer practice and there were always too many other things going on during these occasions to ever permit us to make a positive match.

And so the perverse demons of the night which had succeeded in their design to soil Matt and me, were able once again to revert to their guises as ordinary everyday Academy students, and despite the "hang tough" optimism that we had started off our Thursday with, feelings of paranoia and foreboding were soon getting the better of us. So as much out of fear as from feelings of defiance, Matt and I started sticking together like Siamese twins, or in other words, we became inseparable. If one of us needed to go back to the room for a book, we both went back to the room. If one of us needed to go to the bathroom, we both went. We resolved that if there wasn't anyone else at the Academy for us to go to for help, we were determined to rely on each other. Just the same, an experience we had at lunch on Friday didn't help matters any for us.

The meal started off normally enough. After we had all been seated, Mr. Stuart tapped his glass as he always did with his spoon to get our attention. If I remember correctly, a group of students were scheduled to be driven by one of the teachers down to Providence in the school's van later that day to hear a performance of that city's symphony, and we were given the details of their departure and eventual return times. Mr. Stuart also gave us information about the intended times after Saturday morning classes when the van would be made available to take those of us who wanted to go to and from town for shopping or whatever. And then after that, our headmaster sat down again and lunch was begun.

Matt and I had already decided that on the next day, we would catch a ride into town in the van so we could find a phone to use in secret. Then, Matt was going to try to get in touch with his aunt, while I would try to reach someone in my dad's office out in Denver. The only problem we saw with this plan was that since we were going to be making these calls on a Saturday afternoon, there was probably little hope that either of us would be able to reach anyone. And this was before the time when answering machines came into use. But we had decided that if there was no one in Massachusetts who could help us, we needed to do what we could to find ourselves some help from someplace else. At the very least, we figured we had to try to let our families in on the activities we were being forced to participate in at the Academy.

As our lunch was brought out to us by the kid who was assigned to be our waiter that day, Matt and I were horrified to see that the lunch for this day was hamburgers. So once the meat and the buns had been passed around the table, the other kids began to grab for the squeeze bottles of mustard and ketchup.

While this went on, Matt and I sat motionless and, I guess, just stared at the bottles without grabbing for them ourselves. A feeling of disgust came over us both very quickly as we watched our friends squeeze out the contents of these bottles all over their food. Even after some of the kids at our table and elsewhere had begun to eat, Matt and I continued to sit transfixed by what we were watching. So I guess it had to be that after a bit, our odd behavior would catch the attention of someone sitting next to us.

"Hey, how come you guys aren't havin' any ketchup or mustard? I thought you guys liked that stuff?" Frank finally figured he had to ask. He loved to say something when others were behaving in ways that he thought looked weird.

"Oh ah," Matt attempted to offer our friend an explanation as he picked up his dry hamburger and raised it to his mouth to take a bite. "Ya just never know where those things have been."

Later that day after our afternoon classes, soccer practice and dinner had been completed, Matt and I kept ourselves around other people as much as we could. There was never any study hall on Friday nights, so we started off our evening by staying a few hours in the TV lounge. It always seemed to me, and Matt too, that the shows the rest of the student body wanted to watch were never the sort of programs that we found interesting. Because of this, I rarely ever went into the TV lounge. But on this occasion, it seemed the safest place available for us to be.

Later on in the evening, though, when the cigarette smoke in the TV lounge became too much for either of us to put up with any longer, Matt and I left the lounge and found a group of kids talking in the library. So for the rest of this night we hung out with these guys until the time finally arrived when we had to head back to our rooms for lights out.

Neither Matt nor I were all that thrilled with the idea of going to sleep on this night. So far this week we had received visits from the upperclassmen every two nights, which meant that if they held to their pattern, we'd be having another encounter with them tonight. Nevertheless, since there was nothing we could do about it, we soon were in our beds, and a short time later had both fallen fast asleep.

***

"Wake up, I say wake up there, son."

My first conscious thought was *Oh no*! *They're in our room again!* I opened my eyes and saw the improbable face of a rooster, or rather the cartoon image of a rooster painted onto a Halloween mask which was staring down at me as I lay in my bed.

"Wake up, Matt, let's go, kid."

I looked over at my roommate and saw a second figure standing over him wearing a "Casper the Friendly Ghost" mask. The ghost was trying to awaken Matt by patting him on one of his legs.

"Come on, Matt. We didn't give you guys any sleeping pills tonight, so you ought'a have no trouble waking up now. So let's go." The ghost then placed a hand on Matt's chest and began to shake the boy.

When Matt did finally begin to stir and open his eyes, he gasped and froze when he saw that we had visitors again.

Fog Horn then took a step backwards to give me a little room. "Sit up, boy," he commanded in his best Harvard Square version of a southern accent.

I was outraged that they would give us drugs without our knowing. "What do you mean you gave us sleeping pills?" I asked as I sat up in my bed suddenly.

The ghost then turned his head and looked at me. "Huh? Oh, yeah. When we wanted Matt to sleep we put sleeping pills in his mashed potatoes, and when we wanted you to sleep, we put 'em in yours. But you only ate half of your mashed potatoes the other night and we were kind of worried that you might not stay asleep when we came for Matt. But you did."

"Hey, shut up!" the rooster said to his comrade. "Now we can't use them anymore," he said about the pills.

Once I was upright, I could see that both of these yo yo's were upperclassmen, after all who else could they have been, and I found myself dumbfounded by what I was hearing. I couldn't believe how cavalier these guys had been with our health. "I can't believe you guys would actually put sleeping pills in our food," was all I could get out on the subject because I was equally angered over the fact that these guys were invading our privacy again. "We don't want you in our room at all. So damn it, get out of here!" I shrieked. "We're trying to sleep." It galled me to think about the nerve these characters were showing by entering our bedroom at such a late hour of the night.

"Let's go, little guys," the one closest to me then said, ignoring my rant. The southern accent now was dropped, which presumably meant that in their minds, the time had come for everyone to be serious. "We've got big things going on tonight."

I didn't care about big things. I wanted to be left alone so I could go back to sleep. A quick glance at my alarm clock told me that we were having this exchange at ten minutes after two in the morning. So instead of cooperating, I began to yell even louder. I guess I was hoping at that moment that someone nearby would hear me and come to our rescue. "We're not going anywhere with you guys. Not now, and not ever. So get the hell out of our room!"

I guess I was too blind with anger to see it coming, but as soon as I had said my last word, the rooster swung his right arm around and slapped me hard across my face.

"Auhauh!" The blow flattened me.

"Now listen up, both of you," the rooster had become mad too. "You *are* coming with us one way or another. So my advice to you both is that you shut up and do as we tell ya. Now move it! Out of bed, both of you!" The rooster then stepped closer to Matt to roust him out of bed which, considering the small space they had to operate in between our two beds, caused the ghost to have to side step closer to me. "Come on! Right now, Matt!" the rooster crowed.

"Yeah, you too, Clint," the ghost was now looking at me. "Get your ass out of bed now, or else."

"I don't think so." By this time I had sat back up again and was feeling more defiant than ever from the hit I had just taken. "We're not goin' anywhere with you two slime bags." I had had it.

The ghost then became angered as well by my refusal to comply and began to swing his right arm so he could slap me in the same way his partner had just done. But this time I was ready. Instantly I threw a block with my left arm and stopped him before he could reach my face. Then, before he had a chance to recover, I grabbed the bones on his wrist with the thumb and first two fingers of my right hand, and I twisted his wrist while I used my left hand to hit and then reverse his arm at the elbow. In the midst of it all, I switched hands so that when I had completed the move, I had turned him around one hundred and eighty degrees, and I was holding his arm behind his back with enough pressure to snap it in three places all at once.

"Auhauh!" The ghost cried out in pain.

I was determined to make my point with these assholes so I was keeping the tension on his wrist, elbow and shoulder pretty high. This was actually my favorite karate technique. I had practiced it plenty of times in the past, but what amazed me when I did it this time was that I was able to execute this move perfectly while still being seated on my bed.

"Auhauh… God!" The ghost continued to complain about my treatment.

It felt good to finally be able to hold my own against these bastards and inflict upon them a little of what they had been doing to Matt and me. "All right," I began to announce in a loud and confident voice. "This is the way its gonna be. Either you two jokers get out of here right now, and then you and the rest of your band of perverts stay the hell away from us forever, or I'll break all three joints in this guy's arm right now."

"All right, Clint!" Matt then smiled and sat up. He believed that I had finally turned the tables on our adversaries. And so did I.

The sudden feeling of power from being able to control our own lives once again was intoxicating. "So you decide," I went on. "Which way is it gonna be?" I tried hard to make myself look and sound as if I meant business… because I did.

"Auhauh… Come on, kid. You're killin' me! Auhauh!"

I added still more pressure to my hold so I could further demonstrate my resolve. It was clear now that I had beaten them. This whole miserable business they had been putting Matt and me through was about to be over for good—or so I thought.

By the time I saw it coming, there was nothing I could do to stop it. Both of my hands were already occupied, and I couldn't move around really or use my feet to defend myself because I was still sitting on my bed. The rooster hopped over to the other side of the ghost and then slugged me full out in my face.

"Auhauh!" The blow laid me out completely, and as I lost control of my body, my hold on the other guy's arm was released.

"Clint!" Matt called out in a panic when he saw me get put down. "Clint!" He wanted to jump over to help me, but at that moment, the just-freed ghost had moved into his way.

With the ghost now turned loose, the rooster reached down and grabbed me by the front of my T-shirt and then lifted my limp body up off of the bed. With rage in his eyes, he then readied his fist to finish me off. I just hung there in the air, unable to move and waiting for his inevitable blow to end it all for me.

"Hey, hold on, man!" The ghost suddenly came to my rescue. "If you wipe him out now, he's not gonna be any good to us all night. And that'll mess up everything. You understand what I'm talkin' about?"

"Yeah, all right," apparently the rooster understood. Reluctantly then, the bigger kid who had just bested me released his grip on my T-shirt so my lifeless body could drop back to my mattress with a thud. "Fine!" He glared down at me as I lay again on my bed. "I'll let you off the hook this time," he hissed, "but if you ever pull any of that shit on any of us again, I'll end it for you permanently. And just so you understand what I'm saying to you… the next time I have to put you down, I'll cripple you for life. And don't think I won't do it, either."

When the ghost had finally cleared out of the way, Matt jumped out of his bed and came to my aid. "Clint, are you ok?" Matt sat down on my bed next to me, as I lay there barely able now to move.

"Yeah, I think I'm gonna live." My jaw ached and my mind felt sort of foggy.

"Can you sit up?" Matt then wedged one of his hands under my back and took hold of my right arm with his other hand. Slowly then, he helped me to sit up again.

As the rooster watched Matt render me assistance, he became irritated at the amount of time we were using up. "Come on, we don't have all night. Get up and let's get going. Feet on the floor, now!"

"Just hold on a minute!" Matt snapped back. "Ya really hit him hard."

I still didn't want to leave the comfort of my bed, but it didn't seem as if we were being given any alternative. So, a moment later I was on my feet and able to travel.

"Ok, you guys now get on your sandals, and then go stand by the door and wait," the rooster ordered.

Without any idea by this time of what we could do otherwise, Matt and I slid our feet into our flip-flops and then stepped over to the door. As we waited for whatever outrageous acts awaited us next, I realized suddenly that the rooster was the leader. The acoustics in our room and through his mask made him sound different, but now I was sure about who he was—whoever he was. I mean, Matt and I still couldn't figure out who any of these guys really were except we were reasonably certain, at least, that they were all students at the Academy.

"Ok, open the door and let's get going," the leader commanded.

Without any argument this time, I reached out and turned the knob on our door and then I pulled it open. When Matt and I then stepped out into the hallway, we were surprised to be greeted by six other upperclassmen who were also wearing all types of Halloween masks to conceal their faces from us. Apparently these guys had been waiting there the whole time while their two compatriots had been in our room.

"Halloween's not for another six weeks, guys." I felt I had to say something to announce our arrival into their custody.

"That's very funny," the leader replied without humor. "Now let's get going. Go to the left and then out the door at the end of the hall and up the stairs outside."

That week a hurricane had slammed into North Carolina, or someplace, and the resulting storm had worked its way up the east coast and into New England. For two days we had steady sheets of rain which drenched us every time we had to go between the main building and our dorm. Matt and I had tried to cut down on the number of times we needed to go between the two buildings, but we were still getting ourselves very wet at least six times a day, plus our soccer practices which actually had been a lot of fun under these conditions. When the two upperclassmen had entered our room that night, it had still been raining. But by the time the ten of us had swung open the large wooden door at the end of our hall so we could all go outside, the rain had finally ended.

For the second time that week, and this time with the two of us going together, Matt and I found ourselves being led in the middle of the night across the upper campus with only underpants, T-shirts and flip flops on our bodies. The ground everywhere was soaked and I found that I had to pay close attention to how I was stepping so I could keep my feet from sliding out of my wet flip-flops.

Neither Matt nor I felt at ease about our circumstances, and we both looked at each other with alarm when the upperclassmen escorted us right through the front gate and out onto the winding asphalt road which led eventually down to the highway.

"Where're you taking us?" Matt asked. The fear in his voice was obvious to all of us.

"Don't worry, we're not goin' far," the leader replied.

Two or three minutes later, long after we had crossed over the state line into Connecticut, we stepped off of the road to the right and entered a small clearing which was surrounded by tall straight lodgepole pine trees. At the same time, I remember hearing the sound of bullfrogs croaking incessantly off in the distance somewhere, which meant that there must have been a pond or a back water from the lake close by. As we began to traverse this field so we could get ourselves well away from the view of the empty road, I noticed that the ground we were now walking on felt sort of rubbery from all of the decaying pine needles which carpeted the area.

"Ok, here's the spot," the leader announced finally as we arrived at a low-lying section of the field.

We all came to a halt, then, next to two long puddles of water which lay at right angles to one another. The upperclassmen then positioned me at the base of the first puddle, and Matt at the base of the second. When they had us where they wanted us, with our backs turned toward the water, they stepped away from us for a moment. Matt and I could see that we had been placed at about six feet apart from each other. During this moment of relative peace, we both wondered what it was that these guys were planning to do to us. Whatever it was, it was obvious, at least, that they wanted us to be able to see each other while they were doing it.

As I turned my head and watched our eight upperclassmen divide themselves so that one group of four could stand with me and the rest of them could encircle Matt, I knew by this time that nothing these older kids ever did was random.

Every aspect of the encounter we had each already suffered through with these guys had been planned out to the smallest detail. And as I became aware of footsteps in the puddle behind me, I wished for there to be some way that my roommate and I could escape from this bunch.

"Hey!" I called out. From behind, one of the upperclassmen from my group of four had wrapped his arms around my neck to put me in a headlock.

"Auh! What're you doing!" Matt's high voice yelled as he became immobilized in the same way.

"Shut up both of you!" the leader yelled. "All right, hold him tight and lift him up," the leader said to the guy who was holding onto me.

"Yeah, do the same with him," the guy who was now standing in front of Matt then gave the same order to his comrade.

A moment later, the fronts of our bodies were completely exposed and vulnerable to the upperclassmen in front of us. Since the guys holding onto us were taller than Matt and I were, we each now found ourselves, once again only able to stand on the balls of our feet. What happened to us next, I guess, was expected. The last time these guys had us under their control, they had broken us in. Tonight, it seemed, the time had come for us to be broken down.

"Ohoof! Ohoof!" Without warning the leader then delivered two strong punches to my stomach. Since I couldn't move or even stand fully on my own, it was impossible for me to protect myself or recover at all from his blows.

"Ohoof! Ohoof!"

When I heard those sounds, I quickly turned my head to the left and saw that the guy in front of Matt had just slugged him twice in the stomach as well. The look of pain I then saw on my friend's face conveyed the enormous state of misery he was now in.

"Ohoof! Auhauh!" Another blow to my stomach and then the leader hit me with a right cross to my face. Since he was a black belt, he knew how to make his punches count.

"Ohoof! Auhauh!"

Then I heard Matt get the same treatment. After that, things just got worse for us.

Most of the time we took body punches. Only occasionally, when they really wanted to score a debilitating blow against us, did they slug us in our faces. After all, they didn't want it to look too obvious that we had been beaten up.

They pummeled us this way for what seemed like an eternity, but they weren't interested in knocking us out—although after the first minute had passed, it would have been easy for them to have done so. Instead, they beat us until we were just this side of being knocked unconscious, and then they would let up on us for a few minutes so we could have a chance to regain some of our strength. Once we had recovered, somewhat, the hitting would resume until we would again be nearly ready to black out. Each time they let us recover, we would only be able to gain back a fraction of the strength we had built back the time before, until eventually they had beaten us down to the point where it seemed as if we would never have our strength back again. And then, finally, they stopped.

As I breathed hard and coughed and just hung there in the guy's arms, I glanced quickly at Matt and saw that, like me, virtually all of his strength was now gone from his body and he was only on his feet still because he was continuing to be held there by the bigger kid behind him. Blood was trickling down onto his chin from one corner of his mouth, and he looked to me as if he was about to pass out. Then, since I apparently hadn't been beaten enough, I took another blow to my stomach and one more to my face.

"Ohoof! Uh!" That was it for me. I couldn't raise my head any longer to see what was going on. I had nothing left.

"Ok," the leader spoke again. "Drop 'em in."

With that I felt myself being let go and shoved backwards until I landed sprawled out on my back in the puddle behind me. An instant later, I could hear Matt splash down as well.

"Ok, let 'em lay there for a minute while the rest of you guys get yourselves into your positions," the leader ordered.

As I lay there dazed and no longer able to move on my own, I could feel the water that I was now lying in lapping against my ears. It was at this moment when I found myself wishing for the leader to hit me again. I figured one more good punch would be all it would take to knock me out completely and end this awful night once and for all. But I soon found that I was not going to be so lucky. It turned out that the beatings that Matt and I had just sustained had been intended merely to soften us up for the real event which was yet to come.

The next thing I remember was feeling the hands from two of them wrap around my wrists and pull me up into a sitting position. Now I felt even weaker. Immediately, my head flopped forward as if it were attached to my body by a long string. The two who had pulled me up then each placed a palm on my back behind my shoulders, and gripped my upper arms with their other hands, so they could hold me up and keep me from falling back into the puddle again. Then a third guy got down on his knees behind me and brought his hands up on either side of my head so he could take large hunks of my wet and dry hair into his fingers. He then placed the heels of his hands against my temples and pulled back on my hair.

"Uh!" I groaned as I felt my skull being raised up by these fingers and hands which were now clamped tightly over the top of my head. When the repositioning of my head had finally stopped, I discovered that, from my new angle of view, I was being made to look directly at the lower half of the leader's body as he was still standing in front of me.

Once these guys had my spent body and head set up the way they wanted, I took the opportunity to glance over at Matt. As Matt's eyes shifted slowly and locked onto mine, I could see right away that the other four were handling him in the same way that I was being manipulated. I could see water dripping from the ends of the hair on the back of his head and it made me realize that water was probably still dripping from the hair on the back of my head as well. I also noticed that as his head and body were being held up for him, his mouth was hanging open a bit, while Matt's face stayed absolutely expressionless. To me, he looked as if he were waiting at death's door. His appearance at that moment shook me right to my soul, and I've been haunted by this image of him for all of these years since. They had really worked us over.

Suddenly, my attention was called back to what was taking place in front of me, by the sound of a zipper being pulled down on a pair of blue jeans. I aimed my eyes forward again in time to watch in horror as the leader pulled off his pants and displayed for me his perfectly formed erection.

"How 'bout this, huh?" he stated with pride.

"Oh shit!" Matt blurted out, wearily.

At that same moment, I heard the sound of another zipper going down. I looked over at Matt again and this time I saw him staring in fear at the apparent erection which was now being wagged in front of him. I say apparent, because from where I was sitting, I could only see the guy's bare ass at this moment.

"All right, listen up!"

The leader had my full attention again.

"If you two thought that what we did to you little guys earlier this week was just a one-time thing—think again. The reason why we're all getting together here tonight is so we can show you two a couple of undeniable truths about how your lives here at the Academy are gonna be from now on. One… whenever we want you, we're gonna have you. And two… we're gonna have you all the time now."

What happened next was the biggest shock of my life, and I suppose it added to our growing feelings of hopelessness. The leader then stepped back so we could both see him better, and then he removed his Halloween mask which signaled to the others to do the same. We couldn't believe our eyes. The leader was in fact, the school's head proctor and the guy standing in front of Matt was our head waiter.

Everyone there saw the shock on our faces. "Kind of surprisin' ain't it?" The guy holding onto my hair then peered around from behind me to reveal that he was the proctor from our dorm. And the rest of them were guys that we recognized mostly as leading students or athletes some of whom, coincidentally, just happened to be seated with us at our table in the dining hall. In fact two of these guys were also the upperclassmen who lived in rooms one and four on our own dormitory floor. Yes, that meant that "the Block" was one of them—small wonder I guess.

If there was any doubt about our prospects before, it was clear now that our futures were doomed. The power that these guys wielded on our campus was second only to that of the teachers. And in a lot of ways, these guys could do more. Matt and I each gave the other a fearful glance. Neither of us had been prepared for this. I kept expecting the headmaster or some teacher to suddenly show up and save us from these lunatics. And I couldn't understand how nobody on the school's staff seemed to know anything about these guys. Then, the leader continued his pronouncements.

"And don't either of you think that there's anyone you can run to for help once this night is over. If you speak about any of this to anyone outside of the eight of us you see here now, I promise you we'll make sure that both of you little guys wish that you had never been born. And that goes for trips into town too. From now on you're restricted to staying here. No more trips to town or anywhere else without my approval. Understand me?"

The leader then paused for dramatic effect. Neither of us dared at this moment to say anything in response.

"All right," the leader continued. "So tonight, you little guys are gonna give all of us blow jobs. And don't forget, none of us want to feel any teeth. If we feel any teeth, we'll knock 'em out of your heads. Ya got that?"

I looked down at the ground in front of me and closed my eyes. This was not something I wanted to have to go through again. But before I could have a chance to wallow in my own self-pity, the leader reached out and squeezed my cheeks together with one of his hands and then tilted my face up so I would be forced to look at him straight in the eyes.

"I said, you got that, Adams?"

"Uh huh," I answered obediently.

"Good!" he replied. And with that, the leader tilted my head down a bit so I could look straight ahead again, and then I watched him bend his knees so he could squat down a little to line himself up better. "Yeah, this ought'a be real good," he proclaimed while he still held my face in his hand, and then he forcibly plunged his penis into my mouth.

The shock of having all of that in my mouth again rattled me for a moment. He was big and as it had been for me with the Artist, at first he went down my throat too far and caused me to gag.

"Perce your lips!" he demanded as he adjusted himself to make me more comfortable.

There was nothing I could do other than obey. I still had no strength of any kind in my body. So as I struggled to form my lips around his penis in the way he was expecting, the three who were holding me then began to ungulate my body and head so that my lips could stroke the leader in along his shaft, and then back out again.

"Aaahhhh! That feels great!"

The leader approved of my efforts. I didn't care.

"Make 'em harder. Perce your lips more, and make 'em harder," he ordered.

"Ugk!"

As the leader's cock filled my mouth, and as I continued to feel myself being rocked forward and back by the others around me, I suddenly heard a sound which caused me to gaze over at Matt again. When I saw him, I saw that the head waiter had just shoved his engorged penis into Matt's mouth, and just like me, Matt was now having his depleted body and head moved forward and back for him by the other three guys who were huddled around him.

It was hard for me to see Matt as he sat there so helplessly. It was also hard for me to see how easily these bastards were manipulating him to satisfy their own perverse desires. I could barely stand to see how firmly that upperclassman had stuffed his dick into my friend's mouth. But as Matt's eyes glanced over and connected again with my own, it was harder still for me to realize that my friend was now watching me succumb to the same abuse.

The whole experience was demoralizing as hell. Now that I've had some years to think about it, I've decided that breaking our spirits had been their plan all along. The defiant attitudes that Matt and I had adopted after our first encounters with these guys in the gym now seemed absurd. The events of this night demonstrated to both of us quite clearly that, without a doubt, neither of us was strong enough to help the other and also, neither of us was capable in any way of preventing these bigger kids from doing with us whatever they pleased.

As we sat there in our puddles, all battered and bruised and in more pain from our beatings than either one of us had ever felt in our lives—then or since—and as we both continued to be handled by these guys gathered around us in a way that was intended to cause the penises in our mouths to ejaculate, I kept my eyes fixed on Matt as tears began to slide down his cheeks. The sight of him crying made me aware of the tears which I was also shedding. I guess both of us seeing the other going through this same awful experience at the same time had something to do with it. Because at that moment I could see in my roommate's eyes that the same thought which had just struck me was now in his mind as well.

Our bodies, in fact our very lives, were no longer our own. From this night on, it was abundantly clear to us both, that for the remainder of our existence on this earth, the only role in life that we would be allowed to have would be that of sex slaves. And this thought, as it turned out two weeks later, was exactly what these upperclassmen assholes had wanted Matt and me to believe about ourselves. In this strange and detached world in which we were all now living, these eight upperclassmen had proven their dominance and were now engaged in the act of reaping from us the spoils of their victory over us.

After that, all ten of us seemed to settle into a steady rhythm as Matt and I resigned ourselves to having our bodies rocked forward and back for us so our lips could keep stroking the penises which filled our mouths. Even if we could somehow have found the strength to fight back, we knew now that we would never again try to defy these guys. The price for doing so, frankly, was just too high. Their beating had nearly destroyed us. And because we had been defeated so completely, we knew now with certainty that life for us would never be the same. As it was, it took all of the strength I could manage to keep my lips rigid, and I had no doubt that the same was true for Matt.

For a while then, I just sort of set myself on automatic. Since the three guys holding me were doing all the work, I just tried to relax and allow them to use me as much as they wanted. Before long an odd feeling of peace seemed to come over me. As I thought about this new rush of good will, I decided that it was my reward for accepting my rightful role in this new world as a submissive. I then looked over at Matt and observed that like me, he had stopped crying and was now looking unfazed by it all as well. So our transformation, it seemed, was complete. The boys we had been at the beginning of the evening were now dead and we had emerged from the water reborn. From this night on, Matt and I belonged to the upperclassmen. And without question, this new fact in our minds we now held as incontrovertible.

A short while later, the time had come for the leader to climax. He strained and breathed quickly in the usual ways until I could begin to feel his penis pump his semen into my mouth. Then I heard him let out a long sigh, and he was finished with me.

By now I felt as if I was an old pro at this stuff, so the experience didn't seem to disgust me as much as it had that night in the gym. But when he pulled himself out of my mouth, the guy behind me suddenly yanked back hard on my hair which forced my face to tilt upward again so I could see the leader's face as it now filled my view.

"Swallow it!" he demanded.

"Auh!" I gasped. The way that the guy behind me was pulling my head back was not only painful, but he was making it harder for me to do as I was being ordered.

"I said swallow it! I wanna see that Adam's apple move," the leader barked.

"Ah!... Ah!... Um!" I swallowed.

"Good! Good boy."

Finally some praise. Instantly then the guy behind me relaxed his tension and tilted my head back down a bit so I could look straight ahead again.

"Swallow it!" the head waiter was now demanding of Matt.

I glanced over quickly and saw that Matt's group was doing the same to him.

"Ah!... Um!" Matt swallowed too.

"All right!" the head waiter then acknowledged. "Way to go."

And so it was one down and three more to go for both of us. I tried to get Matt's attention by staring at him, but he seemed more intent now upon preparing himself for the next penis. Then, in a move which I now understand was orchestrated to obliterate any remaining threads of independence we might still have possessed, I got slapped hard across my face.

"Auhauh!" I cried out in pain.

"You forgot to suck!" the leader yelled at me. "In the gym we taught you that you're supposed to suck when you give a guy a blow job, and you didn't suck me off just now."

At the moment of impact, the other three guys had let me go. The force from the leader's hand spun my head around hard enough to take the top half of my body along with it. I then landed face down in the water behind me. Uncertain then, as to whether or not I had yet regained enough strength to move on my own, I became afraid that I was about to drown. But before I could panic, I felt hands grab me and pull me back up into my sitting position. The three sets of hands then returned to their assigned places on my back, upper arms and hair which was now soaked clear through.

"Are you gonna remember to suck from now on?" the leader thundered.

"Yes," I gasped. "I promise I'll do better," I said as I felt water pour from my bangs and down over my face.

"Auhauh!" SPLASH!

I then looked over in time to see Matt land on his face in his water. The guy in front of him had just slapped him as hard as the leader had slapped me. Immediately then, another guy put his hands on Matt and sat him upright again. As I then watched water pour from Matt's bangs and flow down over his face, I could tell from his expression that this experience had shaken him. Then the head waiter spoke again.

"You didn't suck when you did me either. Are you gonna remember to suck from now on?" the head waiter demanded.

"Ah huh," Matt agreed. "I'm sorry. I won't make that mistake again. I promise, too." Although I could tell that he wanted to cry again, Matt was too frightened at this moment to do so.

"All right then," the leader spoke again. "If you guys wanna try to do a better job this time, we'll give ya another chance.

"Thank you," Matt answered. "Yes, I wanna try to do it better."

"Yeah, me too," I said also. And we really meant it.

The guy behind me then removed his hands and I felt my wet head flop forward again until my chin was resting on my chest. As the leader then walked around behind me to take over this guy's job, I tried to lift up my head on my own, but I still couldn't do it very well. A moment later, I could feel the leader's fingers making their way through my soggy strands as he clamped the heels of his hands against my temples. When I could look ahead again I watched as another pair of jeans came off and another penis in full erection was presented to me.

I glanced over at Matt again and saw that another bare ass, from my vantage point, was standing close to his face. Then hands grabbed our cheeks and penises were jammed into our mouths again.

This time, Matt and I tried harder to please our masters. But in our still weakened conditions, all of our effort took their toll on us, and we began to groan every time we pressed down hard with our lips—which was every time we did a stroke.

"Ummmph! Ummmph! Ummmph! Ummmph!" Matt began to groan first. Throughout the encounter so far, I had been trying to keep myself from making any noise. I figured that any sound I made would distract the current occupant of my mouth and make him mad at me. But before long, the strain became too much and I could no longer hold it back either.

"Ummmph! Ummmph! Ummmph! Ummmph!" Just like Matt, I began to groan with every stroke. But the hits for not keeping quiet never came. In fact, the sounds that Matt and I were now making actually seemed to stimulate these guys even more. So for the next twenty minutes or so, as the rest of them took their turns with us, the steady groans from two thirteen-year-old boys joined the chorus which rose into the late night air from our rain-soaked field, and sounded much like two high-pitched bullfrogs—just croaking away peacefully in their ponds.

Chapter Four
The Training Begins

When the wake-up bell went off the next morning, Matt and I found that we ached everywhere. At first, just getting out of our beds was a struggle. But with a great amount of effort, we somehow managed to pull ourselves together and make our way over to breakfast on time.

Besides some bruising and some swelling on our faces, the cut on the corner of Matt's mouth was still visible, and I had acquired a black eye from one of the things that had collided with my face—the leader's fist or the ground. If we had walked into a school room back home in Colorado looking the way we did, the kids there would have been all over us with questions about what had happened to us. But people in Massachusetts were different. I guess they had all been raised to not involve themselves in the lives of others or something, because as Matt and I entered the dining hall and sat down at our table, none of the sixty other kids or five teachers in that room said a word to either of us about our appearance. It was only after we had begun to eat when Frank, naturally, finally perked up and offered a question.

"You two get into a fight or something?" he asked.

"No," Matt answered succinctly.

And that was all that was ever said on the matter. Nothing more was ever mentioned to either of us again by anyone. It made Matt and me wonder if the entire school was in on this bizarre lifestyle which we were now so thoroughly caught up in.

After that morning, things for us just became stranger. For the next two weeks, the eight upperclassmen made it a point to occupy almost all of our free time. What surprised us both was that these perverts began to treat Matt and me as if we had become their best buddies. Apparently, since we had gone through the first phase of their "initiation" and emerged from the ordeal the way they had wanted, we were now considered to be part of their gang and as such, were entitled to experience their version of camaraderie and reward. Matt and I went to our classes and attended all of the meals as usual, and every night we continued to observe study hall and lights out just as if everything in our lives was unchanged, but the rest of the time there was nearly always at least two of them hanging around us.

This next phase of our initiation into—we had no idea what—commenced the night following the encounter in the pine field which, coincidentally, happened to fall on a Saturday night. Most weekends, the headmaster left the campus and stayed away until early Monday morning. This weekend, as it turned out, was no different for him. Nobody ever knew where he went all these times, but presumably he tried to use these occasions to pursue a private life of his own. One thing we were all pretty sure of, though, was that our headmaster most likely spent all of these days and nights in an altered state, and these excursions into weekend-long drunkenness made it possible for him to remain mostly sober when he was with us during the week.

On this particular Saturday night, two of them appeared at our door at about the time the warning bell sounded for dinner. They told us that we would not be eating in the dining hall that night and then they made some vague statement about having something special planned for us instead. After that, they walked us over to the headmaster's house, which we knew had been vacated by the man only a couple of hours earlier. It was there where we then met up with the rest of the gang.

As head proctor, the leader had keys to everything. So it didn't seem odd at all that one of the keys on his ring opened the front door to the headmaster's house. At first Matt and I figured we were in for more of the same sort of activity we had participated in the night before, and we decided right away that having to perform inside, at least, would be better than being cold and wet outside. But instead, we were amazed to learn that we were being treated to an evening of pizza and a movie. Apparently one of the eight had been able to borrow the school's van and had returned from town with a bunch of pizzas for the ten of us. They had also, somehow, gotten their hands on a copy of *It's a Mad, Mad, Mad, Mad World*. So our exclusive little group spent that Saturday night eating pizza and watching the movie on the school's projector, in the headmaster's living room. It was almost fun.

I say almost because by this time, I no longer felt as if humor could ever be a part of my life again. As I watched the movie, I saw a lot of actors I liked, and there were plenty of scenes which I normally would have found very funny. But except for the scene at the end, where Ethel Merman slips and falls in front of the others in the hospital—how could anyone not laugh at that—I didn't laugh once throughout the entire film. And it was the same for Matt too.

When the movie had finally ended, the leader then stood up in front of us and began to speak. The time had come, apparently, for the ground rules to be laid down for just how we were going to be expected to conduct ourselves from here on out. In the process, we learned a little more about this gang's version of life at the Academy, which, of course, was information which had been left out of the school's catalog.

It seemed that every one of the eight bigger kids who were there in the head's house with us that night had been where we now were. All of them had, at one time, been first-year students who had been culled from their grade and forced into going through the same sort of initiation that Matt and I had just suffered through. Then each year, as a new crop of younger boys came along and new slaves were selected, their seniority had allowed these guys to move up in the pecking order—which they referred to, of course, as "the pecker order." We were all expected to perform sex acts on demand, but only for people who were older than we. Also, it seemed that as these guys had aged up, sex duties were gradually replaced by some other activity, but we couldn't figure out just what that was on this occasion. The one exception to these rules was the leader. Because he was the gang's leader, he had won the right to have no such requirements placed on him.

Matt and I were further told that if we stayed attentive and always did as we were instructed, without complaint or hesitation, we would be part of a privileged few and entitled, therefore, to special rewards like this pizza party. At the same time, it was made very clear to us that any failure by Matt or by me to execute these requirements would result in the most dire of punishments being meted out to the both of us. So although Matt and I were powerless to help each other when these guys were really after us, if we remained compliant and obsequious, we did possess the ability to prevent each other from being beaten up.

So, as it turned out, things would improve for us somewhat once we got older, but at the same time there was no doubt to either of us that our lives had indeed been changed forever and our roles as sex slaves were permanent. Then something happened that Matt and I probably should have expected, but hadn't.

That night, after the pizza and the movie and the speech, this group of eight introduced Matt and me to marijuana. Despite its popularity in those days, nether Matt nor I had ever had an interest in experimenting with drugs. It just didn't fit the kind of kids we were. But knowing full well what we would be in for if we refused to go along, we accepted the joints they placed in our hands and began solemnly to draw the smoke into our bodies.

At first we had the typical reaction that boys will have when they take up smoking. Throughout the rest of the evening, we spent more time coughing than we did inhaling, and as a result, the drug never seemed to have any effect on us at all. But for each day that followed, the upperclassmen kept after us to keep trying until by about the third or fourth day, we had managed to overcome our urges to cough. On that day, for the first time in our young lives, Matt and I both discovered what it was like to become high—and we liked it. From then on, we couldn't get enough of the stuff.

As the days wore on, Matt and I tried each day to smoke more pot than we had smoked the day before. This pleased the others so they made certain that we always had an ample supply of the drug. Before long, we were running back to our room after lunch every day to have a joint, and then after classes we'd smoke on and off for the rest of the day until lights out.

Drugs were everywhere at the Academy and there was never any effort made by the faculty to interfere with their use. Actually, looking back on it now, I suspect the teachers preferred the students on drugs because it tended to subdue them so that the occasions for conflict were reduced. As long as we didn't pull out a joint in the middle of class and light it up in front of the teacher, the school always looked the other way on the subject of drug abuse. After all, every enrolled student was a paying customer for the school's owner. And a tuition check from a parent whose kid was allowed by the Academy to become strung out on drugs was better than no tuition check from a parent whose boy had gotten kicked out of school for drugs.

Eventually, Matt got so into pot that he started carrying around a roach clip all the time so he could sneak outside behind Ulster Hall and take a few tokes between classes. At our ever increasing rate of consumption, it didn't take long before Matt and I gave up altogether on the soccer team and chose instead to hang around the upperclassmen all afternoon so we could continue to get high. These daily retreats were usually held in the leader's room since his was bigger than anyone else's and because he was the only student at the Academy who was allowed to have a TV. It also became routine for Matt and me to service at least a couple of these guys every day at these gatherings.

"Clint, come over here, kid." It would always start out this way. One of them would summon me over to stand in front of him. Usually this would

and his head and legs fell, drained of their energy, back down until they crashed onto his sheets.

Immediately then, the guy stopped what he was doing to Matt and sat up again. "How was that, little guy?" he asked.

It took a moment for Matt to recover enough to be able to speak. He was now completely out of breath. When he did answer, he said only one word. "Wo!"

I then felt a large hand placed against my bare chest. I didn't turn my head to look at him when I felt the guy gently push against me. I just lay down knowing that to do so was expected of me. Then, as soon as I was horizontal, I could feel two hands take hold of my underpants on either side of the elastic and then pull them down over my legs and off of my body so that, like Matt, I was naked now too.

"Sit up and watch," the guy on the other bed said to Matt.

With my eyes still fixed on my roommate, I watched as he leaned up and propped himself on one elbow. He looked calm and rather peaceful now as his eyes met mine. And I remember thinking to myself that the marijuana and the sex had really had a powerful effect on him.

I was still looking at Matt when I felt fingers begin to handle me. I then saw Matt smile faintly at me as his gaze seemed to convey something like... "...hold onto your sheets, you're gonna love this." I then turned my head away from him so I could stare up at our ceiling there in the darkness. And as I felt myself beginning to be stimulated, I closed my eyes and decided that indeed I was going to make every effort to enjoy this!

***

So the continual on-demand pleasuring of our masters, the marijuana, and the nightly rituals, quickly became integral parts of our daily routine at the Academy. Still there was one more thing that the upperclassmen introduced to Matt and me during these first two weeks after the pine field, which further instilled in us the patterns of addictive behavior. Alcohol. They started us off by giving us beer and, like the marijuana, encouraged us to drink as much of it every day as we could. It took me a while to adjust to the taste, but like the pot, Matt dove into it just as quickly as it was given to him.

The high we got from alcohol was completely different from what we had become used to from pot. Our attempts to sustain it, though, always caused us to fall asleep. So we smoked during the day, and saved the beer for after lights out. Usually then, instead of a joint, the upperclassmen would give us beer and wait until we had a pretty good buzz going. Then they would make us lie down so we could receive our blow jobs. Afterwards, while they cleaned us up, the upperclassmen would continue to get Matt and me drunk, and this would go on until we'd pass out for the night. I guess after that the upperclassmen always left our room, because they were never there when we awoke the next day. The only negatives to this routine were the hangovers we wound up with in the mornings. But in time, we learned to adjust to those too.

The Saturday night after the pizza party—one week later—was an evening which saw our use of alcohol peak. To this day, I still can't remember much of what happened to us that night. It began with a message from the leader saying that once the headmaster had departed the campus for the weekend, we were expected to be at his house again for another dinner and evening together with our gang. By this time, I guess, the upperclassmen had figured that we no longer needed to be escorted around everywhere. After all, where could we have gone?

Matt and I were already nicely stoned when we appeared at the head's house on time. On this occasion, we found only six of them attending instead of the customary eight. Throughout the evening, we tried to find out why the other two were absent, but we could never get anyone to give us a straight answer to our inquiries. Dinner was burgers cooked on the headmaster's grill outside in his backyard. By now we were having the kinds of lively conversations with these guys that kids our age normally had with their friends. So the party went along fine until they pulled out something new for us to try.

Sometime after dinner, Matt and I were presented with our own fifths of cherry vodka, and told to enjoy them. My dad used to drink vodka on the rocks every so often and I remembered trying a sip of it once and thinking that the stuff tasted like lighter fluid. So the idea now of having to down a fifth of vodka in front of these jokers didn't thrill me. But when I took my first sip, I found that the cherry flavor masked the alcohol taste enough to make this task seem possible to me after all. And Matt seemed to take to our eighty-proof dessert right away. So before long, Matt and I were sitting next to each other on the couch and slugging back our bottles of booze.

I don't remember much more of what happened after that. A little while later, of course, Matt and I fell into stupors and subsequently lost touch with everything around us. From then on, instead of having memories of that night, I only have vague impressions of things the others did to us once we were incapable of refusing them.

I do know that we both had to be carried back to our room by several of the upperclassmen, and I remember that once I was lying on my bed again, my clothes were pulled off of my body—seemingly all at once. I also recall Matt and me being sat up on my bed and cradled in their arms like infants while we were fed more vodka from our fifths which the bigger kids handled like baby bottles. And I have faint recollections of choking as vodka spilled from someone's attempts to pour more liquor into me than I could apparently consume.

And so, once again Matt and I had been subdued by our tormentors. The methods which these miscreants were employing to gain control over us were mounting. This time, though, the results for us had been the worst yet. In the past, whether they had used beatings or intimidation or marijuana or even beer to break down our defenses, Matt and I were always alert enough to know what was happening to us. On this night, all of that changed. The vodka they gave us dulled our brains to the point where we were no longer people. Instead we had become nothing more than warm, barely animate objects for them to play with and handle in any way they chose. And the scary thing about it all was that these guys could have been devil worshipers or ax murderers, and in our less than conscious conditions, we would never have been able to raise so much as an eyebrow if our lives had actually become threatened. As it was, I suppose, Matt and I were lucky that all these guys wanted from us was to commit sex acts with young boys.

The next morning, Matt and I woke up naked and together in my bed. Our heads and torsos were lying next to each other and our arms and legs were entangled. Cherry stains were all over our faces, chests and stomachs and also all over my sheets. And there was dried semen on our penises and lower abdomens.

It took a little while, but when we were finally awake enough to understand our circumstances, Matt and I unsnarled ourselves so we could sit up.

"I think they laid us down side by side and then they gave us both hand jobs at the same time to see which one of us would spout off the highest," Matt moaned as we both looked ourselves over.

"Who won?" I asked.

"I have no idea." The pitch in Matt's voice dropped with his last word which signaled to me that he wasn't feeling much like saying anything else for the moment.

As we then strained to get to our feet, we knew that despite the way we had found ourselves on this morning, we had both been made too utterly drunk the night before to have been able to initiate any sort of activity with each other—sexual or otherwise. But as I fought with my worst hangover yet to remove the ruined sheets from my bed and put on a clean set from our closet, we both understood that once again something for us had changed. Matt and I knew that we had no interest in each other in a sexual way. After all, we liked girls. In fact we tended to regard our odyssey together as a bad ride at an amusement park which we had just happened to step onto by mistake. We still had hope that any time now Mr. Stuart would conclude his investigation and then we could, in effect, jump off of this ride and have our lives back. But in spite of how we felt about each other, the direction in which the minds of our masters was now heading, and what that foretold to us about the sort of events which were likely coming up soon, made what we were in for next seem obvious.

For the rest of that Sunday, after we had taken turns washing the cherry stains, the semen and whatever else there was off of our bodies in the shower, Matt and I stayed pretty much on our beds as we struggled to reclaim ourselves from the night before. Around noon I decided that the time had come for me to begin a letter to my parents. Since we weren't permitted to contact our families by phone, I figured that a slower means of communication would have to do.

In the afternoon, both of us threw up—which helped a little—and by dinnertime we were able to stagger over to the dining hall for a light meal. After that day, neither of us wanted to even look at a bottle of cherry vodka again. In fact, just recounting the experience now makes me feel ill. But no matter how much I'd like to forget about it today, the Saturday night which followed a week later ended up trumping our experiences with the cherry vodka, even though at the time we hadn't believed such a thing could be possible.

***

For the next week, our lives fell into the routine that the upperclassmen had established for us. Every day they made sure we were well supplied with marijuana and as a result, Matt and I began to get into the habit of staying high throughout each day, even during the free time we had before breakfast. Our afternoon retreats to the leader's room afforded us the opportunity to hone our skills in the practice of oral sex on demand by increasing our stamina and improving our technique. And every night, Matt and I eagerly awaited our turns to receive blow jobs from the masters themselves, as well as to become embalmed by the beer they poured into us to the point of passing out blissfully until the wake-up bell the next morning would drag us, bleary eyed and hung over, back to consciousness.

As we descended deeper into the pit which the bigger kids had dug for us, a number of things attitudinally began to change for us. I suppose the biggest change was that the trading of blow jobs with these guys no longer seemed to us to be any big deal. The act of wrapping our lips around another kid's erection became as normal to us as shaking hands or brushing our hair. We also began to think of these older kids as our closest friends and confidants. It seemed as if we could talk with these guys about almost anything, as long as we continued to give them all good head. But we weren't won over to this new lifestyle entirely just yet. We still understood that despite our willingness now to engage in whatever behavior they demanded from us, we were being forced to live this way against our wills, and an event on Thursday of that second week reminded us that our newfound complacency toward these guys was dangerous and perhaps not the best way for us to handle our relationship with them.

It happened after we had returned to our room that evening from having dinner. By now, if Matt and I weren't in our classes or at our meals or with the upperclassmen, we tended to keep ourselves in our room and isolated from the rest of the student body. Whether it was real or imagined, we had begun to believe that the other kids at the Academy were treating us differently than they had before this whole business with the gang had gotten started. So to avoid questions and other discomforts in social situations, we felt it was better for us to simply keep to our dorm if there was no place in particular where we were needing to be. I suppose, then, this was why they had no trouble finding us when they came looking for us.

I was sitting at my desk which stood along the east wall of our room near the door while Matt had decided to lie down on his bed for a few minutes before getting started on his homework. My mind, at this moment, was focused on the task of remembering what assignments had been given in class that day when a serious knocking on our door commanded us to respond.

"Come in…" I called out as I turned my head in time to see Matt sit up on his bed.

Immediately then, our door blew open and the leader and the head waiter stormed in. "Ya blew it, Clint!" the leader announced as he walked quickly through the room and over to stand next to Matt. "Ya screwed up!"

The head waiter then closed our door behind him and took up a position next to me.

"Stand up," the leader barked out his order at my roommate.

Matt shot me a questioning look for an instant, and then he placed his feet on the floor and stood up in silence. It was obvious to us both that something was up and I could tell that Matt was now gripped with fear. I was afraid too. Because neither of us had any idea of what this was all about.

"I don't understand," I said as I tried to deflect the leader's attention away from my friend.

"You wrote a letter to your parents about us and you tried to mail it today, Clint," the leader thundered.

Instantly I felt butterflies in my stomach in the way I used to when I was a small child and I had just been caught at something I had known I wasn't supposed to be doing. At the same time, it angered me to learn that the leader had intercepted my letter. But I held my tongue and refrained from offering any response, since I couldn't think of anything to say at the moment that wouldn't have made things worse for us. *Tampering with the U.S. Mail,* I thought to myself instead. *Well that's one more felony we can add to the list.*

The leader then continued with his rant. "I warned you both what would happen if you didn't cooperate completely with us." And with that, the leader turned and slugged Matt hard in his stomach.

"Ohoof!" Instantly Matt doubled over in pain from the blow.

"Now hold on a minute!" I yelled as I stood up to help my roommate. But before I could take a step, the head waiter slugged me in my stomach also—"Ohoof!"—which forced me back down into my chair. "Ah!"

"Stay in your chair and keep quiet," the head waiter demanded of me.

The head waiter wasn't as good at throwing a punch as the leader was, but the blow I took from him was painful enough to get the job done, and it caused me to have to keep my arms pressed together against my stomach while I sat bent forward and facing the floor in front of me. And before I could recover, I felt my assailant suddenly grab a large hunk of my bangs and raise my head so I would be forced to watch the other things the leader was about to do to poor Matt.

When the leader could see that I was watching again, he then grabbed a hunk of Matt's hair and pulled my roommate's head up in the same way. "Ok, Clint. If Matt had screwed up, I'd be doing this to you. But because you fucked up, I'm now gonna punish Matt. So I hope you enjoy watching this." And with that, the leader threw a right cross at my roommate's face.

"Auhauh!" As it connected, the leader's punch forced Matt's small body to sail backwards through the air until he landed sprawled on his back cross-wise on his bed.

The leader then reached down and grabbed the front of Matt's shirt with his fist and lifted the boy off of his mattress until my roommate was hanging hopelessly in the air above his bed. "Remember, Clint, this is happening to him because of you." With his right fist, the leader then threw another punch at my friend's face.

"Auh!" The force from the leader's blow drove Matt's body down hard onto his bed again. In response, Matt coughed once then he rolled his head to one side, groaned slightly and finally bent one of his arms at the elbow. He was being devastated by the beating he was taking.

Still not finished, the leader grabbed the front of my friend's shirt again and lifted Matt above his bed one more time.

It was awful to watch. "Uh!" Once again the force from the leader's punch propelled Matt downward until his battered body slammed helplessly against his bed. This time, once he was down Matt lay still. A quick inspection of his condition revealed that he no longer seemed able to move on his own and I watched anxiously for any signs of life from his head or his arms which were now extended like crooked tree branches from his body.

"No! Don't hit him any more!" I pleaded.

"Shut up!" the head waiter yelled at me. He then let go of my hair so I could continue to watch this spectacle on my own.

The leader acted as if he hadn't heard me at all. Instead he bent over Matt's quieted body and began to unbutton my friend's shirt. When he had it undone all the way and had separated the two halves to reveal Matt's torso, the leader went on to unbuckle Matt's belt and unhitch Matt's pants. The side of the mattress was hitting my roommate at about mid thigh, causing his legs to hang out and away from his bed. So when the leader unzipped Matt's pants, he was able then to pull the boy's pants and underpants down along his legs until he could leave them to hang around my friend's ankles.

With Matt's naked body now exposed for all of us to see, the leader wasted no time in placing his thumb and forefinger onto Matt's penis so he could begin to stimulate his victim sexually. As the head waiter and I watched the stroking begin, it didn't take long before Matt's body was beginning to react to what the leader was doing to him.

"Hhhha!" Matt exhaled sharply and then he rolled his head to his right. He wasn't unconscious, but he had definitely been wiped out by the violence which had just been waged against him.

When the leader could see that Matt was responding to his efforts, he quickened the pace of his stroking. In no time he had worked the boy's penis into a solid erection.

"Uuh!" Matt groaned and rolled his head over to his left. It was obvious now that he was feeling the surges of stimulation all throughout his battered body. "Uuh!... Uuh!" Soon apparently, Matt was approaching his climax.

There wasn't a thing I could do for my roommate at the moment. I knew that if I said or did anything right now, the head waiter would hit me again before I could get myself out of my chair. I did manage, though, to get a quick glance at him and I could see that he was smiling as he watched my roommate respond to his hand job.

"Ah!" Now Matt sounded as if he was about to pop. "Uhoof... Uhoof... Ah!" And with that, Matt's entire body flinched as we watched his semen begin to spurt out.

The leader continued to stroke Matt until his throbbing ended. Then the leader let go of the boy's swollen member and wiped his hand off on Matt's face. "There!" he proclaimed. "Now he ought'a feel better." The leader then turned his head and looked at me again. "Now remember this, Clint. This all happened to Matt because of what you did. So don't screw up again. Got it?"

"Yes, sir," I answered obsequiously. I just wanted these guys to get out of our room so I could tend to my friend's needs.

"Remember, I own you two. You guys can't do shit around here without checking with me first, and I can do anything to you I want. Got it?"

"Yes, sir." This time I looked down at the floor when I gave my answer. I was worried that if I looked directly at him, he might take that as an act of defiance and wind up staying in our room longer to do or say something else to us.

"All right, come on." The leader then said to the head waiter. "Let's get the hell out of here." A moment later they had gone, and I jumped out of my chair so I could cross the room and sit down on the bed next to Matt.

"Are you ok?" I asked not knowing what else to say.

"Ah!" was the only reply that Matt seemed to be able to give me at the moment.

"Matt, I'm so sorry this happened to you. If I had any idea they were gonna stop our mail, I'd never tried to send my letter out." I then began to inspect Matt's body to see what his needs were going to be. "Oh shit! You're bleeding!"

"Huh?" Matt replied.

"He opened up that cut again on your lip. It's not too bad, but I need to go get something for it." I then stood up again and stepped quickly over to our closet. We always kept a roll of paper towels in our room, so I tore off a few sheets, and then I threw open our door and dashed across the hall to soak them in cold water from our bathroom sink. A moment later I was back and sitting on Matt's bed again. He was still lying there on his back. "Here," I said. And then I placed the wadded-up wet paper towels against the cut on my friend's lip.

"Thanks," Matt said as he raised one of his hands to take over the job of holding the compress to his lip. "What an asshole," he exclaimed.

"Who, me?" I was worried that Matt blamed me for what had just happened to him.

"No, the leader. That was really weird." Embarrassment was beginning to set in.

"Yeah, no kidding," I agreed.

Matt continued to speak as he began his struggle to sit up again. "I think we're gonna have to be a lot more careful about these guys from now on."

Chapter Five
There's No Way Back: The Line Is Now Crossed

Weekends in boarding schools are usually pretty dull. Going into town and wandering the streets of Ulster, or shooting baskets alone or with other students on the campus were about the only activities there were for us to do. But once Matt and I had crossed over into the seamy world of the eight upperclassmen, our weekend boredom became unbearable. By the time the second Saturday after the pine field had come around, we were seeing life exclusively through a haze of marijuana smoke. Since we were restricted from going into town, and since neither one of us felt inclined to exert ourselves enough to play basketball, we were left to do little more than lie on our beds and listen to my stereo.

"Start it over again will ya, Clint?" Matt asked me when the forth side of the *Tommy* album by The Who had finished playing. It had seemed to me to be a fitting couple of records to put on that day.

"Aw, why don't you put the record on this time?" Just lying there on my bed, I was feeling too comfortable to move. Besides, the temperature that day was up in the high eighties and moving would have required sweating, and I really hadn't wanted to do either.

"Oh, come on, Clint," my roommate protested. "You're closer."

This matter now required a moment of thought. "All right. I'll put the first side on again. Give me a minute, though." I wanted a little time to work up the steam I was going to need to drag myself off of my bed.

By the time the warning bell had sounded for dinner later that afternoon, it seemed apparent that, since we hadn't been told otherwise, there was not going to be a special party given for us at the head's house this week. Neither

Matt nor I said anything to each other about it at the time, but we both knew that in the eyes of our masters, we were now compliant enough to cause them to believe that they no longer needed to make special efforts to keep us obedient. So with a huge sigh of relief, we sauntered over to the dining hall for dinner that night by ourselves. It felt kind of liberating to finally have a break from the gang. "Maybe," we hoped, the bigger kids had grown tired of us so we could be left alone for a while.

After dark, perhaps a half hour or so before lights out, we were back on our beds when our lethargy was interrupted by a knock on our door. When I hollered for whoever it was to come in, I remember being surprised to see that it was Artist and one of the other upperclassmen who were paying us a visit. At first, Matt and I were confused by their timing. Artist was the one who usually gave me my nightly rituals, but it was too early just yet for us to go to bed.

"Good evening, boys," Artist announced as he rushed into our room.

"Hey," the other guy said as he carried into our room a large brown grocery sack filled with bottles of some sort which clanked together as he set it all down on my desk.

"You're a little early tonight aren't ya?" I couldn't believe it, but after barely talking to anyone all day, I was actually relieved now to have people other than my roommate to interact with. Even if they were slime balls.

"Oh, no. We're not here to do our usual thing this time. We've got a whole new program for you little guys tonight." Another thing that seemed odd was that both of these guys were wearing the same clothing—gym shorts, T-shirts and flip-flops.

"Like what?" Every time the older kids changed their pattern, Matt's first reaction was to become concerned.

"Oh don't worry," the other guy tried to reassure us as he closed our door. "You guys are gonna love it tonight."

"I've heard that before." Matt was not going to be persuaded so easily.

Up until now, Matt and I had not yet been taken by this bunch to a place where we were beyond the point of no return. To be sure, we had been introduced to behaviors and substances which we had never before experienced, and there was no question that our lives had been altered forever. Indeed, our habit now was to perform sex acts on demand with these guys any time and virtually any place they wanted, and to do so willingly and without delay. But if the upperclassmen were to suddenly become caught and thrown out of school—which we believed was about to happen now almost any day—

Matt and I then would have ended our foray into this world of homosexuality and resumed our pursuit of the fairer sex. It was true that we now liked the way it felt to get high and drunk, but with the pressure off of us, we would have continued our abuse of pot and alcohol at a greatly decelerated rate to quickly become like virtually every other kid at the Academy. So neither of us had any idea when we saw Artist pull from his pocket a small clear plastic bag filled with some kind of white powder, just how thoroughly transformed our lives, as well as our relationship as roommates and friends, were about to become. In fact, the things that happened to us later on this night affected me so profoundly, I've wound up using some of its events years later as elements in the story lines for some of my other writings.

"What's that?" Matt asked nervously.

"This?" Artist acted as if he didn't know that we were watching his every move. "Oh, nothing special."

"No really?" My curiosity was now piqued as well. "What is that?"

"Oh, for heaven sakes, just hang on." The Artist then began to look around our room for something. "I'll tell you all about it in a minute." Artist always seemed to us to be a bit effeminate.

It was tall and gross and about to fall apart, but it was exactly what Artist was needing at the moment. Matt and I watched as he laid the bag down onto the top of our dresser and then he pulled an oversized woman's makeup compact out from his other pocket and placed it next to the powder. "Do either of you boys know what this is used for?" he asked as he pointed at the compact.

"You brought it because you wanna make yourself look pretty?" Matt replied.

Suddenly I found myself smiling and chuckling out loud while I listened to the other guy laugh too. Matt was good at zinging these guys whenever the opportunity presented itself.

Artist frowned. His usual carefree attitude was now replaced by one which was far more serious. "No. Just watch for a minute and learn." He then opened the compact and pulled from it a razor blade which he also placed on our dresser.

Matt and I then looked at each other for a moment. It was a bit unnerving to us to see any of these guys with a sharp object in their possession. Neither one of us had ever been threatened by them in this way, but it seemed to make good sense to keep ourselves aware of such possibilities—just to be safe. I could tell when I looked at him that my roommate was still clueless over what was about to take place in our room, but I was pretty sure by now that I knew what was going on.

Thoughtfully, the Artist opened the plastic bag and poured a small amount of its contents onto the mirror that was housed in the lid of the compact. When he was satisfied he had the right amount, he sealed the bag and laid it back down on our dresser. Carefully then, right in front of the picture of Matt with his parents, Artist picked up the razor blade with his right hand and began to chop the powder into finer parts. This was a task he seemed to take seriously because he spent more than a minute at it—chopping and mixing, then chopping some more and mixing some more. And when he had the substance the way he wanted, Artist then spread the powder around into two equally proportioned lines which he made extend all the way across the surface of the mirror.

Once again I turned my head and looked at Matt. He caught my gaze and returned it just for an instant. It was evident to me that he didn't want to break his concentration on the bigger kid who was standing next to our dresser. "What did ya do that for?" Matt asked. We could both clearly see everything that Artist was doing.

"It needs to be chopped up into smaller pieces so it'll work better," the Artist replied.

The answer only caused my roommate to have more questions. "Work how? What's it do?"

"Just hold on, and I'll show you." Artist then began to look around our room again. "Give me that," he said to the other guy as he pointed to a disposable pen I'd left lying on my desk.

Obediently the other guy picked up my pen and handed it to Artist. "Here."

"Thanks." Artist took the pen. He then pulled off the point with the ink tube attached from one end, and he removed the stopper from the other end which left him holding a hollowed-out cylinder. With his preparations now completed, he turned his head to look one last time at Matt and me. "Now watch this," he said with his first smile in minutes. Artist then resumed his focus on the powder. He hunched himself over our dresser again and placed one end of my empty pen barrel into one of his nostrils, plugged his other nostril shut with a finger from his other hand, and then he guided the opposite end of the pen along one of the lines of powder as he sniffed it all up loudly into his nose. As soon as the first line had disappeared from the surface of the mirror, Artist removed the pen from his nose and stood straight up again. "Ah!" he exclaimed. "Wo!" Suddenly he began to act as if he had just eaten a jalapeño pepper. "Man, that's good stuff," he continued. Then, with his finger still pressed against his other nostril, Artist gave a few more loud sniffs so he could suck the powder up farther into his nasal cavity.

"Gee." It was clear that Matt had never known of anyone doing something like this. My roommate seemed a bit shook by this spectacle, and not at all certain about what he should make of what we were witnessing.

With renewed purpose, Artist continued by bending over our dresser again and, this time switching nostrils, snorted up the other line of powder into his nose. "Oh, man! Ow!" he exclaimed again as he sniffed several more times.

This time I looked at the other guy to see what his reaction was to all of this. I could see that his eyes were aimed at the powder, and he seemed to me to be inpatient to have his turn at the substance.

"Ok, Clint," Artist was now speaking in complete sentences once again. "I'm gonna cut up a couple of lines for you next."

I had done a report on cocaine the year before in school, but this was the first time I had ever seen it for real. It was startling to us both to watch someone actually take the stuff into his head. At this time in the 1970s, we were still a few years away from cocaine becoming the fashionable drug of choice in discothèques and private parties all across the country. So far the white powder, or "snow" as it was sometimes called, had only begun to show up in a few major cities which, coincidentally, included Denver and Boston. This was why I had some knowledge of the drug. I knew from the research I had done for school the year before that it seemed as if some people became addicted almost right away while others were able to use cocaine occasionally with no problem—seemingly. But I also knew that eventually, if a person used cocaine long enough, the drug would take over and become addicting, and that this point of addiction was different for everyone.

This was without a doubt, something I wanted nothing to do with, but it was clear that this substance was about to become another in the growing list which Matt and I were expected to abuse. This was not good. I knew this could lead to ruined lives for both of us, but at the same time I took some comfort in the belief that using cocaine one time probably wouldn't make us addicts. Also I knew that cocaine was expensive, and I didn't figure these characters for having the kind of money it would take to keep us high all the time in the same way they were doing to us with the pot and the beer. And so I watched with a sort of detached resignation as Artist poured some of the powder onto his mirror for me and resumed his chopping with the razor blade. While nobody spoke, I rationalized to myself that since I was not the one who was initiating my use of this drug, there was no need for me to feel guilty for what I was about to be doing. And yet at the same time, it made me feel sad to realize that I was about to be crossing over yet another line which I had never wanted to come anywhere near during my lifetime. "What's it cut with?" I asked as I tried to show off my limited knowledge.

"Well! My little man knows something about this stuff, huh?" Artist didn't stop to engage me in conversation. He kept right on chopping the powder for me as he spoke.

"I know a little," I declared. I did know that by the time it made its way to the streets, some other substance was always mixed in with cocaine. In my reading the year before, I had learned that sometimes dealers would use speed as the other substance, and I had even read of a case once where strychnine had been used. So since I had no idea where this cocaine had come from, I felt it was important for me to find out at least this much about the stuff before it was too late.

"Ah... milk sugar and I think some lanolin too," Artist replied. "All of our stuff comes from a guy who's real reputable. In fact, you'll both be meeting him tomorrow."

"Oh yeah?" I looked at Matt to see how he was handling this news. Right away I could tell that this whole business was beyond him because his expression at this moment was blank. "How come?" I asked.

Artist began to separate the powder into two long lines again. When he had finished his job, the bigger kid turned and looked at me once more so he could dismiss my curiosity. "We'll talk about that later. Now, come on over here, Clint. It's all ready for ya," Artist stated this command in a businesslike tone. And for the first time since this whole craziness had begun, I found myself with the impression that there was a bigger agenda at work here for Matt and me than either of us knew.

I hesitated for an instant. This was a big step for me and my earlier attempt to take it all in stride was now giving way to a more realistic sense of pure terror.

"Come on, Adams, let's move it," my master was now offering me some encouragement.

At this moment, I knew with certainty that I really didn't want to do this, but at the same time I knew that if I refused, the bigger kids would just slap me around—or worse, they'd slap Matt around—until I'd agree anyway. So I planted my feet on the floor and stood up.

"Well, come on, Clint. There are others waiting ya know."

I then took a step or two to bring me alongside the Artist, and then I waited for what was to come next.

"Well?" Artist was now becoming exasperated with me. "Pick up the pen and do like ya saw me do."

Slowly then, I took my eyes off of Artist and aimed them over at what he had laid out for me on the dresser top. What I saw were two neatly prepared lines of white powder which he had spread across the surface of the mirror for me to suck up into my head. I remember thinking at this moment that I ought to be clever enough to figure out some way to keep this from happening to me.

"Clint! Pick up the damn pen and do it now!" Artist wasn't going to put up with any more delay.

And so the two weeks of training which had been beaten into our bodies and stuffed into our orifices took over and I saw my hand pick up my hollowed-out pen as I leaned the upper half of my body over the top of our dresser. I wiped off the pen with my shirt and then I placed one end of the implement into a nostril while I positioned the opposite end at the beginning of the first line of powder—and then I hesitated again.

"Any more delays, Clint, and we're gonna start hittin'. Is that understood? Now get on with it!" Artist's patience had reached its limit.

"Yes, sir," I replied quickly. I understood that I had run out of time. And so I plugged my other nostril with a free finger, and I sucked hard through the pen.

"At a boy, Clint!" Artist seemed pleased with my first attempt. "Now keep goin' and finish that line."

I didn't like it. The powder irritated the membranes on the inside of my nose. Not enough to make me sneeze, but enough to cause me to think again about my desire to find some quick way out of this mess. Also, because it felt so strange to me to have what seemed like a huge wad of something up my nose, I stopped and pulled my head up after snorting in only about half of the first line. But with Artist hovering over me, I knew I had no choice but to continue, so I repositioned the pen and resumed my efforts to suck the cocaine up into my system.

"Go, Clint, go! Yeah, ya got all the first line, man! Good boy! Keep sniffin' 'til ya work it all the way up in there. How do ya feel?" Artist was suddenly a one-man cheering section for me.

"Fine," I answered as I stood up and continued to sniff the powder up higher into my head. I figured that Artist didn't want to hear how I really felt at this moment.

"Good! All right then, bend back over the dresser and do the other line." Artist didn't want me to have any time to reconsider my views, apparently.

And so I leaned over our dresser again, switched the pen to my other nostril, and then I sucked in harder than I had before. This time I made it about three quarters of the way through the second line before I had to stop. It still irritated the inside of my nose, but I paused only long enough to take a breath, and then I continued until I had vacuumed up every last grain of powder from the surface of that mirror.

"Ok, wow, man! I guess you really like that stuff. Huh?" Artist was exuberant.

At this moment, I was just relieved to be done with the deed. "I guess," was all I could think of to say in response as I continued to sniff this new hunk of cocaine up into my sinuses.

"Yeah, well all right! You go back and sit down now on your bed and wait for it to take effect. You should start feelin' it in a few minutes." Artist then turned his head and looked at my roommate. "Matt, I'm cuttin' a couple of lines up for you next."

I then sat down on my bed again and looked at Matt. He met my gaze and seemed to be asking me with his expression if I was all right. I tried to give him a reassuring nod, and then I looked back at Artist again as he began to pour some cocaine out for my friend.

"All right," Artist continued to speak as he began to chop up the powder again. "This is gonna give both you boys a nice sexy high."

What the hell does he mean by that? I wondered as I worked now to keep myself alert for any changes in my brain.

For the next ten minutes or so, things in our room continued to go along in pretty much the same way. Once again, nobody spoke until Artist had finished his chopping. Then, when he called for Matt, my roommate walked solemnly over to our dresser and took his turn at snorting the drug into his system. The other guy also took his turn after the rest of us had finished and before long, we were all feeling our highs from the cocaine.

"Man, this stuff's pretty good!" Matt volunteered once his high was in full swing.

"Yeah, no shit!" I agreed. We were both now enjoying the way the Artist's white powder was making us feel to the extent that the slight discomfort we had endured to get this way no longer seemed important to us.

"So ya like this stuff, huh?" Artist asked us both.

"Man, do I ever!" Matt answered enthusiastically.

"Oh, yeah," I concurred. But as splendidly as we were now feeling, the high from cocaine struck me as being overrated. What I mean is, it wasn't as mood altering as pot sort of is, nor was it debilitating like alcohol. It was just… a simple high which, by the way, didn't seem to last as long as the other substances we had become used to abusing. But like the other drugs, cocaine seemed to loosen our tongues so that in a short while, we were all sitting down and talking about things with these guys that we hadn't dared to talk about until now.

"Wo, what's in the sack on Clint's desk?" Matt's natural curiosity was on display again.

"Oh, you mean this grocery bag?" the other guy asked back. For some reason, people from the east used the word "bag" instead of "sack" in these instances. And there were lots of other habits of speech around here which Matt and I found bizarre. For example, instead of saying a "bar" of soap, people from this part of the country would refer to a "cake" of soap, and I don't even want to get started on all the strange names they had for milk shakes.

"Yeah," Matt confirmed. "It sounded like there're bottles in there."

"There are," Artist then took over the conversation. We watched him as he stepped over to my desk. "We're gonna have gin and tonics tonight also," he announced.

"You're kidding?" I couldn't believe this.

"No, I'm not. Why do you think I am?" Artist began to pull out the bottles and paper cups that he and the other guy had brought to our room.

"Because there's liable to be nothing left of us by morning if ya make us drink all that stuff too." I still didn't know how the cocaine was going to effect us long term and to introduce something similar in my mind to cherry vodka, struck me as downright dangerous.

"Don't worry," Artist tried to reassure me as he poured me my first gin and tonic. "The tonic will keep you from getting too drunk, and we're only gonna have a few of them. It's just to sort of put an accent on the evening." Artist then handed me the drink.

"Ok," I answered as I accepted the cup. I still wasn't sure what to make of all of this, but like everything else, what choice did I have? And when I took my first sip, I decided that I liked the way my gin and tonic tasted. "Mmmm! It's good."

"I thought you'd like it." Artist began to pour a drink for Matt. As he did, he began to talk about all sorts of subjects, and for the next fifteen minutes or so Matt and I mostly listened as our highs grew. The way we were feeling was of far greater interest to us than anything that Artist had to say, until he brought up a matter related to our first encounters with these guys in the gym shower which touched a nerve in Matt. "You know what else is good is the way you feel when you take a bone up your ass." Artist then began to pour us both our second round.

"Are you nuts?" Matt reacted without thinking.

Fortunately Artist wasn't put off by my roommate's outburst. "No, really!" he said as he handed us our new drinks. "The nights we made you guys take it in the ass, you were all upset because it was your first time and everything, and you didn't know how to deal with it. But think about it for a minute." Artist then looked directly at Matt. "Do ya know how it feels when you've got a really hard and long turd that won't come out right away? And when ya finally get it moving, it slides out real long and slow and even, and it takes a pretty long while before you get it all the way out. Do you know how that feels?"

"Yeah," Matt answered tentatively.

"Well, while it's sliding out of you it feels really good, doesn't it?"

"I guess." The look on his face told me that Matt was now trying to imagine the experience.

"Ok, well, if you relax, it can feel just as good in your ass while someone is slidin' his cock in and out of you." Artist then sat back with his gin and tonic and seemed pleased that he had just been able to impart this bit of wisdom to us both.

"Really?" Now Matt was actually sounding a little intrigued by what Artist was saying.

Man, he sure lost his anger in a hurry, I thought to myself. And then I remembered, finally, that cocaine was also supposed to intensify one's sexual appetite. *Oh, that makes sense. I guess that's maybe why Matt seems interested now in the positive things that Artist is saying about being raped.*

An hour or so after the bigger kids had first appeared in our room, Matt and I had each consumed three gin and tonics and two more lines of cocaine. The upperclassmen had gotten us thoroughly plastered and high, but we were not so far gone yet that we were completely out of control. Our conversations had stayed pretty much on the sex theme, and I remember a point in our discussions where we both admitted that we looked forward every night to receiving our blow jobs.

"Well tonight you're gonna get blow jobs too, but they're gonna be a little different from what you're used to," Artist revealed.

"What do ya mean?" I asked with an inebriated-sounding voice.

At that moment, we were interrupted by a knock on our door. "Come in!" Artist called out.

"When did this become your room?" Matt suddenly felt indignant.

When the door was opened slightly, we could all see that it was the leader who had come by. "Hey." He was sticking just his head through the opening so he could speak to Artist. "Are these guys ready to go?" Our leader seemed in a hurry, as if he had someplace where he was supposed to be.

"Yeah, I think we're all set here." I hadn't been paying attention to how many gin and tonics the Artist or the other guy had been having, but it didn't seem to me as if either of them were particularly interested in standing up and moving along at this moment.

"Ok," Leader continued in a rush. "We're all heading now to the lower campus. We'll meet you guys in a few minutes in the parking lot in front of the Annex." The leader then closed our door and left the dorm through the east door.

"Ok, we'll see ya there," Artist replied a little too late.

"So what's up now?" I asked.

"Do we have to go outside at night again?" Matt whined with his speech sounding slurred now as well.

"Yes," Artist admitted. "We've got a special night planned for both of you."

"You're not gonna hit us again are ya?" I was worried about this. We hadn't been made to do anything outside by this bunch since the pine field.

"No… no. There's no need for beatings anymore. You guys are broken in. You've been behaving just fine."

"So why do we have to go out now?" Matt asked. It was his turn.

Artist then sat up straight in his chair. "Look, this isn't going to last very long and you both are gonna love it. So stand up and let's get ready."

Matt and I looked at each other first, and then we both put our cups down, placed our feet on the floor and stood up.

"Fine," Artist was pleased. "Now, take your shirts off and put on just a plain old undershirt. Oh, and take off your socks and put your flip-flops on, and then we'll be ready to go."

Silently, Matt and I obeyed. Even in our altered conditions, we still knew that we had to do as we were told to keep from being punished. So a few moments later, we were attired as ordered and ready to receive our next set of instructions.

When they saw that we were ready to go, the bigger kids then stood up and prepared themselves to leave. "If you've got anything in your pockets, you'll probably want to leave them here," the other guy offered.

Matt and I accepted the advice and removed whatever we had in our pockets.

Artist then walked over to the front of our room and opened our door. "Ok, guys. Let's all go to the lower campus."

And with that, Matt and I followed the Artist into the hallway and out through the large wooden door on the east side of the building. Once we were outside, we were surprised to find how warm the temperature still was. We were also surprised to discover that lights out had occurred a half hour earlier. Apparently we hadn't noticed the bell while we were imbibing in our room, and for some reason the AOD that night—who if I remember correctly was supposed to be Mr. Foot, our Spanish teacher who lived in Ulster Hall—never came through our hallway to check on us.

The other guy brought up the rear as we began to descend along the set of cement steps past a pole with a single dim lamp hanging from it, until we had made our way on down to the lower campus, and then he left us to join the others when we finally caught up with the remaining six upperclassmen in the Annex parking lot. It was strange, but everyone there was dressed the same in gym shorts, undershirts, and flip-flops. Were we going to a late-night beach party at the lake?

"Welcome, boys." As it had been for us in the coach's locker room, the leader again sounded pleased to have us there. This time, though, he didn't wait for us to respond. "Ok, listen up. We are going off campus again tonight, but we're not going far. We've got a little hidden spot picked out just over the second hill heading that way." The leader then pointed his arm along the road which ran past the south side of the Academy below our dorm window and wrapped around the lake to the east toward our friend Jamie's house. "You don't have to worry about any of this because we're not planning any punishment for you little guys tonight. As long as you keep doing as we say, you should have a pretty good time tonight. All right?"

Again Matt and I chose to say nothing in response. We would go along with these guys, but we saw no reason to cheer about it.

"Fine." The leader acted as if we had responded in the affirmative, anyway. "Ok, there is one thing, though. We are going to require you two tonight to keep eye shades on for the whole time until we're done."

"Oh, man!" Matt then reacted verbally.

"Yes, well, I'm sorry, but it is necessary." Then to a couple of the upperclassmen who had apparently been selected ahead of time, "Ok, you guys go ahead and put them on the kids now."

I then watched as two of the upperclassmen placed the elastic string from a black pair of eye shades around the back of Matt's head and then they pulled the blinds down over his eyes. Once Matt could no longer see, I watched further as the two bigger kids then lifted thick handfuls of Matt's fine black hair out from under the elastic string all around his head and smoothed his hair down again with their hands so that the shades would fit him more snugly. Then, a moment later they repeated this procedure on me. And when the two sets of hands had finished fussing with my hair, I could hear the leader begin to speak again.

"Ok, we're ready. Let's go."

And with that I felt a hand wrap itself around my upper arm and give me a tug so that together one of the eight and I began to walk. Because it ran right up to the beach, there was sand all over the surface of the parking lot which crunched under the rubber soles of my flip-flops every time I took a step. When I stopped hearing this sound I knew, as we progressed, that we had left the campus and were walking, finally, along the asphalt road.

Matt and I stayed silent as we were led in blackness to wherever these perverts were taking us. I really hated being treated this way. As we walked, I recalled that first night two and a half weeks earlier when I had been led at night in this same manner to the gym. And then I remembered my meeting the next morning with Mr. Stuart and I found myself wondering what possible reason the man could have for taking so long to catch these guys. *How hard can it be?* I asked myself. *Here, a big noisy group of us have just walked freely off of the Academy grounds a half hour after lights out, and nobody has noticed us?* All I could figure was that our headmaster's love for the bottle was the thing that was causing him to move so slowly. And considering how looped I was feeling at this moment, a deep appreciation for why a person would want to stay drunk all the time was beginning to develop in me.

"Everybody stay on the side of the road in case a car happens by," the leader called out.

"At this time of night?" the head waiter responded. We were in a semi-residential area and a lot of the houses we were passing were summer cottages which had already been closed down for the winter.

"Yeah well, let's play it safe anyway. Remember, we've already got a lot invested in these kids," the leader reminded.

What the hell does he mean by that? I wondered further.

"What is he talking about?" Matt asked his guide.

"Shshsh!" was the response from my roommate's upperclassman.

We walked for about five or six minutes before I felt another yank on my arm, this time to pull me away from the lake to my right. With zombie-like compliance, I then changed my course so I could follow in the direction I was being led. Right after that, I was able to feel a change through my flip-flops as we moved from asphalt to high grass and weeds. Quickly I adjusted my stride so I could handle this change in the terrain and then we walked down a short embankment and out onto a level area toward the south. A moment later, we came to a halt at a spot which I perceived to be the center of this field we were all now standing in.

"We'll hold here," the leader called out, as he sounded once again like a military man.

"Ok, now just stand still for a while," a voice close by me said. It wasn't the guy who had been guiding me who spoke, so I figured it had to be the bigger kid who had been leading Matt.

"Ok," Matt replied.

Good! Now I knew, at least, that Matt was standing nearby. Soon after that, the others seemed to gather in more closely around us and begin to converse with one another. The bigger kids just ignored Matt and me, but in a minute heavy paper cups were placed in our hands and we were told to drink what was in them. It turned out that Matt and I had each been given our fourth gin and tonics for the evening. After walking to this place, I was ready for another drink, so I downed mine fairly quickly and it seemed to me as if Matt wound up doing the same. Apparently someone had brought a thermos of them or something, because it sounded to me as if everyone around me was drinking after a while.

And so I found myself at one of the strangest cocktail parties I had ever attended. Matt and I stood blindfolded, talking to no one, while all who were around us carried on as if everything on this night were perfectly normal. And five minutes later, the only changes that could be heard were the sounds of Matt and me sniffing up the remnants of the two new lines apiece of cocaine which the bigger kids had just given to us. Then a few minutes later, around the time the new gin and the new cocaine in my system were coalescing to dull my brain and excite my loins to levels I had never before experienced, I could hear the others around us snorting up their own portions of the drug. It was also at about this same moment when I came to understand for myself that everything I had heard in the past about how cocaine makes people who use it feel super horny was true. I was now aching for sex and I didn't care who or what they were going to make me have it with—I just knew I had to have it, and I had to have it right now! And finally, when I was about to explode and ask out loud why the hell we were here, the leader began to speak again.

"Ok, let's get started." He knew that we were both now stoked from the cocaine and ready to perform any sex act they wanted from us.

I wasn't sure but, when I focused just then on what the leader was saying, I got the impression suddenly that more people were now with us in this field. But there was no time for me to consider this new idea because as soon as the leader had spoken, hands were grabbing at my belt and zipping down my fly. A moment later these hands had succeeded in pulling down my pants and my underpants so that both garments could lie useless around my ankles.

"Lean forward and put your hands on my back," a voice instructed me.

I did as I was told. I placed my hands along the undershirt-clad back of an upperclassman who had bent over in front of me, while his hands helped me out of my pants, underpants and flip-flops. Once they were finished with me, I heard the bigger kids then put Matt through the same routine. A moment later, we were both standing in the middle of this field, in front of who knew how many people now, drunk, high and naked from the waist down. Whatever it was that the upperclassmen had in store for us on this night, it was quite clear now that things were about to begin.

"Ok, little guys, lay down on the ground," the leader commanded.

Matt and I did as we were told and lay down on our backs. I was glad that I had been allowed to keep my undershirt on because grass always made my skin itch. It's never seemed to bother me that much to have grass against my butt or my legs, but it has always made my back uncomfortable.

"Ok, guys. Pick 'em up."

Somebody then reached down and rolled me over onto my stomach.

"Wo!" Matt called out as two sets of hands grabbed his wrists and his ankles and lifted him up into the air.

"Hey!" An instant later I had left the ground as well.

We didn't know it yet, but our field was adjacent to a yard and a house which had been closed down for the winter. Somehow the upperclassmen had managed to get the water at this house turned back on and for the past three days or so had been letting it run through a long garden hose out into a deep and thick patch of mud which measured about fifteen feet square and sat menacingly along the eastern edge of our field. Then, at around noontime on this day, the bigger kids turned off the water and allowed the sun and the late summer heat we were having to bake the ingredients so that by the time we arrived, the area had become a soupy sloppy mess.

"Ok now… we understand that you two love to be given blow jobs." The leader was sounding a bit over animated by now.

A general clamor of laughter then rose from the crowd in response.

I was being carried prick down across the field to a destination which I assumed had been picked out ahead of time. But with my blindfold on I had no idea where they were taking me or what was going on at this moment.

"So tonight we're gonna sixty-nine you two so you guys can give each other blow jobs at the same time. Ha ha," the leader then laughed along with the others.

We're gonna what? I wondered. And then before I had a chance even to speak, I was placed face down onto someone's stomach and my legs were released into some sort of a cool mushy substance.

"Clint, get up on your knees and elbows, man. Your dick's in my face."

It was Matt. They had placed me on top of Matt. I realized, then, that they must have laid my roommate here on his back first. Immediately I did as he asked and planted my knees and elbows into the ooze so I could lift myself slightly off of my friend's body. And as I did this, I realized that Matt's penis was pressed up against my face as well. *Sixty-nine?* I thought. *When both numbers are placed together, they look like the same number with one of them inverted. I get it. Matt and I are now sixty-nined.*

"Ok, you two… take each other's dick into your mouth and start giving each other a blow job. And you guys can't leave here until each of you have cum. So get going!" The leader's speech was sounding a bit slurred by now from the gin and tonics I figured he was enjoying.

Mud! I could smell it now, it was mud they had stuck us in. And considering how much of a struggle I was finding it to move in this stuff, poor Matt must have been sunk about halfway down.

"Come on, boys," the head waiter then yelled. "Start suckin' on those dicks!"

Oh shit! I thought as the reason for why we had been positioned this way finally sunk in. Matt and I had been worried that something like this was going to happen, ever since that morning a week earlier when we had awakened in my bed together. Instantly though, I felt Matt search for a moment with his tongue and his lips, and then I felt him take my penis into his mouth. As soon as he had me, Matt began to swirl his tongue around my crown and slide it up and down my shaft, and I found myself surprised to notice that right away my penis was beginning to swell. In fact, my roommate was doing such a terrific job on me, I was actually finding it hard to continue to move. *This kid's got real talent,* I thought to myself. And then I realized that the cocaine in my system was probably causing me to respond so profoundly to Matt's stimulation.

I then could feel my penis set free like a projectile from Matt's mouth, so I did the same with his.

"Ok now, I want you two to hug each other and roll over so that Clint will be on the bottom and Matt will be on top."

Since we had been taught to obey, I dug my arms down into the mud until I was able to wrap them around Matt's bare butt, and when I felt his arms around mine, I strained to pull us over. A moment later I felt my entire backside plop down hard into the thick and gooey mud and as Matt settled himself on top of me, I could feel the back of my head sink down a ways into the mess.

"Ok, now take each other's dicks into your mouths and keep going down on each other until you both cum." The leader sounded so pleased by what he was making us do, he was almost giggling now.

When Matt and I landed together in our new positions, I had felt his hard wet penis slap against my cheek just as I had felt my own penis hit him in his face. Neither of our penises had moved away from our faces when the leader gave us his order to resume, nevertheless Matt had me in his mouth and was working me before I could get going on him again. But in another moment, we were both fully engaged in our attempts to get the other to ejaculate.

"At a boy, Clint," one of the upperclassmen called out. "Give Matt a good one."

For a while then, this was the scene. Matt and I tried to please our masters by lying in the mud and working hard to please each other. And I suppose the cocaine also gave us both hair triggers because in a short while I could feel Matt's penis throbbing between my lips as his semen was released into my mouth. And then about the time I could feel the tension leave my friend's body, I lost control and emptied myself out into his mouth.

"All right!" the leader shrieked. "You guys are really close friends, now. Remember, friends always swallow friends' cum."

And so we did. Now, besides being roommates and friends, Matt and I were sex partners. It hadn't been something that we had wanted, but it seemed to be a dimension to our relationship which we both now had to live with. And then before we had a chance to absorb the full impact of what we had just done to each other, I felt Matt's body lifted up and away from me suddenly as hands grabbed my wrists and ankles at the same time. I was then lifted into the air, spun around so I could be pointed in the opposite direction, scooted over to my left a bit, and then plopped on my back into the mud again. Matt was deposited on his back in the mud just next to me to my right. Immediately after we were settled again, hands then began to shovel mud onto our bodies to cover us over completely.

"Ok, now… we're gonna keep your faces free of mud, but the rest of you we're gonna bury. We want you guys to think of yourselves as part of the earth now, and as soon as you're done, each of us here are gonna come by and plant our seeds in ya. Ha, ha, ha." The leader then led the rest of the crowd in even more laughter.

As mud continued to be heaped onto my body, other hands tied ropes around my wrists and then pulled my arms over my head, spread them apart, and then staked them down into the mud. Once my arms were immobilized, I felt ropes then tied around my ankles. My legs were then spread apart and staked down in the mud as well. With my movements now restricted, mud continued to be pushed onto me until my legs and arms had become just as hidden from view as the rest of my body.

"So how are we doing here?" I heard Artist ask me as he knelt down next to me and slopped a bunch of mud into my hair.

"I don't know, you tell me. What the hell is all of this about?" For obvious reasons, I was becoming terrified over what was being done to me.

"Well, there's no reason to be afraid. I'm gonna do a little mud sculpting on you to get you ready, and then you're just gonna give blow hobs to any of us who happens to come by to shove a dick into your mouth. And then when we've all been serviced by you two, we'll let you both go and you guys can go back to your room for the rest of the night. Ok?"

"I guess." It wasn't as if I had any choice in the matter, but I was grateful that Artist had been willing to clue me in. So I settled in to become a mud sculpture, or a part of the earth, or whatever the hell it was that they were wanting me to be for them.

"Now you're gonna find out how I got my name," Artist revealed.

"Ok." I was ready to learn. I then felt Artist slop more mud into my hair, and he kept doing this until he had my hair completely saturated. Artist then spent about a minute shaping the mud so it would look pretty much the same as my hair usually did—with bangs and over my ears mostly.

"Ok," Artist continued. "There's one more thing I need to do with you."

Next I felt him reach down around my groin and dig out my penis. He brushed some of the mud away and then he began to stroke me with his hand. Like most guys, it normally takes me at least fifteen minutes or so to recover after ejaculating. And at first I was worried that Artist's stroking was going to be painful for me. But again the cocaine really seemed to be doing a number on my sex drive, so immediately I began to feel stimulated from the friction and the feeling of his hand on me. "Uuh!" I moaned as he began to set up a steady rhythm. In no time he had worked my penis into a fully hardened erection and I felt as if I was quickly being launched into a state of ecstasy. "Uuh… Ah!" And as my body began to tense, and as I was getting ready to enter the home stretch, Artist let go of my penis, stood up and walked away.

"Where are you going?" I called after him in a panic. "Aren't you gonna finish me off?"

"That's all ya get for now," was all he said as I heard him walk away to do the same to Matt.

More laughter then rose from the crowd. This was obviously part of their plans to torture us.

And so, since I seemed to have a few minutes, I lay there quietly and tried to listen to the many conversations which were going on around me. As I concentrated, I found it didn't take too long before I began to notice that I was able to hear a few full-grown male voices in the crowd. This, of course, caught my attention right away, so I tried to sort out these adult voices from the others so I could figure out if any of them sounded familiar to me. At about this same time, because I was lying down and because it was late, I suppose, the alcohol and the pot in my system seemed to be taking me over and I realized all of a sudden that I was falling asleep. As the seconds were ticking by now, I was finding it increasingly difficult to keep myself conscious until soon I was beginning to blink in and out. When I was awake, I decided that the grown-up voice that was talking with the leader seemed to be the one that was the closest to me. But just as I would begin to focus in on what the man was saying, I would blank out again for a few seconds.

"Yeah, it was a good idea to let them keep their undershirts on. That way they can retain their body heat longer while they're in the mud," the man's voice said. "I think with the next two you ought to…"

Huh? I was awake again, but I didn't see why I needed to keep fighting sleep anymore. After all, I was pretty comfortable now just lying here and…

"Oh, I think you boys have done a marvelous job with these kids. They're gonna be our best ones yet," the man continued.

…Best? What did he mean by that? This last comment struck me as something I ought to be concerned about, but at the same time, did it really matter all that…

"You know I'm certainly glad that neither of these boys ever went to see the baba."

WHAT! I was awake now and staying that way. *Did I just hear what I thought I heard?*

"If either of these kids had gone to see the baba, then they wouldn't have this great-looking cock-sucker hair they've got now."

"Cock-sucker hair?" the leader asked. "What's that?"

"Oh, well.. their hair is so nice and long and straight and fine, that whenever they're giving someone a blow job and their heads get jerked suddenly, it makes their hair ripple across their heads. Our customers love that. That's why we call it cock-sucker hair."

I was stunned beyond words. The voice I was hearing belonged to Mr. Stuart. This was a nightmare which had just become a reality. I now understood that our leader had a boss, and that boss was our headmaster. No wonder he never caught these guys. He had always been one of them. Now I knew there was no hope for us. There was never going to be any rescue. Matt and I were truly doomed to live this way for as long as… And then I wondered suddenly what Mr. Stuart had meant when he had talked about customers.

"Uuh! Ah!" Matt groaned as he responded to the stroking he was receiving from Artist's hand.

"Ok, I'm done," I heard Artist say a moment later. And then I heard him stand up and walk past me to where the leader and the headmaster were standing.

"But aren't you gonna finish?" Matt called out. His voice sounded so pathetic to me now. "Hey! Don't leave me like this!" There is nothing worse for a guy to be started up and then not allowed to finish.

The leader laughed again with the rest of the crowd, and then he resumed his announcements. "All right!" the leader then called out to everyone who had assembled around us. "It's time to start planting our seeds. So let's get to gardening."

A cheer then went up from the field and I began to hear the sounds of fabric swishing all around me as everyone there, I guess, began to slip off their gym shorts and flip flops.

Some joke, I thought. I then noticed a light rain beginning to fall as I waited for whoever was going to be my first customer. (Now I was thinking like Mr. Stuart.) The drops felt good on my face and I listened as our headmaster seemed to be the one who was coming closer to me.

"I've had my eye on this kid ever since the first day he walked into my office with his parents. I just love blonds, you know, and this one's really cute."

And then I felt the rain on my face being blocked by the headmaster's body as he got down on all fours above me. "What the hell?" I shouted without thinking. It was still so hard for me to believe that our headmaster was actually about to do me. But the table had been set, and the rules had been stated. And now my real debauching was at hand.

"Shut up, Adams," the head of our faculty barked. And then Mr. Stuart placed his hand on my face and squeezed my cheeks together to purse my lips.

There was nothing I could do. With the headmaster's hand now holding my face, I couldn't move my head, and with the ropes holding me down, I couldn't get away. And frankly with the drugs and alcohol so strong in my system, I didn't have the will to even try to stop any of this from happening to me. And so, I accepted the headmaster's penis when it was thrust into my mouth. Then a moment later as he removed his muddy hand from my face and placed it in the mud above my head to steady himself, I made my lips rigid and I sucked on his penis as hard as I could so I could demonstrate to this man the thoroughness of my training and deliver to the person whose responsibility it was to look after my welfare, a really fine blow job.

Every so often I could hear someone speak to Matt, or I could hear Matt make the smacking sounds as he performed his service on others. So I figured that the crowd had divided itself into two lines so that everyone there could have a turn at one or the other of us. Also, I guessed that the cocaine was giving everyone hair triggers tonight because it seemed as if they all were moving right along. In no time, I could feel the headmaster's cum filling my mouth, and then he pulled himself out of me.

"Good job, kid," I heard Mr. Stuart say as he moved himself away from me and allowed the rain to fall once again on my face. "I always knew you'd be a good addition to the Academy." And when he was on his feet again, I heard him speak next to someone nearby. "You see? If you always keep their mouths filled, they can't complain."

A moment later I again couldn't feel the rain on my face, which told me that another person was now hunching over me.

"Ok, Clint. I want you to remember to suck me this time."

It was the leader who was in position above me now. I then felt his fingers become wrapped around my penis and then he began to stroke me. "Uuh!" I moaned right away. In no time his steady stroking had my erection back, and soon after that the leader had me breathing in short sharp gasps. I was now completely under his control and eager to have him continue until he would bring me to another ejaculation. I was loving this. I never wanted his stroking to end. *Oh, man,* I couldn't believe it! The leader had now put me into a world of ultimate pleasure and as my body began to tense and I prepared myself for the time that was soon to come when my penis would go into frantic spasms which would yank the rest of my body in sweet splendor along with it, he let go of my penis and squeezed together my cheeks with his hand as he then plunged his penis into my mouth. Instantly I reacted by sucking as hard as I could while I clamped my lips down hard on him. I was wild with stimulation and I was going down on him as ferociously as my smaller body would allow.

"Aw yeah! That feels great, Clint!"

Now I was causing the leader to gasp. I had his penis under my control and I wasn't letting go until it had issued forth fully.

"Priming the pump, huh?" a voice from the crowd observed.

"Yeah! Ah… God! It works great! Go, Clint! This is one of the best ones I've ever had. Aw yeah!" The leader was most definitely enjoying the blow job I was giving him.

They didn't "prime my pump" every time a new person took his turn with me. They didn't want to take the chance that I might ejaculate and then lose my drive. So every second or third guy would stroke me and put me back into the stratosphere for a short while, and then he would plunge his penis into my mouth and I would automatically convert all of that sexual energy into giving him the best blow job I could. And it sounded to me as if they were doing the same thing to Matt. Every so often I could hear him begin to moan and breathe as if he was getting close to having an orgasm. And then the sounds would stop and all I'd be able to hear then would be the smacking sounds we both made as we performed our jobs. There also would be some laughter from the crowd around him after every occasion like this. I suppose there was laughter around me too whenever they pulled this trick on me, but I didn't care. I was always too swept away by the emotions of the moment to notice.

After the leader had finished with me, I stopped waiting for the next guy to grab my cheeks and squeeze them to force me to open. Instead, I just opened my mouth automatically and then waited for my next customer every time I felt the rain blocked from falling onto my face. This response to every newcomer worked fine for a while until some other man came along to take his turn with me. I wasn't sure, but I suspected that this man was our cook. The reason why I didn't know his identity for certain was because we rarely heard Thomas speak. On this occasion, he smelled like liquor and was mighty mean when he took his position over me. Once he was settled on all fours, he grabbed my face hard with his large hand and then he shook my face as he squeezed my cheeks together.

"You're lyin' here in this field an' just thinkin' that everyone who comes to do you is gonna be nice 'nd all. Well let me tell ya, I'm now gonna shove my big black dick into your lily white mouth and I expect the best damn blow job you've ever given anyone. Otherwise, I'll start beatin' on you, boy, and I won't quit 'til you're all broken and bloody and cryin' for mercy." And then he stuffed himself into my mouth.

This time it didn't take any priming of my pump to get me going. I sucked and clamped down on him as hard as I possibly could. And when it was all over I figured that I must have done a decent job in satisfying him because he never hit me.

At some point during the evening, Mr. Stuart made an announcement while Matt and I were both in the middle of servicing people. "After you're all done here, we've got a little celebration planned for all of you big people here. Little guys can't come. I want all of you to meet up in the Annex. We've brought in two carloads of hookers down from Worcester for you all tonight. I think we cleaned out that whole town of hookers, frankly. Anyway, we've also got plenty of nose candy and booze to go around for everyone. Including the girls. So as soon as you're done here, go get cleaned up and meet us in the Annex."

A cheer then rose up from the field again. I wasn't sure why they were celebrating, but under the circumstances, I was just as glad that Matt and I weren't invited. And then after that, I turned my attentions back to the guy whose penis was filling my mouth.

***

I don't know how many guys I serviced that night. I suppose it was maybe eight or nine penises which had been shoved into my mouth before the event was over. I just remember coming to all of a sudden and realizing that no one was around me anymore. The rain was still falling on my face and when I moved my arms I found that the stakes which had been holding them down earlier were now pulled up out of the mud for me. And so I brought my hands to my face and pulled off my eye shades so I could finally get a look around.

I saw that indeed the bigger kids and the men had left us behind. I then looked over to my right and saw Matt still lying with his body and his limbs completely covered over with mud, looking to me to be unconscious. "Matt!" I called over to him, but he didn't move. "Hey, Matt, wake up!" Again he didn't respond. So I sat up and spent the next minute or two untying the ropes from my wrists and ankles. Once I was free again, I stood up and walked over to help my friend. When I reached him I saw that he was still staked down. There were muddy hand prints and semen on his face and I thought I could hear him snoring. *Hmmm,* I thought. *Artist did a nice job of sculpting his hair. Very life-like.* "Come on, Matt," I hollered out loud. "We've gotta go. You're gonna freeze if you stay out here all night."

"SNORE!" Matt was clearly sleeping.

There was no time for this. We were both going to be freezing soon if I didn't get us going. So I got down into the goosh again—this time on my knees—and I circled my friend slowly so I could untie the ropes which were still restraining his movements. Then I sat back on my legs alongside the boy and spoke to him again. "Matt!"

"SNORE!"

He looked so peaceful there, I hated to disturb him. But we couldn't stay out here in the cool mud and survive the night. So I thrust my arms into the slop the boy was lying in until I had them under his back and then I hefted my friend up into a sitting position and shook his face and body to wake him while I also pulled off his eye shades.

"Huh? What are ya doin'?" he asked me as he became conscious again.

"Come on, Matt, we've gotta get back to the dorm and get ourselves warmed up."

But Matt wasn't going to be convinced so easily. They had used him to the point of utter exhaustion, and it was hard for him now just to sit. "I just want'a sleep, Clint. Just let me sleep here, ok? I'll be fine," he begged.

"Not here. We gotta go back to the dorm first. And then I'll let you sleep. Ok?" I then stood up and as the rain ended, I began to pull up on him by his arms.

"Ok." With my help then, Matt rose to his feet.

Next, I looked around for our clothes. As before the others had taken our pants and underpants but this time, at least, they had left us our flip-flops. So with my arm around my friend to steady him as we both began our journey back to our dorm, I walked us over to where the felons had left our footwear and I helped Matt on with his pair before I put on my own. Once this task was completed, it was time for us to leave the field. As I looked around for the way out, I was surprised to see how secluded the area really was. There were plenty of trees and bushes around the perimeter which made this place pretty private.

After another minute or so had passed, I had managed to put us back on the road again and headed toward the Academy. As we walked I worried that someone might drive by and stop to inquire if we were all right. I figured that two boys walking along a back country road in the middle of the night, naked from the waist down and completely covered in mud would be more than a little difficult to explain. So I kept trying to get Matt to walk faster, but the best he was able to do was a moderately paced shuffle.

Seven or eight minutes later, we were standing in the parking lot in front of the Annex. Finally, we were back on Academy ground. Rock music was playing loudly from inside the coffee house, and we could hear chatter and the sounds of people having fun. I still wondered what the celebrating was all about, but for the moment I decided that it didn't matter.

"Come on, Clint, let's go to our room."

"Just wait a minute, Matt. We can't go to bed all covered in mud like this, and we can't get it off of us in the shower. This much mud would clog the drain before we could get clean. So we're first gonna have to go into the lake to get as much of this crap off of us as we can."

"Oh, Clint, no. Do we have ta?" Matt was barely able to keep himself upright.

"Yeah, I'm afraid we do, Matt."

I then led Matt across the parking lot and onto the sandy beach. We walked past the Annex and straight into the lake.

"Oh, Clint. This water's cold," Matt complained.

"I know." As the rain began to fall on us again—this time it was coming down much harder—I pulled my friend's undershirt off over his head and then I did the same with my own so I could throw them both over onto the beach and out of our way. "Use your hands to wipe the mud off of your body while I dunk myself."

"Ok."

I took a deep breath, and then I bent my knees and went under the surface of the water. While under I ran my hands through my hair and over my face so I could get rid of as much of the mud as possible. But after all that the others had put us through that night, I found I didn't have a lot of wind, so in another moment I popped my head back above the surface so I could gasp in some air and fill my lungs again.

"Clint, I don't know if I have enough strength to do that."

"That's ok. I'll help you." As water drained from my hair and face, I stepped closer to my roommate so I could stand directly in front of him. Next, I grabbed hold of his arms. "Ok, now bend your knees and I'll do the rest."

"Oh, Clint! Isn't there some other way to do this?" Matt sounded so tired.

"Come on, Matt. Here's your big chance to go swimming in the lake, finally."

"Ok." And with that, Matt took in a deep breath, allowed his knees to buckle beneath him, and down into the water he plunged.

In the same way I had done for myself, I began to run my hands through his hair and over his face to get as much of the mud and other stuff off of him as I could. And because I figured that Matt's wind was as short as mine seemed to be on this night, as soon as I could feel more boy than mud I quickly pulled on him to raise him back above the surface. As he came up I watched as water poured from his head and left his black hair hanging down over his face nearly to the tip of his nose. While he coughed and gasped for air, I used the heel of my hand to push his hair up and away from his eyes so he could see again. "Ok, Matt. Let's get out of here and get inside."

"Ok, Clint," Matt stammered as his body began to shiver from the coldness of the water.

Immediately we turned around and waded out of the lake and then one more time we walked across the beach. When we were standing on the pavement in the parking lot once again, I turned us to the right so we could make our way to the cement steps which by now seemed harshly lit by that single lamp on the pole which was located about halfway up the hill in front of us. No one ever took a break from their revelry in the Annex to come outside and check on our conditions, but if anyone had come looking for us a few moments later, they would have observed two naked boys on the steps with rain water dripping and streaming in silhouette from every inch of our heads and bodies. And it was in this manner that we slowly made our way up the hill to our dormitory.

Several times on our way up I had to stop as the rain just poured down over us, to give Matt a chance to catch his breath, but eventually we made it to the landing and on into our hallway.

"Bed!" Matt called out as soon as we were inside. "I'm ready for bed now, Clint." Matt was so tired.

"Not yet," I commanded. "We're too dirty still. Plus we're both freezing." By now I was shivering too. "We're gonna have to take a shower first."

"No, Clint." Matt protested weakly. "I've just had a bath in the lake and a shower in the rain. I wanna go to bed, man!"

"We need to get into the hot water so it'll warm us up. Plus we're not really clean yet. Now come on," I said as I pulled Matt with me by his arm into the bathroom.

Once we were inside the small room, I closed the door behind us and turned on the water in the shower. While we waited for the water to get hot I reasoned that I couldn't put Matt aside while I showered first and Matt didn't look to me to have the strength to clean himself if I put him in there first, so I figured that we would both have to go into the shower at the same time. The single metal stall was barely big enough for a full-grown man. It would be a tight squeeze for the two of us in there but under the circumstances, I couldn't see how we had any other choice.

A few moments later, when the water was finally hot enough, I pulled on Matt's arm again. "Come on, Matt, let's get in."

"Ok, Clint." He wasn't arguing with me anymore. He knew that in another moment he'd be warm again.

And so I stepped into the shower first and then I pulled my friend in to join me. Right away I found my task with him was like trying to wash a baby. Matt was having trouble standing on his own so I figured I was going to have to lean him up against something to keep him upright. At first I tried to lean him against one of the walls so I could rub the soap over different sections of his body and then angle the shower head toward him whenever I needed to rinse him off. But I kept having to keep one of my hands braced against his body all the time so I could prevent my roommate from collapsing. So finally, the only practical solution I could come up with was to turn him to face the front of the shower, and then pull the boy backwards until he was able to rest against the front of my body. In this way, at least, I was able to have both of my hands free to wash us.

And so I embarked on an effort to wash us both as if we were one person. I began by taking some of my shampoo from the shelf just outside the shower where I kept it and pouring it into both of our hair at the same time. After some rubbing and once I had the lather built up for both of us, I then put our heads under the stream of water together so I could rinse us off at the same time. After all, considering how intimate we had been forced to become earlier that night, I saw no sense in worrying any longer over where we were touching each other now. Even so, it took me a couple of moments to work up the nerve I needed to place my hands all over the boy's groin area and inside his butt crack so I could wash him in those places.

"Clint?"

"Yeah, Matt?" With him leaning backwards against me still, I had my arms extended out in front of us both so I could finish washing his chest and neck. To steady myself, I was letting his weight pin me against the back wall of the shower.

"Do me will ya?" He wasn't shivering any longer, but his speech was still a little slurred.

"What?" I wasn't sure I understood what he was asking me.

"I said do me. With your hand. Those guys kept stroking my dick and getting me all worked up, and then they never let me cum. Clint, I'm so tensed up inside, I'm about to explode. I need your help 'cause I'm not strong enough to do it myself right now."

"Well then jerk off once you're in bed," I suggested.

"No, Clint. I don't wanna get cum all over my sheets. Please do me, Clint. Do me now. I need a release. It's drivin' me mad."

"I… I don't know, Matt. It doesn't seem right." I was conflicted. I wanted to help him any way I could, but I didn't want us to start doing things like this with each other all the time.

"Come on, Clint. After everything we've been through tonight, I need you to help me with this." And then Matt reached up and took hold of my soap-covered left hand.

If it had been any other time I would have pulled my hand away from his immediately. But the cocaine in me was still incredibly strong and my appetite for sex—any sex—seemed beyond my power to control. And I was certain that Matt was suffering in this same way. Plus after all the changes we had gone through for the past two weeks, I guess I was curious now to see just how far Matt would actually go. So I did nothing as my roommate began to take my hand down to his groin. I then watched as he placed our fingers around his penis and then together he caused us both to begin to stroke him. After the first couple of strokes had been executed, Matt let his hand drop to his side as his head fell back to rest against my shoulder and the side of my head.

"Ok, Clint. Keep it goin'. Do me, man. Do me good." Just that much effort had seemed to tire out my friend again.

Since I had already begun, I figured that it would make no sense now for me to say I couldn't do this, so I continued to stroke his penis. And so by default, I guess, the decision was made for me to help Matt to release his pent-up pressure. Because our bodies were pressed together so tightly, soon I was able to detect even the slightest reactions inside of him to my hand movements. As I sensed these twitches and muscle tightenings, I immediately began to feel an almost spiritual connection to the boy as if I no longer existed separately and instead had become part of my friend and he of me. Every time I felt these changes inside of Matt, it was as if the same muscles were constricting inside of me. And whenever Matt inhaled sharply and then held his breath, I held my breath right along with him. And as I quickened the pace of my stroking, and I was able to feel his body stiffen all over, my body tensed up also. It was an amazing experience. In fact, I was so moved by the closeness we were sharing, it almost felt to me as if I was conducting a science experiment of some kind and had discovered religion instead.

"Uuh! Ah!"

Matt's moaning encouraged me to quicken the pace of my strokes once again. I then reached out and readjusted the shower head so the running water would hit us in our chests and faces.

"Uhoof! Uhoof!" In no time it sounded and felt to me as if Matt had nearly reached his climax. Faster still I moved my hand on his penis, and then three times in a row I felt him take in a breath and hold it, and then Matt stopped breathing altogether. Should I stop? No, I decided I needed to keep up the friction. And so I squeezed his penis harder and as soon as I did this, I felt it begin to pump his semen past my fingers and out onto the shower floor.

"Ahahahahhhh!" Matt's body then jerked forward as I kept stroking his penis. As I felt his pumping continue, Matt jerked his body then to his right, and then he jerked it again to his left. Instantly after that, I felt the pumping end, so I stopped my stroking and squeezed the upper and under sections of his penis at its base between my thumb and forefinger, and then I ran my fingers up his shaft to push out any remaining semen. At this point, I knew that any further handling on my part would be painful for my friend, so I let him go. As I did this, I could feel a shiver make its way quickly down Matt's body, and then he relaxed against me more completely than he had before.

"Ohhhh!! Thanks, Clint," he was out of breath and still leaning his head against the side of my own.

"You're welcome, Matt." I was a little winded myself. Of course now a bit more washing was in order, so I reached up and took the bar of soap into my hands. When I had a lather worked up, I returned the soap to its plate and then I reached down to gently wash off Matt's penis for him.

"Oo, careful," he cautioned.

"Don't worry, I know it's tender after cumming." At first I didn't realize what Matt was doing. I was too busy trying to wash him off. But in a moment, I could feel that he had reached around between us, and had taken my penis in between his fingers.

"I've been feeling your dick against my butt and I can tell that you need a release too, Clint."

Because I had been paying such close attention to Matt's needs, I hadn't noticed that more than ten minutes of having my own penis rubbing up against his skin had apparently given me a substantial erection. "No, Matt. I'm fine, really." My mind was working sensibly for the moment, but I knew that if he didn't let me go now, in no time my rational thinking would be out the window. And then I felt him begin to stroke me. "Uh, Matt!"

"Come on," he stroked me again. "You need a release really bad too, man."

"Uuh!" As I felt another stroke, I realized that my roommate was right. It had been an awful trick for the upperclassmen to get me all jazzed up as they had, and then not allow me to finish. And I had to admit, Matt's stroking did feel… "Uuh!" He did it again.

"Come on, Clint. You need this and you know it." And then Matt stroked my penis again.

"Uuh!" And with that stroke, he had me. I couldn't resist it any longer. I gave up by leaning my head back so it could rest against the rear wall of the shower and by letting my arms drop to my sides. The control of my body was now given over to Matt. I would do nothing now to prevent him from stroking me as much as he wanted. "Uuh! Uuh! Uuh!" It did, after all, feel incredible!

For the next thirty seconds or so, the only sounds being made in our bathroom were the sounds of the water running from our shower and the sounds of my groans after each of Matt's amazing strokes on my swollen penis. And then Matt spoke to me again while he continued to stroke me. "Clint?"

"Huh?" I was quickly on my way to a better place. "Uuh!"

"I don't have enough strength to go all the way with you with my hand, so I want you to put that baby oil you've got on your dick and do me in my ass."

"What? Are you kidding me? Uuh!"

"No, really. I've been thinking about what Artist said tonight, and I want'a try it again. Please, Clint. Do me in my ass." Matt began to stroke me harder to get me to give in. "Please, Clint."

"Uuh! No, Matt. Come on, you don't really want me to… Uuh!"

"Come on." Matt began to chant with every stroke.

"Uuuh! No… Ah!"

"Do me in my ass!"

"Ah!"

"Do me, Clint!"

"Uuh!"

"You need it, Clint, do me!"

"Uuuh!" This time he had me. I couldn't put up a fight any longer. "Ok! Ok, I'll do it, Matt. I'll do it!" I gasped. Any willpower I had possessed earlier was now just an inconvenient memory. I then felt Matt's hand drop away from me, and I watched him as he bent himself forward and away from me.

"I figure if I lay my arms across the cold and hot water handles like this, and I bend my knees a little and spread my legs apart, that'll give you the right angle to get your dick into me." Matt then got himself ready to accept my erection. I didn't know where Matt had suddenly found the energy to stand on his own like this. Again, perhaps the cocaine which was still with us both was drawing from his last little bit of strength. In any case, there was no denying that he was serious about having me go through with this act.

"All right," I agreed. My toiletries were in a bag which was lying on a shelf just outside the shower. So to keep the baby oil from washing off of me, I re-angled the shower head so that the water would pour down now directly onto the back of Matt's head, and then I pulled the curtain back slightly and reached out to get the bottle I had purchased in town during our first weekend at the Academy. An instant later, I had the bottle in the shower with us and was pouring some of its contents onto my fingers. As I had learned from the leader the night he had raped me in the gym shower, I then stuck my oily fingers up into Matt's anal cavity. Once I had him oiled up, I then poured more of the oil over my penis and stroked myself with it until I had the oil all over me and I had made my erection rock hard. I then bent my knees and guided my penis with my hand to Matt's hole while I placed my other hand on his hip. "Are you sure you want me to do this?" I figured I'd better give Matt one more chance to change his mind.

Matt responded by reaching behind him once again so he could wrap his fingers around my penis to stroke me a few more times. "Do me," he chanted.

"Uuh!" As before, I responded right away.

"Do me…"

"Ah!"

"Do me, Clint!"

"Aahhh!"

"Do me!"

"Uuuhh!"

"Do me now!"

"Ok," I gasped again. I couldn't take his tormenting any longer. If he wanted it, he was going to get it. And so I spread some more oil over my penis, and then I squared myself up and I jammed my projectile into his ass.

"Auh!" Matt reacted when he felt me enter him.

I went in easier than I had thought I would, so I continued to push myself in until my penis had disappeared entirely into my friend's anus.

"Auhauh! Ugh! Ah!" Matt worked to get comfortable with me inside of him.

"Are you ready?" I asked. The time had passed for giving him the option to quit. I was inside of him now and I was liking the way it was feeling.

"Ah!" he gasped. And then he took three quick breaths. "Hhhh! Hhhh! Hhhh! Ok," he said as he sounded out of breath. "Go for it!"

And so—so help me—I began to rape my roommate. Every time I'd pull back he'd sigh, and every time I'd thrust in again, he'd cry out. But after a little bit of time had passed, he got used to me, somewhat, and then it seemed as if he was trying to enjoy me. And I think from then on he did enjoy me.

"Ah.. ok…that's auhauh! feels ok… yeah… ouw! oh… ok…"

I hated to admit it, but it felt fabulous to be up in Matt's ass. And when I finally ejaculated into my friend, and after I had pulled myself out, I felt utterly satisfied and grateful that Matt had insisted that I rape him. At the same time, I wondered how Matt was going to judge our encounter.

"Well…" Matt started to speak as he stood up and placed his backside under the water to rinse himself off one more time. He then looked at me and smiled as water dripped from his chin and ear lobes. "Artist was right!"

***

Daylight! Reality presented itself with a vengeance the next morning. As soon as my eyes were open, I found myself confronted by a cascade of emotions which were not going to let me off the hook. The biggest of which was embarrassment! It wasn't so much the embarrassment from being made to perform blow jobs while everyone watched and cheered me on. As humiliating as these experiences always were, I had already learned to deal with my feelings in these situations. No, I was embarrassed over my inexcusable behavior with my roommate while we had been in the shower the night before. I felt guilty for my breach of his trust and I believed that my sexual dalliances with Matt were unpardonable.

Matt had been in serious trouble last night and it had been up to me to help him… not help myself to him. So where in the world had the idea come from to shove my erection up his ass? That was not something I had ever aspired to do. And of course, the answer was obvious. Matt and I hadn't just been groomed over the past few weeks for this kind of sex. We had been indoctrinated. We were now sexualized to the extent that behaviors like last night were just occurring in us naturally, and I found it disturbing as hell to realize this.

There was also no doubt in my mind that the high levels of cocaine in our blood streams shared, in equal portion, in the blame for last night's shower orgy. Never in my life had I felt myself in such a constant and extreme state of horniness. It was as if Matt and I had been compelled by the drug to quench our sexual appetites by any means we could find. And frankly, I suspected that if either of us had found ourselves in the shower with a golden retriever instead of a roommate, we would have found a way.

I was beside myself with shame. Despite my understanding now of how we had been manipulated by the upperclassmen to engage in the sexual acts we were now guilty of having committed on each other, I still felt awful over what I had done last night to my friend. What, I wondered, was I going to say to Matt once he was awake? How was I ever going to be able to face my friend again? I couldn't bear to think that I had taken advantage of him for my own selfish gratification at a moment when he really needed me to take care of him and look out for his best interests. How in the world was I going to get past this?

"Clint?" Matt spoke.

At first I didn't know how to respond—or for that matter, even if I dared to. "Yeah?" I decided that I couldn't ignore my friend. That would only make things worse.

"Are you awake?" Matt sounded tired.

"Yeah… I'm awake, I guess." I was holding my breath now in anticipation of my roommate's wrath.

"Thanks."

Of all the words I was expecting to hear just then, this hadn't been one of them. "For what?"

"For getting me back here last night and for getting me cleaned up. I never would have made it if you hadn't been there to help me. Who knows? They might have left me there all night long. I could have died for all they cared."

I then turned over in my bed and looked at Matt. "Yeah, but then I…" I couldn't find the words. "I… I fucked you."

Matt saw how I was struggling, and he smiled. "Oh, yeah. You sure did."

"I know, and I shouldn't have. You were weak from what they had done to you and I… I should have been stronger. I'm sorry, Matt. I shouldn't have done that to you."

"Are you kidding? Clint, I wanted you to. Hell, I made you fuck me. You know, you needed a release last night just as badly as I did. And you had done so much to get me back here safely and to get all of that mud and crap off of me, I figured it was a way I could pay you back right away. So I'm glad you did it."

"You're glad?" I was relieved that Matt was being so kind to me, but this still didn't seem right.

"Well sure. After all, I got something out of it too. Remember? I told you that Artist was right." Matt then smiled again.

"Oh yeah, you did. Did I really feel good to you when I was in there?" After all, a guy likes to know these things.

"Well, there were a couple of times when you shoved your dick in me so hard, I thought my eye balls were gonna pop out of their sockets. And I think maybe I need some more practice so I can get more used to it but… yeah, I'd say overall, you did feel pretty good."

"Really?" This whole conversation had suddenly become astonishing.

"In fact, if it doesn't bother you too much, sometime I might ask you to bone me again."

"Well…" Now I *was* surprised. What a difference two and a half weeks had made. "Let's, maybe talk about that some other time, ok?"

"Yeah, ok." Matt thought for a moment and then continued to speak. "Clint?"

"What?" I answered. I couldn't wait to hear what Matt was going to come up with now.

"I can't get out of bed."

"What do ya mean?" This made no sense either.

"I mean, before you were awake, I got up and went to the bathroom, and I was barely able to make it back to my bed—I was so tired."

"Really?" I began to think of why Matt would feel so drained of energy this early in the day. Surely the… liberties I had taken with him the night before, hadn't sapped his strength *that* much.

"Yeah, and every so often now I'll try to sit up, but the most I can stay up for is only about thirty seconds. Then I have to lay back down again. What about you? How do you feel this morning?"

"Fine, I think—other than this giant headache and a queasy stomach."

"Yeah," Matt added. "I've got those too."

I also needed to go to the bathroom, so I pulled the covers off of me and got out of bed. Neither Matt nor I had bothered to put on any clothes after our shower the night before, and this morning I discovered that I no longer felt self-conscious about walking around naked. We had both spent so much time in the buff around others over the past few weeks, it just no longer seemed to matter to me anymore who saw me undressed. "I'll give it a try," I said once I was on my feet. Immediately then, I walked straight out of our room and into the bathroom across the hall. "Oh shit!" Another first. In my entire life I had never before felt what I experienced then. When I closed the door to the bathroom behind me, it was as if all of the strength in my body had suddenly vanished. If the toilet hadn't been there for me to sit down on, I would have collapsed right there on the floor.

"Clint?" Matt called out when he heard me curse.

"I'm ok, Matt. But I see what you mean," I called back. And then I didn't want to use up any more of my energy by yelling.

"Can you make it back?" Matt called again.

"I don't know!" I responded weakly. "Give me a couple of minutes." Since I was sitting in the right spot, I went ahead and did my business, and then I remained there on the commode for a few minutes longer with my head between my knees. Eventually, I reasoned that I couldn't spend my day sitting there, so I decided to make an attempt to get myself back to my bed.

I figured that being upright was the thing that would wear me out the fastest, so I decided that once I was standing, I would move as swiftly as I could. "Here I come!" I called out to Matt.

"Good luck," came the response.

With grit determination, and after taking in a deep breath, I stood up, threw open the bathroom door and then raced back into my room. When I made it to the chair at my desk, I wanted to stop there to rest, but I forced myself to keep going until I collapsed utterly drained onto my bed.

"Ya made it!" Matt sounded relieved for me.

"Barely," was all I had the wind to say in response. It took a few more minutes after that before I was able to move myself around enough to lie down properly in my bed again. And when I had finally managed to pull my covers over me once more, I discovered that I felt relieved because, among all the other strange things that were happening to me this morning, I was also finding it hard now to retain my body heat. "What the hell is going on with us?" I blurted out in frustration.

"I don't know, Clint. Try sitting up now."

"What, do you like to see people struggle?" I asked as I shivered under my covers.

"No, I mean it. I'm up to forty-five seconds now. When I started trying I could only sit up for ten seconds before I'd have to lie down again."

All of this seemed so impossible to me. "All right," I agreed. I then pulled my body into a sitting position and I resolved to stay this way for as long as I wanted. But ten seconds later, I had collapsed, drained again of all of my energy. "Jeeze! What is this?" I gasped.

"I don't know," was still the only answer my roommate had for me. We then spent the next few minutes lying quietly in our beds, just waiting to feel the energy return to our bodies, when Matt finally spoke again. "Maybe if we ate something?"

"No, I'm not really hungry. And I'm not even sure if I could keep something down right now anyway."

"Yeah, me neither." Matt then thought for another moment, and then in a more serious tone, he spoke once more. "Clint?"

"Yeah?"

"Was that cocaine they gave us last night?"

At first I thought this was a really stupid question for Matt to ask me. But then I remembered that the word "cocaine" had never actually been said throughout the entire evening. "Yes, Matt. That was cocaine they gave us," I answered thoughtfully.

"Oh, no!" Matt then began to cry.

I figured he was upset because I had just confirmed for him that we were now using hard drugs. In those days most people in our generation believed that using the so-called soft drugs like marijuana and alcohol was practically harmless. But hard drugs like cocaine and heroin were substances which only hard-core users indulged in, and were to be avoided at all costs by average and younger people like us. And then my friend said something to me that I wasn't prepared for.

"Clint, I think we're addicted now," and then he continued to cry.

"I can't believe that, Matt. Not after one time."

Matt tried to pull himself together enough to explain. "We used it four times last night. Listen, a bigger kid who used to live down the street from us in Michigan had this happen to him after only using cocaine for one night. After that everyone said he was hooked. Clint, what are we gonna do?" And then Matt broke down completely. "Clint, I don't want'a be a drug addict," he sobbed.

I hated to see Matt this way. "Come on, Matt. Maybe it's not as bad as you think. Let's just lie here for a while and give ourselves some time to gain our strength back. I'll bet in an hour or so we'll feel a lot better."

"Ya think so?" Matt sniffed.

"Sure. We've got a couple of hours 'til lunch anyway." Besides, there were other matters we needed to discuss which were equally as compelling. "And there's something I need to ask ya, anyway."

"Like what?" Matt had managed to compose himself again.

"Did you notice that last night there were more people taking their pleasures with us than just the usual eight guys? And did you also notice that some of the ones who were using us were grown men?"

Now Matt became pensive again. "Yeah, one of the guys that did me sounded a lot like Mr. Werbick, our history teacher."

"I'm sure it was him," I observed.

"No shit? Then that means the other man I sucked was Mr. Foot, our Spanish teacher?"

"Probably," I acknowledged.

"Unbelievable! Jeeze, my teachers came in my mouth. How the hell am I gonna face them in class on Monday?"

Actually, it was a question that I had asked myself. "Well, they may think that because of the blindfold, you don't know who they really were. Especially when you figure in how much booze and drugs they had filled us with."

"Yeah, maybe," Matt conceded. "You know I've been worried all along that there were more people here at the Academy who were involved in this crap than we were being shown. So now I guess we know, don't we?" Matt was unsettled by this information.

"Yeah, well, you don't know the half of it," I offered.

My comment caused Matt to raise an eyebrow. "Oh, yeah? Ok then, tell me."

At this moment, I realized how upset I still was over my discovery. "I think Thomas Jefferson was one of mine."

"No shit? That guy's huge."

"Yeah. And he was pretty scary too. He kept threatening me."

"Really?" Matt was giving me his full attention now. "Like, how?"

"Oh, he grabbed my face a lot harder than anybody else did, and he threatened to hit me if I didn't give him a great blow job. Stuff like that." Then I thought for a moment about what else I could say. "And I think he's got a lot of rage in him."

"Huh. Well maybe that's why everyone's always too afraid to ask him for seconds." Matt then chuckled a little. "Was there anyone else who did ya?"

If Matt's reaction to my news seemed caviler, it was because by now we were both resigned to our roles as sex slaves and as such, we had become jaded. And actually, I wanted to chuckle along with my roommate, but the rest of my story was just too depressing, and I knew would prove to impact our lives profoundly for the rest of the time we lived at the Academy. "Yeah, well, the first guy who did me last night was Stuart."

Matt's face drained when he heard my news. "Stuart? Our headmaster? The man you told me we could trust to get us out of this mess? Stuart? Clint, do you know what this means? This means that the things they've been doing to us are school policy. Shit! Clint, it's the policy of this school to take kids in their first year and turn them into sex slaves. It's not just some group of renegade students. It's the way things are done here. Damn it! Clint, did he say anything last night?"

"What do ya mean?" I asked. I was still taking in everything that Matt had just said.

"Was he talking to anyone?"

"Yeah, he talked to the leader first, and then he talked to me a little."

"Well, what did he say?"

"Oh, well, I was gonna tell ya this part also. He said he likes blonds and he's been waiting to have a chance to get at me ever since I got here." I continued to recall as I spoke. "I was kind of goin' in and out of consciousness when he was talking to the leader, but I did hear him say something about two more kids to train and he talked once about customers." I then stopped to see what Matt's reaction was going to be.

"Yeah? Ok. And was there anything else he said?" Matt was emotional now and pressing me for my recollections.

I was ready now to go on. "Yeah, there was. He used the word 'customers' when he said that you and I both have great cock-sucker hair and that customers love that."

"We have what?"

I went on to explain our headmaster's theory of what it was that made for an appealing young blow job artist. And after I was done, Matt became even more agitated.

"Clint! Why the hell didn't you tell me this last night? Didn't it worry you?"

"Well yeah, kind of. But with all the drugs in me last night, I guess it just didn't hit me fully until this morning. And Matt, don't forget you were way too out of it last night to handle any kind of information like this, anyway. That's why I waited until now to talk to you about it."

Matt was then quiet for a moment. He was reviewing in his mind everything we had just discussed. A moment later he had reached his conclusion. "Clint?"

"Yeah?"

"I think, when you heard Stuart talk about customers, he was talking about selling us!"

"Selling us? He can't sell us."

"Oh yes he can. Clint! He's talking about child prostitution!"

Matt's words hit me like a brick on the back of my head. I had briefly considered the same idea several times on my own since last night, but hearing Matt actually say the words out loud, now made the whole idea seem plausible all of a sudden. And if my roommate was right, then we were truly in very serious trouble. "So what do we do, then?"

"I don't know about you, but I'm leaving this place right now. I don't care if I have to go begging on the streets of Boston, I am not going to be sold as a boy prostitute."

"I didn't think there was such a thing as child prostitution in this country."

"Are you nuts?" Matt was now acting hyper. "Every year over a half a million kids go missing from their homes in this country. That's like…" Matt began to run some figures in his head, "…almost seventeen times the population of Ulster that just disappears off the face of the earth every year, and their families never see them again. And they all aren't just runaways, either. A big percentage of these kids wind up in child prostitution rings."

"How in the hell do you know something like that?" I asked. I was amazed at my friend's knowledge on this subject.

"I read an article about it in a magazine after my aunt told me she was sending me off to a boarding school. Huh! I guess I was worried that I'd never be seen again, or something."

"Yeah, well, how are we gonna get out of here when we can't even get ourselves out of bed? And you know, if we don't get a really good head start so we can have the time we need to get all the way down to the highway and then find someone to give us a ride, the leader or someone else from here is bound to catch up with us in the school van long before we'll be able to walk all the way into town."

The reality of our physical limitations was now back with us. "Well, let's start by seeing how long we can sit up." Matt always looked at things methodically.

"Ok," I replied. I was game if he was. And so we both pulled ourselves into sitting positions, and our determination held us there for nearly a full minute before we both fell backwards onto our mattresses again, out of energy and out of breath.

"Oh!" Matt gasped. "Clint, what are we gonna do?"

I was also breathing hard. "Ah… well, as soon as we've regained our strength, we need to try to make a run for it, I guess."

"And when's that gonna be?" Matt now sounded as if he believed it was hopeless for us.

"I don't know. Maybe in a couple of hours," I was still finding it hard to catch my breath. Neither of us said very much after that. We both figured that the less we did or said, the faster our strength could return to our depleted bodies.

An hour later it was time again to see if we had gotten any better. "Do ya want'a try sitting up again, Clint?" Matt asked me.

"Yeah, ok." And so we tried, and this time we were able to sit up for nearly two minutes before our bodies gave out and we crashed back down again.

"Oh, Clint!" Matt was again out of breath. "How are we gonna keep them from selling us? We can't stay here anymore, but there's no way we can get out of here, either. In fact, I don't know how we're supposed to meet that guy they said they wanted us to see today."

"Oh, yeah." I had forgotten that Artist had mentioned something last night about plans for us today to meet the guy they were getting their drugs from. And then I wondered what sort of a man would have an apparent formal relationship with a school in order to supply numbers of its student body with drugs.

At that, our door blew open and the head waiter walked in. "Well good morning, boys. And how are we feeling today?" He then pulled out my chair from under my desk, placed it in between our beds, and sat down in it.

"Don't you ever knock?" I asked. I was irritated that he had just acted as if our privacy meant nothing to him—which obviously it didn't.

"Why? Are you worried we're gonna see what ya look like without your clothes on or something? Huh? Ha, ha, ha!" The head waiter was amused by his own words.

A second upperclassman then walked into our room and closed our door behind him. "Hey, guys," he said as he walked straight over to our dresser.

The head waiter didn't wait for either Matt or me to respond. He had things he had come to say to us, and so he proceeded to speak. "No, really. How are you guys feeling today? How come you're still lyin' around in bed?"

"You know why we're still in bed," Matt replied. "For some reason, we don't seem to have enough strength to get onto our feet—let alone stay there. You wouldn't happen to know anything about any of this would you?"

"Yes, well," the head waiter continued. "The reason why you two have no strength anymore is because your bodies have gone through a change. From now on, they'll only work when you're using cocaine. Your bodies now crave the stuff and this weakness you're feelin' is your bodies' way of tellin' you that it wants more cocaine and it isn't gonna work right again until you do a couple more lines. So when you're not on the stuff, you're gonna be wiped out and helpless, like you are right now." The head waiter then grinned. "So sorry, boys, but you're both hooked now and the only way you can ever feel better is to keep doin' the drug so it always stays in your systems. And fortunately for both of you little guys, we just happen to have plenty of it around all the time so you won't ever need to worry about not being able to feel good after this. I can guarantee yuz that we're always gonna make sure that we take good care of you two."

While the head waiter was pronouncing our sentence, the second guy was getting busy at his assigned duties for the morning. Without saying a word, he reached into one of his pockets and pulled out another oversized compact.

"Are you guys issued those things at the beginning of every year, or something?" Matt asked.

"No, we buy them ourselves," the second guy answered as he pulled out another bag of cocaine and placed it and his compact onto our dresser. "Time for a little hair of the dog, boys. I'm gonna start cuttin' up some lines for ya," he said in a patronizing tone.

By this time, I was fuming mad. It was obvious now that these guys had never regarded us as real friends. Not even in the twisted way they defined the word around here did they care about us. Instead we understood that we were nothing more to these upperclassmen assholes than a means. A means to some end which we suspected we were going to be learning a great deal about later on that day. "Well I'm sorry," my voice began to rise in volume, "but you two can just take that crap and get the hell out of here! Matt and I have no intention of becoming drug addicts."

My words quickly shifted the head waiter's condescension to anger. Immediately he rose to his feet and began to come toward us. "You're already drug addicts, you moron!" The head waiter then moved to stand next to Matt and as I watched, he grabbed Matt's wrist and pulled my friend's weakened body up into a sitting position. Then, in a move which had obviously been planned ahead of time, the head waiter backhanded my roommate across his face.

"Auh!" The blow forced Matt down again to his mattress with pain from the sting of the bigger kid's hand now added to his misery.

"What the hell are you doing?" I shouted. For the moment, that was all I could do.

"Shut up and watch this." The head waiter yelled back at me as he then grabbed Matt's arm and pulled the boy upright again.

"Uh!" Matt was struck again, and as before, he fell beck down to his bed with a thud.

"God damn it! Stop hitting him!" I shrieked.

"Oh, you want me to stop hitting him?" The head waiter asked me in a childish tone. He then took two steps toward me. "Fine!" he said as he took hold of my arm and pulled me up into a sitting position.

I was still in no better shape than Matt. So when the blow came, there was little I could do to prevent the impact. "Auh!" And as expected, the force caused me to fly backwards until I landed flat on my back again.

"There… is that better?" The head waiter was now practically screaming at me. "Would you like another one? Huh?"

Once again I felt the bigger kid grab my wrist and pull on the upper half of my still limp body until I was upright again. "Uh!" His slaps were really painful and I wondered how much more of this abuse we were going to have to take as my body crashed back down again onto my mattress.

What happened to us next was just strange. As we continued to lie helpless in our beds, the head waiter then began to yell at us as he kept himself moving back and forth between us so he could slap us at random whenever the urge to hurt us some more moved him to do so. "I can't believe it, but you boys still don't seem to get it."

"Uh!" Matt reacted again to getting slapped.

"Neither of you two have a say anymore in how your lives are gonna be run. We own you now. You two belong to us!"

"Uh!" With still no strength in my body, I felt as if the head waiter's slap was going to rip my head off of my neck.

"You belong to us like a dog belongs to his owner."

"Uh!" Matt cried out again.

"We own you two and I don't ever want to hear either of you object to anything we tell you to do ever again!

"Uh!" *Damn it, that hurts,* I thought.

The head waiter then stood still for a moment. "Are there any questions?"

I could hear Matt whimpering again and I wasn't too far from tears myself at this point. Neither of us would now dare to say a word to this maniac.

"All right, fine." The head waiter then seemed pleased that he had been able again to beat us into submission. Then he spoke to the second upperclassman. "Are you ready yet?"

"Yeah, I've got the first two lines ready. Who do you want to go first?"

"This one," the head waiter said as he pointed to me. I guessed he had figured it would be better if Matt were given a few more moments to compose himself. And so, a few minutes later, Matt and I were all fixed up again and well on our way to spending the day high. Once the upperclassmen were satisfied that their job for the morning had been successfully discharged, it was time for a little more talk.

"Ok, listen up, boys. Pretty soon you'll start feeling better, so I want'a see you both at lunch today. Then at five o'clock this afternoon, I want you both dressed in white shirts, school ties and your school blazers and ready to travel. The van will be waiting for you down in the Annex parking lot and you'll be off campus then after that until just before lights out when we'll bring you back."

"Where are we going?" Matt asked as he continued to sniff the drug up farther into his head.

"We'll tell ya once you guys are in the van. Ok?" The head waiter then looked at us both to see if we were going to say anything more. But neither of us did. Satisfied then, that he had again gained his supremacy over us, he next spoke to his cohort. "Fine. Let's get going."

Matt and I then watched as the two upperclassmen left our room. But before he closed our door behind him, the head waiter stopped so he could say one more thing to us. "Oh, and in case you guys get any funny ideas today about trying to leave or something foolish like that, I want you both to understand that escape attempts will be met with the most dire of punishments to you both. And don't forget, when the drug runs out, you guys can't do anything. So the only way you two can stay righteous from now on is to keep doin' the drug and right here is where you will always find an ample supply to feed your habit. All right?" He then closed our door, and a moment later they were gone from our building.

A minute or so passed, and then I heard Matt sigh. "Well," he offered. 'That about wraps it all up for us."

Chapter Six
The Man Who Was Really in Charge

As ordered, Matt and I presented ourselves to our masters, dressed in our school uniforms, at precisely five o'clock later that afternoon. Just as the head waiter had promised, the van was already waiting for us in the Annex parking lot when we reached the bottom of the steps.

"Let's go, boys. Hop in," the leader apparently didn't want us to waste any time.

Without delay, Matt and I climbed in through the double doors on the side and sat down on the bench immediately behind the two front seats. The hair of the dog had long since done its job on us. The cocaine we had been given in the morning, plus the two extra lines apiece the upperclassmen had made us snort an hour or so earlier, now had us feeling high and horny once again. Just the same, Matt and I were generally pissed off at this bunch. Even though there were still some details about this trip which we were lacking, we now believed that we understood the full purpose for the incredible amount of manipulation we had been put through, and we didn't like it.

Next the leader slid into the seat behind us while the head waiter opened the door on the driver's side and sat down behind the wheel in front of us. "Here he comes," he announced.

We then turned our heads in time to see our headmaster emerge from the Annex and begin to walk toward us.

"How come you're driving?" Matt asked as he looked back at the head waiter.

"Are you kidding?" the upperclassman shot back. "It's after five already. Do you want *him* driving us?" the bigger kid said referring to our illustrious school head.

A moment later Mr. Stuart reached the van, opened the front door on the passenger side and then hefted his short frame up and into his seat so he could take his place for our journey. Immediately once he was in the vehicle with us, Matt and I could smell the booze on him. Normally we would extend a friendly greeting to the man in a situation like this, but since we now understood that this asshole was really the enemy in scholar's clothing, we chose instead to stay silent. So when all of the doors had finally been closed, he turned around to face Matt and me. "I decided that since you boys have this all figured out now, I'd come along and make sure you understood completely about what's going to be expected from you two from now on."

With some surprise over the man's newfound insights, both Matt and I then looked over at the head waiter again.

When the bigger kid saw us looking at him he must have been able to read our expressions because quickly he smiled. "There was almost always at least one of us listening in the hall outside your door this morning until I came in," he admitted.

"Here," the leader then said to us.

From behind, Matt and I were then handed our own thermoses which had already been filled with something.

"Start drinking," the leader added.

The head waiter then turned himself back around and started up the engine while the headmaster continued to look at us. "Well? Open them up and start drinking, boys," he ordered as well.

Matt and I looked at each other first, and then we did as we were told. We already had a sneaking suspicion about what was inside, and a moment later after we had taken our first sips, our fears were confirmed. Gin and tonics again!

"You boys get started on those and once we're on the highway, we'll talk some more," the headmaster then turned himself around also so he could face forward again. "Let's go," he said to the head waiter. And off we went.

By the time we had passed the town of Worcester and were well on our way toward Boston, I was beginning to feel the alcohol as my senses started to dull again. So I figured, before I became too far gone to care, I'd better gain whatever information I could. "So where are we going today?" I called out to Mr. Stuart.

The man heard my question and turned around to look at me. "We're headed to Boston so a man that the Academy does some business with can meet you two."

"Why do we need to meet this guy?" Matt then joined the conversation.

Our headmaster paused for a moment to consider my roommate's question, and then he continued. "Look boys, I know you're both bright kids, so I'll just lay it all out for you now, and then we'll be done with it. All right?"

"Ok," I agreed. *A little honesty would be a nice change,* I thought.

"Tuitions just don't pay like they used to. As I think you know, enrollment this year alone is running at only about half of what our capacity is. So in order to keep the Academy open, our owner decided some time ago that we needed to find a secondary source of income for the school. Otherwise, he would have had to have shut the whole place down."

"That would've been a tragedy," Matt said sarcastically.

Mr. Stuart ignored my friend's comment and continued. "So eventually we got hooked up with the guy you're going to be seeing this afternoon. He supplies us with all the cocaine we can use, and then the older students in our little group go up to Harvard Square in Boston, or to the bus station in Worcester, or to other places we know in the area to sell the stuff on Wednesday and Saturday afternoons. And we even sell a lot to people around Ulster too."

"Ah huh," I acknowledged as I took another swig from my thermos.

"Well, this man in Boston, also showed us how we could rake in a bunch of money if we turned out a few of our youngest students to service a very special clientele that he has."

"Turned out?" Matt asked. "You mean sell us?"

Mr. Stuart shifted his gaze to look at my roommate. "Well, sort of. 'Rent' would be a better word for it, I think."

"Rent?" Matt asked back. He already knew the answer, but he wanted to hear the head of our school and our supposed protector actually say it again.

"Yes, well, you two boys will begin to perform your special kind of services for this elite group of customers with—let's say—their very particular tastes, and the money we make from your work plus the cocaine sales, will help to pick up the slack where tuitions leave off, as it were."

"And do we do all this in our dorm or what?" Matt asked.

"Well…" Mr. Stuart continued. "No, we'll set you up someplace off campus where you two can work without worry of being interrupted."

"Where?" I pressed.

"Well, we have a special arrangement with one of the local lodges in the area. On Wednesdays, you'll mostly be taking care of our local customers from around Ulster. And also on those days, some people from Worcester may come down every so often to be serviced by you boys as well. But on the weekends you'll get to go on trips to places like Boston, or New York… and you guys are even going to get to go to Florida. Won't that be fun?"

Suddenly I got the impression that our headmaster was trying to sell us on all of this. It seemed that the closer we got to Boston, the more nervous he was becoming. "I've already been to those places," I answered blankly.

Ignoring my response, Mr. Stuart then looked at his watch before he turned his head to speak to the head waiter. "I think we're going to be right on time." Then he looked back at Matt and me again. "Yes, well… you boys hurry up and finish what's in those thermoses, now. We're passing Framingham right now, so we'll be downtown soon." It then looked to us as if he had finished saying what he had wanted us to know and was about to turn around and face forward again, when he looked back at us to say one more thing. "By the way, I have a standing rule about all of this which can never be broken."

Matt and I glanced at each other quickly. We couldn't imagine what was coming next.

"I will never let either of you boys go it alone. Whenever we send you out to be with customers, you will always go together. That way you two can always look after each other and keep each other safe. Ok? Oh, and I want you both to learn each other's blood type. Tomorrow morning we'll get that information for you out of the nurse's office. And you can expect me to quiz you on it from time to time so be sure you memorize 'em. Ok?" Then for real this time, Mr. Stuart turned himself around so he could gaze out through the windshield for the rest of our trip into Boston.

Neither of us knew what to make of these pronouncements. It seemed as if our headmaster had meant to comfort us in some way, but instead his news just made us feel even less secure than we had before.

"Keep drinking," the leader urged us from behind.

And so, as the song "Lola" by The Kinks played from the radio in the dashboard, Matt and I drank faster, so we could dull our minds and our muscles as much as possible before we arrived at our destination. Later, when we got into downtown Boston, we turned into a garage beneath some tall building which was located near the Prudential Building which, besides the Callahan Tunnel, was about the only structure in Boston I recognized in those days. When we stopped, we could see that we were parked next to double doors which led to the building's elevator. Then the engine was turned off and the double doors on the side of the van were thrown open for us.

Once Matt and I had stepped out of the van and were standing on the cement, we could both tell that the gin and tonics in our systems were doing their job because we were both now feeling nicely plastered again.

"You two wait here with the van," Mr. Stuart gave his order to the leader and the head waiter. And then, a moment later Matt and I were in the elevator alone with our headmaster and heading for the penthouse level.

"Now listen," our headmaster had something he wanted to say to us before the elevator stopped and the doors opened. "From now on you kids are to be seen and not heard. You don't say *anything ever* to *anyone* unless they speak to you first. And when we get in there, after we've said our hello's, then I want you two to go and sit down quietly on the couch in the living room and wait there until you're called. You boys are professionals now, so no horse play and no wise cracks. Got it?"

"Yes, sir." My parents had always raised me to do as I was told, so I accepted what this adult was requiring of me without question.

"Yes, sir." Matt too had been raised properly by his parents.

"I mean it," Mr. Stuart felt the need to press his point with us even farther. "These people will chew you up and spit you out and never think twice about it if you cause them any trouble. So don't ever forget about what I've just said to you. Ok? Remember… do as you're told. Always! All right?"

"Yes, sir," I answered again.

"Yes, sir," Matt responded too.

A moment later a poorly lit hallway was revealed to us, so we stopped our conversation and stepped out of the elevator. As it happened, the door we were interested in was right there in the hallway where we had appeared. So as Mr. Stuart pressed the doorbell to announce our arrival, I tried to take a quick look around to acquaint myself with the surroundings. It looked to me as if there were one or two other penthouses on this floor, but the dimness of the light, along with the dullness of my condition, made it impossible for me to know about this for sure.

An instant later the door in question was opened and we beheld a tall, balding, fat man in a bathrobe. "Come on in," he said smiling. "You're right on time."

"Oh good," Mr. Stuart then placed a hand on each of our shoulders and quickly guided us into the front entryway of the man's apartment. "The traffic wasn't so bad this time. I guess people aren't returning from their weekends away from town until later on tonight."

Matt and I were then stopped and turned around to face our host.

"This is Clint," Mr. Stuart said pointing to me. "And this is Matt."

"Hmm." The man looked us over. "And you say they've been trained?"

"Oh yes," Mr. Stuart sounded eager to reassure the taller man of our qualifications. "They're green, but they know what they're supposed to do."

The man continued for a moment longer to stare at Matt and me. "Ok," he finally said. "You boys go sit down on the couch in the living room and wait there," our host said dismissively.

Without a word from either of us, Matt and I then turned and walked like the little drugged automatons we had become into the man's living room and then we sat down on his couch. As soon as we were seated, Matt and I noticed immediately that there were two silver hand mirrors placed on the coffee table in front of us with two lines of cocaine spread across the surface of each.

"You boys go ahead and do those two lines of coke I've left out for you," our host called over to us.

Next to the mirrors, a box of short straws was lying on the table as well. So I picked up the box and pulled out two straws, and then I handed one of them to Matt. Eagerly then, Matt and I proceeded to do as we had been told so that a moment later, there was not even a trace of the powder left behind.

It's a funny thing about cocaine. The more of it you do, the more of it you want to do. So as Matt and I sat back on the couch and continued to sniff our gift from the fat man farther up into our heads, the two men continued to talk quietly in the entryway. We tried to listen to see if we could make out what they were saying, but they were keeping their voices too low for us to be able to understand any of their words. One thing we did observe, though, was that Mr. Stuart seemed to be awfully obsequious around this man. Matt and I were astonished to see this because we had never known our headmaster to be fearful of anyone.

"Hey, I'm Joe." Neither of us had noticed him when he entered the room suddenly from the kitchen where he had been waiting, but now we were aware of another large man and this one was standing in the living room right in front of us. "What's your names?" Joe then put out his meaty hand to shake mine first.

"I'm Clint," I answered as I watched my smaller hand become enveloped by his.

"And I'm Matt." My roommate then took his turn and shook the hand of the man who looked to us sort of like a stevedore.

"Oh good, I see you boys have met Joe," our host said as he and our headmaster then walked into the living room to join us. "Joe here is another member of my team. I call him our straightener."

Matt then looked at the fat man standing next to Mr. Stuart and couldn't resist asking the obvious question. "What's a straightener?"

"Oh," our host replied promptly. "Well, if anyone ever gives us any trouble, I send Joe here to straighten them out for me. Right, Joe?" The fat man then looked over at his near equal in size, but noticed that Joe had already moved his mind on to the task of sizing up Mr. Stuart.

"Huh?" Joe replied when he realized that his boss was speaking of him. "Oh yeah, yeah. Right! Ha, ha, ha! And I always straighten them good too. Ha, ha, ha!"

Our host then gazed back at us with a pained expression on his face. "You'll have to excuse Joe, boys. Sometimes he's got a rather short attention span."

Matt and I just looked at each other in amazement. Even in our altered conditions, it was obvious to us both that this guy Joe was as dim as the lights out in the hallway.

The fat man then wheeled around on one heel and walked across the room to open a closet door. With the rest of us watching in silence, he removed a baseball bat from inside and then he closed the door again and returned to where we were all still gathered.

"Here you go, Joe," our host said as he presented the bat to the muscular man. "I got this for you yesterday while I was over at Fenway dropping off a delivery for some of my buddies over there."

"Oh, no! You're kidding!" Joe was obviously overwhelmed by his boss's gesture of kindness. "This is so great! An official Boston Red Sox baseball bat."

The fat man then raised one of his fat fingers so he could point to some writing we could all now notice on the bat. "Yeah and see," he announced with pride, "I even got five of the players to sign it for you."

"Oh, man," Joe continued to gush. "This will go great with the rest of my collection," And then, as if he felt the need to let us in on what the whole fuss was about, Joe looked at Matt and me. "I love the Red Sox. How 'bout you boys? Don't you just love 'em too?"

My roommate and I then squirmed a bit in our places on the couch. "Ah, sure," we both answered. In reality, neither one of us could understand what the big deal was.

"Well, you're very welcome, Joe. I always like to reward those who work hard for me and do a good job."

Suddenly I found myself wondering if this entire little drama was being staged for our benefit.

"I knew you were a big fan," the fat man continued. "So I just figured I'd pick this up for you. Do you really like it?"

"I sure do. Thanks a whole lot for this." Joe kept running his hands along the grain in the wood and was stopping every so often so he could feel with the tips of his fingers each name that had been scribbled into its surface.

"Well, good." Then the man in the bathrobe looked at his watch and instantly Matt and I could see a change in his demeanor. "Ok then, Joe." It was obvious now that our host had other matters—like Matt and me—on his mind. "Thanks for stopping by."

Joe then looked away from his bat and over at the man who was now giving him the bum's rush. Instantly he understood that his fatso boss was wanting him to leave. "Huh? Oh yeah, ok. Right. I need to be going anyway."

"And why don't you ride down the elevator with Stuart, here." It was clear now that our host was wanting to move on to the next item on his agenda for the evening.

Apparently surprised that he too was being dismissed, Mr. Stuart then turned his head to look at our host. "Oh… right. I guess it is time for me to be leaving now as well. I'll be back for the boys then at nine." And with that the head of our school turned and began to slink back over to the front door so he could leave the two of us behind in this strange man's apartment to be subjected to God only knew what.

As he watched Joe then walk out of the room too, I could see that Matt was about to say something. I figured that he was now as distressed as I was that we were about to be abandoned. But before he could speak, I elbowed him on his arm to remind him that we had been warned to never speak unless we were being spoken to. And I succeeded, apparently, in communicating my meaning because after that Matt just sat back and folded his arms across his chest.

It only took Fatso another thirty seconds or so to get rid of the two men. And then he closed and locked his front door. "Sweetie!" he called out.

Immediately then, we saw two big double doors across the room, which we gathered led into the apartment's master suite, fly open and issue forth a small woman with rich-looking, long, straight brown hair which she allowed to fall past her petite shoulders. Her appearance caused Matt and me to automatically remember our manners. We assumed right off that this person was Fatso's wife as she rushed over to the spot in the living room where Matt and I were now standing, clad also in nothing more than a bathrobe.

Doesn't anyone around here ever wear real clothes? I wondered.

"Oh, are these the two new boys?" she asked. "Well, aren't you both just the cutest little things?"

She was a fine one to be calling us little. The woman herself was only about five feet three inches high. And she was wearing enough makeup, nearly, to be mistaken for a kabuki dancer.

Fatso then walked over and stood in front of me. As if now seeing us for the first time, he looked us both over much more carefully, and then he spoke again. "Ok, boys, stand straight."

In our inebriated and high states, standing still now seemed a bit too difficult for us to pull off. Nevertheless, we did our best to comply with the man's order.

Fatso then reached over and rested one of his fat hands on my shoulder. "I'll take the blond one first," he proclaimed to his wife.

Sweetie then stepped over to stand next to Matt so she could wrap one of her arms around his shoulders. "Well then, I'll just take the one with the black hair," she announced with a big smile. This woman was pretty and perhaps twenty-nine or thirty years of age, and it was funny to see her as she stood next to Matt because she was so short. Together the two of them looked like a pair. "We'll just see you two in a little while then," Sweetie remarked sprightly.

I continued to watch as Sweetie then took Matt by the hand and led the boy away into the master bedroom. "Come along, my little dear," she beckoned. Matt made no protest, and in another moment had disappeared with his new admirer behind the double doors. Then Fatso moved his hand onto a spot on my back between my shoulder blades and gave me a little shove to let me know he was ready for me to walk with him.

Together we then walked through the front entryway and down a hall on the other side into, what I presumed, was their guest bedroom and bath which turned out to be complete with a large walk-in shower. My host kept walking until he had reached the large double bed in the room and had sat down on its edge. He then placed his hands on my upper arms and squared me up so I could stand directly in front of him. After all that Matt and I had been through over the past several weeks, I found that I wasn't phased when Fatso helped me off with my jacket and undid my tie for me. And I hardly noticed it when he undid my buttons and removed my shirt. But when he began to unbuckle my belt and unhook my pants, it occurred to me that this was something I probably needed to lodge a complaint over. But if I had learned anything in all of my trials at the Academy so far, I had learned that I needed to keep my mouth shut unless someone around me was wanting to put something into it. And besides, by this stage of the evening the cocaine he had given us plus everything else they had filled our bodies with had made me pretty pliable. So I simply stood there for the man and allowed him to undress me.

up without finishing me off. *Doesn't anybody ever finish anything these days?* I thought as I remembered similar feelings of frustration from the night before in the mud pit.

"Yes, I think you'll do nicely," he said, obviously pleased with the offering my headmaster had made of me. I felt as if I was a turkey being picked out and prepared in advance for a Thanksgiving meal. Then he stood up again. "Follow me, son."

Now my senses were overwhelming me again. I felt frazzled and I hated this technique of manipulation that people kept putting me through. I wanted to scream out as loudly as I could manage… "Hey, sit back down on this bed and put your damn hand on me again and finish what you started, you walrus." Fortunately though, my mind wasn't so far removed from reality yet that I actually believed that saying something like this would be a smart idea. So instead I simply refrained from saying anything at all and, a bit stiff legged at first, I followed my host as he led me into the bathroom.

All I can remember still of the adjoining room was mirrors and green tile everywhere. Across the room from where I entered was a large door with clear glass in it which separated the bathroom from a huge walk-in shower which looked big enough to me to be able to hold eight or ten people in it—if there were ever any reason to do so.

Fatso gripped the metal handle on the door and pulled it open for me. "Go on in," he grumbled.

Obligingly I did as I was ordered and didn't stop to turn around and look back at him until I was standing in the middle of the shower on top of a larger than normal drain cover. I then watched as Fatso followed me into the room.

Once his bulk had cleared the doorway, the man sighed and pulled off his robe to reveal every revolting detail of his flab to me. And as every bad fat joke I had ever heard went whizzing through my brain suddenly, my keeper continued with his plan by throwing his garment back out into the bathroom and then closing the glass door so that the two of us were now naked and standing in his guest shower together.

"Ok, sit down there in the middle of the floor where the drain is and face the front."

"Yes, sir." Again, I did as I was told. At first the tiles on the floor felt cold against my bare skin, but in a few moments my body heat managed to warm them up for me. Fatso then walked over to join me in the center of the room and once he was standing alongside of me, he reached up toward the ceiling and pulled down some sort of leather harness in two pieces that was tied to one end of a rope which was running up through a pulley he had hanging from a hook which had been set permanently into the ceiling. Because it had been placed so high above me, I hadn't noticed this rig of his until he had stretched out his arm to bring it to him. And despite the temptation I felt suddenly to remark about the leather and rope I was now looking at, I maintained my composure just enough to keep me from saying something to the man, even though this situation was rapidly making me nervous.

I don't know how he did it, but a moment later I watched in amazement as Fatso managed somehow to sit his blubber down on the tiles in front of me. He was ugly with his clothes off, but it surprised me to discover that I wasn't as repulsed by his appearance as I had thought I would be. As I sat quietly on his shower room floor, this large man reached out with one of his large hands and grasped my left foot and then he lifted my leg into the air a ways so he could push onto my ankle and lower calf one of these wide leather strappings he was holding onto. I didn't know the name for these things, but after he had placed the other one around my other ankle, he spent the next several minutes lacing them up as tightly as he could for me. When this job was finished, he fastened my ankles together with a hitch that was sewn into the sides of these leathers and then he got back up onto his feet.

Once he was vertical again, Fatso appeared ready for action. The next thing he did was to walk over to the front wall of the shower and turn on the water. At first the water came out only through a small faucet that was mounted low on the front wall. The pressure from his plumbing was enormous and for the next minute or so as the spray hit my lower body and as the cold runoff touched my legs and buttocks as it flowed past me into the drain, Fatso kept his fat toe inside the stream so he could test the water until the temperature had risen to the level he wanted. "Ok, here we go!" he announced. And then he opened a couple of valves on the front wall, and water came shooting out at me from all directions.

I was drenched instantly. The largest outlet for the water was positioned in the ceiling directly above me. As soon as the water from it hit my head, it flattened my hair completely. The sprays which were coming at me from several spots on each of the four walls filled the other areas of the room as they also covered me, which I didn't mind any longer because by now the warm water was feeling pretty good to me.

"Ok, scoot yourself forward a little, and then lay down on your back and put your legs up into the air for me."

What's gonna happen to me now? I wondered. With no other alternative available to me by this point, I complied with the man's wishes and adjusted my body so I was positioned the way he had said. A moment later, when he saw that I was ready, Fatso reached out for the other end of the rope he had attached to my ankles and pulled down on it hard until he had hoisted me entirely off of the floor to hang upside-down in the middle of his shower.

"HOLY SHIT!" I yelled out. As my arms hung down now past my head, I could still touch the floor with the tips of my fingers, but I felt as if he had raised me up too high.

"Don't worry," he tried to reassure me. "You're in there solid. You're not going anywhere." Then he tied off his end of the rope to a cleat that was mounted near him on the front wall.

As I moved back and forth like a pendulum with water running off of every part of my body and with my wet hair hanging straight down, I struggled for an instant to regain a measure of equilibrium. Right away I realized that breathing was my biggest challenge. Inverted as I was, water was pouring into my nose from the shower head above. Happily, I discovered right away that tilting my head back a bit more or simply raising one of my hands to block the water from filling my nostrils solved this problem. And at about the time I stopped my swinging, I decided that I couldn't imagine what deviltry this obvious pervert was intending to do with me. *Just try to be calm,* I kept repeating to myself. But as I felt the blood begin to rush to my head, I became frightened again when I remembered something I had heard once about how after a person is placed in bondage, a beating is customary.

"Ok, just relax and be still while you hang there, son." Fatso said this to me while he was walking over to take a position in front of me. "Just take it easy, now." When Fatso's large stomach first pressed up against my chest, I could see, finally, what this whole elaborate business was about. He had raised my body to a height which had placed my mouth at essentially the same level as his genitals. And when the closeness of his body left me with no choice but to look him over more carefully, I saw that he had already developed the largest erection I had ever seen on an animal with only two legs. *Well, here it comes.* I now understood and was a little surprised at myself for not seeing what was happening here until now. *It's the drugs and the alcohol,* I decided.

And so as I resigned myself to performing the job I had been trained to do so well, I waited as Fatso put his right hand into my wet hair so he could place his palm across the top of my head. Then he guided me toward him until he had my face positioned close enough for him to insert his penis into my mouth. Since

I knew what was expected of me, I opened my mouth and braced myself when I saw the time was at hand so that when he was ready, I accepted him.

"Auch!" Unfortunately, I gagged when I felt him try to shove his penis down my throat. His was by far the longest one I had encountered so far, and I was unprepared for his bulk.

When he heard me gagging, he immediately pulled himself back out and then he bent himself over so he could look me directly in the eye. "Sorry, kid. Haven't you learned yet how to relax your throat so you can give deep-throat blow jobs?"

"No, sir." I was still recovering from the shock of feeling him go down my throat, so it was hard for me to say anything else at the moment.

"Do you want me to teach you?"

"Not while I'm upside-down," I squeezed out through my vocal cords. I knew that this answer was a bit cheeky, but with all of this intimate activity now going on between us, I believed it was now possible for me to be able to get away with saying something like this.

"Ok, then you can just purse your lips together and do the best you can. And no teeth! If I feel any teeth, I'll knock them out of your head. You got that?"

"I got it, sir," I answered submissively. So much for my attempt to assert myself with this guy.

With his hand still in my hair, he stood upright again and guided my head toward his penis until he had inserted himself into my mouth once more. "Use your tongue," he ordered.

While he held my head in position for me, I created a suction and began to massage him with my tongue. After a minute or so of that, I reached out and wrapped my arms around his flabby thighs so I could take over the initiative by bobbing my head in and out without his help.

"Oh yeah! Good going, kid!" The boss approved.

For the next few minutes then, I put the full extent of my training into practice. As I worked, I could tell that Fatso was enjoying my efforts because every so often I could feel him tremble inside. He also kept yelling at me.

"Oh yeah… you're really good at this, kid."

Oh yes, I thought to myself. *This is why I've come to boarding school. So I can excel at everything I do.*

After that, I guess I settled into a rhythm on him. I figured that this was probably all there was going to be to our encounter together, but I found myself taken off guard by the plans that this strange man had in store for me. It turned out that my genitals were dangling at a convenient proximity to his mouth. And

I hadn't expected it, but about the time I was beginning to slow down from exhaustion, my host surprised me by wrapping his lips around my penis and taking me into his mouth. Almost immediately I responded by doubling my efforts to get him off, and in no time he had gotten me hard again as I performed my service with a vengeance. After that, we both continued to work on the other and I never knew how he had managed it, but somehow he had worked out a way to time everything so that we both ejaculated at nearly the same moment.

"Wo!" I exclaimed with an enormous amount of satisfaction when it was all over. By now I had released my host completely so that my arms were once again hanging down past my head. As usual, I was depleted of my energy, but on this occasion I felt better than I usually did because the perspiration I normally generated during these sessions was being washed off of me by the shower.

"That was pretty good wasn't it?" my host inquired of me.

Well what do you know? I was actually charmed by the fact that Fatso seemed genuinely concerned over how I was feeling now. "Yes, sir!" I answered enthusiastically. This was certainly a new twist on what had become a very old routine to me.

***

After the water was turned off and I had been released from my bonds, I was left to dress alone in the guest room. Once I had my tie on again, I was unsuccessful it seemed in my search for a brush or a comb I could use to put my hair back into place. So instead, I toweled off my head and I did the best I could by using my fingers as a comb. When I was finished and I had my jacket on once more, I walked out of the guest room and made my way back to join the others who by this time were all waiting for me in the kitchen.

"Oh there you are," Sweetie said when she saw me appear in the doorway. "You come right ahead and sit down here at the table next to your friend."

"Thank you," I replied. *Doesn't she ever stop smiling?* I wondered to myself. As I entered this small room, I could see that Matt was dressed again too and seated already at the kitchen table. So I walked across the linoleum and sat down in a chair next to my roommate.

"Your hair's wet," Matt said to me quietly and with some surprise.

"I know," I answered back softly. I couldn't put my finger on it, but Matt's demeanor just then seemed changed somehow from the way it had been only thirty minutes earlier. It was as if during the brief period we had been separated, a light bulb had been switched on inside of him and he was now more mature than he had been when we had first arrived at this couple's apartment.

"So how was yours, Sweetie?" Fatso asked his wife. He was apparently not concerned about critiquing our performances while we were right there in the kitchen with him.

"Oh he's wonderful. Very sexiful." Sweetie then bent down and gave Matt a big kiss on his cheek. "I just love him to death."

Shyly, Matt smiled. Even so, I could tell that my friend was pleased to have received this stamp of approval from our hostess.

"How was yours?" Sweetie asked her husband.

"This kid did a nice job. He's got good lips and he gave me a really good one." And then Fatso looked directly at me. "And I bet you loved the blow job I gave you too didn't you, son?" Fatso then lowered his large hand into my damp hair and began to rub the top of my head as a gesture of his newfound admiration for me.

"Yes, sir," I answered obsequiously. *Oh well, who the hell cares how my hair looks anyway,* I thought.

"Oh, that's great, honey." Sweetie was busy now at the oven as she worked to heat up something for us to eat. She then reached into the refrigerator and pulled out two bottles of beer, opened them, and placed the alcohol down on the table for Matt and me to drink. "We don't want that buzz you boys have to get away just yet, now do we? So you two go ahead and start drinking those beers, and I'll have some dinner ready for you in just a few minutes."

Matt and I then looked at each other as we took our first swigs from the bottles. These two grown-ups were certainly not like any parents that either of us had ever known.

Soon after that Sweetie placed a serving bowl on our table which was half filled with some sort of left-over casserole, and then she and her husband departed from the kitchen in order to give us a little time to ourselves. As soon as we were sure that we could speak freely again, Matt was quick to ask the first question.

"So how *did* your hair get wet, anyway?" he asked as he served some of the casserole onto his plate.

"We had a shower," I answered dryly.

"Oh," Matt thought about my answer for a moment as he put a fork full of casserole into his mouth. Then in a moment he spoke again. "I guess that means I'm gonna be getting wet, too," he lamented.

"Yeah well, I hope you're not afraid of heights," I remarked with a slight tone of disgust in my voice. I still hadn't made up my mind over how I was feeling about my soggy encounter with our host.

"Huh?" My comment confused my friend.

"Never mind," I answered. I decided it would be too hard for me to explain and too outlandish for him to believe. "What about you?" I figured it would be better for me to change the subject while I helped myself to a serving of Sweetie's casserole.

As soon as he had heard my question, Matt stopped his eating and turned his head to look at me. "Clint, I can't believe it! I've just had sex!"

I was taken off guard by this declaration of his and I didn't understand Matt's state of sudden elation. "So," I replied with no emotion. "That's practically all we've been doin' for weeks now, Matt. What's the big deal?"

"No!" Matt was frustrated now by my lack of insight. "I mean I had real sex. You know, on top with a woman on the bottom. Clint, I had real honest-to-God sex for the first time ever in my life!" The enthusiasm he was feeling for what he had just experienced seemed boundless.

"Oh, yeah?" Now I understood. "And how was it?"

"Are you kidding? It was incredible! I can't tell you how great I feel now. I really think she likes me, Clint."

"Really?" I was intrigued now by the things Matt was saying. "So you're telling me that sex with a woman is better than the stuff they've been making us do at the Academy?"

"There's no comparison. I mean, everything we've been doing up until now has been like… I don't know, just playing with people's dicks or something. But when I was in her bedroom and with her in her own bed…" Matt then shivered. "It was like… man! I couldn't believe how great it felt." Matt then returned his attention to his dinner.

As I sat there and absorbed Matt's revelations for a moment, I found myself feeling a little jealous all of a sudden. Matt was right. Everything we had been doing so far had been nothing more than a sort of perverted horse play. I suppose I might have felt differently about our sexual escapades if I had been inclined that way, but I wasn't. To be sure, the things that the upperclassmen had done to us and had trained us to do were probably the best ways for males who liked males to express themselves sexually, but it wasn't meaningful—other than the momentary thrill we felt every time we ejaculated—to either of us. *Hmm?* I then thought. *Maybe I'm beginning to mature some too?*

"I'm telling ya, Clint. Real sex with a woman's got it all over the crap we've been doin'." Then Matt smiled as he looked at me again. "I wonder if I could maybe convince this guy to take you again so I could have another turn with his wife?"

"I don't think that's the way these two are doing things around here," I observed. "Besides, if real sex is as good as you say it is, I'm gonna want to have my turn at it. Jeeze, I'm already itchin' to pop off again, anyway." I was still feeling as it all of the cocaine we had been given that day and the day before was raging stronger than ever through my system.

"Yeah, me too," Matt confessed as he concentrated more on his meal. We were both hungry and after that we said little more to each other until we had finished with our dinner.

When our plates were finally cleaned, we knew the time had arrived for the grown-ups to make a switch of their young sex partners and resume their debauchery. So once we were on our feet again, I watched as Matt solemnly followed Fatso down the long hallway to the guest room. And then, when I felt Sweetie take my hand into hers, I knew my time had come as well to leave the kitchen.

"Ok, now… what is your name again?" Sweetie asked me.

"I'm Clint," I answered politely.

"Oh right, Clint. Well come on with me, my little Clint."

Obediently, I followed the woman as she led me into her bedroom. A moment later, after we had entered the master suite, I had to make an effort to adjust my eyes to the darkness because Sweetie had turned off the lights and had drawn all the curtains shut. Once I was all the way in the room, I turned around in time to watch my soon-to-be sex partner as she closed the big double doors behind us and then locked them. I couldn't imagine who she thought might be interrupting us in here because in another few moments I was certain that Fatso would be soaking Matt down in the guest room shower.

"How about some music, Clint?" Sweetie asked sweetly.

"Ok," I agreed.

Through some dusky light which was seeping through a small gap in one of the curtains, I watched then as Sweetie took a couple of steps to place herself in front of a shelf with a stereo resting on it. Without the need for any additional light, she switched on the power and then clicked the changer so it would drop the arm down onto a record which was already sitting on the turn table. A moment later, the song "Evil Ways" by Santana filled the room and then she turned around once again to look at me. It was at this moment that I realized

She's right, I thought to myself. *So far I've been acting like a boy. I've been waiting for her permission to touch her.* So with no more encouragement needed, I took this woman into my arms. I didn't try to become the aggressor, though. I knew my place. I was participating now, but I was careful to maintain my position as the one who was submitting to the sexual demands of the other because it was obvious to me that this was the way that Sweetie wanted our encounter to be. So as I held my hands against the same places on her body that she was holding on me, I wanted to scream out with joy as I felt my aching erection squeeze up against her pubic area.

"No don't…" I said to her when she finally pulled herself away from me.

"It's ok," she assured me. "Come with me." She then led me by the hand and took me across the room to her bed. "On your back, lover," she instructed once we had climbed up onto her king-sized mattress.

Once I was lying still and looking up at her, she brought her head down and began to place her lips anywhere she wanted on my body. It was clear that she didn't want me to move, so I remained motionless and enjoyed the feel of her warm, soft, and wet lips while her luscious hair fanned out to lie all across my torso. "Ohhhh!" I sighed as I took large hunks of her silky hair into my fists.

"That's right. Just relax, my little man," Sweetie said as her tongue played with my nipples.

We continued this way for a few minutes. During this time I was more than content to simply lie there on her bed and enjoy the splendor she was creating for me. But as the minutes ticked by, my mind seemed to focus solely on my penis and how wonderful it was going to feel when Sweetie would wrap those lovely lips of hers around it. And then finally, when she took my penis into her mouth, and as I felt those lips begin to slide their way down my shaft and back up again, I realized that just as it had been for me the first time in the gym shower when Artist had introduced me to the practice, I again cocked my head backwards and prepared myself for a life-changing experience. But as quickly as my blow job had begun, it ended with Sweetie sitting up suddenly and telling me to do the same.

"Huh? What do you mean?" Reluctantly, I did as she asked and then she gave me another order.

"Now scoot over and let *me* lie down there."

And so I did as I was told, and then I watched her as she lay down on her back and spread her legs before me. She then took my fingers and taught me where to place them and how to insert them into her, plus she showed me ways in which my tongue could pleasure her. I felt as if I was receiving on-the-job training to become a boy gigolo. And looking back on it now, I guess I was.

A moment later she pulled a small square packet of something out from under her pillow and then she opened it and rolled a lubricated rubber down over my penis for me. "All right, lover, now lay on top of me," she said softly.

My arms trembled under my weight as I tried to position myself properly. Then, as soon as I was on her, she used her fingers to guide my penis inside of her and… "O… h my Go… d!"

***

I watched as Fatso, in his robe again, peered through the peephole in his front door soon after he had heard his doorbell ring. How he could see anything in the darkness out in that hallway was a mystery to me. At this same moment, I was dressed once more and sitting on the living room couch again with Sweetie this time sitting next to me in her bathrobe with her arm around my shoulders. Apparently I had done all right for my first time with her—even though the stimulation I experienced from being with her had proven too much for me and I had lost control of myself far too early.

"Come on in, Stuart," Fatso said as he held the door open for my headmaster. It seemed as if nine o'clock had come along a lot sooner than I had been thinking it would.

The shorter man then shuffled into the apartment and took up a position in the entryway as Fatso closed the door behind him. "Nnnn are the boyz ready?" It was obvious to all of us as soon as he spoke that Mr. Stuart had been drinking during his absence from us.

"You do have someone else driving don't you, Stuart?" Fatso inquired.

"Oh sure… no problem there. Are they ready?" The little man spoke quickly as he kept looking down at the floor to avoid having eye contact with Fatso. I figured this meant that our headmaster was aware of his impairment and wanted to spend as little time as possible being observed by other adults.

"Yeah," Fatso answered. "We're just waiting for the black-haired boy."

At the very moment Fatso was giving his answer to Mr. Stuart, we all were able to see my roommate suddenly as he emerged from the guest room at the far end of the long hall and began to walk toward us. At first I though Matt looked frustrated by something, but as he drew closer to all of us I decided he was just plain mad. He was fully dressed once again, although he had neglected to straighten his tie, and because he had felt rushed, he told me later, my friend had not taken the time he had needed to dry his hair so drops of water were falling every so often onto his jacket or his white shirt or his tie.

"Ok, let'z go. Come on byz," Mr. Stuart said. And then he turned and opened the front door again so the three of us could leave the penthouse.

Sweetie then gave me a big kiss on my cheek. "Well so long. We'll see you boys again sometime soon. Ok?"

"Ok," I answered sheepishly. I really didn't know how to react any longer. That's the way it is with life-changing events sometimes. It takes a little while to figure out if you're still the same person afterwards.

"Yeah, so long, boys," Fatso bid us his farewell also. Then he turned his attention to our headmaster again. "Stuart, these two are some of the best ones you've ever trained out at that school of yours. You go ahead and turn these two out this week, and then I'll call you in a few days to let you know where I'm going to want them to be sent next weekend. All right?"

"Yeah. That'z good." By this time our headmaster was already out in the hallway again and pushing the button for the elevator.

"Your hair's wet," I said as a friendly jab at my roommate once the three of us were going down together in the elevator. After all, he had made the same crack about me earlier in the kitchen, so I figured that turn about was fair play.

"Yeah!" Matt replied in disgust. And then he said nothing more to me. I concluded then that my friend had probably no appreciation for the acrobatic nature of his water party with our host.

Our ride to the Academy that night was uneventful. Apparently all three of our escorts had bided their time in Boston somewhere rather than return to Ulster only to have to turn around and come back for us a short time later. And since nothing was said by anyone during our trip home that night, I figured that the older three had probably had as much of each other's company as they could stand for one night. Plus by now we knew what all of the older kids at the Academy knew about Mr. Stuart and how things were whenever he got himself into this sort of condition. Without exception, whenever the head of our faculty was drunk, things around the man had to be kept quiet. This was the reason why lights out was one of the few rules at the Academy which was actually enforced. Clamor around Mr. Stuart when he was three sheets to the wind as they say, could be calamitous for any boy who didn't watch himself in this regard. So other than the moment when we first entered the van and the head waiter had kidded Matt about his hair being wet still—both the head waiter and the leader had gone through the same indoctrination when they had been our age—nothing more was said by any of us during the entire hour-and-a-quarter drive back to the campus.

Naturally, the long ride back left me with time to review in my mind the events of this bizarre evening in Boston. I wondered how many other boys had been hung upside down in that incredible shower and how it was that such a nice woman like Sweetie could have such a warped penchant for thirteen-year-old boys. And how in the world could a couple be married and still do the things they had done with Matt and me on this night. But mostly I wondered what it was that Fatso had meant when he had told Mr. Stuart to turn us out during the upcoming week and why it was that we were going to be traveling somewhere on the following weekend. What did these things suggest about our immediate futures and would we ever be able to gain control over our lives again? Of course I was sure I already knew the answers, but these questions occupied my mind more than anything else that night as I sat there in the darkness and watched the front porch lights of probably hundreds of families—all safe and secure in their houses—pass by the window I kept looking out of. In fact I became so lost in my own thoughts, I failed to notice when we arrived finally at the Academy and the van had been stopped in front of our dorm so we could get out.

"It's past lights out," the leader said once Matt and I were standing on the outdoor basketball court. "So you two go on back to your room and get yourselves to bed right away."

"Yes, sir," I replied obediently.

"Yes, sir," Matt answered in the same subordinate tone.

As Matt and I then walked down the flight of cement steps to our landing and continued on into our building, we did so without speaking a word to each other. It had been another day of enormous change and emotion for us. There was a great deal they had done to us once again and it was going to require some time for us to absorb it all, plus by this hour of the night we were too exhausted to think straight any longer. So as soon as we were in our room, we both lost no time in pulling off every stitch of our clothing and falling gratefully into our beds so we could welcome sleep and the end to this miserable day.

Getting to sleep for both of us was easy, but waking up the next morning was another matter. As soon as the first bell of the day had sounded, the leader rushed into our room with our morning doses of cocaine. "Good morning, boys! Time to get up." He had already showered and dressed for the day.

Matt and I answered this guy's cheery greeting with grumbles and an obscenity or two.

"I'm going to prepare some lines for you right now and then after this you two are gonna have to do this for yourselves." The leader wasn't put off by our lack of enthusiasm for his visit. The kid knew as he placed his things onto the top of our dresser that our attitudes were now changed from the way they had been the day before.

As we sat up in our beds and rubbed the sleep from our eyes, Matt and I watched as the leader then chopped and mixed the white powder for us. And then when the time came for us to snort the drug up into our heads again, we did so without so much as a hint of argument this time. After all, cocaine was our life now. The draggy way our bodies were feeling told us that the head waiter had been right. We were indeed hooked on cocaine now and we needed the stuff so we could make it out of bed and through our day.

When we were finished, and Matt and I were sniffing the remainder of what we had just inhaled so it could go farther up into our nasal passages, the leader then went on to inform us of how our lives as drug addicts were going to be. "That ought to hold you two until lunchtime. After lunch come find me, and I'll give you guys some more to hold you through the afternoon. Then after dinner I'll give you two enough coke to use one time for the evening, and then again for tomorrow morning so we won't have to keep coming here every day. Understand?"

"Yes, sir," Matt answered.

"Yes, sir," I said also.

"Fine." The leader seemed pleased that we were now so cooperative. "All right now, here's a hand mirror and a razor blade for you guys to use." The leader then placed the items down on our dresser next to the picture of Matt with his parents. Then, with his responsibilities toward us discharged for the morning, the leader turned and walked over to the front of our room and opened our door again. "You guys go ahead now and get up. You're still expected at breakfast this morning and you still have to attend all of your classes."

"How?" Matt asked painfully. You could almost hear the tears in his voice.

"What do you mean, how?" The leader was surprised by my roommate's question.

"How are we supposed to go to class when some of our teachers did us the other night when we were in the mud?" Matt really seemed bothered by this issue.

"You don't have to worry," the leader tried to reassure my friend. "They won't say anything about it. Besides, all of us have had faculty cocks in our mouths at one time or another. It's really no big deal. Now let's get going." And with that the leader then walked out into the hallway and closed our door behind him.

"Are you ok?" I asked Matt after I had heard the leader leave our building through the large wooden door at the west end of our hall.

"Yeah," my roommate replied in a lost-soul sort of way. "It's just... after having sex with Sweetie last night, it reminded me how much I hate being made to have sex with guys."

"I know," I agreed. "I hate it too. That's why I try not to think about it and just go along with the things they make us do. It makes it easier to put up with, I guess."

"Yeah, I know," Matt sighed. "Also, now that I've had some time to think about it, I'm not sure what I think about having sex with another man's wife. Even if he did want me to do it." Matt sighed again. "It just seems like we're breaking every rule in the book these days. Ya know?"

I understood the spiritual implications of what my roommate was saying to me. I had been feeling the same pangs of guilt, myself. "Yeah, I know, Matt. But I think in a few more days the number of people we have sex with and their marital status is gonna become a blur to us, anyway. So I don't think it's gonna do us any good to think about these things anymore."

"Yeah, you're right," Matt agreed. "Besides, I think the cocaine is starting to kick in now so... who the hell cares anyway? Right?"

I then smiled at my friend. "Right." By now I was beginning to feel pretty good too, so I swung my legs over and planted my bare feet onto the cold linoleum and stood up. "Come on, we'd better get going." And then I began to look around the room for something I could put on to wear for the day.

The rest of that Monday went normally for us—if you could call our lives at the Academy normal. At lunchtime new table assignments were posted and Matt and I found ourselves assigned once again to the headmaster's table. It was creepy too because during the entire meal I felt as if the man kept staring at my mouth as I ate. Then in the afternoon, we were told that since our training was now over and we were going to be put to work this week, we were no longer permitted to hang out with the gang in the leader's dorm room. It didn't make any sense to us, but neither did anything else in this crazy place.

For dinner, Thomas made mashed potatoes once again. This time though, we were served our dinner family style. And when Matt and I tried our food, we found that everything we had been given that evening tasted fine—if you could define anything that Thomas prepared for us as tasting fine. And so we figured that the sleeping pill caper was over for us.

"Pass the bread please," Matt asked of one of the kids who was sitting across our table from him.

By chance I happened to take a moment to look around the dining hall once everyone at our table had been served their food. I guess I had the idea to see for myself if all of the other tables were serving the meal family style which, as I've said before, was the usual practice at the Academy. To my dismay, I noticed an instant later that the plates being handed out at the head proctor's table had once again been prepared in advance in the kitchen before they were served. In order to see this, I had to make myself appear as if I was simply gazing around the room in a casual manner while I concentrated hard to peer between the several dozen other kids who were seated between the spot where Matt and I were now sitting and the table across the dining hall which had just captured my interest. And then I saw them. I don't know why I was surprised, but sitting in the places where Matt and I had sat the week before were two new first-year boys. "Look over there," I whispered to Matt.

When he glanced over in the direction where my eyes were indicating, Matt saw what I had just discovered. Carlos and Juan, our two Venezuelan next-door neighbors, were now sitting at the head proctor's table and they were surrounded by the upperclassmen. "Oh shit! They're eating their mashed potatoes," Matt said to me under his breath.

"Yeah," I acknowledged quietly.

"Who's eating their mashed potatoes?" Frank suddenly butted in.

Startled suddenly by the sound of Frank's voice, I responded by launching into him. "How is it that you're sitting with us every time we're moved to a different table, Frank?" Besides being upset about Juan and Carlos, I was feeling a little annoyed over the fact that Frank seemed to always be hanging around us and wanting to involve himself in our affairs. Also, I wanted to throw the guy off the subject of Juan and Carlos.

"I don't know," Frank replied. "I guess you guys are just lucky or somethin'. How 'bout you tell me how come youz two are always eatin' together when everybody else who's roommates gets split up at mealtime?"

It was a good question. Matt and I had wondered the same thing several times ourselves and all we could figure was that the answer probably had something to do with the fact that the head waiter was the one who made the changes in the seating assignments every two weeks. "I have no idea," I answered in a way that was intended to portray me as being utterly innocent.

"Yeah?" Frank stared at me for a moment while his mind mulled over my answer. "So who's eatin' their mashed potatoes?"

"We are, Frank. Aren't you?" Matt jumped in suddenly and saved me from having to come up with an answer that I probably wouldn't have been able to sell.

"You?" Frank now looked confused. "But that wasn't who…"

"How come you don't like mashed potatoes, Frank?" It was my turn now to send in the next salvo.

"Huh?" Our misdirection seemed to be working. Frank now appeared to be thinking more about what we were talking about now than what we had said earlier. "I like mashed potatoes!"

"Then why aren't you eating yours," Matt lobbed another one at our friend. It was amazing how much we could both tell what the other was thinking these days.

"I am eatin' them!" Frank was now exasperated with us. His Brooklyn short fuse was starting to work in our favor.

"Then why did you tell us that you weren't eating them?" I chimed in again.

"I didn't… Aw what the hell!" Frank then gave up and looked down at his food again. "Never mind." And then he looked up at Matt and me one more time. "Just don't talk to me anymore. You guys are screwy."

Matt and I then gave each other a glance of knowing satisfaction. We both understood how close we had come just then to revealing information about what was really going on in this place to an outsider. Most of the other members of the student body, including Frank, went about their business every day living their lives as normal prep school kids. Their routine was the cover the upperclassmen and the participating members of the faculty needed to keep the secret about the heinous things they were doing to us from becoming known by the outside world. We had been told time and again to never speak of what we were doing to anyone outside of our little gang and to do so would invite the harshest of punishments upon us. We knew from our experience in the mud pit that there were more than just the eight students we were aware of who were involved in the activities of our gang, but without knowing for sure who these other kids were, we could never be certain if telling someone about our plight would get us saved or beaten up. It was an effective way for the upperclassmen to keep us in line. And so Matt and I were constantly having to guard ourselves against slip-ups that might allow information about our tormentors to leak out accidentally. As for Frank, he was a bright kid and if he had been able to put together from something that we had said about the way our lives at the Academy really were, the upperclassmen probably would have dealt with the problem by hauling him off to the gym shower one night and putting him through the same initiation that Matt and I had been forced to go through. So at the least, we figured that we had just saved our friend from a life of drug addiction and embarrassment over being forced to perform blow jobs on demand. Preventing bad things from happening to Frank was one thing, but keeping Juan and Carlos safe was a different matter altogether.

All during study hall that evening, Matt and I discussed whether or not we should say something to Carlos and Juan about what we believed was in store for them later that night. After a lengthy debate, we concluded that foreknowledge of the events upcoming would do nothing to prevent the upperclassmen from getting their way. Just like Matt and me and all of the other first-year students for that matter, Carlos and Juan were trapped at the Academy with no place else to go. Also we knew that if we were to say something to our next-door neighbors beforehand, reprisals for our disobedience would soon follow. So even though it went against our instincts, we decided that saying nothing to our friends was, in the end, the only prudent way for us to handle the situation.

"Why do jou suppose I am so tired tonight?" We heard Carlos ask Juan just before the ten o'clock bell went off as the two boys returned to their room together after using the bathroom.

"I have no idea, man. I guess you just are, that's all." Juan spoke perfect English. His father was actually an American who was working at that time for an oil company in Maracaibo. The man had married a Venezuelan woman and bilingual Juan had been the result of their union. Our friend preferred to be called Juan, but on his right wrist he always wore a small silver ID bracelet which was engraved with the name "Juan" on one side and "John" on the other.

At lights out we waited for two of the upperclassmen to appear to give us our nightly rituals. With the cocaine in our systems all the time now, both Matt and I felt as if we had been walking around all day with what is referred to in the vernacular as perpetual hard-on's. And it surprised us when after some time had passed, nobody had come to our room. It may sound odd, but it felt strange to us to be lying there in our beds by ourselves. So as we continued to wait in vain in the darkness for anyone to show some interest in us, we soon grew tired and fell asleep, which marked this day as a milestone in our recent lives at the Academy. Because for the first time in weeks, Matt and I had gone through an entire day without being manhandled and made to ejaculate.

Later, at around ten minutes after two in the morning, I was awakened briefly by the sound of something—or someone—being slammed up against the wall which separated our room from the room of the Venezuelan boys. As I became conscious somewhat, I thought I could hear the sounds of kids shouting at each other. There seemed to me to be one high-pitched voice and two lower voices making all this racket. Next, I heard something like a vase

Since we seemed to be in agreement, I figured that any sounds or sharp breathing or sudden movements made in the darkness would now be overlooked by either of us as an urgently needed remedy for a problem which, under normal conditions, is profound for all teenaged boys. So since stealthy movements were now unnecessary, I shoved my hand noisily under my covers and prepared myself to get a firm grip on the situation.

"Wait," Matt blurted out suddenly. "I've got a better idea." He then threw his covers off of him and stood up on the floor.

"What?" I asked as I turned my head to look at my friend.

"Stand up," Matt insisted.

"Why?" After all, I was warm and comfortable by now under my covers and I had just begun to give myself a happy ending to the day.

"Just stand up," Matt urged.

I stopped what I was doing and sighed. "Ok," I agreed. And then I pulled my covers off of me and stood up to face my friend. "Now what?"

"Now close your eyes."

"Oh?" I couldn't believe it, but in an instant I decided that this could be interesting.

"Yeah, close them. I've got an idea."

"Ok," I relented. And so I followed my friend's instructions and I closed my eyes.

Matt then reached over and laid the picture of him with his parents face down on the top of our dresser, and then he took hold of my T-shirt from around my waist and pulled the garment up and over my head until it was off of me completely. "Keep 'em closed," he warned.

"I will," I promised.

When the T-shirt had come off, it had messed up my hair. A moment later I could feel Matt's small hands smoothing out and arranging my hair to put it back into place. As I remained still, I then felt his hands begin to lightly feel their way down onto my shoulders and then continue on down farther to my chest and finally they made their way onto my stomach. As he did this, he made sure to move his fingers very slowly along my skin. I stood there as he did these things to me and tried to put myself into the right frame of mind. A moment later, I was surprised to discover that I was suddenly finding this experience to be incredibly erotic. So by the time his fingers found their way into the elastic of my underpants, my penis was already becoming swollen from the anticipation he was creating in me.

Matt saw my bulge and commented. "So is this ok?"

"Oh yeah!" I breathed.

Next Matt knelt down in front of me and slowly peeled down my underpants until they were left to rest around my ankles. When he saw that I was nearly erect already, he put out his tongue and swirled it around my crown. Like a good mechanic, he knew how to use the right tool for the job.

"Uuh!" I reacted. It was obvious to me now that Matt knew what he was doing with me.

An instant later, Matt took my entire penis into his mouth and then he began to work me.

"Hhhh!" I exhaled. The sexual sensations began to shoot through my body. Matt then placed his palms onto my buttocks and began to squeeze each cheek as he clamped down harder on me with his lips. And as I felt Matt begin to create a suction in his mouth around my penis, I opened my eyes and looked down at his hairy head so I could watch it as it moved in and out on me with increasing vigor. Then his stimulation became too much for me and I threw back my own head and felt my body stiffen.

"Uugh! Hhhh! Hhhh!" At this rate, he was going to have me ejaculating in no time.

Then he stopped and removed his mouth from around my penis. "Ok now, go lay down."

Silently, I stepped out of my underpants and moved backwards so I could do as my roommate had commanded. A moment later I was flat on my back in my bed again and watching as Matt's face hovered over my groin area once he had climbed up onto my bed with me.

"Are ya ready?" he asked.

"Oh yeah!" I gasped.

Matt's head then sank as his mouth enveloped my penis and resumed its stroking with his rigid lips. The friction and the suction quickly transported me off to another world. *Ah, go Matt!* I thought to myself. He had learned from the best and there was no doubt in my mind now that he was no longer an amateur. And for that matter, neither was I. Because a few minutes later, after Matt had taken me through a hard ejaculation, I stood up again and had my roommate shut his eyes while I pulled off his clothing and prepared myself to do the same for him.

Chapter Seven
Being Put to Work

Finally the dreaded day came for Matt and me to be turned out. On Wednesday afternoon after lunch, we climbed into the van with the other kids who were going into town that day, for our first trip into Ulster since the whole process to convert us into the drug-addicted, sex-crazed boys we now were, had begun. Once we were in town and had pulled into the parking lot at the Duncan Donuts, Matt and I remained in our seats while everyone else in the van got out. As we sat there with Artist sitting in the seat behind us, we watched as our friends began to disperse to more exotic destinations like the record shop or one of the pizzerias in town.

"Hey, aren't you guys comin' too?" Frank asked when he noticed that Matt and I were still sitting in the van.

"Ah…" I said as I tried to think up a quick explanation for why we were breaking with the standard practice.

"I agreed to drop them over on the other side of town at the Grants Department Store," Mr. Foot said quickly. "Now close the doors, will ya?"

Apparently satisfied with our teacher's explanation, Frank shrugged and then reached out and slammed the two doors shut on the side of the van. For an instant after that, he looked at me with an expression which seemed to convey a sense of confusion and disappointment, and then Frank took a step backwards while Mr. Foot threw the transmission into drive again and drove us back out onto Main Street and away.

A few minutes later, Mr. Foot maneuvered the van onto the grounds of the business which we were about to become intimately familiar with. He said nothing until he had taken us around the drive and up to the front door, and then he stopped the vehicle to let the three of us out. "Ok, you guys. Everybody out now."

"The Friendly Inn? Are you kidding me? They're gonna let us do our stuff here?" Matt expressed the amazement we both felt. We had thought that we were going to be stuck away in some seedy little house or something off Main Street in downtown Ulster. We had no idea that we were going to be offered up to anyone who was willing to pay for thirty minutes with us in a place as out in the open as this.

"This is the biggest motel in the area. It's right off 193 and next to the lake!" I announced. "And customers are gonna come here to see us?"

"Yeah well, we want people to be able to find you, you know," Artist explained.

"Let's go, out!" Mr. Foot apparently didn't want anyone to see him dropping kids off at a motel.

And so Matt and I climbed out of the van and prepared ourselves to report for our first day of work. As soon as Artist was standing on the pavement with us, the three of us then walked in through the single wide automatic front door and on into the main lobby as the van roared away. This was the first time, by the way, that I noticed the strange briefcase that Artist had brought along with him.

"Are you boys from the Academy?" An older woman of indeterminate age and horn-rimmed glasses asked as she handed us three room keys from behind the front desk. "You'll have to wait a couple of minutes. The maids are just finishing up with those rooms right now."

"Ok, thank you," Artist replied as he took the keys and slipped them quickly into his pocket. Then he turned around and guided us away from the view of the half dozen or so people who were sitting around the lobby and watching every move we were making—or so it seemed to me. "We'll go wait in the pool room. It's usually empty around this time of the day."

Is the whole town in on this? I wondered as we made our way to the motel's indoor swimming pool.

"We'll be fine for a few minutes in here," Artist proclaimed once we had gone through the glass and metal door and had entered the pool area.

"How in the world did the Academy arrange for us to be here?" I probably shouldn't have asked this question, but I was still so shocked by the thought that the acts we were about to perform were going to be so public.

"Oh well, some years ago your new friend in Boston made the arrangements with the owner or the manager or someone like that here. So ever since, we've been bringing the first-year kids we've trained, over here to work. You know, it's a nice clean place and the guy here who set everything up for us takes a piece of your action for his trouble."

"And what about that woman behind the front desk?" Matt asked. "Does she get a piece of our action too?"

"Well sort of," Artist replied. "She probably gets a hundred dollars a week or something like that slipped to her under the table for assigning our rooms and giving us our keys and helping us out in other ways.

"Oh, man!" Matt replied in amazement.

There wasn't much more for us to talk about after that, so Matt and I began to look around to see what kind of pool facilities this place had to offer. The water looked inviting and there was a doorway leading to a couple of locker rooms just beyond the diving board at the opposite end from where we had come in. "Wait a minute!" I couldn't believe what I was now seeing.

"What?" Matt asked.

"Oh this is too much!" I was now exasperated nearly beyond words.

"What?" Matt looked at me with worry in his eyes.

"Well look!" I shouted. "This is the pool that's in the damn catalog!"

"Really?" Matt looked away from me and back at the water again.

"Yeah, look at those funny sort of translucent wall tiles over there, and the steel pillar in the middle of the cement, and that ladder coming up out of the water, and the patio furniture. This *is* the pool those Academy kids were swimming in that I saw in the Academy's catalog! I don't believe it!"

Artist then smiled at me. "That's right, Clint. Man, what a memory you've got. Those were first-year students in that picture. They were on a break from their duties in the rooms they were using here that day.

"Incredible!" I replied with disgust as if being lied to about a swimming pool was more heinous than being turned into drug addicts and boy prostitutes.

A few moments later, Artist decided the time had come for us to move on, so we left the pool and headed for the bedrooms we had been assigned to use for that afternoon. The plan, as it turned out, was simple. Matt and I were placed in adjoining rooms with the door between us closed when customers were there, but left unlocked all the time. In this way, Matt and I could be available to come to each other's aid should the need arise. Between customers, as it worked out, we preferred to keep this door open so we could talk with each other and look each other over to make certain that we were both all right after each session. Also, we were expected to work until just before dinnertime. When he figured that we had labored long enough for one day, Artist would come for us and take us to the van which by this time will have returned to take us home. And except for the few free minutes we had between customers, Matt and I were never given a break once we started to perform our unique services.

"I'll be in a room in a different part of the motel for security reasons," Artist explained once we were all settled in what was to be my room. And then he opened up his briefcase and revealed to us the largest quantity of cocaine in one place we had ever seen. "By now the woman at the front desk has written my room number on a piece of paper and has stuck that paper in the lower left corner of the bulletin board they have out there in the lobby. Then, she'll place a small alarm clock she has up onto the counter there at the front desk every time she's ready to let the next person, who's waiting out there in the lobby, to come to my room."

"So all those people I saw sitting around the lobby were customers waiting to come and have sex with us?" I interrupted.

"That's right," Artist confirmed. "Anyway, after a person leaves the lobby to come to my room, the woman then puts her clock away until I call her to have her send me the next customer. So when these people who are interested in purchasing your services today come to see me in my room, I'll ask them first if they prefer a boy with black hair or a boy with blond hair, and then after that we'll negotiate a price and I'll send him or her to one of you with a slip of paper in his or her hand. This paper is how you'll know that the person who's knocking on your door is a legitimate customer."

"Are you gonna write something on the paper for us?" Matt asked.

"Yes," Artist answered as he pulled out some cocaine and began to prepare it for us. "There's a code you have to memorize because different customers are gonna want to do different things with you."

"Like what?" Matt asked as I began to prepare to snort up my afternoon ration of happy powder.

"Ok well, the number one means you take it in the ass. Number two means you give it in the ass. If you see a three on the paper it means you're supposed to take it in the mouth and a four means you give it in the mouth. Then a five means you accept a hand job, and a six means you give a hand job."

"Shit!" Matt reacted as I began to sniff the drug into my head.

"Well, we charge different prices for different services." Artist then resumed his chopping and mixing as he explained. "A one, for example, is more expensive than a five. But don't worry. Most of the time you'll be taking it from them, so you're not likely to get all used up. But if you find after a while that you can't cum anymore, then just fake it." He then looked at my roommate. "Ok, Matt, snort away, kid." Artist then stood aside so Matt could get close enough to the mirror to take in his cocaine.

"Ok," Matt answered. "SNI…I…F"

"And then before they leave me to come to see you guys," Artist continued, "I also sell them whatever amount of cocaine they want to buy from me this week. So if you're really nice to them, they might be willing to give you guys a little taste from time to time." Artist then looked around my room to see if there was anything else he needed to do, and then he closed up his briefcase. "Ok, you guys get ready. I'll start sending them to you in a few minutes. And then when you've finished with the first one, put your clothes back on and make the bed, and then call me on the phone to let me know that you're ready for me to send you the next customer. And if you go too long and I don't hear from you, I'll come down here and check on you myself. And if I have to do that I'm gonna be pissed. So keep 'em moving through here. Ok?" And with that our master opened the door and walked back out into the hall. "Oh, and one more thing. If either of you guys get any funny ideas about placing an outside phone call to anyone, you should know that the phones in this place are turned off at the front desk and the woman there is keeping her eye on the panel to make sure your lights don't go on without mine going on too. And if I ever get a call from her telling me that either of you were making calls to anyone else in this motel besides me, the night you guys spent in the pine field will seem like a walk in the park compared to how you'll both be feeling after we've finished with you two. Get my drift? And the same goes for what will happen to you guys if either of you decide to leave your room. Our operations here have been going on now for years. So there are a lot of people around town and in this motel even who are interested in seeing what we do here continue. These people would let me know immediately if you guys were wandering through the halls or worse, actually walking out on the grounds by yourselves. So do your jobs, don't screw up, and everything will work out just fine here. All right?"

Neither Matt nor I said anything in response. We just stared at the kid.

"Ok, then." And with that, Artist left us and began to walk through the hall toward his room.

"I think I'm gonna be sick," Matt said as he closed my door to the hall. "Clint, how the hell did we end up in a spot like this?" My friend then sat down on my bed and looked dejected.

"I have no idea," I answered glumly. "One day I was all excited about getting to go to the boarding school of my choice, and the next thing I know I'm standing here in a motel room in the middle of God knows where waiting for a hundred or so strangers to have sex with me."

"Yeah. This stinks." Matt was then silent for a minute or so before he felt like speaking again. "On the other hand, I can feel the cocaine starting to kick in now, so maybe this won't be all that bad after all."

"Yeah," I agreed. "I know what you mean." I was beginning to feel better too.

A few minutes later we heard someone knocking on Matt's door.

"Oh shit! They picked black hair first," Matt then stood up and began to walk toward his room.

"Are you gonna be all right?" I asked.

"How the hell should I know?" he shot back as he closed the door between our two rooms and then he went on to answer his door to the hallway.

Since I had nothing else to do for the moment, I tried to listen through the adjoining door to hear how things were going for my friend.

"A three, huh," Matt responded after he had extended his greeting to the stranger. "Ok, come on in."

I then heard the customer enter Matt's room and close the door behind him. After that I heard silence for a few moments as I imagined them both taking off their clothing and getting the bed ready and then… KNOCK! KNOCK! KNOCK! Someone was now knocking on my door. So I left Matt and walked over to open it.

"Hi." A man I judged to be in his early thirties wearing a business suit and smiling at me then handed me a scrap of paper. When I unfolded it I could see that it plainly had the number one written on it.

"Ok," I answered. "Come on in."

***

On Saturday after lunch Matt and I were picked up by Joe in his blue 1963 Cadillac convertible. We had been told to pack overnight bags and that we were going to be spending the night at an estate down in Connecticut somewhere. For some reason which neither of us ever really learned, Joe was supposed to be our chauffeur for this trip. I found Joe's driving alarming and at one point on Route 44, we had to pass a car while traveling at over one hundred miles per hour so we could barely miss hitting a car that was coming toward us from the other direction. And through it all, the man kept droning on about old girlfriends and people he had beaten up. The entire experience was nerve-racking, to say the least, for both of us. And as a way for us to release some stress—I suppose—my roommate and I found ourselves offering comments throughout the trip which were humorous to us as boys, but less than flattering to our driver.

By this time, Matt and I had thoroughly debriefed each other about the customers we had serviced on the previous Wednesday. The only really upsetting incident of that day had been the one time Matt had opened the door between our two rooms because he had believed that I was in trouble—which I kind of was.

"Get the hell out of here, kid!" The giant man who was raping me at that moment yelled at Matt. Upon seeing that I wasn't being murdered at least, Matt felt he had no option then, but to comply with the man's order. I explained later that this customer had shown up with the number four written on his piece of paper. So after he had finished giving me a blow job, he then ordered me to turn over and get ready to take it in my ass. When I sat up and protested that he had only paid for the service we had just completed, he hauled off and slugged me full out in the face. He was a big man and his punch had spun me around and left me lying in the bed on my face. The man then squared up the lower half of my body, dipped his penis into the jar of Vaseline we always kept on the night stand, and then proceeded to take from me what he had really come to my room to get.

As I lay there dazed and not entirely coherent, I guess I must have yelled out each time he thrust himself into me because my screams, apparently, were what had triggered Matt to enter my room.

"I didn't know what else to do," Matt had said when we talked about this later.

"That's ok, Matt. There wasn't anything you could have done. After all, it wasn't as if you could have pulled the guy off of me or anything. So don't worry about it."

"Yeah, but I should have been able to think of some way to help you." Matt was clearly torn up inside because of his inaction.

"Forget about it." I really didn't want Matt to feel bad. I simply figured that in the future, I wouldn't worry about what sort of money the Academy was collecting for our services. The ache I still felt in my jaw on this Saturday afternoon caused me to decide that from that point forward it would be in my best interest to permit the customers to do whatever they hell they wanted to me and allow Artist, or whatever other upperclassman was escorting us that day, to worry about the rest.

I can't say the name of the town or the person who had ordered us up for this weekend, but our latest customer turned out to be a famous actor who Matt and I recognized immediately once we were deposited on his front drive. He was friendly and, we found, very easy to talk with. We also found his place to be magnificent. The large house was set well back from the tree-lined road, and he said that he owned about twenty-four acres of land around us. And after the man had helped us with our bags and had shown us to the room we would be staying in, he had us meet him around in back by his swimming pool for an autumn afternoon in the still warm Connecticut sun.

We arrived at the pool before he did so we waited in the chairs on his patio for him to show up and give us permission to jump in. When the man did finally appear, he did so in a terry cloth robe. He informed us then that his family was away for the weekend so we men had the run of the place. "So I say we ought to go skinny dipping!" he announced. Matt and I then watched as the man pulled off his robe to reveal himself in all of his splendor, and then he jumped into the pool.

Matt and I then looked at each other and smiled. Skinny dipping sounded like great fun to us, so we pulled down our swim suits and jumped into the water in our birthday suits to join our host.

Matt and I were both fans of the man's television show, and we had seen his movies, also. So the time we spent with him that afternoon was magical. It was almost like spending time with a wild and uninhibited uncle. We had lots of questions about his show and the other members of his cast, and he was happy to spend the day talking about himself. And we barely gave it a second thought when, at different times, he had us swim over to him and then float on our backs so he could go down on us. We were finally away from the Academy and free from the constant scrutiny of the upperclassmen and the colluding members of the faculty. It felt wonderful to us both to be out in the world again.

It turned out that our host was an excellent chef. So for dinner that night he prepared Chateaubriand for us with wild rice and asparagus. After weeks of eating the garbage they gave us at the Academy, I felt as if we had been sprung from prison. Our host also introduced Matt and me to French wine, and he taught us a little about which wine went with what sort of meals. And I liked the high I got from wine. It seemed to come up more gently and wasn't such a right cross to the jaw as hard liquor was, and I thought it mixed better with the cocaine the three of us enjoyed later on. After dinner, though, once we had helped him to clean up his kitchen, our host's secret plan for us was revealed.

When the time came, Matt and I followed this guy upstairs to his bedroom. Once there, he pulled out some costumes and makeup and then he helped us for the next fifteen minutes or so to get dressed up. Apparently this macho star of the big and small screens had a thing for *The Wizard of Oz*. So while Matt and I were looking with disbelief into this guy's full-length mirror at the

***

During the next few weeks, we became accustomed to our new routine. On Wednesday afternoons and evenings we provided the services we had been trained to perform on whatever local area customers happened to show up at the inn, while on our off nights, to quell our raging urges, Matt and I usually found ways on our own to relieve each other's tension. And then on weekends, depending upon how our time was scheduled, we would either go out on two one-day excursions, or we would pack our bags and leave the campus for an overnight trip.

We were also aware of the progress that Carlos and Juan were making as they were put through the same training that we had been forced to endure. Carlos was shorter and had thick curly hair, while Juan was taller and had his hair cut above the ears and combed over on top. On the weekend they were scheduled to go into the mud pit, I wondered how Artist's mud sculpting would make each boy appear. Matt and I weren't permitted to have much contact with either of them during this period, but we found out from some of our gang that even after the beatings and the drugs and the booze, Juan was still being defiant every so often while Carlos had succumbed fully as we both had.

On that same weekend, Matt and I were driven down to New York City to stay overnight with a man who lived alone off Third Avenue in Manhattan. We never really learned very much about this guy other than he worked in an office on Wall Street and he treated us with great kindness. Until this trip, Matt had never been to New York, but I had already visited the city a few times by this point in my life. We had been told to bring dark suits with us and fortunately Matt and I each owned one because this man wound up taking us out to Sign of the Dove for dinner that Saturday night. He had warned us ahead of time to say that we were his nephews in from Chicago for the weekend should anyone who knew him happen to stop by our table for a visit.

"Most people who know me know that I live alone, and I wouldn't want any of them to get the wrong idea about me," he explained as we were seated next to one of the mirrored walls in the restaurant.

"You mean the right idea," I replied softly and with a smile on my face.

A bashful sort of an expression then came over the man. "Well, yes I suppose you're right. But you know what I mean." Then, as soon as the waiter had taken our orders, our host continued in a voice which was just loud enough for the two of us to hear.

"You know, I would never ever hurt anyone or force anyone to do something they wouldn't want to do. I admit that I like boys. In fact, when I have a steady young friend I feel happy all the time and complete. Like I'm a whole person, finally. But I would never want to do something that would harm a boy in any way."

At this point Matt and I looked at each other and I could see that the very same thought which had just crossed my mind was in my roommate's brain as well. And that was… if what our host was saying to us was true, then why the heck were we here?

"I've dated women, you know," the man continued. "I've even gone to bed with them, but I could never get excited about being with them… if you know what I mean."

"You mean they never got you aroused?" Matt asked. By now we had become used to speaking plainly about sexual matters.

"Well… that's right. No matter how hard I try, I just don't seem to be able to be interested in women in a sexual way," he told us.

"What about men?" I asked. I was now finding this conversation a bit intriguing.

"Well, I finally got to a place in my life a few years ago where I decided that if women didn't turn me on, I must be interested in men, instead. In New York there are places where gay men can go to find other gay men, so I began going to some of these places and looking for a guy I might find interesting. And after a while I found a man who seemed interested in me."

"What happened then?" I asked when our host paused for a moment to take a sip of water.

"Well, we went out for dinner and then later on we wound up back at my apartment."

"Did ya do it with him, then?" Matt was now into this guy's story as much as I was. And I had to admit, our host was a very engaging fellow.

Undaunted by my roommate's frankness, our host then went on with his story. "Well, after we had both had a few drinks, we did go to bed together. But just like the experiences I had with women, going to bed with another man just didn't excite me either. So the evening turned out to be a complete disaster and we never saw each other again."

"That's too bad," I remarked without thinking.

The man then looked at me and smiled. "Thank you. No matter how hard I've tried to deny it, and no matter what I've tried to get around it, I could never get over the fact that boys are where my interests really lie. And it's not just

"He said he did. So I rubbed him back. He liked it, so I rubbed him back some more. And pretty soon I had his pajamas off and I was giving him a full body massage. And once I had him completely relaxed, I gave this boy his first ever blow job. He loved it, of course. And it wasn't too many days after that before I had taught him how to give me blow jobs too. 'It's only fair,' I used to tell him. 'Whatever I do to you, you have to do to me.'"

"How old was this boy?" Matt asked. Neither of us were eating now. We had both become transfixed by this guy's story.

"This happened when he was eight," the man answered.

"Eight?" I asked in amazement. I then looked at Matt and saw that he couldn't believe what he was hearing either. Somehow, this guy had misconstrued innocent childish horse play for sexual advances. We felt it was extremely doubtful if this boy had possessed any idea at all of what he was doing when he first rubbed the man's groin. So how, we wondered, had this guy not understood that? And then the story continued.

"Before long whenever he'd come up to my apartment, he'd be out of his clothes in no time and telling me that I had to take mine off too. And so I would. Ohhh..." he sighed. "We used to have so much fun together."

"What happened to him?" Matt asked.

"Oh, his mother finally married some guy and they all moved out to Flushing. After that, I never saw him again."

"How old was he when he moved away?" I asked.

"Twelve," our host answered sadly.

"So that means you two had sex all the time for four years?" I calculated.

"Yes," the man answered with a far-away look in his eye. "They were the best four years of my life."

The waiter was back then with our meal, so we all stopped talking about this man's four-year affair with his neighbor boy and turned our attention to our food. And because it was so clear to us that our host was still greatly saddened by the fact that this young friend of his was no longer in his life, we changed the subject after that and tried not to bring the boy up in any of our further conversations for that weekend.

After dinner our host took us to see the musical *Hair*—we were glad to see that we weren't the only ones being made all the time to take our clothes off—and then when the show had ended, we returned to his apartment and drank alcohol until we had all become blitzed. Right before bed, however, there was one thing our host made us do to earn our keep.

As it turned out, this man liked showers also. He didn't have one as large or as elaborate as the one that Fatso owned, but the one in his bathroom was big enough for all three of us to fit into at the same time. So after we had undressed, Matt and I followed the man in and then took turns wetting ourselves down.

"Ok now each of you pick up a cake of soap," the man instructed once the steam from the hot water had raised the air temperature in the shower to a comfortable level. "Then I want you boys to use the soap and your hands at the same time to wash every inch of my body from my shoulders down."

By this time in our careers as boy prostitutes we had heard crazier requests, so obligingly we did what was asked of us.

"Ahhhh!" As soon as our hands began to rub the soap around on his skin, our host instantly closed his eyes and began to relax. He had been tense all night and even the alcohol he had consumed with us hadn't managed to calm him all that much. So as our hands worked up a lather on him, the only thing we could see that wasn't relaxing was his penis. The longer we rubbed, the more swollen it became. I remember thinking that his penis reminded me of a balloon being inflated by a bottle of compressed helium as he continued to be aroused by our touch. This went on for a while until the man finally opened his eyes again and spoke to me.

"Ok, you can stop now. Next I want you to take a step back and sit down for a few minutes. Ok?"

"Ok," I answered obediently. And then I planted my bare bottom on a little triangular seat which had been set into one of the rear corners of his shower. Once I was sitting, I then watched our host speak to my roommate.

"Ok now, and you… I want you to stop washing me and I'm going to pull you toward me so you can hug me for a little while. All right?"

As water dripped steadily from the ends of his hair and his ear lobes, Matt looked soulfully up into the man's eyes as he listened intently to these instructions. Our host had treated us very kindly all night and yet our presence that evening seemed to do little to cheer him up. His sadness over the recent loss of his relationship with the neighbor boy was profound. And despite our misgivings over the way he viewed his relationships, and the world in general, he was a gentle man and Matt and I did grow to like him during our visit. So by this time Matt and I had come to a point where we sincerely wanted to do for this man whatever we could to help him to feel better. So when he asked us for something, we wanted to do it for him.

The man then backed himself up until his shoulders were pressed up against the front wall. Then I watched him reach up behind him and adjust the angle of his shower head so that the water would flow down directly onto him, and then he reached out, took my friend into his arms, and quietly drew Matt to him so my roommate's front could lean against his own front. Once their bodies were pressed together in this fashion, the two of them simply stood there with their eyes closed and their arms wrapped around each other in blissful silence while the water poured down all over both of their bodies.

"Ahhhhh!" Matt then sighed also, which surprised me a bit to hear. Our pity for this man notwithstanding, as a rule Matt and I tried never to let ourselves become emotionally affected by our customers. But the two of them hugging the way they now were, seemed to give each of them a chance to finally let go of a great deal of disappointment they were both so clearly carrying around with them. And when my friend was finally relaxed enough to be pliable, and the man could move the boy's body around like a limp piece of spaghetti, our host then poured some shampoo into Matt's hair and began to wash it for him. Soon, as the lather grew, and the suds began to drop down onto Matt's shoulders and back to drain away eventually between the two cheeks of his buttocks, Matt continued to keep his eyes closed and his body resting against the man whom he still had his arms around.

"Now start kissing your way down my skin until you reach my dick and then blow me," the man ordered softly.

Never before had Matt or I ever kissed any of our customers. We and the upperclassmen considered kissing a part of love and we weren't there to love our customer. But I watched with some further surprise as, reluctantly at first and without bothering to rinse the suds from his hair, Matt turned his face inward toward the man and began to gently kiss his stomach. Quietly then Matt's body slowly sank as he continued to kiss his way down along our host's hairy abdomen until finally my friend was resting on the tiled floor on his knees. Then, without being asked, Matt opened his mouth and took the man's erection in between his lips and then he began to bob his head in and out as he went all out to give our customer the service he had paid so handsomely to the Academy to receive.

The next morning after we were up, our host took us out for brunch to a little sidewalk café on Third Avenue. He had us order Virgin Mary's and when the wait staff wasn't looking, he pulled out of his jacket pocket two small bottles of vodka he had apparently gotten from a recent airline flight and poured their contents into our drinks for us.

"There," he proclaimed proudly. "Try those."

Matt and I each drank our Bloody Mary's and like them immensely. And it pleased us a great deal when he ordered us another round and then managed to produce two more little bottles of vodka for our drinks.

After our meal we returned to the man's apartment and stripped off our clothes once more for another shower. When we were all soaked down again, our host had us repeat the performance we had done on him the night before, only this time when the washing was over, it was Matt's turn to sit down while I was the one who got pulled to him until the fronts of our bodies became pressed together as if we were one.

At first I felt uncomfortable having to hug a man whom I barely knew in such an intimate way. But something about the way he held my head against his chest and the feel of the warm water as it rushed over us both caused the tension I had in my muscles to just give way. So before long my body had become as peaceful and supple as my roommate's had the night before. And as I felt his confident hands swirl my wet hair around within the shampoo lather and as I noticed his sturdy fingers massage away the months of stress which had accumulated within my scalp, I couldn't help but lean against him and enjoy the experience he was giving me.

"Ok, now start kissing your way down my body, and then blow me," the man ordered in a voice which was still barely audible. And without hesitating or thinking about the suds that were still in my hair and draping over my ears, I turned my face slowly into his body and began to do as he had asked. So that once I was on my knees in front of him, I opened my mouth and stuck out my tongue first so I could swirl it around his crown. An instant later, I took his erection into my mouth and gave to this man the best blow job I could muster.

***

Dinner at the Academy on the following Tuesday night was held a half hour earlier, so the entire student body would have the time needed to board the two chartered busses—which had shown up during our meal and were waiting for everyone out on the front drive—and make it down to Providence in time to see a play put on by the Trinity Square Repertory Theater Company. I liked stage productions and getting to see two in one week was a real treat for me. In all, I believe, the Academy had arranged for us to attend six plays in Providence throughout that year and today I am only able to remember one of them, which was entitled *Helter Skelter*. I remember this particular play still because the whole thing made no sense to me. I suspect the reason for my confusion that night had to do with the song by the same name which a three-piece rock band in the production kept playing on occasion to punctuate whatever drama the playwright had been trying to portray. I could never figure out what the heck those guys thought they were playing, because what they kept blasting out at the audience bore no real resemblance to the original work done by the Beatles.

I don't recall ever seeing Mr. Stuart or any of the other offending members of the faculty with us on these trips. But with the school vacated for a number of hours, it seemed reasonable to me to suspect that the freedom these guys suddenly had was used for snooping through our rooms.

The next afternoon, when Matt and I were taken to the inn, Carlos and Juan were made to come along with us. The day had come, apparently, for our friends to be turned out as well. At some point during their night in the mud, they had been informed of our status with the gang, and so by now we had been granted permission, finally, to speak with our next-door neighbors and do what we could to help them cope with their new lives.

Besides getting their own adjoining rooms in another part of the motel, Carlos and Juan also got their own upperclassman to come along and manage their fees and schedules for them. And later that night, when the four of us were back on our floor in the dormitory, we learned that despite the fact that they had been serving a completely different clientele from the one that we knew, they too had done a steady business that day. In fact, I wondered at the time how it was that so many people seemed to know all of a sudden that our Venezuelan friends were now on the job.

During the weeks that followed, our foreign friends fell into the same routine that Matt and I were now used to. On the weekends, though, their duties were similar to what we were doing, but with a twist. Every Saturday afternoon Carlos and Juan were driven up to Logan Field—usually by Joe—so they could get on board Fatso's private jet and be flown to a spot along the Gulf of Mexico—usually Florida. Apparently then the boys' unique services were offered up to Fatso's Spanish-speaking associates as partial payment for the cocaine they would bring into the country for him from South America. According to what the two of them would tell us upon their return to our dorm every Sunday night, the machismo in Fatso's associates always kept the boys accepting it in their asses throughout the night. It was only because the boys were always made so utterly drunk by these men, that it was possible for them to sustain themselves at all during these night-long sessions. And besides being sex objects, Carlos and Juan were also used as mules for Fatso's deliveries. At night, while some of these South American associates were having their way with the boys, other men would pack the latest shipment of cocaine into our friends' over night bags. So then after the jet had flown them home the next day, Carlos and Juan would first be taken to a warehouse someplace in downtown Boston for offloading of Fatso's merchandise before they would be driven back to the Academy.

So at long last Matt and I understood what this whole business we were now so deeply involved in was all about. Thanks to the services which we four boys were being forced to provide, Fatso had been able to build for himself a drug business which was like no other. His ingenious approach was to sell sex with his cocaine, only the sex he was selling wasn't with ordinary prostitutes. The sex he was selling was with us.

By this time in our real-world education, we had learned that boys were considered a rare and highly prized commodity in the sex trade, and Fatso was using us to entice both his customers and his suppliers to do business with him. We had become integral tools to his livelihood.

To be sure, Fatso's business plan had already been implemented long before the time that Matt and I had appeared on the scene, but according to what the others were telling us, we were outperforming by volume every last one of our predecessors. And this particular year marked the first time that Fatso had extended his operations to provide sex to his supply chain. So by putting both of our ends to work for the cause, so to speak, we were insuring that both ends of his business were well taken care of. And like all good businessmen, Fatso had made certain that his customers and his lines of supply would always be maintained by the arrangements he had made with the Academy for a steady stream of young boys. He was making bundles of money off of us, and the Academy was in for a solid share.

So now, besides being drug addicts and boy prostitutes, we were part of an international drug trafficking and distribution business. And apparently business was booming because as the weeks went by, it became very clear to us that the volume of customers we were taking care of was growing. The very idea that we could be mixed up in this type of an enterprise was an overwhelming concept for us to grasp.

"Well, in for a penny, in for a pound, I guess." Matt tried to reconcile himself to our fate one afternoon. After all, what else could he say.

"Ya mean, in for an ounce, in for the whole bag?" I asked trying to make a joke about the cocaine end of Fatso's business.

"Whatever." He didn't think my joke had been particularly funny. In fact, there really wasn't much of anything that autumn to break up the tedium of our routine until the end of October.

The next time we all got together socially as a gang was the night of Halloween. This occasion, as one might imagine, was a special holiday for the upperclassmen. I actually had hopes on this night of being given the chance to go out into the two small neighborhoods around the Academy to do some trick-or-treating. The idea I had was that an outing like this would give us an opportunity to become introduced to some of the neighbors, and then we could assess which ones might be willing to help us if we decided later to run from the Academy. But as things worked out, we were restricted, as usual, to staying on the campus.

And so when Matt and I arrived at the headmaster's house after dark that night and found the festivities well underway, we too were concealed by masks. We had been "urged" to buy them in town during one of our recent trips to the motel. And once we had made our selections, we were told to hang onto our masks always and to never lose them. To the upperclassmen, it seemed, owning a Halloween mask was a sort of final rite of passage into their world. Now that Matt and I had our own masks, we truly were full members of this group and thoroughly prepared for the next school year when we would be participating in their late-night raids into the dorm rooms of the next crop of unsuspecting and innocent first-year boys to harvest new members for the gang.

"Here they are!" a very drunken leader announced as we appeared in the living room. "Somebody give them their party favors."

Instantly after that, fifths of some sort of bourbon were thrust into our hands. "We gotta start drinking now?" Matt asked.

"Yup!" the leader blurted out. "Start drinkin'."

Apparently we were behind everyone else on their journey to inebriation, and the upperclassmen were eager to see us catch up. As I unscrewed the cap from my bottle and looked around the room, I could see that everyone there had a fifth of one thing or another in their hands. So submissively Matt and I began to mingle around the room and in a moment, we had caught up with Carlos and Juan. A quick inspection of our friends told us that they were already too far gone for useful conversation.

"Hi ya, Clint! Hi ya, Matt! I sure hate the shit they make us do around here, but the fringe benefits are great! Don't you think so?" As he slurred his words, Juan tried to express to us his obvious approval for the way the bourbon was making him feel.

"Are you ok, Carlos?" Matt asked our other neighbor.

Carlos just stared at nothing for a little while with a silly sort of a grin on his face and then, in a delayed reaction to Matt's question, he flinched and turned his head with a bobbing motion to look at my roommate. "I'm fine," he answered in an obviously impaired state. And then he continued to smile as he resumed his staring. It was clear to us both, then, that our Venezuelan friends were just as drunk as everyone else in the room.

"Come on you two, drink up! We've got plans for the four of you guys tonight," the head waiter revealed. From the way he was acting, we could tell that he was what I had often heard people refer to as a sloppy drunk.

Full members of this group or not, as we began to drink from our fifths we understood that until there were new first-year boys to replace us, the four of us were destined to be the entertainment for these gatherings. So a little while later, when it was obvious to the others that Matt and I had downed enough bourbon to become nearly incoherent, the bigger kids then decided that the time had come for us to begin the real festivities.

"Ok, everybody outside in the back yard," the leader announced.

A moment later we had all gathered on the lawn around a kiddy wading pool which had been filled earlier in the evening with cold water and apples. "Ok, now. You little guys start bobbin' for the apples. Huh? Ha, ha, ha?" the leader then broke out into laughter.

The whole crowd around us then began to laugh, so we laughed too. After all, this wasn't going to turn out to be another example of wanton debauchery. This was just going to be clean, silly fun. Or was it?

As the four of us younger guys huddled in closer around the kiddy pool and began to wonder how cold the water in it really was, I suddenly got an idea. "Hang on for a minute," I announced to the bigger kids. "Let me give everyone some instructions first. I used to do this all the time back home and I've got a strategy for it."

"Sure, no problem." The leader's speech was still sounding slurred.

As I brought my three friends closer to me so I could explain to them how I thought we should all proceed, I looked up suddenly toward the west and saw the neighbor kid Danny standing in his back yard looking at us and smiling. "Can I come over and try that too?" he called out to us from behind his chain-link fence.

The boy's voice caught our leader's attention right away. "Yeah, come on over, Danny," he hollered back.

We all then waited for a few moments while the twelve-year-old disappeared from our view briefly so he could walk through the gate which opened into his front yard. In no time after that he appeared in the headmaster's back yard with his German shepherd at his side. "So when do I get to go?" he asked as he joined us around the wading pool. Once the dog saw where his master was going to be standing for a while, Bandit then walked around us all until he found a spot nearby that he liked, and then he sat. Danny was known by nearly everyone on the campus. He and Bandit were always over to play basketball or just hang out with many of us. In fact, since he knew that I was from the west, one day he had asked me a question about the Unicameral of Nebraska because he had studied in school that it was the only state in the country with a single legislative body.

"You can be the first one to stick your head in the water, Danny," the head waiter offered.

"No wait!" Artist suddenly stopped the boy as he was beginning to bend over. "First you gotta drink some of this." Artist then handed Danny his fifth of cherry vodka.

With a sheepish sort of a look on his face, Danny then smiled broadly. "Really?" It was immediately obvious to all of us that Danny wasn't opposed to this idea.

"Yeah, go ahead!" Artist confirmed. And then he passed the bottle of liquor into the boy's hands.

All of us then watched in silence as Danny first turned his head around to look behind him toward his house so he could make sure that no one from his family was watching him through their windows. An instant later, after he was convinced that the coast was clear, he turned his head back around to face us again, and then he placed his lips around the rim of the bottle and threw back his head to take in his first belt.

"Ugk!" Danny then quickly brought his head back down and began to choke and cough from the harshness of the drink he had just consumed. It was quite clear to all of us now that the boy had never before tried hard liquor. But as soon as he had managed to compose himself, Danny put himself through the ordeal three more times before Artist finally wrenched the bottle out of the boy's hands.

"Jeeze, kid!" It was as if Danny was wanting to get as drunk as he could, now that he had been given the opportunity to do so. "Ok, now. Wait a few minutes until you begin to feel it, and then you can bob for an apple. Ok?" Artist half ordered and half asked.

"Ok!" Danny gasped as he tried to calm his breathing down.

"Hey, why don't we move all of this into the gym?" the head waiter suggested as he stared at our young guest and smiled.

"Naw, this is fine right here," the leader answered firmly. Then to change the subject quickly, he looked at me. "Let's go, Clint. Let's finish up your little meeting, now."

"Ok," I responded just as rapidly. I then returned my focus to the now four young boys who were standing in front of me. "Now look, guys. What you want to do is commit yourself to the apple. If you try to keep yourself from getting wet, you won't get the apple and in the end you'll still wind up getting wet anyway. So just pick the one you want and then shove your whole head straight in after it until you have it pinned against the bottom of the pool. Then you can sink your teeth into it and bring it out of the water. Ok? So who's gonna be first?" I asked.

"I'll go first," Matt volunteered. His speech was slurred by now too.

And so we all watched as Matt got down into the grass on his knees, bent the upper half of his body over the water, selected his apple, and then submerged his entire head into the water in pursuit of his prize.

"Give me some more, will ya?" At this same moment, Danny yanked Artist's bottle from his hands and began to slug it back again and again.

"Ok," Artist relented. "If you want ta get roaring drunk, it makes no difference to me."

"Uk!" Matt gasped when he brought his head up out of the water with an apple in his teeth.

"Way to go, Ramsey," the head waiter called out.

After that, Carlos and Juan and a few of the upperclassmen took their turns bobbing for the apples. It was funny to see but between the joking and the insults and the all-around good time, each one that went after an apple followed my instructions and dunked their entire head under the water. And as this lighthearted fun went on for something like fifteen minutes, Danny continued to take large gulps of Artist's cherry vodka. After Juan had gotten his apple and had raised his head up out of the water to display himself to the rest of us with his bangs lying down flat in his face and his apple firmly caught between his teeth, Danny let us know that he was finally feeling drunk. One by one, heads continued to go into the water and one by one apples continued to come out. And then, when everyone else had gone who had wanted to try, it was Danny's turn to bob for an apple.

"Ok, Danny," I said. "It's your turn next." I was actually becoming worried about the kid. After all, he was likely going to have to be going home pretty soon to be with his family again. I didn't think that his parents would react well to their son becoming drunk at the hands of some Academy kids.

"Give me back my bottle, you lush," Artist said as he ripped his bottle of vodka away from Danny's hands.

"Huh?" Danny now seemed a little disoriented. "Oh yeah. Ok." Then, not realizing that his feet were up against the side of the wading pool, Danny tried to take a step forward and nearly wound up falling full out into the pool. Fortunately, the boy's swan dive was stopped in mid-flight by Artist and one other upperclassman who managed to grab him just in time and keep him from going for a late-night swim.

"Wo! Thanks, guys!" Danny offered once he had regained his footing. The boy then sank to his knees and prepared to throw his head into the water.

"Go whenever you're ready, kid," the leader gave his permission.

Danny then stopped his preparations for a moment and looked up at the leader. "Ok, thanks." The boy then looked back at the water below him again, and then he plunged his head under the surface as he chased after one of the last remaining apples.

A moment of silence then followed as we all stared down at the boy's head while it continued to stay submerged before our eyes. And then Danny's head shot up out of the water and he sat back on his legs with an apple in his mouth. Great volumes of water then poured from his hair and drained over his face as we all watched and waited for him to say something. With a hand which was just as wet as his head, the boy then removed the apple he had snatched from the pool and spoke to us again. "Man, Clint! Your stragedy worked great!"

Everyone then laughed again. If it hadn't been obvious before, it certainly was now. The Academy's twelve-year-old neighbor was drunk.

"That's great, Danny," I replied.

"Danny!" Suddenly we all froze from the sound of an adult voice calling for his son. Danny's dad was now standing in his back yard and looking at us all. Instantly Bandit stood up in anticipation of their departure.

"Oh, oh!" Danny whispered. "I guess I gotta go home." Instead of turning around to look at his parent, the kid held his back to the west. "Yeah, Dad!" His piercing high-pitched voice suddenly shattered the upperclassmen's mood.

"It's time to come in now," the father ordered. "It's getting late and you've got school in the morning."

"Start eating the apple and then eat a candy bar when you get home," Artist advised quietly. "That way they'll never smell the booze on your breath."

"Really?" Danny was eager now for advice on how he could stay out of trouble with his parents.

"Yeah, well, when you get home, just go to bed right away so they won't catch you doing anything dumb." The head waiter now joined in with his bit of wisdom.

"Yeah?" Danny replied. "That's a good idea, too." Then Danny got an idea of his own. Quickly he turned his dripping head around and looked at his dad. "There's only one more of us to bob for an apple. Can I stay here and watch for another minute? I'll come in right after that, I promise."

Danny's dad thought for a moment, and then he gave his son his answer. "All right, but only a few more minutes, and then I want you inside. Got it?"

"Yes, sir. Thanks, Dad." Danny then turned his head to face us again and this time he was facing me. "You haven't gone yet, Clint," he observed.

My friend was right. And although I knew he was stalling so he could go into his house by himself in a few minutes—after his dad had already gone in ahead of him—and thereby avoid getting close to his parent, I also realized that time had run out for me. Unfortunately, I had been continuing to take sips from my fifth during this entire time outside, and now I felt as if I was about to pass out. Nevertheless, I rallied and got down on my knees, anyway.

"Go, Clint!" Juan yelled.

"Yeah, let's see how the expert does it," Danny chided. He was starting to become obnoxious as a drunk.

And so, as I plunged my face into the cold liquid before me, I found that because of the high level of alcohol that was now in my blood stream, I had to plant my hands out in front of me in the pool as well to prevent my entire body from falling into the water. Then, once my head, hands and arms up to my elbows were submerged, I discovered that bobbing for apples while drunk was a scary endeavor. Looking back on it, I would never recommend it to anyone. Because as my severe inebriation kept me flirting with unconsciousness, I kept having to raise my head abruptly above the surface and then endure brief sessions of coughing and choking while water drained from all sections of my hair and face to fall noisily back down into the pool below me. I had always been comfortable in the water and although it was never something I would do under normal circumstances, on this night I seemed every so often to forget myself and allow a tiny amount of water to seep through into my lungs.

"Come on, Clint! Don't let that apple beat ya!" Artist called out during one of my choking sessions.

On one or two occasions I honestly thought I might drown. But finally, I was able to get a firm grip on the apple with my teeth and I raised my head in triumph. Then in less than heroic fashion, I gasped as I tried to breathe through the water that was pouring over my face from my bangs which were now flattened against my forehead.

A cheer then rose from the crowd. It seemed as if I had succeeded in providing them all with a decent amount of entertainment.

"Well, I gotta go," Danny said once I was on my feet again.

"Ok, see ya, Danny," I replied.

"Yeah see ya, Clint," he answered back. "See ya guys." And then Danny looked at his companion. "Come on, Bandit!"

In the moonlight, I could still see water beaded up on the boy's face, and as a few drops fell from his hair, he turned and began to walk back toward his house. *There he goes,* I thought to myself. *He's been saved from this bunch by his family.* It gave me the shivers to think of what these bigger kids might have done to Danny on this night if they had been able to get him into the headmaster's house. A move, by the way, which I was certain was going to be attempted next. But the boy had been plucked from their clutches just in time by his family. Without him even knowing how close he had come to going down a road he could never return from, the kid had been rescued. Much in the way I longed for my own family to rescue me.

"Ok, everyone back into the house," the leader called out. He now sounded drunker than ever.

And so I turned my drenched upper body and head and began to walk back into Mr. Stuart's house with the rest of my gang. And as I took one last quick look in time to see Danny and his dog disappear around some trees, I thought about how lucky he was to be going back inside his house to spend the rest of his evening with his family, and I ached for the chance to get my own family life back again. Right there in front of me, just beyond my grasp, was Danny and his normal family life. Suddenly a normal life didn't seem as distant to me as it had for the past few months. Yes, it was right there! *Oh why,* I thought, *couldn't we have checked this place out first?*

"Come on, Adams. Let's go!" The head waiter noticed that I was lagging behind.

"I'm coming," I groaned. And as I entered the house again, I resigned myself to having to continue to live the way I was now living—a drug addict and a sex object.

"Danny's a dead man as soon as his dad smells his breath," Artist offered once we were all back inside with the door closed.

"And you told him to eat a candy bar," the head waiter responded critically.

Once we were all back in the living room again, the bigger kids ordered us to keep drinking. The cold water and the cool night air had sobered everyone up a little and the remaining activities, it seemed, were going to require we younger ones especially to be much more out of control than we were at the moment.

"Let's have all the little guys sit down on the floor together," the leader ordered. "And arrange yourselves so that you're integrated. You know, one U.S. kid, then one Venezuelan kid. Then another U.S. kid and another Venezuelan kid."

And so, Carlos and Matt and Juan and I all sat down together on the carpet in the center of the headmaster's living room.

"Now drink, ya little bastards!" The head waiter this time issued the command in a way which expressed what we believed to be his true attitude toward us.

Without any argument, the four of us did as we were told and began to take rapid gulps of our fifths. A short while later, once we were all on the brink of passing out once again, the bigger kids—feeling impatient with our slow progress I guess—assumed control over us. Suddenly a hand pulled my bottle away from me while other hands guided my upper body down until I was lying on my back on the floor. I then felt these same hands begin to undo my belt and unhook and unzip my pants. And while I watched in my drunkenness as my clothing was pulled away from my body, I happened to look over at my friends and notice that they two were being undressed.

"Since some of them are still wet, just throw all the clothes into the kitchen," the leader instructed. A minute or so later, all four of us were lying naked on the carpet.

"Ok," the leader continued. "Little guys sit up again, and big guys feed 'em some more of their bottles."

This time, after the hands had helped me to sit up again, I felt one of them hold on suddenly to the back of my head while the other tried to force me to down the remaining half bottle or so of bourbon which I hadn't been able yet to consume. Of course as soon as I felt the alcohol enter my mouth, I began to drink it, but in a few moments the inevitable happened and I began to choke on it and spit it out. But this time, the hands didn't give me a break. As soon as I had regained myself and had stopped coughing, the hands again forced me to drink more.

Enough already! I remember thinking to myself as the bigger kids kept up their efforts to force even more liquor into me. And it wasn't just me who was being put through this hell. I could hear the others around me choking and gagging as they too were force-fed their alcohol. Eventually, I guess, the upperclassmen grew tired of this game, and left us alone. But as we sat there with bourbon spilled all over our faces and torsos, I don't think any of us were surprised by what they made us do next.

"Now we're gonna have you boys form a square on the carpet with your bodies. So U.S. kids lay down parallel to each other on your backs but separate out a little bit and Matt… you face the other way. And then Juan, you lay down on your stomach perpendicular to the U.S. boys at one end of them, and then shove your dick into Clint's mouth and take Matt's dick into yours. And then Carlos… you lay down like Juan but at the other end of the U.S. boys and face the other way so you can put your dick into Matt's mouth and then take up Clint's dick into your mouth. Ha, ha, ha!" The leader then began to give his drunken laugh again.

In our trashed conditions, these instructions were complicated for us to follow. But with the help of the upperclassmen, we eventually got our bodies and penises arranged in the ways the leader had ordered. And as I waited for the next order to be given, I realized that we were all about to get to know each other a whole lot better.

"Ok, now go down on each other, and don't stop until you all cum." And then the leader laughed again. In fact, this time the leader led the entire room in laughter. They were now clearly amused by the spectacle we were making of ourselves.

At the same time I felt Carlos take my penis into his mouth, I could feel Juan searching for my lips. When he got close, I opened my mouth and took him in to save time. And then we all began to do what we had been trained so well to do, and our first ever foursome was begun.

As always the crowd around us yelled and cheered as we all worked to arouse one another. And eventually, despite the fact that we all had to fight to stay conscious long enough to get our jobs done, we all ejaculated into the mouth of the boy lying close by.

"Stay where you are," a voice said once we had all finished. Blankets were then draped over us and the lights in the room were turned off. It was obvious to us then that we were expected to go to sleep this way. And considering how drunk we all were by this point, it was no problem for us to do as expected. So a few minutes later, after a little bit of adjustment so I wouldn't wind up with one of Juan's legs lying across my throat, we had all fallen asleep where we lay.

***

"Hey, how 'bout shootin' a few hoops with me?" Frank asked as I passed through the basketball court in front of my dorm one afternoon after classes.

"Naw, not today, Frank," I answered.

"Oh, come on, Adams. What do ya have to do this afternoon that's so important, anyway? Ya quit the soccer team didn't ya?"

"Yeah," I replied.

"So come on!" With that Frank passed the basketball to me.

Instantly I dropped my books onto the small lawn in front of my dorm and caught the ball. *Why the hell not,* I thought. *I haven't done anything like this for too long.* "Ok, you're on," I said. And then I dribbled over to the backboard and made a layup.

"Not bad, not bad." Frank then took the ball back to the foul line and waited for me to set myself up to defend against him. "But let's see if you can keep me from doing this!" Frank then ran past me and made his shot as if I hadn't been there.

"Not bad," I said a little winded. "But I'll show you how it's really done." I then took the ball back to the spot where Frank had started and prepared to make my drive for the basket. A moment later I was off, but Frank got me all tangled up and was able to take the ball away from me and sink his own shot.

"Ya know we're supposed to get betta as we get olda, not worse," Frank said in his native Brooklyn tongue.

"I'm just warmin' up," I said out of breath. In the past weeks my jaw and my neck had gotten stronger, but the rest of my body had apparently fallen apart. "Just take the ball out and let's go, wise guy." Even though I was breathing hard, I didn't want to let on that I was already wanting to stop playing.

"Hey, what did ya get on that English assignment today?" Frank asked as he blew past me again.

"I don't know. An F I guess." It was my turn now and instead of trying to fancy foot my way around Frank, I decided to try a shot from way outside.

"An F? Didn't you used to get A's?" Frank set himself up to block my shot.

"Yeah, I guess." I took my shot and missed the rim by a mile.

"You guess?" Frank then ran over into the lawn in front of the headmaster's house to retrieve the ball.

"Yeah, I don't know. I guess I just didn't get the assignment. That's all." I was starting to feel as if Frank was putting me through some sort of an inquisition.

"Bullshit!" Frank was never one to mince words. He now was standing in front of me with the ball in his hands. He had a look of frustration on his face and it was obvious that he wanted to say something to me. "Somethin's goin' on with you, Adams, and your roommate too. Both of youz have changed. Neither of you two are doin' nothin' anymore. You know I like you, Adams. You're a kid from the suburbs, but I always thought you were all right. Matt too. But now both of youz are turning your lives into shit, and I can't figure out why."

"I don't know what you mean, Frank." Now I wanted to leave. It had become obvious to me long ago that Frank was one of the students at the Academy who was not in the confidence of the upperclassmen. And my masters had very strict rules about not telling outsiders about our activities. "Come on, Frank, are we gonna play ball or not?"

"We're not!" Frank answered abruptly. "Adams, you're really pissin' me off. You've got everythin' goin' for ya, and you're blowin' it. You're blowin' it big time, and I can't figure out why. But I will."

"I don't know what you're talking about, Frank."

"Don't give me that," Frank countered.

"I don't," I tried again.

"I said don't give me that, Adams! Jeeze!"

I then took a step closer to my friend and lowered my voice. "Leave it alone, Frank. Really. It's no big deal. I'm just goin' through a phase, or somethin'. That's all." I was trying to deflect his attention from the real problems I was facing.

Frank was now fed up with my answers. "Bullshit, Adams. Bullshit! That's a load of crap and you know it." Frank then turned and began to walk away from me. "You go on and keep fuckin' up your life. But don't stand there and insult my intelligence by tellin' me that you're goin' through a phase. That's bullshit, Adams, and you know it." And then he walked around the front corner of Ulster Hall and was gone.

I was surprised that the changes in me were so transparent to my friend. I actually hadn't thought that anyone had been able to notice.

So with no reason to stay on the court any longer, I picked up my books so I could continue on into my dorm. But as I began to walk again, I could hear Frank's voice carrying on the breeze from the front steps of Ulster Hall.

"And you suck at basketball too!"

Chapter Eight
Finally a Break… Sort Of

Thanksgiving was too short of a holiday for me to go to Europe to see my folds, and Matt's aunt was just as happy not to have him under foot that weekend. She was apparently on the hunt after a ski instructor in Aspen whom she believed might marry her as long as she didn't let on too soon that she was encumbered by a kid. Also by now, our full-fledged cocaine addictions called into question any number of logistical concerns over how we could manage to keep ourselves high while not giving anything away to our loved ones once we were with them again. So Mr. Stuart had assured my parents and Matt's aunt that he would see to it personally that we were both sent home with a nice Academy family to spend the holiday with. And so, on the Wednesday night before Thanksgiving, after we had finished up our duties at the Friendly Inn, Matt and I found ourselves in a car headed for Boston to spend Thanksgiving with Fatso and Sweetie.

We had been up to see them several times since the first night we had met them, and in a strange way they were beginning to seem like surrogate parents to us. During the ride, though, I took some time to open a letter I had received from my real parents. In it I was stunned to read my mother's congratulations for having gotten all A's on my midterms.

"Huh!" I grunted under my breath. Then I folded up the letter again and put it back into my pocket.

"Well there you are! Come in, come in," Sweetie said as we walked through the front door of their penthouse a little later on that night. She then raced over to give each of us a big lip sticky kiss on our mouths. "Take off your coats. You boys must be starving by now. I've got a casserole all ready for you and keeping warm in the oven. So just come right on into the kitchen and take your places at the table."

It was late when we had finally arrived at their apartment that night, so after dinner, Matt and I climbed into the double bed in their guest room and went right to sleep. Fatso and Sweetie knew that we had been working hard all afternoon and evening, so they didn't ask us to do anything with them that night. Also, Matt and I always left each other alone on the days we worked.

The next morning, we got up early and prepared ourselves to fly to Florida so all four of us could spend the rest of the holiday together at Fatso and Sweetie's house down there. As soon as we had finished breakfast and had taken our showers—Matt and I had decided to use Fatso's big shower at the same time, but because we had a schedule to keep, they left us alone that morning too—we were off to Logan Field. During our journey to the fixed base operator where Fatso kept his Lear Jet, I asked him about Carlos and Juan. He told me then that because they too could not return to Venezuela for only a few days, our friends had wound up going to spend their weekend with Joe at his house just outside of town. After hearing this, Matt and I looked at each other and knew that we were getting the better deal.

By this time we had learned that Fatso was a successful businessman in Boston and that he owned a pretty good-sized company there. I never found out the name of his firm or what type of business it was, but Fatso seemed to be well known around town because he and Sweetie were always going out to benefits and other social events in the area. It was also clear to us that his legitimate business interests made it possible for Fatso to pursue his not so legitimate interests like child prostitution and the cocaine trade.

Fatso had a car waiting for us when we landed in Ft. Meyers. Once our luggage was all loaded into the trunk, he then took us directly to a local restaurant for a full Thanksgiving dinner. It was actually one of the best Thanksgiving meals I had ever eaten. The management at the restaurant apparently knew Fatso and when he was asked if we were his sons, he explained that we were actually his nephews who were down from Portland. So immediately Matt tried to sound as if he was from Bar Harbor.

After our noon dinner, we all piled back into the car and Fatso drove us straight to a nearby marina where a fifty-foot Daytona with a flying bridge—which he apparently owned—was tied up and ready for us to board. I loved the ocean and boats. Besides the trips we had taken to Cape Cod, my dad and I had done some pleasure boating up and down the Inter Coastal between Miami and West Palm Beach over on the east coast of Florida. So I felt right at home when I stepped onto that deck, and I was eager to help with the lines when the time came for us to shove off.

"Where are we goin'?" Matt asked once we had cleared the harbor and could increase our speed.

"Captiva!" Fatso answered as he nudged the throttles forward a bit more. "That's where our house is."

"Where's Captiva?" Matt had never heard of the place.

"It's an island off the west coast of Florida. It won't take us long to get there." Fatso really seemed to love to pilot his boat. It was funny to see him in the skipper's hat he was wearing because it covered his bald head so thoroughly.

"It's a lovely place," Sweetie added. "I'm sure you're both going to love it there."

After a while, when there was nothing more to see but the water that was all around us, Matt asked if he could go exploring through the boat.

"Sure!" Fatso said appreciatively. "I'd show you myself, but I can't leave the wheel right now. But Clint, you know boats. You go ahead and take Matt on a tour. Ok?"

"Aye, aye, Captain," I accepted Fatso's request. Besides I was interested in snooping around below myself. But a few minutes later, while Matt and I were inspecting the master's cabin, Sweetie suddenly appeared in the doorway.

"Take your clothes off, boys," she ordered. And then she came on in with us and closed the door behind her. "We've decided that during this trip we're going to teach you boys how to do three ways." At that, Sweetie began to pull off her own clothes. We did as we were told and in a moment, as the engines droned on, the three of us stood there naked and looking at each other.

"Ok now, let's all get on the bed together," Sweetie said.

***

When we finally made the island, we tied up for a short while at a marina on the leeward side so we could take on more fuel and provisions, and then we continued on around to the island's windward side. There, eventually, we tied up at our hosts' private dock. And when we stepped off the boat, the thing that surprised Matt and me the most was how secluded the place was. Although we had passed other homes while we were cruising around the island, there were no neighboring buildings of any kind in view from this property.

"See," Fatso began to explain. "You boys can swim here in the ocean any time you like."

It was true. Fatso and Sweetie did have their own private beach. And when we walked up to the house, we discovered we were in for a few more surprises.

"How do you boys like the pool?" Sweetie asked.

"Cool!" Matt replied.

"Great!" I agreed.

The rambling one-story house had a large cement patio in back facing the ocean with a big rectangular-shaped swimming pool set in at one end. Neither Matt nor I could believe it. For the next three days, we were going to be living on an island paradise with complete privacy. No upperclassmen coming around to bother us, or to listen in on what Matt and I were talking about. The whole idea was exciting to us both.

"I'll show you boys where your room will be, but first we need to tell you about our rule that you must observe while you're here." Sweetie's tone suddenly sounded ominous.

"What's that?" I asked. *Oh great,* I thought to myself. *Just when it was starting to seem good around here.*

Sweetie then turned her head to look at her husband. "Honey.... why don't you tell the boys about our rule."

"Oh right," Fatso then looked at both of us with a serious expression on his face. "Ok, boys, the rule of the house is that as long as you two are here, you cannot wear any clothing at all. We don't wear clothes either when we're here."

"Really?" Of course this wasn't the first time we had been told that we couldn't wear our clothes all weekend. But the idea of running around naked for a couple of days in this hot tropical paradise sounded like a lot of fun to us. So after looking at each other quickly and smiling, my roommate and I decided that complying with this rule would be no problem. "Yeah, we'll do that," I agreed.

"Ok, sure!" Matt's grin made me think that he was ready to pull his things off right now where he stood.

"Now," Fatso continued, "you can wear your flip-flops if the ground gets too hot or if you need to protect your feet when you go down to the beach. And at night it usually gets a little cool here so you can put on only what you need to make yourself warm. Like maybe a sweater and nothing else for example. But during the day... absolutely no clothes. Got it?"

"Yeah," I confirmed.

"Sure," Matt did too.

"Ok, then," Sweetie continued. "Let's go inside and get settled."

When we followed our hosts into their house, I found it odd that the place seemed to be unlocked and already occupied. The room that Matt and I were given had one huge king-sized bed in it. When we saw it, Matt and I gave each other knowing smiles, and then we set our bags down on the floor.

"Take off your clothes now and then come join us in the living room, boys," Sweetie said to us. And then she left us alone to carry out her instructions.

A few minutes later—now naked—Matt and I walked into the living room and discovered something else about this weekend that we could become excited about.

"Oh come on in, boys," Fatso said when he saw us. "I want you both to meet Conchita. Say hello to the boys, Conchita."

"Hola!"

For an instant Matt and I were embarrassed and we instinctively reached down with our hands to cup them over our genitals. But then we realized that this ravishing girl of eighteen or nineteen was just as naked as we were.

Fatso saw our reaction and smiled. I guess it amused him to see that in spite of all the people that Matt and I had been naked in front of for the past few months, we still had a tendency toward modesty. "Conchita just came to us recently from El Salvador. We're training her right now as our housekeeper."

"Hola." I smiled.

"Me too," Matt added.

That night, Fatso took Matt and me into his room with him to continue the threesome theme we apparently had for the weekend. He told us that there was more money in threesomes and so he wanted us to be able to handle them as well as we were handling everything else we did. And we found his training to be pretty thorough, too. At first he had Matt and me team up to work on him, then he took Matt as his partner and the two of them worked on me, and then finally Matt became the object of our efforts when Fatso and I paired up. Matt and I were always very careful to do everything that Fatso asked of us. He always treated us kindly, but at the same time it seemed to both of us that if provoked, he could become very abusive and even dangerous if he felt the need.

The next day, Matt and I went skinny snorkeling in the ocean, a short distance down the beach from Fatso's dock. Matt and I were both finding our visit to Captiva to be a truly enjoyable experience. In every sense of the word we were on vacation, and all of the pressures we had been carrying around since our arrival at the Academy were now more than a thousand miles behind us. And as we peered through our masks at the world below the waves, and watched an angelfish which seemed more curious about us than we were about it, I couldn't help but be reminded of the great trips my dad and I had taken to places like this. And then Matt and I surfaced together to talk.

"Did you see that?" Matt was excited as the waves washed past us.

"Yeah," I answered as I pulled my mask off of my head and planted my feet on the sandy bottom.

"He came right up to my mask and looked at me, and then he swam away." Matt's voice sounded as if his nose was pinched shut—which of course it was.

"That was pretty cool, Matt!" I observed as I felt salt water dripping from my hair and face.

"Man, that's the first time anything like that's ever happened to me." Matt then pulled off his mask too. Once he could speak normally again, my friend was ready to change the subject. "Clint?"

"Yeah?"

"You never told me what was in that letter you read from your folks the other night."

I was surprised that my roommate was selecting this moment to bring up a subject like this. On the other hand, this was the first time in months where we knew for certain that we could talk freely and without being spied on. "Oh, well, my Mom just congratulated me for getting all A's on my midterms."

"What? Clint, you blew your midterms. Come to think of it, so did I." Matt's excitement was now tempered by reality.

"Yeah well, I've been thinkin' about it and I've decided that the Academy must have changed all my grades before they mailed the report card to my parents."

"No shit?" Matt suddenly sounded excited again. "Huh! That means that I probably got all A's too."

"Probably," I agreed.

"Man! I never got all A's before in my life. I came close a bunch of times, but this is the first time I ever got A's on everything all at once."

"Yeah well, just so long as your aunt doesn't get suspicious or anything," I cautioned.

"Naw," Matt assured me. "I don't think she ever bothers to open the envelopes when they come."

I suppose we should have taken this matter more seriously, but for a while now grades had ceased to be important to us. And now, if the Academy was going to just give us A's anyway… well, I guess Matt and I simply figured that if the Academy didn't care how we did, then why the hell should we be concerned. Then Matt had another idea. "Hey! Maybe we ought'a just skip going to our classes altogether now?"

"Naw, I don't think so, Matt. After all, the place is still supposed to be a school and most of the kids there don't know anything about the stuff we're doin'," I reminded my friend.

"I suppose," Matt now sounded depressed again. Then, in a quieter voice, he changed the subject again. "Clint?"

"Yeah?"

"Does it still bother you to have sex with guys?"

"No. I don't think it does anymore. How 'bout you?"

"It used to. But it doesn't seem to now. It just seems like having sex is having sex. It doesn't really matter anymore who I'm having it with."

"I know what you mean. It's like… I don't know, shaking hands with a bunch of people in a crowd. As soon as I've shaken the hand of one person, it's over with and it's time to move on to shake the hand of the next person. Only we're shaking dicks instead. Do you know what I mean?"

"Exactly," Matt understood my simile. "Jeeze… I'm so horny all the time from all the coke we've been doin', I'm usually willing to stick my dick into any hole I can find—male or female."

"Yeah," I agreed. "Me too."

"Of course, I still enjoy boning the women when they come to the inn," Matt wanted to make sure I knew that he hadn't abandoned the straight life altogether.

"Well, sure," I agreed. "So do I. In fact, how much you want'a bet that we're gonna get a crack at Conchita tonight?"

"No bet!" Matt then shrieked and launched himself backwards into the water until he was floating on his back in the waves again. "I heard Sweetie say this morning that it's now her time of the month so she wants us to train with Conchita tonight. Yahoo! I can't wait to stick my dick into her," he hollered. And then he took his penis between his thumb and forefinger and started to stroke himself as if he were beginning to masturbate right there in front of me. "Owoo!" he shrieked again.

Matt's actions caused me to laugh. And then I watched Matt stop his hand movements suddenly and stand up in the water again.

"Hey, that actually feels pretty good."

"I'm sure it does," I understood.

"Hey! I've got another idea. Let's put our masks back on and then float on our stomachs and jerk off in weightlessness in the water to see what it feels like."

At first I was a little embarrassed at this idea. "Are you kidding?"

"No really! It'll be cool. Come on, let's do it!" He wouldn't stop encouraging me to go along with him on this one.

"Ok," I finally gave in. And so I put my mask back on while at the same time I watched my friend put on his. And then once we both had our snorkels back in our mouths, we resumed floating face down so we could discover together the unique feeling of freedom which comes from ejaculating in a weightless environment.

Chapter Nine
The Pace of Our Work Increases

The weeks between Thanksgiving and Christmas that year seemed to go on forever. As word spread about the availability of young boys at the Friendly Inn, we began to receive customers from all over New England and New York. Before long, the sheer volume of customers waiting to have their turn with us had grown to the point where the four of us were made to add Monday and Friday afternoons to our work routine. It was obvious to us that by some method, the services of boy prostitutes were being heavily promoted. But what we couldn't understand was how it was that people in law enforcement weren't hearing about us. We kept hoping for the day when the local police or the FBI would kick in our motel room doors and save us from our tormentors, but no one ever came. And even if the advertising for us was being done only by word of mouth, how was it that the authorities could not have heard about us? After all, didn't they live in the same towns as our customers?

With Tuesdays and Thursdays now the only days that we had to ourselves, we were becoming worn out. Despite our youth, the larger work load was more than we could cope with. Even the trips we continued to make over the weekends had begun to lose their intrigue for us. So in no time, Matt and I found ourselves longing for the day when it would be time for us to leave the Academy for Christmas break.

During stolen moments when Matt and I believed that we could talk without fear of being overheard, we decided that our upcoming vacation would be the occasion we would use to leave the Academy for good. To keep from arousing any suspicions, though, we reasoned that we would pack normally for our trips, and then we would leave all of our other belongings behind. If later on the Academy would end up shipping our things to us, everything would be fine. But if they chose, instead, to keep our things and not return them to us, we figured...

so be it. After that our plan called for me to talk with my parents and for Matt to talk with his aunt about arranging for us to be sent somewhere else together—preferably out of the country since we had no idea how vast Fatso's network of associates really was. Because even though Fatso was normally very nice to us, we were certain that the man was capable of meting out reprisals against us if we didn't show up after the break to do our part to keep his empire going. And if need be to get our point across, we were prepared to tell our families everything about what had been happening to us. We knew that revealing to our loved ones the truth about what we had been doing with strangers in motel rooms would be a hard thing for us to handle, but getting off of cocaine was bound to be a lot harder. Yes, on top of everything else, to accomplish our goal of breaking free from the Academy forever, we each figured that we weren't going to be able to avoid going through withdrawals to get off of the drug. But in our naive and drug-addicted minds, we determined that somehow we'd find a way to tough it out.

"That's one of the reasons why we make you little guys do only one year of this duty," Artist told me after I had confided in him one morning about how exhausted Matt and I had become from the constant grind of having to perform sex acts all the time.

It was also during these weeks when Fatso introduced us to the system he had for enabling us to remain high while away from the Academy for extended periods of time. A couple of weekends before we were scheduled to leave for Christmas break, Matt and I were up at their place in Boston to spend Saturday night and Sunday with them again. This time they had turned up their heat and were requiring us to go around naked all the time again. That way, if either of them wanted to have sex with us, they would simply grab Matt or me and have at us. Sometimes we'd go off into a bedroom for privacy, and on other occasions, we wouldn't waste the time. In any event, at some point during this visit, Fatso presented Matt and me with specially designed cans of shaving cream. When we pressed in on the can at just the right spot and then twisted the bottom, the outside would then come off and reveal an inside compartment which could hold about a week's worth of cocaine for one person—at our current rate of use.

"Cool!" Matt said as he tested the workings of one of the cans for himself. "And look! Shaving cream even comes out of it." Matt squirted out a palm full of the foamy soap, and then he smeared it all through my hair.

"Hey!" I cried out as I felt myself under attack. After that, I allowed a moment for things to calm down again, and then it was my turn. "Yeah, you're right," I agreed as I acquainted myself with the mechanics of a second can. "This is cool. But what if somebody notices that we're not old enough yet to shave?" I then filled my hand with shaving cream.

"Well then you tell them that these cans you're carrying are a gift for your dad," Fatso offered.

Immediately then I retaliated by smearing the mound in my hand all around in Matt's hair.

"Hey!" Matt protested.

"He who lives by the sword, dies by the sword," I proclaimed. And then, using all the shaving cream in the apartment that we could get a hold of, the battle was on. Sweetie managed to keep herself out of the fray, but Fatso was quick to join in and eventually, when all three of us were covered from head to toe, we ended up using the shaving cream on our bodies to give each other hand jobs. After that, we all went into the guest room shower to clean up.

"Ok, now we're going to have a couple of rules while we're in here today," Fatso began as he turned the valves to get the water flowing at us from all directions. "We can't leave the shower now until all three of us are clean, and nobody is allowed to clean himself."

"What?" I asked as I stood next to Matt and away from the paths of the various streams until we were given permission to enter the water.

"I mean, in order to get clean, we each have to be shampooed and soaped down and then rinsed by hands other than our own." Fatso then smiled. This was just the sort of little game he liked to play with us all the time. "So we'll start with Matt. Matt, you stand here in the center and then we'll get you clean." Fatso then motioned for my roommate to walk over to him.

"Ok," Matt accepted Fatso's invitation and walked over to stand next to the large man. Then he closed his eyes and made his body pliable so when I walked to the center of the shower to join the two of them, he was ready to allow us to handle him in every way necessary to get him clean. "It was kind of fun," he told me later on. "I just pretended like I was an emperor or something, and it was the job of my servants to wash me."

"Yeah," I agreed. "I kind of liked having all that done for me too."

***

Whenever we were out on the weekends, we were always given a safe number—a special telephone number for someone who would always be close by—to call in case a problem developed or our safety was threatened.

Sometimes the number would be to a pay phone in a restaurant down the block with one of the upperclassmen sitting next to it. Other times, we didn't know who would be at the other end. Normally, Fatso was very careful with who he agreed to place us with for these outings. So for a long time we never had a need to call one of these safe numbers. But on the weekend before Christmas break, all of that changed for us when we were taken to an appointment in Worcester that Mr. Stuart had set up for us.

Some restaurant up there had a party shack out in back on its property which it rented out to private groups for private functions. When a group would rent the place, it would apparently have the option either to have the restaurant's staff serve the party, or to send its own people over to the restaurant's kitchen and bar to collect the food and drinks it needed. When Matt and I arrived that Saturday night, the member of this group who was acting as the party's bartender was just finishing up his efforts to set up the bar and open the tap on the keg of beer they had brought in.

At first this group seemed ok. In total, there were about eighteen men who were fairly crude in their behavior, but by now Matt and I had seen worse. And as they drank that night, they encouraged us to drink right along with them. Matt and I knew better than to get into the hard stuff, so we both stuck with beer that night so we wouldn't lose ourselves completely. As I remember, Matt kept filling his cup from the keg every so often, while I preferred one of the brands they had at the bar in bottles.

As the evening progressed, we were treated as if these men were making us members of their club. Each person we talked to wore a name tag with just his first name written on it, which made me believe that although the guys at this party shared some sort of common interest, they didn't actually ever see each other all that often. There were also the initials "I.L.B.S." printed on each tag. After a couple of beers, I had worked up enough courage to ask one of these guys what these initials stood for.

"It's the I Love Boys Society," the man answered in a drunken voice.

Well that figures, I thought to myself. *After all, it's not as if they called us here to sell them boy scout cookies or something.* As soon as the chance opened up for me to do so, I let Matt in on what I had learned.

This party shack was actually a two-room structure. The room in which Matt and I and all of the other attendees were mingling had a bar, a ping pong table, and a couple of pinball machines in the back along with a couple of small tables with chairs around them. The other room was all tables and chairs and had been set up for the dinner they had yet to serve to themselves.

About an hour and a half into the evening, several of the men began to get pretty belligerent, and started to make their advances toward Matt. While I talked with other society members in another part of the room, I tried to keep my eye on Matt to make sure that he was all right. And then it happened.

"Auh!" Matt cried out in pain.

I excused myself and raced over to a spot near the keg to back up my roommate. I reached him just in time to see him get slapped again.

"Auh!" This time the force from the man who was hitting him knocked Matt off his feet.

"That's enough!" I shouted out to the drunken man. "We're not here to be bashed around!"

"Oh really?" The man looked at me for a moment and then he bent over my friend, who was still lying on the floor at this moment, and grabbed Matt by his shirt to lift him off of the floor and back to his feet. "Well how are you gonna stop me, little man? Huh? I can do any damn thing I want with you two little pricks. So if I want to slap a boy's face to watch his reaction…"

"Auh!" This time Matt was able to remain on his feet.

"Then that's what I'm gonna do," the assailant concluded.

To me this guy looked as if he was about to increase his level of abuse against my pal. Also, nobody in the room seemed willing to come to our aid, so I made a snap decision to divert this guy's attention away from my friend and onto me. "Yeah well, regardless of what you think, I'm not gonna let you hit him again." I then set my beer bottle down on the ping pong table and immediately put myself into a horse stance which did, then, take this guy's attention off of Matt and place it squarely onto me.

"No, Clint!" Matt blurted out to me in fear as he held a hand to his face.

"Just stay out of the way, Matt." I was too committed now to back down.

"You're challenging me?" the guy was amused and irked at the same time by my brazen behavior. "All right, you little shit. Let's see what you've got." The man then prepared himself to actually fight me.

There was nothing I could do now. As I drew him out into a more open area of the room, I kept wondering why the others in this group weren't stopping this guy. I then realized that most of them weren't even paying any attention to us yet.

"Hey, Sully," the guy behind the bar finally spoke out. "Leave the kid alone, will ya?"

"Shut up!" the guy responded with his characteristic eloquence. And then he threw his first punch at me.

I blocked him successfully and then delivered a forward punch to his chest in response. I figured that this would demonstrate to him that I was capable of defending myself, but I wouldn't hurt him enough just yet to make him become even more mad at me.

"Hey, guys! Sully's fighting one of the kids." At long last, some other guy in the room called out to everyone else.

As all the other men in the shack suddenly stopped what they were doing to watch us, Sully threw his next punch at my head. Again I was able to block it with no trouble, but this time I gave him a forward punch to his stomach and as I did, I tried to put all of my weight behind it.

"Uhoof!"

An "oo" sound then rose up from the crowd as Sully bent over a bit from the force of my blow. And then everyone in the room began to laugh when they realized that I had actually managed to land a good one on my opponent. Apparently, though, I had also embarrassed Sully. He didn't like having his friends see that he could be bested by a boy half his size. And I guess he figured out also that he was too drunk to be able to land a punch on me, so he picked up my beer bottle from the ping pong table and cracked me over the head with it.

Since I had never learned a technique for blocking an assault from directly above, I wasn't prepared to stop this guy from hitting me in the head. And so I lost consciousness after that. To recount what happened to me next, I have to rely on what Matt told me later.

"Hey, you knocked him out," some other guy in the crowd hollered.

"Yeah, it's about damn time too, " Sully snarled. And then he put down the beer bottle and bent over me. I had landed on the floor stretched out on my stomach, so when he pulled my shirt off over my head, he made my arms extend out in front of me. Sully then reached down again and lifted the middle of my body just enough to get his hands under me so he could undo my belt and unfasten and unzip my pants. Then, after he had removed my shoes and socks, he reached around under my waist to get a firm grip on my pants and underpants, and with one good yank as my outstretched palms slapped the linoleum, he pulled both garments off of me so I was left to lie there naked and still unconscious on the floor in front of the entire society. As he did these things to me, Sully was also working the crowd. Each time he removed a piece of clothing from my body, he would hold it up in the air for the rest of the men in the room to cheer over. Then he would throw the article off into the crowd and bend down over me again to remove something else. "All right! Are you guys ready for some action?" Sully yelled out after he had separated my underpants from my pants and had tossed them both into the air.

A loud cheer then rose from the crowd again as he picked up my limp body and, with little concern for my well-being, threw me down abruptly across the top of the ping pong table so he could bend my lower half over its edge. "Ok, the line starts behind me," he yelled out. And then Sully reached into his coat pocket and pulled out a small jar of Vaseline. Apparently he had intended to do something like this all along. And then, without wasting any time, Sully dropped his pants, greased up his penis to make himself hard, and then he penetrated me in my ass.

"Oh man, this boy's nice and tight," he yelled as he began to thrust himself repeatedly into my body. "Ah! Hey! Where are you going?" he yelled at the bartender as he noticed the man moving toward the front door of the shack.

"It's time for me to go and get the dinner," the bar tender responded nervously. "Don't worry, I'll be right back."

"Jerome, you go and help him. Huh?" Sully said to a friend of his in the room that he knew he could trust.

"Yeah, ok," Jerome answered. And so the bartender and Jerome left the shack together.

Matt knew he was powerless to do anything to keep these guys from raping me. And as he watched a line of men form behind Sully so that more of them could have a turn with me, Matt decided that the only way he could help us both was to make himself look unavailable and thereby keep the others, hopefully, from knocking him out as well. So while no one was paying attention to him, Matt sat down on the floor against the wall next to the keg, and then he allowed the beer in his cup to spill out all over his crotch. As soon as he felt his appearance was convincing, my friend then closed his eyes and slumped down against the wall so he would seem to the others in the society to be passed out. At the same time, though, he did peer at me through partially closed eyelids every so often so he could keep a watch over the men as one by one, they greased up their penises and took their turns at gang raping me.

In all, Matt told me that nine of them rammed their penises into my buttocks. And all the while the bartender with help from Jerome, kept running back and forth through the bar so they could carry in the food for everyone's dinner and get things set up in the next room.

At about the time the ninth guy was ejaculating into me, Matt told me that he suddenly heard a voice call out from above him. "Hey, what's with this kid?" It was Sully, and he was apparently looking to do the same with Matt that he and the others had just finished doing to me. "Is he passed out, or did somebody knock him out too?"

"I don't know," Jerome hollered back from the other side of the room. "He's been like that for a while now."

"Well let's wake him up then," Sully proclaimed. With the beer keg only inches away, Sully then bent down and grasped Matt's head between his two palms and then he moved my roommate's head sideways a little until he had placed my friend directly under the tap, and then he threw open the handle all the way so that the beer could flow out. "Ha!" Sully exclaimed with a sense of devilish fun. Immediately beer began to gush down all over the top of the boy's head. "Hey, wake up, kid!" As Matt's hair became soaked down by the beer, Sully grabbed my friend's wet face with one of his large hands and began to shake Matt's head around in an attempt to awaken the boy.

"Dinner's ready!" the bartender cried out.

"Aw, what the hell." With Sully's attempts to revive my roommate not working, apparently, he shifted his thinking to another subject which was equally close to his heart. "I'm always hungry after sex, anyway." Sully then released Matt's face and stood up to allow my friend to remain under the flow of the cold beer as it continued to rush from the keg and drench my friend thoroughly. Despite it all, Matt was able to hold himself together so he could keep up the pretense that he was unconscious. "Let's come back and fuck the other kid after we eat," Sully announced. But then, as he was about to turn and walk into the dining room, he got an idea. With a new sense of purpose and while the bartender was turning off the tap on the keg, Sully walked briskly over to the fireplace which stood along the front wall of the shack, and removed a loose stone from its hearth. He then walked back to stand next to my still unconscious body, selected my left index finger, and then drove the stone down hard so he could smash my finger with it. Matt said he saw my entire body jump when the bone in my finger broke.

"Hey, what'd ya do that for, Sully?" the bartender asked with a measure of trepidation.

"Because I want this little son of a bitch to never forget what we do to smart-ass kids like him," he snarled. "All right, let's go eat." The man then left my side and walked off into the dining room to enjoy his meal.

The crowd then, in general agreement with Sully's proposal, followed this monster into the dining room.

As soon as the bar room was empty, Matt then got up onto his feet again and with beer now sloshing around in his tennis shoes, raced over quickly to see what my condition was. When he confirmed that I was still breathing, he ran to a pay phone near the front door and put a dime in to call our safe number for that night. After he heard a voice answer on the other end, Matt's conversation was brief. And then he hung up the phone and returned to the ping pong table to be with me. At about this same time, the bartender returned from the dining room to see what he could do to help.

"You know I like a good poke with a boy as much as the next fellow does," he said. "But doing what Sully did to this boy just isn't right."

"Well, help ought'a be here in a few minutes," Matt replied as beer still dripped occasionally from his chin and hung like little yellow balls from the bottoms of his ear lobes. "Help me gather up his clothes and get 'em back on him, will ya?"

"Sure, kid. We want to get you two out of here before they finish their dinner and come back in here lookin' for more."

Apparently Matt and the bartender succeeded in getting me dressed and out of there before the society returned to the bar room, because when I came to, I found myself lying in the only bed there was in our little infirmary at the Academy. Matt, Mr. Stuart, and some doctor I had never seen before were standing around the bed and staring down at me with worried looks on their faces. As I became aware of myself, I realized that I had been banged up pretty badly, and my head and anal area, not to mention my finger, were in excruciating pain. "Uh… what happened?" I groaned. "Ow… ow my ass! And my head! And what happened to my hand? Oh my God, I'm never gonna be able to play the guitar again!" It was almost more than I could bear.

"There now, son," the doctor tried to calm me down. "I just gave you a shot for the pain, so you should be feeling better in a few minutes.

With my left hand in a cast, I then raised my good hand to my head and felt a bandage wrapped around it. "What's this for?"

"You took a nasty blow to the head and it opened the skin a little and was bleeding for a while. You didn't sustain a fracture there, but I do think you have a concussion. So that's why you feel the bandage. Also, you had some blood coming out of your rectum. I'm guessing that they caused a small tear somewhere inside you. So I've prescribed a mild laxative I want you to take for the next few days to keep your stools soft so we can give that tear a chance to heal. And then the cast on your arm is going to need to stay there for eight weeks. Your left index finger has a compound fracture. It was chewed up pretty bad by whatever hit it, but I think I did a decent job of putting it back together, so it should heal all right for you."

"Am I gonna be able to play the guitar again?" I asked fretfully.

"Well, you'll probably have some scarring there, and you'll need to do some special exercises with that finger once the cast is off. So I think it's possible, but we'll have to see for sure in eight weeks. Ok?"

"And what about Christmas break? How am I gonna go to Europe now?" I was feeling miserable.

"We'll talk about that later, Clint," Mr. Stuart said to me. And then my headmaster turned his attention to the doctor. "Thanks for coming out here tonight. It would have been a lot tougher on us if we'd had to take this lad to the hospital." Mr. Stuart then began to usher the doctor out of the infirmary.

"That's ok, Don. You'll get my bill," the doctor joked. And then the two men left the room entirely and began to walk away from us along the hallway toward the lobby.

Now that we were alone, Matt felt as if he could speak to me, finally. "How are you feeling?" he asked quietly. His voice was filled with concern.

"Like shit," I replied. "Did you get me out of there, or something?" I couldn't figure out how everything had ended.

"Yeah," Matt replied. "I did."

"How?" I asked.

My roommate then told me all that had happened after I had lost consciousness, and then he apologized to me for not doing more.

"Are you kidding? You did great, Matt. You saved my life, maybe. Who knows what those bastards would have done to me next. Or to you." I was proud of how my friend had kept his head and saved us both. And I told him so.

"Well, I think they're gonna want you to sleep in here tonight," Matt observed.

"I don't know why. It's not like they've actually got someone here to check on me or take care of anything for me if I need help." So I tried to sit up, but immediately my body felt heavy and my head began to pound with pain and feel dizzy. "Oh, forget it." I gave up quickly. "I don't know what that doctor gave me, but I can sure feel it starting to work now. So, I guess I'll just stay here for the night after all."

At that moment Frank peered around the corner from out in the hallway, and then he stepped into the infirmary to join us. When we saw him standing there in his underwear with his hair all messed up, we could tell that he had gotten out of his bed to come downstairs and see what was going on with us. "Man, what happened to you?" Since it was past lights out by now, he was taking a chance of getting into trouble just for being out of his room at this hour.

"I got hit by a truck," I answered quickly. Even though I wasn't feeling all that well at the moment, I still knew to keep my mouth shut about what we had really been doing.

Matt then turned and looked at Frank. "Do you want to help us with something?"

"And how come you smell like stale beer?" Frank asked my roommate.

I must have had a look of fear in my eyes when I stared at Matt then, because his expression back to me seemed to indicate that he wanted me to stay calm.

"Look, we'll talk later, but right now I need you to go and do something for me. Ok?" Matt was attempting to bargain.

Frank looked away at me for a moment, and then back at Matt again. "Ok," he agreed.

"Great." Matt then reached into his pocket and pulled out his key to our room. "Go over to our dorm and use this key to get into our room. Then from the bottom two drawers in the dresser, bring me back a clean pair of jeans, some underpants and a clean pair of socks. And then go into our closet and bring me back a clean shirt. My stuff is hanging on the left. Ok?"

"But…" Frank wanted more information on what this was all about.

"Everything I'm wearing right now is all messed up and I need clean clothes so I can spend the night in here." Matt tried to convey a sense of urgency in his tone so he could end any further probes that Frank might think to make. "Now hurry up! Get going before Stuart gets back here."

"All right," Frank agreed as he took Matt's key. And then our friend turned and left the infirmary as quietly as he had come in.

"You're gonna spend the night in here?" I asked with some surprise.

"Yeah," Matt answered simply.

"Where?" There was only one bed in the infirmary and at the moment, I was using it.

"When Frank gets back I'm gonna have him help me bring in one of those big leather cushioned chairs from the library and I'll sleep in that tonight."

"But why?" Matt's idea sounded so uncomfortable to me.

"You said it yourself. The Academy doesn't have anyone to stay here with you tonight, so I'm gonna do it."

"But…"

"Clint, listen! I've made up my mind on this. Now relax. Let the drug the doctor gave you do its job, and go to sleep. Ok?"

In my condition at the moment, it was clear to me that I was outnumbered. "Ok. Thanks, Matt." I was too out of it by now to argue any further. I then could see my roommate smile at me faintly as I rolled my head and looked up at the ceiling. It was easier, I decided, just to do as he said.

The only other thing I can recall from that night was hearing Frank's voice again when he returned with Matt's clothes. "Here are some jeans, and a clean pair of underpants, and the other things you wanted. I don't know if this is enough, though, to get rid of that stench of stale beer and cigarette smoke I can still smell on you." Apparently Frank now figured that he was entitled to more information about what we had been up to.

After that I could hear my two friends continuing to talk while Matt disrobed in front of Frank. As they talked, I guess I must have passed out because I didn't wake up again until nearly lunchtime the next day. And when I opened my eyes, I saw Matt slumped there next to me and dozing in one of the library chairs with a blanket over him. He had indeed spent the entire night by my side so he could look after me.

***

"Hey, wake up," I said gently to my roommate. I then saw his eyes open, blink a few times and then look in my direction.

"Oh. Hi," he responded in a sleepy voice. "How are you feeling?" And then my friend yawned.

"I don't know yet. But I guess I'm hungry and I've gotta take a leak."

"Oh really? Well that sounds like a good sign," Matt said hopefully.

At this moment we heard a knock, and then Frank opened the door and peered into the infirmary at us. "Oh, good. Youz guys are awake now. I looked in a little while ago and youz two were still asleep."

"Hey, Frank," I replied.

"Hi, Frank." Matt still sounded tired.

"Look, it's almost lunchtime, so just stay here and I'll bring youz guys your lunches. All right?" And then before Matt or I could say anything in response, Frank was gone again.

I then sat up and pulled the covers off of me. "Oh, my head," I exclaimed as I put my right hand up to press it against the pain.

"Are you ok?" the sound of concern for my well-being was still with my friend.

"Yeah, I just need to take it easy, I guess. But just in case, will ya walk to the bathroom with me?"

"Yeah, sure." Matt then threw the blanket off of him and stood up. "We can use the bathroom that's off the library," he assured me.

So feeling like an invalid, I stood up and put my good arm round my friend's shoulder. Once we got going, though, I found that except for the pain I seemed to have everywhere, it wasn't as hard for me to get around as I had thought it would be. As a result, in no time we had both done our business and reassumed our residence in the infirmary.

"Man," I exclaimed once I was under the covers again. "It was nice to get up and walk around, but it's nicer to be back in bed again."

"Yeah well, you just plan to take it easy today. Things got pretty rough last night."

"How many guys did you say raped me?"

"I counted nine," Matt replied.

"Jeeze, you'd think they'd all be too embarrassed to rape a kid in front of everyone else like that."

"Yeah, they were bare assed all right," Matt then smiled at the pun he had just made.

I chuckled at my friend's joke just as another knock came on the door and Mr. Stuart walked in. "Well, good morning, boys. How's the patient?"

"Ok, I guess," I responded blankly. Even though he was trying to be nice to me at the moment, I still thought of him these days as the enemy.

"And how are you, Ramsey?" Mr. Stuart asked my roommate.

"I'm ok," Matt's response showed an equal lack of enthusiasm for the man.

Our headmaster noticed our disinterest in him, but continued with what he had come to tell me anyway. "Yes, well." He then sat down in one of the two other chairs which were there in front of my bed. "Anyway, this morning I arranged for a telex to be sent to your father, Clint."

"Oh?" This news, of course, caught my attention. "What did you tell him?"

"Well, the doctor told me last night that he doesn't want you to fly for the next few weeks as long as you're recovering from that concussion. So I thought it best if I inform your parents about your accident and let them know that although you are ok and expected to recover fully, you won't be able to join them for Christmas this year."

This was not the news that I was expecting to hear and I was devastated by it. In just two days I was supposed to be flying to Europe to be with my parents. "No!" I shrieked. "I have to go! My dad sent me the tickets."

"I'm sorry, Clint. There's nothing I can do about this. It's doctor's orders."

"What did you tell them happened to me?" Now I was concerned that my parents might be overly worried about me.

"Well I..." Our headmaster then shifted his weight in his chair and almost seemed nervous. "I told them you were involved in a minor traffic accident. I let them know of the injuries to your head and your finger, but I didn't see the need to worry them any further."

I just stared at the man in disbelief. I didn't want to give up my trip away from this place.

"Also," Mr. Stuart continued, "the doctor said that as long as you have that cast on your arm, you need to limit your physical activity. So regardless of what anybody else says, I'm going to side line you until your cast comes off." In telling me this, Mr. Stuart was hoping to improve my spirits. I guess he figured that if I knew I wasn't going to be working for the next eight weeks, I'd feel better about not being able to see my parents.

At that same moment, Frank walked into the infirmary with our lunches and heard the last part of what Mr. Stuart had just said to me. "What do ya mean side line? Soccer season's over already. And he quit the team a long time ago."

"Oh, that's nice of you, DeVierno, to bring these boys their lunches today." Mr. Stuart tried to intimate with his tone that he wanted Frank to give us our trays and then leave. But Frank wasn't one to do something if he didn't feel like doing it, and at the moment, Frank didn't want to leave.

"If I can't fly to be with my parents this Christmas, where the hell am I supposed to go?" The man's proclamation about an eight-week break from work for me wasn't changing my mood. I was still very upset over this situation.

"Well, I suppose you'll have to go home with one of the other students. Like, what about Ramsey here?" Our headmaster then turned his head and looked at Matt.

"I'm from Michigan. Remember? I'm flying home for Christmas."

"Oh, that's right." Personal information about his students—even his biggest money makers—was clearly an interest which the man did not possess. "Well there must be someone else you can spend the holiday with who lives close by and isn't flying home."

"Yeah," Frank piped up. "You can come home with me. I'm not flyin'. My cousin's comin' up from New York in two days to drive me home. We can make room for you easy, Clint. And you'll love it. My mom's a great cook."

At that moment I must have had an expression of disbelief on my face. This was all going too fast for me.

"No, really." Apparently my lack of response caused Frank to feel as if he needed to make certain that I understood what it was that he was offering me. "You can come home with me for Christmas. I've got a place where you can sleep and everything."

"Well that's a terrific idea. Then it's all settled." Mr. Stuart then stood up again. It was clear that he was feeling uncomfortable with us in the small confines of this room. "I'll make sure your parents know of your plans then, Clint." And then Mr. Stuart looked at Frank. "DeVierno, why don't you come with me now. I'll let you call your mother from the phone in my office so you can let her know that you're bringing Adams home with you for the holiday."

"Yeah, ok. That's a good idea." Frank then followed our headmaster as he left the room. A moment later Matt and I were alone again.

I was almost in tears now. "Matt, I don't know if I can take another five months in this place. The only thing that's been keeping me going for the past month or so has been knowing that all of this was about to be over."

Matt didn't answer me right away. He just stared at the floor for a few moments as if he was absorbing everything that had just taken place. And then Matt looked at me and said something which to this day, I consider one of the most extraordinary acts of courage I have ever witnessed. "Well, if you can't leave, then I'm gonna have to come back here after Christmas, too."

My jaw dropped. "Matt, you can't. We've already planned everything."

"Yeah, and now our plans are all screwed up, so I have to come back."

"No you don't! Matt, even if I can't get away, you still can. It's suicide to come back here when you don't have to. Do you realize that if you come back, you're gonna have to keep giving blow jobs and being raped nearly every day until next summer?"

"I know what's gonna happen to me. I haven't been asleep for the past couple of months ya know. But Clint, I can't leave here if I know you're still having to go through all this crap."

"Of course you can! Matt, don't be an idiot. You've got a chance to get out of here finally. Don't blow it for yourself just because you're worried about me. Besides, Stuart would never make me go out alone."

Now my roommate was mad at me for calling him an idiot. "You can't depend on that. Besides, all he has to do is make one of the freshmen from our gang go out with you. It wouldn't be the same as having me go along, but frankly I don't think a lot of the people we see would care all that much."

This was crazy. Somehow I had to talk some sense into this kid. "Matt, look. I appreciate what you're trying to do, but…"

"Clint, that's it!" My friend was now raising his voice at me as if he were a parent trying to discipline an unruly child. "We're not talking about this anymore. I've made up my mind and that's the end of the discussion. Now let's eat lunch."

And that was it. Any more protesting from me would only cause my friend to become even more angry with me, and considering all he had just done for me the night before, I didn't have the heart to push him any farther on the matter. But I feared for his safety now. So far Matt had held up pretty well against the abuse we had both suffered through. But physically, Matt wasn't as strong as I was. I wouldn't say that he was frail, but he had a slight build and had never struck me as the type who could handle a sustained amount of rough treatment.

Two days later, the time had come for all of the students and the faculty to clear out of the Academy. Matt had arranged to share a taxi to Boston with a couple of other kids, and after we had said our good-byes to each other, he was suddenly out of my life. I had made a couple more attempts, after that morning in the infirmary, to convince him to stay away after the holidays, but my friend had a stubborn streak in him that I had never really noticed until now. So nothing I said to him was able to change his mind.

Frank's cousin seemed nice enough. He was in his mid-twenties and was living on his own. He worked in an office somewhere in Manhattan and made enough money to afford the rent on a small efficiency apartment and to make his payments on the late-model Plymouth Fury he picked us up in. And throughout the entire trip down to New York City, he kept talking about what a big engine his Fury had.

Chapter Ten
New Semester, Old Routine

Winter in Massachusetts that year, once we had returned from our Christmas break, was one of the coldest and snowiest seasons I can remember ever living through. The lake froze so solidly that closer to town, car races were held regularly on the ice. Also, in keeping with this change in the weather, our two day students traded their boats for snow mobiles and rode happily every day across the ice in order to get from their homes to the Academy and back again. And these boys were never content to leave their distinctive conveyances down by the dock. Because of the snow pack, which seemed to cover the ground for months, they chose instead every morning to pilot their noisy contraptions through the Annex parking lot and out onto the south road, past our dorm room window, around the tennis court and in through the front gate on the upper campus so they could park in the circle out in front of Ulster Hall. This act, though innocent in its intention, was torture for the rest of us. Throughout those weeks there wasn't a red-blooded boy among us who didn't gaze upon these gleaming snow machines every day with envy, and ache for an opportunity to jump onto one of them and take it for a long spin across the countryside.

Just as water sports in the lake had been forbidden during the fall for insurance reasons, ice skating and ice hockey were now banned as well. All winter long, the only recreation available to the student body was basketball and despite the fact that the wooden floor in the gym was severely warped in several places, the Academy did manage to suit up a varsity and a junior varsity basketball team that year. At first when the team practices were begun, it seemed as if every day at least two or three boys would get tripped up by the ripples in the floor and fall ass over tea cup onto their fronts. But before long, the Academy players grew used to these varnished waves and were able to travel up and down the court without so much as a stumble. This unique skill always worked quite nicely to the Academy's advantage whenever a competing school would visit our campus to challenge our teams. Just the same, this unusual home court advantage was seldom enough to bring about a win for our teams. The reason why was because, quite frankly, the Academy was a school full of rejects. And although this characterization didn't apply to every student on our campus, it just about did.

The questionable quality of our boarding population notwithstanding, the sport of basketball consumed our lives throughout that winter. Even Frank gave up his wise-guy persona long enough to get himself onto one of the teams. Christmas with his family had been a pleasant experience for me, plus a relief. They had all been very nice to me. Even though it was obvious once we had arrived that his family had little money to spare—Frank had received an ABC scholarship to attend the Academy—they indulged my needs any way they could to make sure that I was well taken care of. For instance, Frank's mother, younger sister and grandparents slept in the three bedrooms of their little Brooklyn apartment, while Frank had a makeshift room set up for him out on the enclosed porch. Since I was his guest, and still recovering from my injuries, Frank gave me his bed and spent the entire time of our vacation sleeping on the couch in their living room.

Mrs. DiVierno was indeed a wonderful cook, and everyone in Frank's family went out of their way to make me feel at home. There were many things about this family which impressed me, but what I found most striking was the strong bond I observed between Frank and his grandparents. I suppose I was sensitive to their relationship because of the fact that my own grandparents had long since passed away by this time in my life, and I missed them. I also noticed that away from the Academy, my host seemed more natural and at ease with himself than he normally did. For that matter, I suppose, I probably seemed more calm as well. Even so, I had taken two of Fatso's specially modified cans of shaving cream with me in my luggage and throughout my stay I found no difficulty in keeping them out of sight so I could continue to medicate myself with the cocaine that was hidden inside of them. And when the time came for us to return to the Academy, Frank's cousin brought around the Fury and drove us both back to Massachusetts.

Once we were back at school again, I found it sort of intriguing to watch Frank on the basketball court. Our break from the Academy had seemed to recharge his batteries. What I mean is, he was really trying to do well for a change. Or rather, he was now allowing everyone to see that he was actually trying. I think Frank always tried to do things to the best of his abilities, but I don't think he ever wanted any of us to actually see that he cared about how he did. It was all part of that wise-guy, street-smart, Brooklyn kid persona he was always trying to project. But since I had become better acquainted with the guy over Christmas, it now seemed to me as if he no longer felt the need to maintain his tough guy facade. Or at least this was the impression I had of him at that time.

"Way to go, Frank!" Matt yelled one afternoon during the Academy's first game of the season after our friend had caught a rebound off of the rim and then popped it back up for two points. My roommate had kept the promise he had made to me and had returned to the Academy after Christmas break. Although I still believed that he had made a terrible decision for himself by coming back, I was glad to have him with me again as I faced this new semester. Before or since, I have never known such loyalty in a friend. And for the first couple of weeks, at least, things for us were not all that bad.

Mr. Stuart had been sincere when he had said that I would not have to work until my cast was off. Matt and I had figured that straight away our headmaster would partner Matt up with one of the upperclassmen and then send them both off together to the Friendly Inn to resume their work as boy prostitutes, but instead my friend was left to kill time with me in the afternoons while I hung out in the gym mostly to watch our teams practice. At first neither of us understood the reason for Matt's reprieve. The only thing we were able to observe was that the need for the Academy to sell Fatso's huge stocks of cocaine, all of a sudden seemed paramount. Every one of the upperclassmen, including the leader, was leaving the school grounds every afternoon to sell as much of the drug as they could. Once they were gone, they were not returning to the campus most evenings until after dark. And this frenzied sense of urgency also affected our friends Juan and Carlos. The skills of these two were being pressed into service every afternoon now, while they continued to be flown down to the gulf coast most weekends to see to the needs of the other end of Fatso's empire. By the time February rolled around, Matt and I were almost feeling guilty over the fact that we weren't doing our share.

Just the same, it wasn't easy living for Matt and me all the time. I don't know if it was because of the weather which was keeping the faculty closer to the campus than usual, or if it was because the newness of our slavery was now worn off and a few of our teachers had decided that the time had come for them to avail themselves of the unique fringe benefits which came with being a teacher at the Academy. But Matt and I began to be summoned individually

"No, I'm sorry," my headmaster then patted me twice on the top of my head which I interpreted as his desire for me to disengage. So I let go of the man's member and sat back in my spot beneath his desk. "I'm afraid I'm not going to send him over there while he's healing, and I'm not sending the other one in by himself. We've already been all over this issue before. You and I agreed years ago that I don't send my boys out on jobs alone. That business in Worcester might have ended up very differently if I hadn't sent them in as a pair. I still have to return these boys to their parents intact, you know."

Apparently Fatso was putting a lot of pressure on my headmaster and I thought as the conversation progressed that I could detect a slight quiver in his voice every so often, but I was surprised at how forceful Mr. Stuart was sounding as he held firm with his Boston benefactor. In the past, whenever I had seem these men together, my headmaster always appeared to me to be afraid to say anything that might be construed as counter to whatever Fatso's wishes happened to be. But on this occasion, the head of our faculty wasn't backing down, and I was grateful that he was finally showing evidence of having a spine, particularly since it was to my benefit that he was. And as I sat there under his desk and listened, I found myself wondering whether or not this man really did care about the welfare of his students after all. And perhaps he even felt a bit guilty for having been the one who had sent Matt and me into that violent bunch of misfits up in Worcester. In any case, I was relieved that he was standing up for us now. I really didn't feel ready just yet to get back out there, anyway. Then, as an obvious reaction to something that Fatso had just said to him, I watched as Mr. Stuart push himself back in his chair a bit and sat up even straighter.

"Are you threatening me?" Mr. Stuart's voice got a bit louder at this point also. "Listen, it's not my fault you overbought from your friends in South America. I've already got all of my other boys out every day for you. Why don't you just siphon the money you need from one of your legitimate operations so you can pay them on time?"

While my headmaster listened on his phone again, I watched as he shoved his penis back into his pants and then zipped up.

"Well, I'm sorry you're having so much trouble these days, but the conditions under which we provide you with boys for the inn haven't changed, and I'm not risking their health or their safety any further than our agreement with you requires." Another brief pause. "Well... yes I suppose you could say that this is my final word on the matter."

Then I could tell that something happened.

"Hmm! He hung up." Mr. Stuart then placed the receiver back down on his phone and pushed his chair way back so he could stand up. "Ok, Clint, you can come out of there. I'm not in the mood anymore to finish."

"Was that Fatso?" I asked as I climbed out from under his desk and stood up again.

"Ah, yes it was." My headmaster then glanced away to avoid looking at me directly.

"Is there something wrong?" I asked with concern.

"Nothing you need to worry about, son. You just run along now and don't worry about anything. Ok?"

"Ok," I answered. I then walked to the door in his office which led to the hallway and opened it. "Do you want me to leave your door open now, sir?"

"What?" Already Mr. Stuart's mind was somewhere else. "Oh, yes. That's fine. Go ahead and leave it open and I'll see you later on, Clint."

"Yes, sir," I replied. And then I left his office, grabbed my winter coat and headed for the front door of Ulster Hall so I could go outside and make my way back over to my own dormitory. I figured that Matt needed to hear about what I had just been through.

***

A few days later, when the weekend arrived, it was time for another of the Academy's extended weekends. I never really understood why it was that we even had extended weekends, but on three different occasions throughout the school year nearly all of the students and the teachers went home after lunch on Friday and then did not return until dinnertime on the following Monday evening.

Scattered in the two neighborhoods which lay just beyond the front gate were four houses which the Academy rented for the teachers who had their own families. Usually one of these poor souls would be made the AOD for the entire weekend. On this particular weekend, Mr. Kelley was assigned this job. Mr. Kelly was a nice man who rarely smiled. He and his wife and his three small children had come to America from Liverpool, England, for a better life and had wound up instead at the Academy. His children were bright and adorable and had become such a visible part of our lives at the Academy, they eventually wound up with their own individual photos in our year book. Mrs. Kelley was always trying to make us feel as if we had a home and were cared for at the Academy. Of course all of us knew better, but we appreciated her efforts just the same.

To make it easier for the AOD to keep an eye on the students who stayed behind because they couldn't go home, all of us who lived in the outer dorms were made to move into rooms in Ulster Hall which were vacated for the weekend by other students. Since Matt and I had still not resumed our weekend excursions, we moved into another kid's room which was located at the south end of the building and looked out onto the circle below. For the entire weekend we would not be permitted back into our own dormitory, so once we had moved into Ulster Hall, we prepared ourselves for another weekend of excruciating boredom.

At dinner that first night, the fifteen or so of us in the student body who were left behind were given box lunches for our meal. In fact, for the entire weekend box lunches were all we got to eat because Thomas Jefferson was one of the staff members who had taken advantage of the Academy's excuse to goof off for four days. And at this particular meal, I recall a discussion about how the local fire marshal had recently visited our not so fair campus and had proclaimed that if Ulster Hall were ever to catch on fire, the entire structure would be engulfed within thirteen minutes. At the time Matt and I simply filed this news away as another bit of depressing trivia about the place we called home. And we went to bed that night—in that building—quite oblivious to the events which were about to change our dreary existence that weekend into one of sheer terror.

The next morning we were awakened abruptly by the sounds of some of the kids running through the upstairs hallway, banging on our door and others yelling "FIRE"! At first we remembered the discussion of the night before and decided that we were the victims of a boarding school prank, perpetrated by some bored striplings who had nothing better to do with their time. Besides, Matt and I were among the youngest students there and bigger kids were always trying to put one over on us. But then Matt leaned over in his bunk and pulled back the blind so he could look out the window.

"Hey, I can't see anything out there but smoke," he announced with alarm.

"What?" I then hurled the covers off of me and dashed over to the window so I could see for myself. "Jeeze! You're right. I can't see anything out there but smoke, either!"

Immediately, Matt and I threw on whatever clothes we could find, and then we rushed out into the hall and made our way down one of the sets of stairs and outside into the circle in front of Ulster Hall. When we were clear of the building, we discovered that part of the reason why we hadn't been able to see out our window upstairs was because of the dense fog which had rolled in off the lake during the night with the heaviest drizzle I had ever been in. Just the same, there was indeed smoke all around us because there really was a fire. However, a quick inspection of the structure before us revealed that it wasn't Ulster Hall that was burning. So as the fifteen of us began to scan the other buildings on the campus, we were all shocked when we saw flames to the south of us shooting out from the roof of the headmaster's house, and there was no sign of Mr. Stuart anywhere.

As our little band of students huddled together in the early morning cold, talk began to go around about the need for one of us at least to call the fire department. But since the phones in Ulster Hall were all locked up, and there was no one among us who had keys to the offices, the fire department had not yet been summoned. So as the others continued to stare at our headmaster's house while it burned and debate the issue, I took off running across the upper campus toward the AOD's house.

Once I was in the trees behind the gym, I picked up a faint trail which led me through the forest and eventually into the back yard of the Kelleys' house. When I reached the house, I banged on the back door and continued to do so for a short while until their middle child—a boy of about six—opened the door, recognized me and let me into their kitchen. I didn't realize it at the time, but apparently I had become drenched by the heavy drizzle because the boy told me later that I was dripping wet when I stepped inside. And while the family was in the midst of having their breakfast, I told Mr. Kelley about the headmaster's house being on fire. After a moment of disbelief, the man picked up the receiver on his phone and called in the emergency to the local fire department. He then grabbed his coat and ran with me back to the scene.

It was terrifying to stand there and watch the flames as they rose from the section of the upstairs where Mr. Stuart kept his bedroom. And I don't know if anyone tried to break into his house to help the poor man, but in just a short time the fire department arrived and went to work immediately to douse the flames. Shortly after that Mr. Stuart emerged from his burning house and seemed to be all right. Though a bit shaken from the experience, he explained that he had been downstairs in his kitchen when the fire had started in his bedroom, and he theorized that when he had fallen asleep a few hours earlier, he had neglected to put out his cigarette. He believed that it had been that cigarette which had fallen onto his mattress while he slept, which had eventually caused the fire to occur.

Before long, the firemen had succeeded in putting out the flames. They had saved the house, but the whole of the insides were a blackened smelly mess and Mr. Stuart ended up having to spend the next two months living somewhere else while the house was rebuilt. For as long as I knew the man after that day, our headmaster insisted that the entire affair had been nothing more than an accident with a cigarette. But the following Tuesday, after the rest of the school was back from their extended weekend away, and even though my arm was still in a cast, Matt and I were driven to the Friendly Inn and made to resume our daily duties as boy prostitutes.

***

For the rest of that winter and into the spring, we continued to be rented out every weekend to customers who were willing to pay the exorbitant fees that Fatso was charging for an overnight of sexual depravity with two young boys. One of the more memorable of these occasions during these months started for us when Joe stopped by the campus late one Friday afternoon to pick us up.

"Where are we going this time, Joe?" Matt asked as he climbed into Joe's car, after I had gotten in, and then closed the passenger door.

"We're headed for Providence this time, boys." Joe would answer our questions usually, but he rarely offered us anything more.

"Is it a man or a woman?" I asked. This was a legitimate question because, as it was at the motel, some of our weekend clients were women.

"It's a man." Joe turned over the engine and then handed Matt a slip of paper. "Here's your safe number for tonight. If you need to use it, I'll be the one who'll be staying close by." Then the large man began to drive us off of the Academy grounds.

"Thanks," Matt said as he stuffed the paper into one of the pockets in his pants.

"Hey, you two are supposed to memorize that," Joe barked.

"Oh yeah," Matt replied. And so he pulled the paper out of his pocket again, looked at it for a moment and then handed it to me. Then he looked at Joe again. "Is the man tonight management or labor?" It was time for us to continue with our little interrogation so we could learn what we could about the things that were in store for us on this night.

"Labor," Joe grumbled.

"Really?" I responded. "People who are labor usually don't make enough money to be able to afford us do they?" I really had no idea what I was talking about. I was just trying to get whatever information I could from our driver.

"Well this one has paid. I guess maybe he's been saving up for a while." Instead of taking a right turn when we reached the highway—which would have taken us into town—Joe turned his car to the left which was indeed the correct way to go toward Providence.

"Is he someone we've serviced already at the motel?" Matt was good at knowing when the time was best for him to take over the task of asking our questions.

"Could be." Joe wasn't always jovial. On this day he seemed distant, as if there were something on his mind which was more pressing to him than answering a bunch of foolish questions from a couple of kids. We had been around him enough by this time to know when he was tired of talking with us. So after my friend had turned around and looked at me for a moment as I sat there in the middle of the back seat, Matt then turned his body forward again so he could look once more through the windshield. These days we were able to communicate so much with each other with just a look. On this occasion Matt had told me with his eyes and with the expression on his face that he figured we needed to cool it for a while with the questions and I had replied through my eyes that I agreed. And so neither of us said another word until we arrived an hour and a half or so later in Providence.

Soon after we hit town, Joe stopped for a few minutes at some little Italian place so we could pick up a couple of pizzas to take with us. The customer himself lived in a small one-story frame house in the middle of a neighborhood that was crammed full of more little houses that all looked the same to us. It was shortly after dark when Joe finally pulled his Cadillac into the guy's driveway.

"When did you boys eat last?" With a half-empty bottle of beer in his hand, the man seemed worried about something when the three of us walked in through his front door.

"Not since lunch," I replied.

A look of relief then came over the man's face. "Oh good," he sighed. "In that case, take your pizzas into the kitchen and put them in the oven for now. Then set the oven on warm, grab yourselves a couple of beers out of the fridge and then come back into the family room and watch some TV for a while. I want us all to get drunk first."

Without missing a step, Matt and I did as we were told and continued on into the man's kitchen. We didn't know right off where his kitchen was, but because the place was so small it wasn't too hard for us to figure out.

"So I'll be back tomorrow at noon, then. Right?" Joe wanted to make sure that the two of them agreed on the arrangements that Fatso had made with this man before he left us for the night.

"Right. Noon," the customer replied.

"All right. That's fine," Joe confirmed. "And remember... no damage. Right?"

"Right," the customer responded. "No damage. I promise."

Matt and I were able to hear this exchange all the way into the kitchen. As I opened the oven door for Matt so he could slide our pizzas in, he asked me a question. "Why do you think that Joe's worried about us being damaged?"

"I don't know," I answered as I closed the oven door and turned on the heat. "He doesn't look familiar to me. Do you recognize him?"

"I can't tell yet," Matt replied as he opened the guy's refrigerator and pulled out a couple of bottles of beer for us. "I don't think he's one of the guys from Worcester, at least."

"Oh," I reacted with some surprise. I hadn't considered this possibility. "Well, that's a relief." I then took the beer that Matt was handing to me and pulled off the cap with an opener I had found lying nearby on the guy's kitchen counter. Immediately after that I began to guzzle down my beer.

My roommate followed my lead by taking a few long drinks from his bottle, and then it was time for us to leave the kitchen. Together we returned to the man's family room and looked around as soon as we got there for his television set. Right away it seemed evident to us both that our customer for this weekend was a person who lived by himself. The place was filthy and his furniture looked as if it had all been discarded by the Salvation Army. There was an old beat-up Lazy Boy by the front window and a couch which straddled the center of the room and faced the back wall where the television was resting on a couple of planks of wood which were propped up off the floor by cinder blocks. Other than a couple of lamps, a coffee table and an end table that had been shoved up against the left side of the couch, there was nothing else in this guy's entire house other than the mattress, box springs and small chest of drawers he had in his single bedroom.

"I guess we sit on the couch," Matt concluded.

"Yeah, I guess so," I agreed. So I walked over and turned on the TV, selected a channel for us to watch and then together we sat down on the man's sad-looking couch.

"Jeeze," Matt remarked as soon as we were settled. "This blanket I'm sitting on is covering up a hole in the fabric."

"Well you better not say anything about it," I cautioned.

Suddenly from behind we heard the man's voice again. "Ok, boys, stand up and take off all your clothes now." Our host then rushed over to the front window and drew the curtains shut. By this time Joe had left, which meant we were now under the charge of this strange man.

"What's your name?" Matt asked as we rose to our feet again.

"You can call me Bob," our host answered as he began to undo his jeans. "From now on until you guys leave tomorrow, I want you two to always be naked." The man was now standing before us in his boxers. "And don't worry about getting cold or anything. I turned up the hear a while ago to eighty-five so we ought to be plenty warm tonight."

As Matt and I began to take off our school blazers and ties, I did notice suddenly that it was pretty warm in this house already. *Oh great*, I thought. *Another guy who wants to stare at our naked bodies all night.*

"No wait!" Bob made us stop what we were doing as he pulled his T-shirt off over his head. "Take turns taking each other's clothes off."

And so Matt and I continued by going through the tedious process of peeling off one article of clothing at a time from the other's body until finally all three of us were naked and staring at each other.

"Ok. You boys can sit down now and go back to drinking your beers." Bob then left us alone for a bit so he could go take care of something in the kitchen.

"Horse," Matt said to me in a low voice after he was sure we were alone again.

"Yeah, no kidding," I answered back. Because it helped us to determine in advance the level of pain we were likely facing, we had developed a three-tiered ranking system to describe how well endowed our customer for the moment happened to be. Horse, sheep or ameba were how we classified the men. Even though this guy was short and thin, he was fairly muscular and his genitalia looked huge to us. This meant that if he elected to give it to us in our asses, it was going to be painful. So both of us began to drink our beers with a greater sense of urgency. We knew from experience that the drunker we were, the less the pain would seem to bother us.

"Good! I'm glad to see you guys are drinking your beers. Here's two more for you when you finish the ones you're working on." After reappearing suddenly in the family room, Bob placed two more opened bottles of beer on the coffee table in front of us, and then he walked over to the Lazy Boy and sat down. "Let me know when you boys are finished with those new ones and I'll go get you some more. The less movin' around you two do, the sooner you'll get drunk."

So for the next forty-five minutes or so, Matt and I did nothing other than sit on this man's couch and drink his beer. Since we didn't get to watch television very often, sitting and watching TV should have been a treat for us. But all we could think about as we felt the alcohol slowly dull our senses was the bulk of this guy's penis and what in the world it was that he was intending to do with it.

"Look at me," Bob called out suddenly once Matt and I had made it about halfway through our fourth beers.

Unevenly and with some weaving in our movements, we complied with the man's wishes and turned our heads to look to our left.

"Yup," he decided. "You two look pretty far gone now. Ok then, I want you boys to start kissing each other," he ordered.

This was a problem. When I turned my head back and looked at my roommate, I saw the same look of horror on his face that I'm sure he saw on mine. This wasn't the same as kissing Sweetie or even as it was when we were kissing our way down a customer's abdomen to give him a blow job as we each had to do with the man in New York. This was the real thing. Of all the intimate acts that we had been forced to do, we had never been required to kiss each other. It was always understood that all of the things we had been trained to do at the Academy were nothing more than sex because kissing was different. Kissing meant love. And love wasn't what any of this crap was about.

"Come on, start kissing each other. And do it good too. You know... French kissing."

Apparently the unwritten rules about how we were supposed to conduct ourselves were unknown to this guy. Even so, there was one thing we knew for certain which outweighed all of our other considerations. Disobeying a customer, short of refusing to do something that would put our safety in peril, was not permitted. On top of that, our host for this weekend was sounding pretty gruff to us by now and neither of us wanted to risk the raising of this guy's ire. On many occasions we had learned the hard way that an angry customer was often a dangerous customer. So with great reluctance, Matt and I placed our bottles on the coffee table in front of us, and then we leaned into each other until our lips were touching.

"Come on... get into it!" Bob was clearly wanting us to put on a show for him.

And so Matt and I began to kiss each other in earnest.

"Come on. French style, guys. Use those tongues."

Immediately after that, I felt Matt's tongue enter my mouth and so I slid my tongue into his. In no time we were putting on the performance that this customer was demanding of us. We continued this way for a short while and after a bit—I figured it was because of the fact that we were drunk—we didn't seem to be as bothered by what we were doing any longer. So another line, apparently, was now being crossed.

"Let's go! Put your hands up around each other's heads and really go at it. Mash those lips and bodies together."

So we did as we were ordered. A moment later I had my hands in Matt's hair and he had placed his hands in mine as we pulled our bodies together and kissed as if it really meant something to us. And in an example of how emotions can sometimes follow actions, I discovered suddenly that there was a tenderness within my friend which was spurring me on to be even more relaxed and passionate with him. Matt must have felt the same way about me because I noticed at this same instant how all that was my friend seemed to melt within my embrace. It was amazing, but we were happy now to stay this way. Each of us giving and each of us taking in equal measure a closeness that was well beyond anything we had felt toward each other during our late night together in the shower or from any other experience we had shared up until this moment.

"Ok, that's enough," Bob commanded.

Instantly Matt and I released one another and quickly wiped our mouths off with our hands in an effort to assure ourselves that the feelings we had just shared for each other had never really happened. We were both too embarrassed at the time to admit it, but to this day I'm convinced that we succeeded in reaching each other that night on the deepest possible level emotionally.

Bob then stood up and walked toward us. He came to a halt when he reached the end table. "Ok, you with the black hair. Stand up and come over here."

With his hand still holding onto mine, Matt then stood up.

"Over here. In front of me, son," Bob urged.

As he stepped past me to walk toward our host, it was easy to see that my roommate was having a bit of trouble now in keeping his balance.

"And you… Blonde. Turn the TV off and then you can sit there on the couch and watch us."

It was now my turn to attempt to navigate my way through this guy's family room. My biggest challenge, I soon discovered, was the coffee table. Both times I had to pass it, the thing seemed to make a serious attempt to jump out and hit me on the side of my legs. In my inebriated state, I nearly didn't make it but in another moment the TV was turned off and I was safe once again on the man's couch.

"Here I am," Matt said in his drunk voice once he was standing next to our host. He was clearly impaired by this stage of the evening.

"Yes you are," Bob replied with a hint of excitement in his voice. He then reached forward and opened a drawer in the end table and pulled out a large jar of Vaseline.

"Oh," Matt remarked when he saw what Bob had placed on the table in front of him. "My mom used to put that on my chest when I had a cold. Or was it that Vic's Vapor... something?" Matt's mind always seemed to wander when he was really drunk.

Oh shit! I thought. In our experience we had learned that Vaseline had only one use for Academy kids.

"Yeah well, it's goin' on another one of your parts tonight." The man then unscrewed the lid and with two fingers from his right hand scooped out a large hunk of the jell. Then Bob placed his left hand on Matt's back at the base of his neck and guided the boy over to stand directly in front of him so that when Matt had stopped moving, the both of them were facing me. Bob then placed both of his hands on the outsides of Matt's shoulders and shook him gently for a few moments. "Ok, now relax and close your eyes," Bob said softly.

As loosened up as he already was from the alcohol, Matt complied with the man's wishes without uttering another word.

"Just relax." And with that, Bob pulled Matt's body backward until my friend was standing off balance a bit and resting his back against the front of this guy's body. Then, with his right hand, Bob reached around and began to apply the Vaseline to Matt's penis. "Keep your eyes closed and just enjoy this," he said. And then Bob began to manipulate the boy.

In no time our host had managed to cause Matt's penis to become engorged. And it didn't take long before the stoking movements his hand was making on my friend caused Matt to vocalize the pleasure he was feeling.

"Ah... Mmh... Mmh... Ohhh... Hahh... Ah... Ah... Mmmh..." There was no question that this man now had control over my roommate's body and mind.

Actually, this whole setup didn't look so bad to me. As I watched the blissful expression on my friend's face, I was hoping that our host was planning to do the same for me next.

"Ah... Mmh... Mmh... Ohhh... Hahh... Ah... Ah... Mmmh..." With his head now tilted back so that his hair was pressing against the chest hair of our host, my friend looked to me as if there was no place else in the world at this moment that he'd prefer to be.

"Ah... Mmh... Mmh... Ohhh... Hahh... Ah... Ah... Mmmh..." Matt's body began then to tense as the hand movements of the man who was standing right behind him took my friend farther along the path to an exquisite ejaculation.

Then Bob pulled his hand away suddenly and placed it on Matt's right hip. "Ok now, lean forward and put your hands on the table," and then Bob pushed on Matt's back with his left hand to force the kid's upper body to bend over.

Automatically, Matt pulled his arms up just in time to place his hands along the edge of the table so he could brace himself against falling any farther. "Huh?" he replied in confusion.

With his right hand free again, Bob then took another scoop of Vaseline from the open jar that was still sitting in front of him on the end table, slathered the jell over his own erection—which he had obtained from rubbing himself against the skin on Matt's lower back—found Matt's hole and then without stopping halfway to give the kid a chance to get used to it, rammed his horse-sized erection into my friend's anus.

"Auhauhahu!" Matt screamed out in pain. It had all happened so quickly, he hadn't the time he had needed to prepare himself.

"Now stand upright again," the man ordered.

After gasping a couple of times, Matt pushed off from the table and gingerly raised the upper half of his body until he was nearly vertical. "That's as far as I can go!" he proclaimed in a voice that was anything now but relaxed.

"That'll be fine," Bob confirmed. The man then wrapped his right fist around Matt's erection again and with his left hand now on Matt's left hip, our host began to stroke my friend in concert with every thrust he made with his penis into the boy's anal canal.

"Auh! Auh! Auh! Auh! Auh!" It was astonishing to watch. Each satisfying stroke that my roommate could feel being made on his penis occurred at the precise instant he felt agony from the huge cock that was being shoved up his ass. The rest of his body was simply left to struggle between these two forces. The combined expressions of extreme pain coupled with extreme pleasure, all being displayed on Matt's face at the same time, was another one of his looks which has stayed with me for all of these years since. It was like watching someone in anguish, only with a half smile and hundreds of times more intense.

"Auh! Auh! Auh! Auh!" Everything about Matt's being now seemed in limbo. It was as if the pain and the pleasure were cancelling each other out and his body had no idea what it was supposed to do next. This state of non-motion with the incredible expression on his face, went on for Matt for several minutes until finally the pleasure component of this spectacle stepped forward and took over his body once again.

To move things along a bit faster, Bob next removed his left hand from Matt's hip and lifted it to take a large hunk of the boy's black hair into his fist so he could pull back hard on it and create an arch in the youngster's back.

"Hhah!" Matt let out a loud gasp.

The change in Matt's position affected my friend in the way in which Bob had intended because soon after that, when Bob could feel Matt's penis beginning to throb, he didn't dislodge himself from my friend's rear end, but as he released Matt's hair from his grip he did suspend his thrusting for a moment so he could give the boy one last hard stroke with his hand and then he squeezed Matt's penis tightly within his fist.

In response, Matt's upper body jerked and lurched forward sharply as his semen spurted out and fell into the man's shag carpet. And then, when his pumping had ended and my friend was emptied out, the natural relaxation of the muscles which follows a sexual climax, aided by his drunken condition of course, caused Matt to allow his upper body to just hang bent over while his arms and his head hung limp as well.

Immediately Bob planted his hands on Matt's hips again and began to thrust wildly into the boy, causing Matt's newly pliable upper section to jerk and fly around in the air continually without the ability, apparently, to stop itself. Although he was standing solidly on his feet, it seemed now as if Matt had lost the will, or perhaps the strength, to control himself. Hair all over his head rippled and flew up every time the upper half of his body was sent by Bob's thrusting to sail past me in another direction. Each thrust of Bob's cock sent Matt's torso, chest and head careening off a different way until finally Matt came to rest once more in the same bent-over position, with his arms and his head hanging down, that he had been in when this whole crazy dance had begun. Then, while my friend's body was silent once again, Bob threw back his head and ejaculated into the boy.

"Auhhhhhhhh! Yeah!" The man yelled out as if he had just won some huge battle. And then he pulled himself out of Matt's ass and with his right hand shoved my friend over onto the floor to land on his side and to slam the back of his head against one of the legs of the coffee table.

"All right!" Bob yelled as he threw his arms up into the air in victory.

"Oww!" Matt cried out from the pain he now felt in his head.

Instantly I was off of the couch and on my knees next to my roommate. "Joe told you no damage, damn it!" I yelled at our host. And then I looked at Matt. "Are you all right?" I asked nervously.

"Yeah," Matt began to use his hand to rub the back of his head. "I guess so."

"Are you sure?" I wanted to be certain.

"Yeah, I'm all right," my friend said as he sat up on the floor in front of me.

I then stood up and looked at the man. "I'm gonna call Joe right now. He said no damage and you just hurt one of us."

"No, don't do that," Bob pleaded. "I'm sorry. Really. I didn't realized that I had pushed him so hard." Then Bob bent over and looked at Matt. "Are you ok, son? I'm sorry, I didn't mean for you to get hurt." Then Bob looked at me again. "Here, help me get him on his feet again."

What a wimp, I thought as I bent down to take hold of one of Matt's arms. *This guy's really a pussy cat.* Together then, we helped my friend to stand on his own once again.

"Are you ok?" The man truly seemed concerned now for Matt's well-being.

"Yeah, it's just a little bump. I'll be all right, I guess."

"And what did you think about our little session just now? Wasn't that something?"

Matt then looked at me and smiled. "You know, I think I really did like it, Clint." Then Matt looked back at Bob again. "I mean you were a little harsh when you first shoved your dick up my ass, but after that it felt pretty good."

"Really?" I was pleased to hear that my friend was all right. "Well it sure looked wild."

"Why don't you boys have your pizzas now, and then maybe later I can do the same for you. Ok?" the man said as he looked at me.

"All right," I agreed.

"Good." Bob now seemed relieved. "Ok then, you two sit back down on the couch and I'll bring everything out to you. Ok?"

"Ok," Matt answered this time.

So as Matt and I settled on the couch in front of the man's TV once more, Bob walked into the kitchen and reappeared in a moment with some vodka for us both. "Here, why don't you both have some of this so you don't lose the buzz you've got gong. Ok?"

Matt and I accepted the man's hospitality. So we ate our pizzas and continued to imbibe throughout the evening as we all watched TV together in the nude. And when I felt that my drunkenness was at its peak, I told Bob that I was ready if he was. Shortly after that I was leaning backward against this man and enjoying the benefits of his manual skills, and when the time came, I did find it easier to permit myself to be flopped around in the same way that Matt had done than it would have been for me to expend the last little bit of energy I had at that moment to hold onto the edge of the end table. And when it was over, I decided that I had enjoyed the experience, tremendously. So that after our weekend in Providence was over, the things we had learned from this man were things we repeated with each other every so often on those occasions when Matt and I were able to have time to ourselves.

***

Eventually, the gray frozen days of our winter in Massachusetts turned into gray warmer days of spring. And the snow mobiles on the lawn gave way to the two boats tied once again to the dock every day, and Matt and I had had it. We had had it with the customers at the Friendly Inn, we had had it with the upperclassmen, we had had it with the faculty, and we had had it with each other. The combination of being cooped up indoors for a long winter and our long-term dependency on cocaine had made us irritable to the point where the slightest annoyance would set us off. Even things which normally would never bother us now seemed impossible for either of us to cope with.

We continued to attend our classes in the mornings—only because we knew we'd get in trouble if we didn't—but we gave up entirely on expending any energy to study. And Matt and I had reached a stage in our relationship where we seemed to bicker with each other all the time. In fact, on several occasions our arguments became so heated, we would have jumped at the chance to move out and cease living together if we had believed that such an opportunity could have existed for us. And the discord from the room next door to ours in East Hall had become equally as intense. The final straw had come one afternoon when Juan had been beaten up by a customer of his who had carried on like a prize fighter. Carlos told us afterwards that he could hear his roommate taking the blows in the room next door at the Inn, but he had been too frightened to intervene until after the customer had left. When Carlos did finally venture into the adjoining room, he found Juan lying on the floor naked and nearly knocked out. After that, Juan seldom spoke to Carlos other than to yell at him in anger from time to time.

Fatso's need for increasing volumes of money now seemed insatiable to us. The year before, he had been easygoing and almost carefree whenever we were around him, but nowadays he looked haggard and always worried about things. And Sweetie wasn't doing any better. In fact, everybody around us now seemed overly tense. Ever since the fire, Mr. Stuart was more pensive and worried than he usually was, and the upperclassmen pretty much ended their efforts to find reasons to gather and have fun at our expense. Also, to satisfy the ever growing demand for our services as well as to help Fatso with his cash flow problems, we began to have our dinners brought to us by room service on the days we worked at the Inn, so we could continue on with our labors for another three hours or so into the night until we would be returned to the Academy in time for lights out. And frankly, it made little difference now whether we observed study hall or not since we weren't doing anything during those hours any longer besides lying on our beds or arguing with each other. To explain our long absences from the campus to the rest of the student body, the cover story was given that we were taking accelerated courses in foreign languages in town somewhere, and working out in a nearby swimming pool so the Academy could comply with new parental demands which had been made on our behalf. In this way Mr. Stuart had hoped to satisfy any pockets of curiosity which might have been aimed in our direction. And because of our increase in hours over at the inn, we were now allowed half-hour breaks before dinner every afternoon to swim unmolested in the inn's swimming pool. Even so, before long they were making us work seven days a week and at that pace, it didn't take any time at all before Matt and I came to believe that any day soon our bodies and our spirits would simply give out and it would be impossible after that for us to continue to perform for our masters.

As I've looked back on these events over the years since, I have come to understand that the pressure everyone was under during this spring was a result of the fact that Fatso had overextended himself to a significant degree with his suppliers from South America. From bits of information I was able to put together later, these troubles with his suppliers were just part of greater financial problems he was having with his entire operation. And of course, all of us at the Academy who were involved with him were being pushed without mercy to help the man make up for his financial shortfalls. So this schedule of nonstop work went on for us until one night when we were back in our dorm, long after lights out, and Matt and I had sneaked over into the room next door because Juan had told us earlier that evening that he had a way for us to end this craziness.

"All right, listen," the boy began while he hugged himself as he sat on his bed. His ribs were still bruised and bothering him from the beating he had taken a few weeks earlier. "You know how at the front desk they keep the phones turned off so we can only call each other in the hotel and not anyone on the outside?"

The rest of us acknowledged that we were familiar with the practice.

"Well, I've been checking the phones every day when we get there anyway, and I've found that sometimes they forget and leave the phone turned on from the person who had the room before me."

"You're kidding?" Matt was surprised by this news.

"Right, Matt. He had us come to his room in the middle of the night so he could pull our legs." This peevish response of mine was typical of the way my roommate and I were behaving toward each other these days.

"I was just reacting to what he said, asshole. You don't have to get all bent out of shape over it." Though Matt was still a timid kid when anyone challenged him physically, verbally he had developed the ability to match barbs with practically anyone.

"Yeah well," Juan wanted to keep going with the point he was trying to make. "Anyway, I figure sooner or later it's gonna happen again. So from now on, each of us has to check the phone in his room to see if we can get an outside line. And the first one who finds he can call out, needs to call the police to have them come and raid the inn."

"Wo, hold on a minute," Carlos seemed alarmed at Juan's plan. "If we do that and they find out that we were the ones who made the call, the bigger kids will punish us. They might even stop giving us our cocaine and I don't think I can live anymore without that stuff."

"Of course you can live without it," Juan shot back. "If that happens, we'll just have to go through withdrawals, then. And that's gonna happen to us one day anyway."

"Oh, man! Withdrawals?" Matt now sounded afraid of Juan's plan as well.

Suddenly Juan sounded irritated with the static he was getting over his idea. "Hey, you guys. I don't know what kind of a fantasy land you're lining in, but we can't be junkies for the rest of our lives, you know." Juan felt indignant that any of us would resist his plan. After all, each of us had already admitted several times recently that we were fed up with our lives at the Academy and we wanted things to change.

"Yeah well, what if they do worse than cut off our cocaine?" Matt retorted. "What if they injure us so bad, we can never recover? Remember, Clint? The leader once threatened to cripple you for life." Matt was right. He had raised an issue which required serious consideration from the rest of us.

"Well while we're on the subject, there's something else we need to think about," I added.

"What!" Juan demanded. We could all now see that our friend's patience were wearing thin with this discussion.

"Don't you think that if the police wanted to help us, they would have done something by now?" I asked.

"What do jou mean?" Carlos' interest, at least, was piqued by my question.

So I continued. "For all these months, customers from all over New England and even New York have known right where they could go to have sex with us. So if all those people can find us with no trouble, how come the police can't?" I paused for a moment to let my question sink in, then I went on. "The only reason I can come up with for why they haven't shown up to save us is because they don't want to. Who knows? Maybe Fatso's paid them off, or something."

"And maybe some of the police have been our customers even. No?" Carlos added.

These were serious matters which demanded careful scrutiny from all of us before we proceeded with any plan to break free from our enslavement. "All I know is," Juan's voice was now quiet and introspective, "I'm gonna go insane here pretty soon if we don't do something. I've just about lost myself completely now, and I'm worried that if we don't do something soon to stop this madness, I won't ever be me again. Do you guys know what I mean?"

We all understood. Each of us felt the same as Juan. In fact, I already knew that Matt and I would never be the same boys we had been when we had first arrived at the Academy those many months ago. But I didn't believe that either of us felt quite as hopelessly trapped as Juan seemed to feel on this night. In the past Matt and I had talked about our feelings a fair amount, and we had both developed the ability to switch off that part of us which was repulsed or ashamed over what we were doing. Even so, we had nearly reached our limit with this way of life as well.

"Ok," I agreed in a voice which was now as quiet as Juan's. "I guess I'm ready to go along with your plan, Juan." Then I looked at my roommate. "What do you think, Matt?" I asked.

Matt looked at me for an instant as if he was grateful finally that I was being civil toward him again. "I don't know," he answered quietly. "I guess I'm in, too."

The three of us then looked at Carlos. This boy was probably the most terrified among us, and we could almost hear the gears turning in his head as he handled the small gold cross he always wore around his neck and weighed the merits of our arguments. His expression kept shifting from fear to thoughtfulness and then back to fear again. "Ok," he finally replied. His voice also was now much quieter. "I guess it is time. I can't stand this anymore neither."

And so there it was. In a matter of a few minutes the four of us had decided to end the months we had endured of sex and drug abuse. Regardless of the consequences, we had chosen to take back our lives. We were going to execute Juan's plan as clandestinely as we could, but we were going to put an end to this way of life which we had become so used to, before it took us over completely and caused us to believe that there would never be anything else for us in life besides prostitution. No longer, we resolved, were we going to be hooked on drugs and enslaved for sex. And as Matt and I said our good-nights to our friends and left the room next door to return to our own bedroom, we had no idea of the peril in which we had all just placed ourselves.

I often think back to this conversation that the four of us had that night and I wish that I had suggested instead that we simply tough it out for another month or so. After all, we had already held on for this long, and in only a few more weeks it was going to be time for us to go to our respective homes for summer vacation. Then we could have set ourselves to the tasks of putting our lives back together and convincing our families to send us to different schools in the fall. But at that age, a boy's perception of time is usually skewed. Especially when he is involved in something he hates: weeks can seem like months and months can seem like years. And so none of us were willing to be patient any longer. Of course now in hindsight, I can see that we were in over our heads when we believed that we had the power to take back our lives in that place. Even with all we had been through by this time, I guess we still didn't understand all that much about the type of people we were dealing with. Because in less than one week after this conversation, we discovered that our plan to call in the police was the greatest mistake of our young lives.

***

A few days later on Thursday afternoon after we were done with our classes for the day, Matt and I ran into Jamie and Charlie, the two neighbor kids who lived behind the Academy. For some reason they had been given the rest of the week off from school and had come across the cove in Jamie's rowboat to see if we were interested in going out on the lake with them. They said they knew of a few places where we would be able to find tadpoles. The boys were waiting for us on the landing when we arrived at our dorm, and since Matt and I had an hour or so to kill before we were scheduled again to be taken to the Friendly Inn, we invited our friends into our room so we could visit with them for a while.

With "I'm Your Captain" by Grand Funk Rail Road playing from my stereo, the four of us then spent perhaps fifteen minutes or so talking about the normal kinds of things that young teenaged boys talk about, and it felt good to fill our minds once again with frivolous kid issues. In the course of this discussion, I began to realize just how much of my youth had been stolen from me since my arrival at the Academy. And as I silently turned this matter over in my mind, I realized further that my enslavement by the upperclassmen and their willing accomplices in the faculty had actually cheated me out of time I would never be able to get back. So as I half listened to the refrain at the end of the song, I took heart in the notion that—thanks to Juan's plan—Matt and I and our Venezuelan friends next door would soon be returning to the lives we were entitled to live.

Eventually, since it was clear that we couldn't go along that afternoon, Jamie and Charlie decided that the time had come for them to leave us and return to their adventure on the lake. And as they were leaving, they walked past Frank as he was coming into our hallway to see us.

"Hey, Clint. Hey, Matt. Can I come in for a minute?" Frank had acknowledged the other boys as he passed them in our hallway, but he didn't stop to engage them in conversation in any way.

"Hey, Frank," I replied first because I was closer to the door.

"Come on in, Frank," Matt called from his bed. We both liked to lie down in the afternoons for a while so we could rest up before going over to the inn, but so far only Matt had managed to make himself horizontal.

Once Frank was in our room he closed our door, and then sat down in one of our chairs before he began to tell us his reason for dropping by. "Say, my cousin is comin' back up here this weekend. I thought if youz guys weren't doin' nothin' ya might wanna come along wit' us. We thought maybe we'd go check out Sturbridge."

Matt and I shot quick glances at each other. The idea sounded like a lot of fun, but we had already been told by the leader to plan on working at the inn all weekend. "Gee, Frank," Matt began. "That sounds like a lot of fun. But Clint and I already planned to get ourselves caught up this weekend on our homework. You know finals are coming up pretty soon."

Frank's expression suddenly changed to a frown. "Are you tryin' to tell me that you're gonna spend this whole beautiful weekend all cooped up here in this room?"

"Well, we might go into town on Saturday," Matt continued. "But otherwise… yeah, probably."

Frank then looked at me. "Is this really what you're gonna be doin' this weekend, Clint?"

I now could tell that Frank didn't believe Matt's story and he was once again trying to probe for an answer to what it was we were really up to all the time. "Yeah, Frank. That's pretty much what we're gonna be doing this weekend. We appreciate your offer though." I now felt as if Frank could see right through me.

Our friend stared at us both for a moment as he studied our faces. And then he let us know what he really thought about our reason for not being able to accept his invitation. "Bullshit!"

"What?" I attempted to act as if I didn't understand.

"I said bullshit, Adams. You guys haven't done a minute of studying all semester. What I think is, you're really gonna go off to wherever it is you two go to all the time. Aren't ya? With that strange-lookin' guy who's always comin' 'round here to pick youz two up in his Cadillac."

For the first time I felt as if Frank really did know something finally about our goings-on. And as I struggled to think of a convincing way to respond to my friend, Matt spoke up first.

"We don't know what you're talking about, Frank."

The boy now looked as if he believed that Matt had just insulted his intelligence and his lineage because immediately then Frank shot to his feet. "I'm not stupid, ya know. I know youz guys are always going off somewhere and doin' somethin'. And I don't buy this business about foreign language classes or swimming workouts."

"Frank, you can smell the chlorine on our clothes. We're in the pool every afternoon." As I tried to make myself sound reasonable, I felt compelled to make an attempt at least to do what I could to salvage our cover at this point.

"I don't buy it!" Frank now was sounding angry. "Youz two used to be really great guys when you first got here. I used to like hangin' out with youz because ya both had a kind of zest for living that was different from everybody else around here. But you've both changed. You're not the guys you used to be, and I think it stinks." Frank then got up out of his chair and opened our door so he could prepare himself to leave our room. He had apparently endured as much of our company as he could stand for one afternoon. "I don't know what the hell is goin' on around here, but you can bet your asses I'm gonna find out." Frank then stepped out of our room and into the hall. "And you can take that to the bank!" And with that our friend slammed our door shut and left the dorm.

Afterward, Matt and I were silent for a moment. Neither of us had realized that our outward appearances had become so different.

"Shit!" Matt uttered finally.

"Really," I concurred.

Chapter Eleven
Good-Bye, Good Friends

Looking back on it, we were just dumb kids, I guess. We had no idea that the things which took place later that day and the next two were even possible. But the day after Frank's visit to our room, Matt and I came to understand that something serious was going on when after classes had ended, the day student who owned the in-board out-board with the wooden hull returned to the upper campus from the dock yelling that someone had stolen his boat. We were on hand to witness this boy's anguish because by this time, we had been restricted to staying on the campus since the events of late Thursday afternoon had rendered our futures at the Friendly Inn doubtful at best.

Ever since the big push had begun to sell more of Fatso's cocaine, the four of us were escorted each day by only one upperclassman instead of the usual two and many of these guys had been allowed to bring their own cars from home to facilitate their duties off campus. Thursday afternoon—a half hour or so after Frank had stormed out of our room—it was Artist's turn to drive us to the inn. And perhaps ten minutes or so after we had all been placed in our motel rooms, and while Matt and I were just hanging around and waiting for our first customers of the day to show up, Artist returned in a panic and told us that we had to get out of our rooms that instant and race back to his car.

As we ran past the lobby, we could see the old woman come out from behind the front desk and move rapidly from one section of the large room to another so she could urge the men and the women who had come to the inn to experience us, to get the hell out of there while they still could. After that it wasn't until we were halfway back to the Academy before we fully understood what it was that had caused this emergency.

"What happened to you guys?" Matt asked. He and I were sitting in the front seat next to Artist while Juan and Carols had already been waiting for us in the back seat when the rest of us had arrived back at the car. Because of our haste, neither of us had really looked at the other boys until now.

I then turned around also to inspect our friends and saw right away that they had been beaten up. "Gee, yeah! What did happen to you guys?" I was surprised as well by their condition.

Juan wouldn't acknowledge that anyone was speaking to him. He kept staring out through his window refusing to say a word to either of us. So Carlos took it upon himself to respond to our questions. "Artist hit us," he answered angrily.

Matt and I then looked at Artist as he guided us south along Highway 193. "Why did you hit them?" I asked.

Artist thought for a moment, and then he took in a deep breath and let it out. "I couldn't think of anything else to do," he answered sharply. "Anyway, they brought it on themselves."

"What are you talking about?" Matt asked. His frustration was beginning to show.

Artist then looked at Matt quickly as my roommate sat next to him in the middle of the front seat. For that instant, we could both see the rage in the bigger kid's face. "Oh, like you two didn't know anything about this," he stated in an accusatory tone.

"Know about what?" I asked in exasperation.

Artist then continued. "As soon as I got into my motel room and was getting ready to welcome in the first customer, I got a call from the woman at the front desk. She told me that she happened to just notice on her board that someone was making an outsie phone call from the room where only a minute earlier I had left our friend Juan back there," he said sarcastically.

"Oh?" I replied.

"Yeah well, so I ran down the hall to Juan's room and when I got the door open, I found both of these guys standing next to the phone while Juan was talking to somebody on the other end. As soon as the little shit saw me, he said 'please hurry' into the phone and then he hung up. So since I'm all by myself with you guys, I figured I needed to take the starch out of them to keep them from running away on me, so I slugged them both a couple of times. Then I called the front desk to let them know that these assholes had just called the police, and then I walked them to my car before I came to get you two guys."

Juan's idea to call the police had not worked out the way we had expected. Instead of elation, we were all now frightened over the consequences we were hurtling toward at sixty miles per hour. In a moment of weakness, I found myself suppressing the urge to point out to our jailer that Matt and I had not been in Juan's room when the phone call had been made. But Artist was the one upperclassman who often showed sympathy toward our plight. So I decided while we still had the chance, to attempt an appeal to his better nature. "Look," I began. "You've already punished them. Maybe you could just let this go this one time if we all promise you that this will never happen again." It was a lame attempt at salvation and I knew it. But at that moment I couldn't think of anything else to try because by now we had turned off of the highway and were speeding toward the forest. And the reality of the leader's black belt was once again beginning to shake me.

"Are you kidding?" Artist shot back. "I don't think you guys realize the damage you've done this afternoon. You've just shut down Fatso's entire operation at the inn. Now that the cops know that something's been going on there, they're gonna be looking for us all the time. So we can never go back to the Friendly Inn again, and we probably can't even set up anywhere else in Ulster. All the money we were making for him was keeping Fatso out of trouble with the South Americans. Now I don't know what's gonna happen because those guys don't play nice when they don't get paid."

Now I felt awful. It was true that Fatso was corrupt, and enslaving us to earn money for him as boy prostitutes was indefensible, but he and Sweetie had always treated Matt and me very well. And even though we hadn't seen that much of them for the past few months, we still thought of them as sort of surrogate parents—in an admittedly weird sort of way.

At first, once we were back on campus, all of us were convinced that punishment for our crime at the inn would be inflicted without delay. But surprisingly, nothing happened to us. And later, once we had trotted off to the dining hall to rejoin the rest of the student body at dinnertime, the four of us concluded that the upperclassmen were preferring to wait until after lights out to invade our rooms and spirit us away to whatever obscure location seemed appropriate to their plan of discipline for our egregious act of defiance. So as the hours wore by, our tension from the fear we were feeling grew, and Juan began to talk again about running away while we still had the chance.

Throughout study hall that evening, as Matt and I sat obediently in our room, we found ourselves wondering whether or not we might be spared from the anticipated reprisals altogether since, in reality, we had never actually done anything wrong that day. And the more we considered the matter from this point of view, the more we were able to convince ourselves that once he had calmed himself down, Artist would certainly have told the others that Juan and

Carlos had been the perpetrators of the phone call and that Matt and I had been doing as we were instructed by waiting quietly in our rooms for the day's first customers. In fact, in time Matt and I came to feel relieved from our belief that we were going to be successful in avoiding any acts of torture this time, and we maintained this sense of complacency right up until fifteen minutes before the end of study hall when the sound of the large wooden doorway down at the western end of the hallway suddenly overwhelmed and ended our silence as it swung open with its customary mid-range groan and then slammed shut again a few moments later as if to announced with finality, the approach of our doom.

"Oh shit!" Matt whispered quickly. "I don't think this is gonna be good, Clint."

I glanced at my roommate quickly and saw the fear which was now covering his face. But before I could respond, the appearance suddenly of two large figures in our doorway drew my attention to the front of our room.

"Well, I'm glad to find you boys here where you're supposed to be, and sitting on your beds too." It was the leader, and he wasn't smiling as he entered our room.

"Hey, guys," the head waiter added as he followed his boss in and then stopped near the foot of my bed. We could hear other upperclassmen remaining out in the hall and one of them, an instant later, appeared briefly to reach in and pull our door closed.

"You guys have had quite a day," the leader continued with a hint of sarcasm.

I now noticed that the leader was placing a small flat box onto the top of our dresser and he was opening its lid. At this moment, I had no idea what this guy was planning for us but I was certain, at least, that I wanted nothing to do with whatever it was he had hidden in his box.

"You know, you guys have been getting harder and harder to control all this year. The cocaine we keep givin' ya just doesn't seem to do the job for us anymore." At that, the leader pulled from his box a syringe and two small vials of a liquid of some kind.

"NO!" Matt shrieked, and then he turned instantly to open our window and try to escape through it. He wanted no part of what the leader was now preparing for him and if there was any chance for him to break away from the Academy, now was the time to do it.

"So to control you guys again, we're going to step you up a notch and put you on the horse." As the leader calmly filled his syringe with the liquid from the first vial, he seemed unconcerned by Matt's reaction.

Of course escape had been lost to us long ago and the head waiter had little trouble pulling my roommate's head and upper torso back inside our room and then sitting on his body to hold him steady for his first dose of this new drug. And as I saw Matt's bare arm lie open and away from the tangle of the two of them, I watched as the leader then bent over Matt's bed, tied a rubber strap tightly around his upper arm, and then as Matt continued to protest, inserted the needle into my friend's arm and emptied the contents of the syringe into his young body.

"No! No!" Matt kept yelling. And then when he felt the heroin enter his system he let out one last pathetic "Nooooooo!" After that he stopped struggling. Once the leader had removed the needle and the strap from my friend's arm, the head waiter pulled our window shut and then stood up again to leave Matt to cope with his new circumstances on his own.

"Ok, Adams," the head waiter then spoke to me as the leader prepared his next injection. "Are you gonna give us any trouble?" he demanded.

I looked at my roommate as his crumpled body still lay in a fetal position on his bed. He was sobbing quietly and rubbing the spot on his skin where the needle had penetrated him. "No," I answered simply. If anyone had told me all those months ago when I was playing in the swimming pool in my parents' back yard in Denver that one day soon I would be shooting up with heroin, I would have told them that they were crazy. The idea would have seemed as impossible to me as life without pizza. And yet now, at this moment of truth, the thought of taking this next step in a downward spiral that had pulled me to such a low level of existence, really didn't seem like such a big deal any longer. So when the leader stepped over to do me next, I extended my arm to him without question and accepted the drug when he put it into my body.

"There," the leader concluded as he put his things back into his box and prepared to leave our room. "That'll hold you two until the morning. See me after breakfast tomorrow and we'll get you two started on regular injections and teach you guys how to give 'em to yourselves." The leader then walked to the front of our room again and opened our door. But before he left he turned back around to say one more thing to us. "The days of your defiance are now officially over." And with that, the two bigger kids turned off our lights as they left our bedroom and closed our door behind them.

Matt and I knew there was nothing that either of us could do. In silence we tried then to make ourselves comfortable while we listened to Juan yell and get knocked around in the room next door. His ordeal seemed to go on forever, but by the time we began to feel the heroin take control of us, we knew that there would be two more boys this night who would be having their first taste of the big "H."

The heroin interacted with the cocaine which was already in our systems and caused a high which was more potent than either of us had anticipated. So by the time the bell for lights out had rung a while later, Matt and I could do nothing more than lie on our backs on our beds with our arms outstretched from our sides, and stare with blank expressions at the ceiling in our room.

The next morning when Matt and I got up, our first thought was of our friends next door and we checked on them right away to make sure they were all right. Juan, of course, had defied the bigger kids the night before and had even tried to fight them off. In the end, though, he had been beaten for his insolence, and made along with Carlos to take the heroin. But with a beauty of a black eye this Friday morning, the boy began to talk again about running away and how we all needed to leave before it became too late for us to do so. Just the same, after breakfast he was lined up in the infirmary with the rest of us for his next injection of our new drug. I had always heard that heroin addicted its victims on the first occasion of its use, and sad to say in our case at least, this information was true.

It wasn't until dinnertime later on that Friday, a few hours after the day student's boat had turned up missing, before we understood that Juan and Carlos were nowhere around. At first Matt and I decided that our friends had stolen the boat as a means to get away for good.

At lights out that night, when we realized that we had gone through our first entire day as full-fledged junkies, we were happy that our friends at least had managed to escape the fate we were now so resigned to accepting. But when we went to bed, it bothered us to know that the room next door was now empty, and our friends were out in the night somewhere with probably no place to stay. In fact, by the time we turned out our lights for the evening, Matt and I had become nearly frantic over the idea of Juan and Carlos being on the run in a foreign country and not knowing who they could trust. And in the morning, when we awoke and prepared ourselves for our Saturday morning classes, we found the room next door vacant still, which caused us to continue our worry over the welfare of our friends.

During breakfast that morning, it was all over school how Juan and Carlos had not come home the night before. Matt and I did our best to have our meal without dwelling too heavily on the topic of the day. After breakfast, the head waiter caught up with us to let us know that a sudden booking for our services for the weekend had come in and we were to have our overnight bags packed and ready so we could be picked up after lunch that afternoon. And as Matt and I walked through the lobby to make our way over to the other end of Ulster Hall so we could be on time for our first class of the day, I remember being surprised to notice through the windows in the front doors of the building that Mr. Stuart's car was driving away.

***

The divers knew right where to look because a woman who lived nearby on shore had heard an explosion the night before and had looked out her window in time to see a boat on fire out on the lake. And by lunch that Saturday, the news had spread all over the campus that the charred bodies of two boys around the ages of thirteen or fourteen which had been pulled from the lake that morning were the remains of our missing students: Juan and Carlos. Mr. Stuart had been able to identify the boys by Juan's ID bracelet and Carlos' gold cross. Both pieces of jewelry were still on the bodies when Mr. Stuart had arrived on the scene.

The theory that our headmaster brought back from the authorities was that our friends had stolen the boat so they could use it to go joy riding on the lake at night. Because of the age of the vessel, a fuel leak—which neither of the boys had probably noticed—became ignited somehow—probably from smoking cigarettes—and had caused the boat to explode once the flames had reached the fuel tank. Of course autopsies would be performed to determine the exact cause of the boys' death, but with what little there was remaining for the coroner to work with, there was little doubt that the final report on our friends would concur with this theory.

"Unless they find bullet holes in their bodies, the deaths are gonna be ruled an accident," Matt observed while we packed our bags in our room after lunch that day. We knew our friends hadn't been joy riding, and we were pretty certain that the in-board out-board had never had a fuel leak. Tom, the day student, had always kept his boat in perfect running condition. This meant only one thing then, and neither of us were able just yet to grasp the idea that we were living and dealing with people who were capable of committing such an act.

"You don't think the leader or the head waiter…?" I asked my friend.

"No," Matt answered quickly. "They're both sadistic assholes, and maybe they could kill in a fit of rage, but I don't see them going to all the trouble to stage something like a boat exploding and then sinking to the bottom of the lake."

"What about one of the teachers?" I continued.

"No," Matt replied again. "They're all too chicken shit to do anything like that. If any of them really had a spine, they wouldn't be teaching here in the first place.

"Yeah," I agreed. "You're right about that."

"That leaves Fatso, or maybe the owner or manager or whoever it is over at the inn," Matt proposed.

I thought for a moment about my roommate's suggestions. Neither of us had any idea who it was at the inn who had arranged with Fatso for us to use his business as a base for our operations. "You know, I'm sure Fatso wouldn't actually do the act himself, and I just can't see him ordering it done, either."

At that moment we were surprised by a severe knocking on our door.

"It's unlocked," I shouted.

An instant later the head waiter opened our door and peered into our room from the hallway. "Hey, your ride's here," he announced unceremoniously. "Let's get going, huh?"

I didn't pay much attention to it at the time, but as I looked into the eyes of this upperclassman who had contributed so willingly to the misery that Matt and I had been put through for the past year, his eyes shifted quickly to avoid my gaze the instant our eyes met. "All we've gotta do is close up our cases, and then we'll be right outside."

"Ok, I'll tell 'em," the bigger kid then left our doorway as quickly as he had arrived.

We were still getting used to having heroin in our bodies, and we weren't entirely certain just yet if we were able to think clearly. Still, it was reassuring to us to engage in the same routine we had been through nearly every weekend since the previous September.

"Are you ready?" I asked as I closed and latched my bag.

"I guess so," Matt answered gloomily as he did the same.

Automatically then, we turned out our lights and left our room. And after we had gone through the large wooden door at the western end of our hallway, and had climbed the cement steps outside until we were on the sidewalk and walking out onto the outdoor basketball court, I happened to look ahead and notice a Plymouth Fury parked over in the circle in front of Ulster Hall. Of course I recognized the car right away and I made a remark about it to my roommate. But when I looked ahead again, I saw something else that I hadn't noticed before.

"Clint!" Matt suddenly stopped in his tracks. "Oh shit! Look at the car in front!"

By now I had recognized it as well. Sitting there in front of the Fury, was a blue 1963 Cadillac convertible, and Joe was looking our way and leaning up against the door on the passenger side. Suddenly the statement that Fatso had made in his living room about Joe on the occasion of our first meeting came back to us.

"You don't think he's here to straighten us out, do ya?" Matt asked fearfully.

"I...I don't know," I stammered. It wasn't all that unusual for Joe to drive us somewhere on the weekend, but it seemed awfully damned coincidental that he was here on today of all days to take us someplace.

Joe saw us standing in the middle of the basketball court and became impatient. "Hey, boys, let's go," and he gave his arm a big swing to motion that he wanted us to come toward him.

"He sounds all right," Matt observed.

"Yeah, I guess," I agreed.

Joe saw that we still hadn't moved, so he called to us again. "Come on, guys, we're gonna be late."

"What do you think?" Matt asked me.

"I don't know. If we run, they're bound to catch us, so I guess we might as well go with him," I declared.

"Ok. If you say so," Matt replied. And then the two us began to walk again toward the car with the big fins.

A moment later as we approached the two cars from the rear, I spotted Frank coming out through the front doors of Ulster Hall, and heading down the front steps until he turned left at the bottom with his overnight bag so he could walk toward the Fury and join his cousin who was waiting for him inside his car. And as fate would have it, a moment later when we met up next to the Fury, Frank couldn't let the moment pass without saying something to me.

"Where the hell are you guys going?" he asked when he saw the suitcases we were carrying. "I though youz two were spending the weekend in your room studying." Frank then glance back at Joe to get another look at the man we were walking toward. "And who's that guy?"

Matt and I had no idea what it was that we were in for, but we figured for sure that Frank would be in trouble, if he made too much of a stink over our change of plans for the weekend. "Just let it go, Frank," I warned quietly as we passed him by. Matt and I then handed our bags to Joe so he could dump them in the trunk for us as he usually did. But before Matt and I could make our escape, Frank turned around and let us have it one more time.

"Let it go?" he repeated loudly. "Let it go?" he said even louder this time. Then he continued. "Yeah, I'll let it go. In fact you can depend on the fact that I'm gonna let it go! In fact, I'm gonna let both of youz go, because you're both assholes. So go on. Just take off with this strange-lookin' guy and I'll be very happy to let youz go!" And with that Frank opened the door on the passenger side of the Fury and got into his cousin's car.

"What's his problem?" Joe asked as the three of us piled into his Cadillac.

"Oh nothing," I answered as I took a position in the back seat by myself again. "Just some school thing." As Joe started up his engine and then began to take us along the main drive toward the front entrance, I figured at least that I had managed to keep Frank from getting caught up in the mess that we were so deeply into. And a few minutes later, when we were finally on the highway and heading north toward the town of Ulster, Matt decided the time had come to ask Joe a question.

"Where are we going this time, Joe?"

Joe then looked at Matt as my roommate sat there on the opposite end of the front seat with his mop of black hair whipping around wildly in the wind. "Today I'm taking you boys to Framingham."

***

Joe backed his Cadillac into the driveway of a nondescript one-story house which was situated in a neighborhood dense with trees. When he had the car parked where he wanted, Joe turned off the engine and then got out to open his trunk for us.

"Whose place is this, Joe?" Matt asked as he opened his door to get out too.

"This is where I've been living for the past year or so," the large man replied.

"Of all the times I've gone by here on the turnpike," I began as I climbed out of the back seat. "I think this is the first time I've ever actually been to Framingham."

"Yeah… well, it's a nice quiet place to live in, I guess," Joe admitted. During our drive, our escort had been the least talkative we had ever known the man to be, and now mentally Joe seemed to be someplace entirely different from the suburban concrete we were all now standing upon. "Grab your things and come inside."

"Sure, Joe." His different behavior today was making us more afraid of him than we usually were, and Matt was reacting to this fear by blabbering more than he usually did. "Is this where we're staying for the night? I guess the place looks all right, but it's a lot smaller than the places we usually get taken to, except for that guy in Providence. Man, he really did me good. Joe, are you having the customer meet us here later today or something?"

"We'll talk about all that later," our host said gruffly. "Now hurry up." It was odd, but at that moment it seemed to me as if Joe wasn't comfortable with the idea of spending too much time outdoors in full view of the neighbors. And in another moment, he had disappeared into his house ahead of us.

When we were finally inside with the man, Matt and I found suitcases, boxes and other things piled up in the middle of the floor in Joe's living room. Our host had already made his way past all of this and was getting himself something to eat in the kitchen.

"What's all this stuff, Joe?" Matt couldn't seem to stop asking questions.

"What? Oh, I'm moving out," the big man yelled to us as he held his head in the refrigerator. "I've just been renting this place and the time has come for me to move on. You two boys go ahead and drop your things where you are and then take all that stuff of mine and put it outside into the trunk of my car."

"Really?" Matt replied. "Then after we've got your things loaded up are you gonna take us to our customer for the weekend? And where are ya moving to, Joe?"

Now Joe seemed annoyed. It was as if he felt imposed upon to be asked so many questions. "Yeah, never mind right now about any of that, you guys. I'll tell you all about everything once you've got my things packed away in the Caddy. Now hurry up!"

That seemed to end any chance we had at the moment for discussion. Even so, there was still one last question that Matt believed he had to risk asking. "Joe, do you want us to take even these two five-gallon cans of kerosene?" Matt had a point here. It seemed strange enough that Joe was keeping kerosene in his living room.

This last question of Matt's got a reaction from Joe that shook us both. It was almost as if he hadn't meant for us to know about the kerosene. "What? Oh, ah," the man fumbled for a moment to find the words. "Look, you guys, just leave those cans where they are and get moving with the rest of my stuff, and do it now!" His usual gruff demeanor was suddenly changed to one of intense irritation.

"Ok," Matt responded quickly. And so the two of us began to lug Joe's heavy belongings out to his Cadillac. As soon as we were outside on the front walk again, I used the opportunity to admonish my roommate. "Next time keep your mouth shut. Will ya?" I wasn't pleased about the work we had been pressed into doing.

"Sorry, Clint," Matt offered. "But I'm guessing that from the way he had everything waiting there in his living room, we were gonna have to be doing this, anyway."

Matt was right of course. Joe would have had us carry his junk out to his trunk even if Matt had been quiet. And if the truth be known, I was feeling nervous over what was happening to us also. After all, at this moment it had only been perhaps two hours or so since we had learned the fate of Juan and Carlos, and as absurd as it would have sounded at the time, we weren't all that certain that we weren't going to be next.

As we packed Joe's things into the trunk of his car, we did our best to perform our task as slowly as was humanly possible. There was something about our involvement in helping this guy to leave town on the very day our friends were found dead which was unsettling to us. Of course we still didn't know who it was who had killed the boys, or for that matter, if their deaths had been the result of foul play—although it was pretty hard for us to believe that any other explanation made sense. One thing that did seem pretty clear to us though, was that as long as we were engaged in an activity we knew was safe, we could avoid moving onto something else which might be less to our liking. But like the upperclassmen, time is a master who will not be reasoned with, so before long our job as midget movers was finished. And when we closed the lid on Joe's trunk, my friend and I stood there on that driveway and wondered again if we should try to make a run for it. Unfortunately, our training and the drugs in our systems had us convinced that there was only one course of action available to us, so together we walked back into Joe's living room to submit ourselves to whatever it was that our host was planning for the rest of that day.

"Close the door and lock it!" This order was issued once Matt and I had returned to Joe's presence inside.

"All right," I answered. I turned around then and walked back to Joe's entryway so I could do as he had instructed. To this day I don't know why I did it. Maybe it was out of a deep sense of contrariness I was feeling at the moment. But when I closed the front door and took hold of the latch handle on the lock, I locked and unlocked the dead bolt in one smooth action so it sounded as if I had complied with my order when I had really done the opposite. Joe heard me handle the lock, but because of a partition which stood between the front door and the living room, he was unable to see that I had actually just left his front door unlocked.

"Do you want us to open the curtains to let some light in, Joe?" Matt asked nervously. It hadn't escaped our notice that our bags were still with us there in the house along with the two cans of kerosene.

The large man then walked back into the living room from his kitchen while he chomped on a ham sandwich he had just made for himself. "No… ah, no that's all right, kid. I think maybe you guys are gonna want the curtains to stay closed, anyway."

"Oh?" I asked as I re-entered the living room to stand next to my friend again. *Here it comes,* I thought. "Why's that, exactly?"

Joe then gave us his first smile of the day. "Because this time, I'm the customer."

"You?" Matt was as surprised by this news as I was.

"Yeah," Joe confirmed still smiling. "Why not?"

"Gee, Joe, I didn't know *you* liked little boys." I wasn't really trying to provoke the man, but as long as we had known this guy, he had always seemed to us as the epitome of the macho heterosexual type.

Now Joe's smile was gone. "Very funny, smart ass. So now you know." Joe then took a few steps closer to us. "All year long, I've been watchin' you boys go out to have sex with practically everybody in New England, while the whole time I've had to keep my mouth shut about what I really wanted to do with you two." Joe then pulled back on one of the curtains slightly so he could take a quick peek out his front window. "No, I never said nothin' about it because a guy in my line of work can't afford to let it out that he likes to do it with kids." He then turned his head to look at us again as he allowed the curtain to fall back the way it had been.

It was hard for us to read Joe at this moment. We couldn't tell if he was about to start laughing, or lunge at us.

"So now it's my turn and you boys better brace yourselves, because I'm gonna want to do everything." Joe now looked sincere in his desire for us.

It wasn't the worst news we had been given that day, but it was a close second, and with a quick glance between us, Matt and I understood that we were both uneasy with the knowledge we now possessed about Joe's true leanings. We were worried now because if indeed Joe preferred to keep this information about him confidential, then after our session with him was ended, he would either have to trust us to say nothing, or do something drastic to insure our silence. And just as I was beginning to contemplate whether Joe was truly the trusting kind, our host went on to finish his thought.

"So strip!" he ordered.

"What?" Matt asked as he was still trying to take this all in.

"Right here?" Perhaps it was the drugs which were making me as slow on the uptake as Matt.

"Yeah!" Joe's voice now thundered. "Right here, right now. Take off all of your clothes right now and just leave them on the floor next to your bags for the time being."

A chill suddenly advanced down my spine and I froze as I watched Matt begin to loosen his tie.

"Come on, Adams!" Joe's yell got me grabbing at my clothes to comply. "I want 'a see your lily white ass too," he admitted sarcastically. "So take 'em off, now!"

A few moments later, as my roommate and I stood naked before this hulking man, his demeanor changed again and once more we could see him smiling at us. "Ok," he continued as his eyes surveyed every inch of our bare bodies. "Let's head for the pool out in back." With his sandwich now finished, Joe led us down a hallway and into his family room which was located at the rear of the house. Matt and I strolled behind the man and stopped to listen when he wanted us to take a moment to admire his pool table.

How clichéd, I thought to myself.

With our arms folded across our chests, Matt and I stood along one side of the table as Joe picked up a cue and began to demonstrate a few of his trickier shots for us. While we tried to act interested, I took the opportunity to scan around the room and right away I could tell that it really did appear as if this guy was moving out. On an opposite wall, the contents from a couple of shelves had been removed and placed into a box on the floor below. *Huh,* I thought as I recognized something familiar. "Hey, there's the bat that Fatso gave you." I blurted this out before I had realized that I was interrupting a quick lesson on Joe's breaking strategy. Nevertheless, all by itself this keepsake with the names of five players scribbled on it was lying precariously in its little cradle-like stand on one of these shelves.

"Huh?" Joe then laid his pool cue down on the table and trained his attention on us once more. "Oh, yeah. That's where I've been keeping all of my Red Sox stuff. I didn't put the bat away yet because I didn't want it to break the pictures I've got in the box." Our host then turned his head and looked at a door with safety glass in it at the back of the room. "Ok, well enough of this chit chat," Joe then raised his hands in the air to about chest level and took a step away from the pool table. "Come on with me and we'll have a swim," he ordered.

A swim, I thought. *Maybe everything's gonna be all right with this guy after all.* Swimming was an activity which Matt and I always enjoyed and I figured that Joe probably knew this about us. So as Matt and I came out from behind the pool table, we watched as Joe raised one of his hands to unlock the deadbolt and then open this door lined with weather stripping so we could walk out to his swimming pool.

It looked to me as if walls and a ceiling had been built out from the house sometime after its original construction to enclose the pool and the cement patio which surrounded it. As we walked through the doorway and felt an immediate increase in the humidity and heat, we looked around quickly—out of habit actually—to see what the layout of the place was and if there were any other way for us to get out which, as it turned out, there was not.

"Wow," Matt observed. "It's really warm in here."

Joe followed us into the pool room and then closed the door behind him. "Yeah, I keep the water temperature set on ninety degrees, so it keeps the air in here nice and hot." Joe then took a ring of keys from his pocket and began to search through them.

Even naked, I could tell that I was already beginning to sweat in this place. "Man, you could grow tropical plants in here." And as I watched with my roommate to see Joe slide a key into the deadbolt on the door and lock it, we realized suddenly that he had locked the three of us in this room. On the inside the lock was operated with a latch, but out here there was no latch. Out here only the key that our host was now stuffing back into his pants pocket could unlock the door for us. Joe then turned around and caught us both staring at the door.

"Is something wrong?" he demanded.

"No, sir," Matt replied in a servile tone.

"No, sir," I answered in the same way.

Joe then began to undo his shirt. "So what do you guys think of the place?"

Matt and I then turned around and gave this room our first real look.

"See," Joe pointed out proudly. "I've got the place decorated like a Hawaiian paradise. It's great isn't it?"

As I looked around, I beheld before me the smallest and the tackiest indoor swimming pool I had ever seen. The pool itself was in the shape of a small rectangle and extended out from where we were standing to the wall on the other side of the room where we could see out through some windows into a back yard which seemed dense with trees. The deep end was closer to us and went down perhaps nine feet. Beyond the cement apron which encircled the pool, there was green Astroturf which covered the patio surface everywhere. For guests, Joe had crammed five round metal tables with chairs all around the room. Two tables were along the side of the pool to our left, two more were on either side of us against the wall that adjoined the house, and the fifth table was closer to us on the right side of the pool. Farther away on the right side stood a badly built bamboo bar with some cupboards mounted on the wall behind it. A couple of plastic palm plants were arranged in the outside corner over on the left, and a topless female mannequin with a grass skirt around its waist and a lei around its neck was standing on its own over in the outside corner to our right.

"And you guys see the lamps?" Joe asked as he slipped off his underpants. Naked he sort of looked like Fatso, only younger and more fit. "I put those in myself."

Surrounding the pool between the apron and the tables were a half dozen or so Tiki lamps which had been permanently cemented into the patio floor. It was still the middle of the afternoon, otherwise I was sure that Joe would have lit these lamps for us.

"Does Don Ho know about this place?" Matt asked.

"Smart ass!" It wasn't the reaction that our host had been expecting, and now he sounded angry with us again. "All right now, you first," Joe pointed his beefy finger at me. Pleasantries were definitely over now. The time had come for us to get down to business. "I want you to get in the pool with me and give me a blow job while you're under water. Let's go." And with that, Joe lumbered over to the edge and jumped into the pool. The loud splash he made echoed quickly throughout the room and woke both of us up to the reality that we were here to work.

When Joe surfaced and swam over to the shallow end, he turned around once he had reached the opposite wall and saw that I was still standing next to Matt. "Let's go, kid!" he hollered at me. "Get in this water now or I'll beat your ass!"

This was it. There was no way that things could be put off any longer. But as I stepped over to the edge of the pool, I worried over how quickly this guy's attitude toward us was able to change. And then I realized as I dove into the warm water, that Joe was like a volcano that was being prevented temporarily from exploding. It seemed obvious to me now that this guy was riled over something and the idea of placing my head under the water at his groin, in a position where I would be unable to keep my eye on him in case he decided to drown me or something, now seemed like an awful risk for me to be taking.

And as I surfaced and felt the water rush from my hair and down over my face, I felt as if the sound the drops were making as they drained from my head and fell noisily back into the pool was drawing too much attention to me. To postpone things a few moments longer I guess, I then turned my head back around so I could look once more at my friend and catch his eye. "Watch my back," I mouthed. I then saw Matt's expression change as he nodded his head which told me that he understood what it was that I was worrying about.

"Let's go, kid! Get over here!" Joe yelled at me.

In the shallow end, at the far corner of the pool on the left were some semi-circular steps. By now, Joe had placed his massive rear end onto the bottom one which permitted him to sit in the water up to his neck. Without any more delays, I stretched out and began to swim over to the far side of the pool to present myself to our boss for the weekend and do for him what I had done for so many by this time. But when I was finally standing before him and getting ready to stick my head under water so I could get to work, a wave of fear rushed through my body and motivated me instead to take a couple of steps backwards. "I can't do it," I declared to my boss.

"What do you mean you can't do it?" At first Joe didn't seem to comprehend what I was saying to him.

"I mean … no, I can't do this. Joe, there's no way I can stay under water long enough to be able to do anything. But I've got a better idea. Why don't we all go back inside the house and Matt and I will give you a really good rub down. And then one of us can suck you off while you suck the other one of us at the same time if you want." My mind was racing now to come up with any sort of a scheme that he might go for.

Joe's face then went red as he stood up in the water. "Come here now!" he demanded.

"No, I can't," I replied nervously as I took a few more steps back.

"I said come here, damn it!" Joe took a step toward me this time. There was no question that I had made this man furious with me.

"Joe, I can't do it. You can't get angry at me for something I can't do." I was now considering how I was going to be able to escape this guy's grasp if he decided to reach for me. But instead I watched as our host turned around instead and climbed the steps to get out of the water. Once on the patio, he continued to walk around the far end of the pool until he was standing in front of the bamboo bar, and then I saw him look at me again.

"Ok," he sounded calmer now. "Get out of the water then and come over here."

I wasn't sure what to make of things now, but to show good faith at least I stood upright again. As water dripped from me all over, I looked at Matt once more to see how he was now sizing up this guy. But when our eyes met, my friend just shrugged his shoulders and looked away. So again I had to make a decision on my own.

"Come on, Adams. Come out of the water and stand over here." Now he sounded almost pleasant.

So I was Adams again instead of kid. That certainly suggested to me that something was on this guy's mind. But I supposed that I couldn't stand around in the pool all day. So slowly I began to move through the water until I reached the steps. Then I climbed my way out of the pool and began to walk along the patio to follow my orders this time as gradually as I could manage. Once I was standing next to the bar, I stopped. "Ok, Joe. Here I am," I said as I dripped water onto the man's Astroturf.

"Yes, so you are." Joe now stared down at me with a look that told me I had just made an enormous mistake. "You know I had hoped that we could have had a little fun together before…" Joe then looked away from me and over at Matt for a moment. My friend was still standing where we had come into the pool room.

"Before what, Joe?" I asked. I was trying to sound compassionate toward the guy. At this time in my life, I was still naïve enough to believe that if I was nice to others they would always, in turn, be nice to me. And as it turned out, I suppose I should have just kept my mouth shut.

Joe then looked directly at me again. "Before I do to you two what I did to your friends last night at the lake."

"What?" Fear now had me paralyzed. "What are you… Ooof!" Before I could finish my sentence, Joe had slugged me hard in my stomach and I collapsed instantly onto the patio.

"No! Joe, don't do that!" Matt shrieked as I looked up at my attacker and gasped for air.

The monster then reached down with his meaty hands and took hold of my sides under my arm pits, and lifted me with no effort off of the floor. "Yeah, I really hoped we could have a little fun before I had to do this." Joe then threw me down hard like a side of beef onto the round metal table next to the bar.

"Auhauh!" I cried out when I landed on my back. The table wasn't big enough to hold all of me so my legs hung over one edge where it caught me at mid thigh, while my head hung off the opposite side.

Joe then turned his head away from me for a moment to look at Matt again. "But maybe you'll blow me later on instead. Huh?" Joe then returned his attention to the boy who was now sprawled helplessly on the table before him.

Matt immediately turned and grabbed hold of the doorknob with both of his hands and tried to force the door open so he could get away and go for help. "Ah!" he exclaimed in desperation.

"You might as well give up, kid. There's no way you can get out of here. You just sit tight while I work on your friend over here for a while."

Undaunted, Matt then scanned the floor rapidly, located Joe's pants, and then bent down to reach into his pockets.

"Hey!" Joe yelled. "Now just leave those pants alone and stay still over there for a while. There's no way you can figure out which key it is and get the door open before I can come over there and pound your ass."

Realizing that our situation was hopeless, Matt then stood up again and gave up on his effort to escape. He did, however, decide to try one last series of appeals as an attempt to save our lives. "You don't have to do this, Joe. We promise we won't do anything to let your secret out."

With his left hand, Joe grabbed a large hunk of wet hair from just above my forehead and pulled my head up until I could look forward and see the rest of my body again. "Auhauh!" I then felt the force and the resulting pain from a right cross which Joe delivered to my face at the same moment he released his grip on my hair. Instantly, of course, my head flopped back down to hang off the edge of the table once again.

"No, you guys don't understand." Joe was able to continue his conversation with Matt while he concentrated on working me over. "That's not why I have to kill you two." Then he lifted my head by my hair again, and threw another punch at me.

"Auh!" The pain from his blow to my face was excruciating. Also, the force created by my head falling through the air afterwards was hard on my neck.

"Well, whatever the reason is, you don't have to do this to us, Joe!" Matt was pleading for our lives as hard as he knew how.

"No, what I mean is, I have orders to kill you two." Again my assailant reached down and mingled his large fingers within my wet strands, and then he lifted my head into position once more and threw another punch at my face.

"Auh!" These were the worst punches I had ever taken. They were far stronger than anything I had been made to endure from the leader.

"Hey, Joe, wait a minute. Look at me. You mean Fatso ordered you to kill us? I can't believe that!" Matt was trying anything he could come up with to get my tormentor to stop pummeling me. But his efforts were of no use.

"Uh!" Another punch and I was now losing it. Until this point, I had been able to regain some strength between the man's blows, but now there was nothing left in my body. This six-foot giant with arms like pile drivers had managed to slug the energy right out of me, and I figured that if he continued to hit me, he would soon succeed in slugging the life out of me.

"No, I don't work for Fatso. He thinks I work for him, but I really work for the South Americans. They're the ones who told me to set your headmaster's house on fire to scare him into making you kids go back to work. And they're the ones who've told me now to get rid of all four of you kids and more, so there won't be no traces left of the prostitution business you guys just wrecked. Hell, I even have to burn this place down after I've finished with you two because of what you guys did. And I've really liked this place!"

"Uh!" By now I figured one or maybe two more punches would be all it would take to have me unconscious.

"But, Joe, you can just let us go and we'll leave New England right away and never come back. Nobody will ever know that you didn't kill us." Matt was trying to offer any idea he could come up with now.

"Uh!"

"No, I can't do that. It'd be too risky for me." Joe then pulled a chair around and sat down in it so he was positioned to look straight at my groin. "But don't worry. I'm not going to kill you two right away. We're still going to have a little fun first. So shut up, before I come over there and start knocking you around."

Matt knew for the time being at least that he was going to have to keep quiet. But it appeared to him as if Joe was now getting himself ready to do something less destructive to me anyway, so my friend figured he could afford to stay silent for a while.

Joe next took hold of my hips with each of his mammoth hands, and then he pulled my depleted body slightly toward him which caused my legs to drop from the table more severely and my head to be propped up finally by the table's edge. This adjustment of my frame, as it turned out, was done just in time because I had felt close to blacking out from my beating and from all of the blood that had been rushing to my head.

"Now try to relax, kid," Joe encouraged. "You're gonna love this."

And then, I felt large fingers begin to fondle my penis. Matt and I had run into people like this occasionally at the inn and, for that matter, I suspected that Sully in Worcester was another who found it sexually arousing to beat or be beaten by another person. "Uuh!" I groaned as I began to respond to Joe's stimulation. He was good. "Uuh!" Right away I began to feel the effects of his efforts and within only a minute or so, he had gotten me hard. *Maybe being beaten is a sure fire way to make sure I'm relaxed,* I thought. It was clear to me by then that Joe was intending to take me all the way. And as I felt the man take my penis into his mouth and begin to work me with his lips and his tongue, I rolled my head over to my left and looked at my roommate to make sure he knew that, for the moment at least, I was doing ok. "Uuh! Ah.. Ah!" Maybe even better than ok.

Matt knew from experience that what Joe was doing to me now would take a great amount of concentration. And with our jailer seated with his back to the door for the moment, Matt used this opportunity to bend down quietly and remove the ring of keys from Joe's pants pocket.

"Uuh!" I didn't know if this theory about sexual arousal being heightened by physical battery was really true, or if Joe was just unusually gifted in this area, but I was heading toward my climax at a pace which was a great deal faster than usual. "Uuh!" I kept groaning out loud so Matt would be able to gage how much time he had to figure out the right key and then use it to get away. But escape, as it turned out, wasn't the foremost thought on my friend's mind at this moment. And then… "Uhoof!" As I struggled to hold myself back, I could see Matt holding up three keys from the ring which he held together and separated from the other keys. He was showing me that he had narrowed the selection down to those three out of the eight or so on the man's ring.

"Uhoooof!" Finally I ejaculated hard and although I was sure that Joe had beaten all of the energy out of my body, somehow I managed to raise the upper half of my body slightly as an involuntary response until I reached the end of my spasms. And then as I collapsed into a prone poison once again, I saw Matt do something that I didn't expect. Instead of making an attempt to get away, my roommate laid the keys down on the floor with the three he had chosen left isolated from the others, and then before my latest sex partner could turn around, Matt covered over the keys with a sleeve from Joe's shirt and then stood up quickly again so he would appear to have been standing quietly the entire time I was being debauched. *Why the hell didn't he try to get away?* I wondered as I lay on the table out of breath. And then I realized what was going on in Matt's mind. My friend was afraid to leave me for fear that I might need him to keep Joe from doing me in while I was still on the table. I have often wondered since this day, how differently things might have worked out if Matt had used Joe's keys to save himself.

"There, that was pretty good now wasn't it?" Joe sat upright again, obviously proud of what he had just caused me to go through.

"Ah!" All I could do was gasp as I lay there incapacitated. I still felt pretty battered and Joe's blow job had just sucked most of my will to resist right out of me.

With our session now ended, Joe gave me another moment or two to recover from my experience. During this time, Matt did his best to keep quiet so he wouldn't invite any unwanted attention from our host. In no time though, I felt Joe pull me upright by my damp hair again. Once I was sitting on my own, I noticed that blood was dripping from my nose. In fact it felt broken and I worried about the mess I was beginning to make on Joe's table.

"Now that I've given you some things to think about, I want you to get up and go stop that bleeding. You'll find paper towels and a sink behind the bar, and then after you've cleaned yourself up, I want you to come back into the pool and do me."

In my dazed state, I believed now that because Joe and I had just been intimate, I stood a better chance than I had before of talking him out of another trip into the swimming pool. At the same time I knew there was an even chance that any objection on my part could cause another barrage of punches from his brick-like fists. But at this moment my mind was made up. I was convinced that if I allowed my head to go under water again, I would most certainly never be returning to the surface and I didn't want to die by drowning. At least on land—or rather on Joe's table—I figured I had a fighting chance to change this monster's mind about his plans for us.

"Joe, I… I'm sorry," I stammered. "But there's no way I can do what you're asking me for. It's just not possible." I remained on the table while I watched for his reaction.

It was as if I had unleashed the fury through the gates of hell itself. The next I knew, Joe was flying at me with a rage far beyond anything I had ever experienced. Instantly he pressed another of his punches into my stomach.

"Ohoof!"

With the total of his bulk behind his assault, the man had me utterly incapacitated as my body reacted to his blow by leaning forward to lie helplessly against his forearm and chest. And like an angry child who takes out his frustration by beating on a broken toy, Joe then wailed on me with his massive fists until I was flat on my back again and nearly unconscious.

As I lay there uncertain as to how long I was going to be able to keep my eyes open, it seemed to me as if Matt had done or said something to get our host to break off his attack, but in my newly debilitated condition there was no way I could be sure of this. All I knew was the hitting had ended for the moment and I was still alive. And curiously, I noticed also that I wasn't feeling very much of the pain I had been feeling any longer.

Joe stood upright slightly and looked over my broken body. "Yeah, how does that feel, you son of a bitch! I tried to do something nice for you, but will you do anything nice for me in return? Huh? I guess not, you asshole!" Next Joe stepped over to the bar and picked up a kitchen knife with a nine-inch blade he had apparently placed there earlier in the day. He then came back to me and reaching forward, stretched out my penis with one hand while he held the cold steel of the knife against the underside of my exposed organ at its base with his other hand. "So, maybe I ought to just go ahead and cut it off. What do ya think?"

Suddenly I was terrified that I was about to lose my penis. "Oh God, Joe, no! Please don't do it. Please don't cut off my dick, plea..e..e…ese!" I began to cry. Raw emotions were all I had left.

"Oh God, Joe, don't do it!" Matt added his voice to the chorus. "Joe, he's a good kid. Don't do it! Please, Joe!"

Perhaps our appeals had an effect. Or perhaps Joe was just following his own twisted plan for me. But through my tears finally, I looked up at my tormentor's face and saw that he was smiling at me. Apparently he was enjoying the torrent of emotions he was putting me through. Then I could feel the knife removed from my groin area.

"That's ok." He tried to sound reassuring as he released his hold on my penis. "I really had something else in mind anyway."

Before I could collect my thoughts to wonder what it was that I was in for next, I felt the cold of his sharp blade rest suddenly against the right side of my torso. Was he going to stab me now? Is this how he planned to kill me, by stabbing me through my heart? Grimly, I began to wonder how many deep thrusts into less vital areas I could withstand before the loss of blood would force me to succumb to his cowardly act.

"Yeah, you feel that don't you?" Joe observed of my apparent reaction to his blade.

Even if I could have summoned the energy somehow to get away, I was too frightened now to risk moving. And so I was faced with the biggest dilemma of my young life. Lying still could get me killed, yet trying to get away could also get me killed. So what was the answer? How was I going to be able to save myself? I decided then to look up and search Joe's eyes for an idea of what I could expect next, but when our gazes connected, all I could see was anger: stark, blinding anger. And then it happened. "Auhauhauh!"

"No! Don't hurt him like that! Please, don't kill him!" Matt yelled at my attacker in vain.

The pain across my gut was beyond description. In one fluid motion, Joe had carved an opening in my skin from one side of my abdomen to the other. But as soon as he had me open, he placed one of his large hands on my body above the slice and his other one directly below. And then curiously he pushed hard to move the two halves of me back together again. Strangely, his cut hadn't gone deep enough to pierce the muscle. Instead he seemed intent only upon creating a gaping wound in my skin—I supposed—to torture me for a while before bringing my life to a bloody and abrupt end.

"Auh…! Auh! Auh!" I was in agony and I couldn't stop screaming from the pain.

"So, you're not such a hot shit now are ya, kid? No clever comments or rich prep school remarks to make old Joe feel like a dunce, now? Huh?"

Matt was yelling almost continually. In a moment, I struggled to collect myself enough to plead with this idiot for my life. "Joe… Agk! Please don't do this. We can work out another way. My parents have money. I'll get them to pay you if you let me live!"

"Too late, kid."

"Auhauhauh!" Unbelievably, Joe carved another opening across my belly.

"No! Joe! Don't do it!" Matt was beside himself with anguish over what was happening to me.

"So how much more of this do you think you can take before you pass out, kid?" Joe asked me as he held the two halves of my new opening together.

"Auh… Agk!" This was about all I could manage to say at this moment. And as my battered and wounded body continued to be sprawled across that metal table top, I realized that I was completely at this man's mercy. Never before in my life had I known such a feeling of utter helplessness. Every aspect of my existence now was dependant entirely upon the whims of this creep who quite clearly had a screw loose. And because I believed Fatso's comment about Joe having a short attention span, even though he was obviously enjoying what he was doing to me for the moment, I figured I only had another minute or two of life remaining before my executioner would put an end to me, permanently.

"Hey, stop! Joe… stop it! Don't cut him anymore! I'll get in the water with ya! I mean it! I'll give ya the best damn blow job under water you've ever had. But ya gotta stop cutting him right now! Ya hear me? Stop and I'll blow ya now, Joe! And believe me, I know how to make it feel real good!" In spite of Matt's fear for his own safety, he was desperate now to distract Joe's attention away from me as he tried to save my life.

"You will, huh?" Joe responded to Matt's offer without taking his eyes off of me.

"Auhauhauh!" For a third time, Joe sliced me open. Now I knew I was going to die. I figured I had to be losing a ton of blood by now so the end for me wasn't going to be far off.

"Yeah well, shut up for now!" Joe yelled at Matt as he once again held my two new pieces together with his large hands. "After I'm finished with your friend here, you're gonna do that shit for me anyway."

The time had come. Matt now understood that if there was any chance still to keep us alive, he was going to have to take action rather than stand by the door and yell. So with that thought in mind, there was only one thing he could think of to do. Quickly then my roommate reached down and picked up the ring of keys he had hidden earlier beneath Joe's shirt sleeve. "Hey, Joe!" my friend hollered. "I've decided I'm not gonna stick around here anymore. See ya later!" And with that Matt slid one of the three keys he had already picked out into the deadbolt on the door.

"Hey! Put those keys down now!" Joe thundered.

"No way!" Matt yelled out as he kept his focus on the lock. The first key was a failure. "I'm leaving now!" Without delay Matt pulled the first key out and slid in the second.

"Why you...!" My friend's play worked. Joe's attention was now distracted from his first victim and aimed directly at his second. Without giving another thought to me, Joe threw his knife down onto the Astroturf and began to jog around the pool toward the door. "Damn it, kid, put those keys down now, or I'll beat the crap out of you!"

The second key was a failure as well. Matt knew he only had seconds now to make his escape. Without so much as a glance away to check on Joe's progress, my roommate slid in the third key, turned it and then he heard the latch on the inside flip over. With no time to spare, Matt grabbed the knob with both hands, turned it and began to pull the door open so he could get away.

"Oh no you don't!" Joe yelled as he placed a hand on the door and slammed it shut again before my friend could slip through the opening. In the process, Joe pressed his enormous body against Matt's which wedged the boy in sideways against the door. "You're not goin' anywhere, you little son of a bitch!"

"Ah!" Matt was suddenly straining under Joe's weight which was now pressing against his smaller frame. "Joe, you gotta let us go! We *both* have families that can give you money!"

The appeal still was of no consequence to our jailer. So the die was cast. Matt's fate was now sealed. Joe continued with what he was going to do to my roommate by forming his right hand into a tight fist and then slugging Matt three times rapidly in his face. Of course Matt and I had taken plenty of punches to our faces since coming to the Academy. But when I saw my friend lose his wits and stagger after just one punch, I realized that these blows were doubly deadly because the sheer force from each of Joe's punches was causing the boy's head to be hurled to his right until it was slammed loudly against the safety glass in the door. And as this awful scene played out, I watched and listened in terror from my perch across the room.

"Auh!" SLAM! "Uh!" SLAM! "__!" SLAM/CRACK!

"Ha! Take that, asshole!" Joe yelled proudly at poor Matt.

On the third SLAM, and as his eyes closed, the force from Matt's head hitting against it cracked the glass in the door. I then watched as Matt's body dropped to the floor to land in a heap against the exit he had nearly been able to escape through. He was now unconscious. Matt's piercing high voice had been silenced. Joe had knocked the boy out.

"What a pain in the ass!" Joe yelled in frustration as he bent down and grabbed my friend's still naked body under the armpits with both of his hands and then lifted the boy into the air. "Nothing works out the way I want, damn it!" Joe proclaimed his anger out loud as he turned with my friend's limp body in his arms and took the few steps needed to move him from where he had been standing to the edge of the pool.

In horror then, I watched as Joe threw my roommate down into the water. "NO!" I screamed. "Joe, no!" But I might as well have been miles away, because Joe did nothing to respond to my pleas. And so helplessly I watched as my friend, my dear, dear friend sank quickly away from my view. It was only an instant before he was gone and I couldn't believe that in another few moments Matt's life would be over. As I stared at the surface of the water and watched the waves settle from Matt's splash, I thought of the picture on our dresser back at the dorm of my friend with his parents. And as tears filled my eyes once more, I thought about the love I knew his parents had felt for their son and how distraught they would be now to see what had become of their boy since their absence. "Don't let him die!" I gasped weakly.

"All I wanted was a fuckin' blow job from one of you kids!" Joe bellowed from the pool's edge as he looked down at my friend's body which was now lying still on the bottom.

I could tell that there wasn't much time left for me either. As I lay there and hoped for a miracle that would cause my roommate to return to the surface somehow and surprise us, I could feel myself sinking gradually into a void from which I knew I could never return. "Please God, don't let the best friend I ever had die!" I couldn't bear the idea of going on without Matt. And then I found that I no longer had the strength to keep myself looking at the water, so I allowed my eyes to roll up and gaze at the ceiling while I waited for my turn to cross over. *At least Matt and I will go together,* I thought. And then like a wave of revelation sweeping over me, I realized that I just didn't care anymore whether I lived or I died. "Come on, you bastard!" I wheezed at our assailant. "I'm fed up with this shitty world. Get your ass over here and end it for me, now. I don't want to wait any longer."

CRACK!

It took me an instant to realize that something had just happened. Quickly I decided to look over by the pool once more to see what it was that had caused that odd sound to occur. And when I did, I beheld the sight of Joe, losing consciousness and collapsing onto the Astroturf. At the same instant, I saw and heard someone dive into the pool, jackknife his body so he could do a surface dive and then slip away from view. Suddenly my battered being was swelled with hope. While I waited for a result from under the water, I looked back again at the patio and saw that it was Frank's cousin who was now standing over our attacker with the bat... that Goddamned baseball bat that Joe had been so proud of which was now poised in the hand of the young man. "You knocked him out by taking a swing at his head?" Without a bit of hesitation I was now a Red Sox fan. Frank's cousin heard me and glanced my way for a second, but then his attention was drawn to something new that was happening in the water.

With a SPLASH, Frank shot noisily through the surface with Matt's lifeless body grasped between his hands in front of him. And while feeling an enormous amount of trepidation, I looked closely at my roommate to see if I could detect any signs still of life. But Matt didn't move and his thick black hair hung flattened and even all around the top half of his head like a shroud.

"Come on," Frank's cousin called out. "Give him to me."

Unable to move, I continued to watch then as Frank swam with our friend's body over to the edge of the pool. A moment later Frank's cousin had hauled poor Matt from the water and had laid my roommate out on the patio so he could administer CPR to the boy. Now at least Matt had a fighting chance to live but as the seconds ticked by, the likelihood of him reviving suddenly seemed to dwindle before our eyes.

"Don't give up!" Frank urged as he sat on the edge of the pool in his sopping wet clothing and dripped.

"I'm tryin'," Frank's cousin confirmed. "But I'm beginning to think its hopeless."

"I don't care! Just don't quit yet!" Frank was as frantic for Matt to live again as I was.

So Frank's cousin continued with his efforts at CPR and mouth to mouth. But a few moments later his movements began to slow, and we were all beginning to share in a feeling of utter discouragement.

"COUGH!" Suddenly Matt spit out a lungful of water onto his face. Immediately then Frank's cousin rolled Matt over onto his side and my friend continued to cough himself back to life. He was alive! My friend was alive! I was overjoyed. Matt was going to live after all. "Aw yeah!" I had never felt such elation in all of my life... and then I blacked out.

***

I opened my eyes to find myself lying in a hospital bed, yet it didn't seem to me as if I was really in a hospital.

"Hey, he's awake!" I heard Frank's voice suddenly so I began to move my head and focus my eyes to see him.

"Well how are we doing?" This was a man's voice and it sounded closer. So quickly I abandoned my effort to see Frank and I looked instead to where I heard this new voice. And when I found him, he spoke to me again.

"Your friends got you here just in time. If you had lost very much more blood, I don't know if we'd been able to save you."

I could see more clearly now. The man was clean shaven, but he had long hair down to his shoulders like some of the kids at the Academy. I decided that he must be a doctor because of the white lab coat he was wearing, but he didn't look like any doctor I had ever seen. Still, he was smiling at me.

"Where am I?" I asked still in a fog. Frankly at this moment, I was amazed to discover that I was still alive. It was also at this point when I noticed the IV in my hand. My eyes then followed the tubing up to the stand which was positioned next to my bed and I saw that they were giving me whole blood and something else. From the way I was feeling, I figured the something else was a very fine pain killer.

"You're in my clinic. I don't think I've ever put so many stitches into one person before. But we've got you all sewn back together again and I've bandaged up your midsection pretty well. And your nose is broken, so you'll notice that I've got some bandaging there as well. So tell me, how do you feel?"

I then glanced for a moment over to where I had heard Frank's voice earlier. When I found him, he was sitting in a chair near the foot of my bed. He was wrapped in a blanket and wearing only his underwear, but his expression conveyed to me feelings of concern and relief. "Fine, I guess," I didn't know what else to say.

"Well, don't try to do anything just yet. I want you to lie here until tomorrow at least before you start moving around again."

"Doc, we've gotta get out of here as soon as we can. I've gotta hide these kids while we're still one step ahead of the people who did this. Ya know what I'm sayin'?" This voice belonged to Frank's cousin.

I then looked up at the doctor again in time to see him frown.

"Well… you can't move him 'til at least tomorrow morning. And he's going to need to be able to stay lying down. He's not going to be strong enough at first to sit up for very long, and he needs to stay on his back anyway so the tissues around his stitches have time to strengthen."

"Well, we're gonna hide them down in New York for a few weeks to start with," Frank's cousin continued. "That way I'll be able to keep an eye on them."

The doctor thought for a moment, and then he spoke again. "And are you bringing Frank back up here after that?"

"Yeah," Frank answered. "I've gotta be back at the Academy by around dinnertime tomorrow night so nobody'll think I'm involved in any of this."

The doctor then thought for a moment longer. "Ok… here's what I think we should do. You guys keep your car hidden in my garage for now. Tomorrow morning then, before dawn you can use my station wagon to transport these boys to wherever you're taking them down in New York. We'll put the back seat down and fix up the back so they can lie comfortably during the trip. Then when you bring Frank back up here in the afternoon, you can bring me back my car. But you better exchange vehicles before you take Frank back to school so nobody sees you in a different car with Massachusetts tags on it. That could cause someone to get curious and run a trace on my car. And I don't need any headaches coming down on me or the people here in my clinic. Ok?"

Frank's cousin then smiled. "That sounds great, Doc. Thanks."

"No problem. You just be sure to hide these boys someplace where they'll be safe."

That reminded me suddenly. "Where's Matt?" I was now worried for the welfare of my friend.

"He's resting comfortably in the room next door," the doctor assured me. "In spite of the fact that he's got a mild concussion and he nearly drowned this afternoon, he's doing just fine."

"Do you promise?" I wanted to make sure that the doctor wasn't just saying what he thought I wanted to hear to keep me from becoming agitated.

The doctor then smiled at me again. "Yes, I promise. Now I want you to get some sleep. You've got a long ride ahead of you in the morning."

"Yeah, I probably ought to go out now and get your car gassed up and pick up some provisions for the trip tomorrow," Frank's cousin announced.

"That sounds fine," the doctor continued. "Come on and I'll get you the keys. Oh, and I've got an extra room upstairs where you and Frank can sleep tonight. Under the circumstances, I think it'd be better if you two stayed close to your friends until it's time tomorrow for you guys to leave."

"Yeah ok. Thanks, Doc. Come on, Frank. Let's let him sleep." Frank's cousin then took a few steps toward the door to leave.

"Is it all right if I stay here and talk to Clint for a minute, Doc?" Frank asked.

"Well ok, but make it quick." With that the doctor then stepped over to the door also and opened it. A moment later he and Frank's cousin had both left, and it was then just the two of us.

"Well, here you are all banged up in a hospital bed again," Frank began.

"I thought you were mad at me?" I was still a little confused over how everything had managed to work out for us.

"Nah… not really. And besides, when I saw youz two get into that silly-lookin' blue finned job, I knew that somethin' wasn't right. So I told my cousin to follow you guys cuz I thought somethin' fishy was goin' on."

This alarmed me. If Frank and his cousin had been close by the whole time, then why had they allowed us both to nearly die before they came to our aid? "Well why did it take you so long to get us out of there, then?"

"Becuz we lost youz after you took your exit off the Pike. It took us nearly a half an hour of drivin' around Framingham before we finally spotted that guy's Caddy."

"Oh," I felt relieved again. "Well thanks for not giving up on us."

"I never have, pal. I never have. Besides, I told you I'd figure out what was going on with youz two."

"Yeah, ya did," I recalled. "So what is this place you guys brought me to?" I now wanted to hear what had taken place after I had become unconscious.

"Well, it's a free clinic, I guess. The doc runs this place out of the downstairs of his house here in Newton."

"We're in Newton?" I was surprised that they had gotten me so far away from Framingham.

"Yeah," Frank confirmed.

"Well how the hell did you know about this place?"

Frank then pulled his chair closer to my bed. "Well while we were loading you two into my cousin's car, Matt filled us in on the stuff I hadn't already figured out for myself. The thing is, nobody seems to know how big these South Americans or this guy Fatso really is. But we figured if their organizations were anything like the setups we've got down in Brooklyn, there was a pretty good chance they'd have people watchin' for ya at the hospitals. So as soon as we could find a payphone, my cousin called this buddy of his he works with down in New York who's from this area originally. And right away the guy told us about this doctor he knew in Vietnam who came back home after his hitch was done and opened up this free clinic not too long ago. So while we were driving here like a bat out of hell, the guy in New York called ahead for us. And since Matt told us what your blood type was, the doc had time to get the blood you were going to need."

"Oh, that's right. They made us learn each other's blood type," I remarked.

"Yeah, so we got you here and then the doc fixed you up. End of story," Frank concluded.

"Thanks." I was truly amazed at the effort that everyone had made to keep me alive. And since my life was now an open book, I figured the time had come for me to bring up one other issue. "Ah, speaking of fix, Matt and I have a pretty heavy drug habit goin', ya know?"

Frank's expression then seemed to become more serious. "I know, and so does the doctor. Actually I knew it when you were at my place over Christmas and you had cocaine stuffed in those dopey cans of shaving cream."

This was news to me. "Really? How did you figure that out?"

"Come on. You're only thirteen. What do you need with shaving cream?"

"I guess," I admitted. "I don't know, it had seemed like a clever idea at the time."

"Anyway, as soon as you've done some healing, you guys are gonna have to kick the habit."

"I know," I replied as I turned my head away and stared at one of the walls in the room. "I guess I've always known."

"Well," Frank continued. "Don't worry about all that stuff right now. Just get some sleep and let my cousin and me worry about everything for a while. Ok?"

"Ok," I agreed. Considering the way I felt at the moment, I was happy to turn everything over to Frank.

The next day everything worked out according to the arrangements Frank and his cousin had made for us. The plan was to hide us both in Frank's cousin's rabbit hutch of an apartment in Manhattan which was located somewhere on the lower east side. Frank's mom was there to welcome us with a hot meal when we arrived, and for the rest of the time we were there, she made it a point to come into the city twice a week to bring us fresh home cooking to eat and to store for later.

In those days there were many who sought different and innovative ways to solve social problems. And sometimes these pioneers had to go against convention to achieve their ends. As for my problems, to keep me from ripping out my stitches during withdrawals, the decision was made to keep us both high—we never knew how our doctor pulled this off—until the time came for Doc to pay us a visit in Manhattan a few weeks later so he could remove my stitches. He no doubt broken a few laws to help us in this way, but there were two thirteen-year-old drug addicts who might not have made it through their odyssey if he hadn't gone the extra mile to help us.

When my wounds were finally healed, it was time then for Matt and me to get off the drugs that the upperclassmen had gotten us hooked on all those many months before. I don't recall any longer just how long it took for us to get clean again, and I won't go into the details of what it was like for us as we sweated and shook and wailed and threw up our way back to sobriety. Instead I'll simply admit that since we were by ourselves most of the time, sometimes I had to hold Matt, other times Matt had to hold me, and still other times all we could do was to hold onto each other. But eventually we did manage to come through our withdrawals and kick our habits. Of course nothing is ever that easy, and in the years which followed Matt had more trouble staying clean than I did. But in that tiny apartment, we were finally able to reclaim our lives.

Chapter Twelve
A Lot of Years, a Lot of Changes

I'm walking now back to my rental car which I left parked a while ago on what used to be the main drive of my old Academy. I've just finished speaking with a very kind woman who lives in one of the three narrow two-story row houses—typical for this area—which now stand on the site where Ulster Hall used to be. She told me that during the many years she's lived here, men who at one time had attended the Academy will stop every so often at her door and inquire as to what ever happened to the old place. Of course I knew how the Academy had met its demise soon after the event had occurred.

As I reach the driver's door and extend my hand to open it, I consider for a moment that I've gone to a lot of trouble today to be here, so I should allow myself a few more minutes, at least, to see everything I can before I get back on the road. Perhaps a quick look around at what used to be the grounds is what I should do next. From where I'm standing at this moment, I can easily see across the field where I once played soccer in a driving rain storm, the other buildings on the upper campus which, I'm amazed to discover, still remain.

East Hall, my old dormitory, now looks to have been converted sometime ago into a single-family home. But even though this building now seems to serve a higher calling, nothing really about it—on the outside at least—has changed. I can say this because I am amused by the black Pontiac I see propped up on cinder blocks on the building's front lawn. I'm not going to take any time to examine my thought more closely on this issue other than to suggest that some sort of poetic justice seems to be at work here today. The headmaster's former house next door seems to be faring about the same. And from where I'm standing at the moment, I can only make out the back side of the second story of the house where the neighbor kid Danny and his family used to live. The woman I just spoke with had thought that Danny had gone off to college when he had gotten older, but she didn't know anything about him or his family beyond that.

Speaking of a higher calling, as I continue my gaze on around now to my right and look past the spot where the tennis court used to be, I'm looking again back along the drive to where the front entrance used to stand, and to the right of that is the gym, still. From the outside the building looks exactly the same as I remember, but I see it's now a Baptist church of all things. This, I decide, I have got to see. So I leave my car for the moment and begin to walk along the drive to the building that I came to know so well on a particular night a lifetime ago.

As I walk, I'm thinking now about what it was that Matt and I had finally told our families. We hated to do it, but for our own safety, we had waited to resurface until after summer vacation had begun so there would be no chance for us to be sent back to the Academy to finish out our term. Actually, Frank's cousin had figured out where my dad's New York office was located. So when we were ready, Matt and I simply walked into the office and announced to the people there who we were. A secretary who had been familiar with the case of my disappearance took us both immediately into the conference room and helped us then to make our phone calls.

Of course, Matt's aunt was relieved beyond words to learn that her nephew was alive and safe after being told by the Academy that we had both run away. Matt did explain that the Academy had turned out to be an awful place where we among many other students had been forced into arduous labor for a local business owner so that the school could collect our wages as a way to earn extra money. And he admitted that the situation had become so intolerable that running away and waiting until after the Academy had closed down for the summer seemed to be the only way out for us. But this was as much information about our year in New England as Matt chose to reveal to his aunt. After all, she probably would have found the entire story hard to believe, anyway. For that matter, if we hadn't lived through it ourselves, I'm not sure that we would have believed it either.

My own phone call to my parents went pretty much the same way. They couldn't understand why I hadn't contacted them sooner, but their relief from learning that I was alive and safe ruled their emotions that day. And as we talked, I told them how close Matt and I had become as friends and that on many occasions he had placed my interests above his own. In fact, I made a point to let my parents know that the two of us had become inseparable. Like brothers. Of course they had questions for me later which I had to find ways to answer but like Matt, I saw no reason to make my parents suffer any more than they already had.

The ride, at long last, was over and that secretary wound up offering to my dad to take us in for a few days and help us to get around the city so we could buy ourselves some new clothes, since we had left everything we had owned back at the Academy. It was actually an amazing experience for both of us to behave and be treated once again as ordinary thirteen-year-old boys. Each day we were with this young woman, we spoke on the phone to our families. And in every conversation with my parents, I campaigned on Matt's behalf. So that by the weekend, Matt and I were both accepting my parents' invitation to fly to Europe so we could join them for the summer. Interestingly enough, Matt's aunt was delighted to place her nephew in our care. It seemed that the Hollywood director she had recently begun to date had been counting on her to spend the summer with him on location somewhere in Canada.

I'm now entering through the same door on the front side of the gym that I went through that night when they first brought Matt here. I don't see anyone at the moment, but the lights are on and the place is open. The pews, the carpeting, the altar at the other end of the room… this is obviously now a church. But I can't get it out of my mind that this building is really just a gymnasium with a bunch of furniture in it now. As I take a few steps inside, it seems to me all of a sudden as if there might be someone in the back somewhere. It could be interesting to talk with this person for a minute or two, so I begin to make my way along an aisle toward the back of the building. Almost immediately as I walk, I can feel how badly warped the flooring underneath this champagne-colored carpeting still is. And then I stop. Suddenly I don't feel like talking to anyone anymore. I've just flashed back on a memory of Frank making a lay up over where the altar now stands, and the image puts me out of the mood to be sociable. Quickly then I turn around so I can get out of here before anyone can discover me.

After they had tucked us away that first day in that tiny Manhattan apartment, Frank did come back here to finish out his year at the Academy. Matt and I knew we would never be back here again and we could deal with the loss of everything we had owned in exchange for our lives. But the more I thought about it, the more I found the idea of never having my guitar again impossible to bear. Also Matt begged Frank to get the picture of him with his parents from our dresser top. For the rest of that semester, Frank kept to his routine and stayed away from our dormitory. But on the last day, as his cousin waited for him out in front, Frank went into our dorm, unlocked our door with the key we had given him and took the two items we had asked him to bring to us. He nearly got away with it too. But before he could stash our belongings into the Fury's trunk, he had the misfortune to run into the head waiter.

Well... since the head waiter played guitar also, he knew every guitar player on campus (I think there were five of us). Frank was not one of those who played, so when he saw Frank carrying my guitar, it didn't take much for the upperclassman to put it all together. With his cousin nearby, Frank was able to get away that day. But before the summer had ended that year, a fire had broken out one night in his mom's apartment in Brooklyn. Frank had gotten his mother and his little sister out safely as the flames raged through their modest home. But when Frank turned around to go back inside for his grandparents, his mother did everything she could to hold him back while she pleaded with him to stay outside. It was tragic, but his grandparents had lived long lives, she reasoned. And the fire had become too advanced now to make a rescue possible. The woman stated emphatically that there was no way any longer for him to get them out. But Frank broke free from his mother's grasp and ran back inside anyway. That was the last time Frank's mother and little sister ever saw the boy alive. Along with his grandparents that night, Frank perished in the flames. The kid who had been such a good friend to me was gone. He had just turned fifteen, and I have not been able to pick up my guitar to play it ever since.

Outside once again, I'm looking back now toward the east where I've parked. I've had enough remembering now, so I begin to walk back toward my car so I can get in it and leave this place for the last time in my life. As I walk, I look once again beyond my car to where Ulster Hall used to stand, and I remember the phone call I made to Jamie the kid who used to live across the cove, from Kennedy Airport right before Matt and I took off for Europe. I had wanted to say good-bye to my friend and to ask him to say so long to Charlie and Danny for me. Jamie was excited to hear from me and was bursting with news he was sure I'd be interested to know.

"What is it?" I asked.

It seemed that on a recent night, Ulster Hall had mysteriously caught fire and burned to the ground. "It made a big orange glow that night," Jamie said as he described the event to me. "My mom and step-dad and I all sat out on our dock in the dark and watched across the water as it burned. It made a big orange glow and lit up the night. I wish you could have seen it. It was really something to watch."

When I spoke with her upon my arrival today, I had asked the woman in the row house if she had ever known Jamie and his friend Charlie. She told me that she had and that Charlie had moved into town once he had grown up and had gone to work as a laborer of some kind. She also told me that Jamie had taken up the guitar and had played in a band for a while. This news caused me to wonder if I had influenced my friend more than I had realized. Later when Jamie had grown, she knew that he had married and moved to near by Thompson, Connecticut, but she lost track of him after that. And before I left her front porch, the woman asked me if I had known what had happened to the Friendly Inn.

"I noticed it wasn't there when I drove past the site a while ago," I admitted. The inn had been a local landmark during the time I lived here, so I didn't consider it odd that she would ask me about it.

"It was a long time ago," she went on. "Back around the time the old school building here burned down. But somehow the Friendly Inn caught fire one night and burned down also. Nobody was hurt though," she continued. "It had been closed for a little while, I think for renovations, so there were no guests or employees there when the fire happened."

"Gee, I replied. "That was a pretty large and rambling facility. You'd think since the place was so close to town, the fire department would have been able to have saved at least some of it."

"I know. That's what a lot of people said afterwards. But they didn't."

I'm now standing at my rental car again. I've seen all I've come to see and it's time for me to continue on now. But as I open the door to get in, I'm stopped abruptly by a familiar sound which seems so incongruous to me in these surroundings.

RING, RING

Immediately I pull my cell phone out of my pocket to answer it. "Hello, this is Clint."

The voice on the other end is as familiar to me as my own. "Hey, I wanted to let you know that we landed at LaGuardia a little while ago and we're just getting into New York now. We thought we'd just go straight to the hotel and wait for you there. How soon before you're here?" It's Matt.

"Well, I made a little stop. You'll never guess where I'm standing at this moment." I hadn't told anyone that I was coming here today.

"I give up. Where?" Matt asks.

I take a brief pause to find just the right words to convey my news. "I'm standing on the main drive at the Academy looking at our old dorm right now."

Matt is silent for a moment. My news has taken him by surprise. "Really?" He can hardly believe what I've just told him. "Well what's it like now?" he asks.

"Well, there are now houses standing where Ulster Hall used to be and the gym is a church, but everything else looks pretty much the same, only I'm finding it kind of hard to think of this place now as an open neighborhood instead of a campus where they used to keep us confined all the time."

"I can imagine. And you say the gym is now a church? For real?" It's hard, given Matt's situation at this moment, for him to have an in-depth conversation with me.

"Yeah," I go on. "It's really strange. But I'll tell you more about everything I've learned today when I see you guys later tonight."

"Yeah, ok. You can also tell me why you decided to go there after all these years."

"Sure," I assure him. Then I sense that I need to change the subject. "Were you able to bring Janet and the kids with you?" I ask.

"Yeah. They're right here in the cab with me. We had to take Frankie out of school for a few days, but it didn't take much for us to talk him into the idea. Look, we're crossing the Fifty-Ninth Street Bridge right now. So we'll see you in a few hours. Ok?"

"Yeah, I'll catch up with you guys at the Pierre. Bye"

"Bye." And then Matt hangs up his cell phone.

As I put my own cell phone back into my pocket, I take one last long look at our old dormitory. I owed Matt everything, and that summer in Europe I knew how I wanted to repay him. And so a few weeks after we had joined my parents, I succeeded in persuading them to adopt Matt and make him my real brother. I wanted to give my friend the one thing he needed more than anything else in the world. So by the time fall came around that year, we had made him a part of our family. With his aunt's blessings, of course, which she wired to us from Banff. And I've never regretted what we did for him. In fact, today we're all meeting down in New York to celebrate my parents'—I mean our parents'—fifty-fifth wedding anniversary. My wife and children arrived in the city with my parents last night and as Matt said, they're all waiting for me now.

Back in the car finally, I start up the engine and begin to drive once more. I guide the car around the circle—all of the trees are gone from it now—and head back along the drive toward what used to be the front entrance. In a moment I'm on the winding country road again and headed for the highway back to town. But before I go too far, I pull the car over to the right and stop so I can look for a minute out the window on the passenger side. There it is. The pine field. This place too looks exactly as I remember it. There's been rain here recently and off in the distance I can spot two small puddles of water. "What do ya know?" I say out loud.

My mind now shifts for a moment to that awful night here in this field when the upperclassmen broke us down. How the experience had caused Matt and me to believe that neither of us would ever have a future. And then I think about the husband and wife who were behind our whole transformation into sex slaves. Ironically, we were on holiday in the South of France with my parents when we learned of the wealthy couple who were presumed dead after their downtown Boston penthouse had been gutted by fire. Their names were never mentioned in the accounts we read, but Matt and I knew it was Fatso and Sweetie the papers were telling about. And although we were sure that the authorities would never have enough information to link all of these fires together, we knew then as we know today that they are all connected.

One thing that was quite clear to us at the time was that Joe had obviously managed to survive the slam in the head he had taken from his beloved baseball bat. Of course since we had all run away from him so abruptly that day, none of us ever saw him again. And I suppose that if I had stopped in Framingham on my way down here from Boston a little while ago, I could have confirmed for myself whether or not he had also burned down that house he had nearly killed us in. But to this day I get a chill that goes deep into my bones and sharp pains which run across my stomach where my wounds used to be whenever I think about that man. I'm sure these symptoms are psychosomatic, but I don't care. Staying away from that killer, even after all of these years, still strikes me as the smartest thing for me to do. So as far as I know, after everything was over, Joe simply slipped back into that slimy underworld from which Matt and I were lucky enough to have escaped.

At the end of that summer in Europe, because we weren't sure if Joe or the South Americans were still looking for us, Matt and I were able to talk my parents into letting us next attend an American school in Switzerland. Staying closer to my parents struck us both as being the smartest decision we could make. During that year and the one that followed—my dad's assignment in Europe wound up being extended for an extra twelve months—Matt and I had long conversations about our experiences in Massachusetts and what type of men we hoped to become one day. At first we thought nothing about going after each other sexually in the way we had been taught at the Academy whenever the urge hit us. But as our conversations evolved and as we gained more distance from our past, we realized that we both wanted to put ourselves back on the track—the heterosexual track—we had been on before we had attended the Academy.

So when we all moved back to the States finally two years later, Matt and I decided that to keep temptation away, we would separate ourselves for our last two years of high school. As a result, I went off to a very fine prep school on the other side of Connecticut, and Matt found a good school up in Maine. And as things worked out, we both had very good years at these other boarding schools.

In those years leading up to our graduations from high school, through sports and other activities, I came to know many other students at a number of other boarding schools. And because I was sensitive to the subject, I became aware of a significant volume of incidents in which sexual liaisons shall we say, occurred between boys—and sometimes between teachers and boys—in nearly every boarding environment I encountered. Indeed, I was even aware of such goings-on—in one form or another—within the new schools we were attending.

For many years after boarding school, however, I dropped the subject from my mind entirely as I worked to build my own family and career, but in recent years I have begun to study these behaviors in greater detail. And although Golding never made mention of it in his classic *Lord of the Flies* I can only imagine that he must have been aware of the phenomenon, and that perhaps the sensitivities of his day had convinced him to leave any description of sex between boys out of his writings. Because I have found, and I suppose I will propose this now as my own theory, that whenever a decent-sized population of boys is gathered—from say the age of eight and above—there will be a percentage of these boys who will engage in sexual behavior with one another, and the degree to which this behavior is forced or voluntary will depend entirely upon how much adult supervision and discipline is present within the community.

To be sure, the experiences that Matt and I and others went through at the Academy should be thought of as occurrences at the extreme edge of the scale. And the obvious question, I suppose, that anyone would ask after reading our story is whether or not we feel as if our lives since the Academy have been irrevocably destroyed in the way so many pop psychologists and self-proclaimed experts seem eager to pronounce every time a case of child sexual abuse comes to light in the media. I know I speak for Matt when I say that such assertions are utter nonsense.

I ask the question. Which is more devastating to a young person: being victimized sexually by another, or being told after the fact by a so-called expert that his future is now thoroughly destroyed? Of course being the victim of a sexual assault can be an enormously traumatic event for anyone. And I will admit that I do feel much better now that I've written about my experiences at the Academy after I've kept them all hidden inside of me for so many years. But I can't say that I feel particularly damaged as I conclude my reflections on the events of those days. On the one hand, the boys we became while we lived at the Academy defined who we were at that time. But in the years which have followed, Matt and I have worked very hard to become the men we have wanted to be. So in the end I would say that our experiences at the Academy have simply been a part of the overall mix which defines who we are today. And since we are both happy with our lives today, I'm not sure that either one of us would want to go back into the past to change anything that had happened to us—even if we could. Suffice to say we have become the men we have chosen to be. Of course there are all kinds of bad in this world and I do not presume here to be all knowing, but it seems to me that as humans we always get only two choices. We can quit when adversity comes around and allow ourselves to be beaten by it, or we can use the misfortunes in our lives as a foundation to make us stronger and wiser. Matt and I merely made the latter our choice.

Although I know thousands of people, today I have just a handful of very close friends whom I trust implicitly. The rest of the world I hold at arm's length. If there is any aspect of my personality which I can point to as a negative result of my experiences at the Academy, I would suspect it is this tendency I have to keep to myself. But I have observed this same response in people who have a physical impairment of some kind and who have suffered ridicule and scorn throughout their childhood at the hands of the others within their peer group. Such behavior today is considered out of vogue, but when I was growing up it was standard operating procedure for anyone who was even slightly different from the others to be subjected to such abuse.

Our experiences do serve notice to parents and school administrators that sexual behavior in children in general does occur and as such is something which responsible adults should, at the very least, be aware of. And there is no question that we should all work to insure that no young person is ever forced into having sex by another. But enough of my post mortem on my life at Ulster Academy. I've really got to be on my way now or I'll miss our dinner reservations tonight at 21.

Once more I look ahead and press my foot down on the accelerator. I should reach the highway in about two minutes. If I remember correctly, I eventually need to find my way to I-84which coincidentally will take me right past the boarding school I attended after I left the Academy. That school is still in business today though they no longer take boarders. The place is now just a school for day students, but they still call me every year to ask for a donation just the same.

It has been a wrenching day for me emotionally as I have relived events from more than thirty years ago. And it suddenly occurs to me that if it had been pre-ordained for me to go through the things they forced me into at the Academy, it was fortunate for me that I wound up having these experiences while I was a boy because as an adult, I don't believe I could have survived the constant physical and mental abuse. Kids are more adaptable than adults. In many ways young people can adjust better to stresses, and withstand adverse circumstances which others force upon them, in ways which those of us who are fully grown are simply not equipped to put up with.

I'm ok these days. In fact, I'm better than ok—and so is Matt. Like my brother, I have a loving wife, well-adjusted and successful children, a nice home, and a career I enjoy. In most ways that mater, I feel as if I have accomplished the things in life I set out to achieve all those years ago. Don't get me wrong, there are still plenty of things I have before me which I still need to complete. But all in all, I feel as if things these days are moving along just fine. And as I turn my car onto Highway 193, I leave the town of Ulster as well as the state of Massachusetts with a feeling of accomplishment. For I have lived in hell on earth itself, and I have come through it all and gone on to build for myself the type of life which any person can be proud of. And this is a fact which no one, despite any experience in my past, can ever take away from me.

Photo of main building and much of the upper campus.
Taken from just outside the front gate.
(Taken from catalog)

My old dormitory
(Taken from catalog)

The gymnasium
(Taken from catalog)

The Annex, the boat house, the lake and the dock

Photo from catalog of swimming pool

My friend Frank
(Yearbook photo)

CPSIA information can be obtained at www.ICGtesting.com
Printed in the USA
BVOW03s1701280414

351936BV00002B/231/P

9 781424 196968